ROBOTIC AMBITIONS

ROBOTIC AMBITIONS

TALES OF MECHANICAL SENTIENCE

Edited by
LESLEY CONNER & JASON SIZEMORE

APEX BOOK COMPANY

For all those who have dreams of a day when robots will be humanity's best friend, and for those who have nightmares that they will one day destroy us all. This one is for you.

ApexBookCompany.com
Lexington, KY

ISBN (pbk): 978-1-955765-13-8
ISBN (epub): 978-1-955765-22-0

FIRST EDITION: NOVEMBER 2023

Cover art by Vincent Lefevre

Jacket design by Mikio Murakami

CONTENTS

INTRODUCTION

MARTHA WELLS

IT'S ALWAYS BEEN IMPORTANT TO WRITE ABOUT ROBOTS AND artificial intelligence. We write about things we need to understand, that we need other people to understand. And artificial intelligence—true artificial intelligence, not predictive text or plagiarism machines—is something that we need to understand not in the future, but now, at this moment in time.

Because so many of the stories about robots are stories about power over others.

Humans creating a sentient being for a purpose, whether it's to be a servant or a tool, has been a metaphor for humans controlling and owning other humans for a very long time. The first work to use the word robot, *R.U.R.* (*Rossom's Universal Robots*) by Karel Čapek, written as a play in 1920, is about a slave revolt by artificial beings created to serve humans.

These stories grapple with the idea that if humans create a sentient being whose only reason and purpose for existence is to serve them, that's somehow okay, and not at all like slavery. (Kind of like the sentient cow in *The Restaurant at the End of the Universe* by Douglas Adams— the comment on the morality of this concept is not subtle.) Not surprisingly, many of those stories end with the artificial intelligence resisting its role and going on a murderous rampage. But the attitudes differ toward the justifiability of that murderous rampage.

Asimov's Three Laws of Robotics (*A robot may not injure a human being or, through inaction, allow a human being to come to harm. A robot must obey orders given it by human beings except where such orders would conflict with the First Law. A robot must protect its own existence as long as such protection does not conflict with the First or Second Law.*) define the relationship between robot and human as adversarial; they seem to imply that robots are going to want to kill their human masters. If not immediately then, you know, at some point.

What's the message then, that an artificial intelligence is a monster that needs to be controlled? That if given any kind of choice it would run out and kill its creators, just because it could? Or that creating a sentient being that is born to be enslaved and subjugated to the will of whatever human owns and controls it is maybe a bad idea? That humans who create artificial beings as slaves deserve the consequences of their actions?

So many "AI goes rogue" stories, when seen from the AI's perspective, are about an enslaved person fighting for freedom from their captors. Guilt and greed are wound up in these stories like barbed wire. It's like we know in our heart of hearts that humans who create an artificial sentient destined for slavery should be punished.

Stories about sentient robots spark other metaphors less violent but not less poignant. Like "Fandom For Robots" by Vina Jie-Min Prasad where the first sentient robot in the world is doomed to obsolescence, and has become a museum exhibit with nothing to do with its endless time. It works out okay in the end, but this kind of story also makes people think about the consequences of their actions. Is creating an artificial intelligence like creating a baby? As its creator, are you responsible for its health and well-being for the rest of its life? Yeah, you kind of should be.

Other stories present becoming human as the ultimate goal of any robot or AI. Because we as humans can't imagine any other sentient who wouldn't want to be just like us. This can be another metaphor for othering; if we can't accept basic differences in body and mind from fictional sentient robots, can we accept them from other humans?

Robotic Ambitions focuses on what artificial intelligence wants as opposed to what humans think it wants, or fear that it wants. It explores the right of sentient artificial intelligences to control their own minds and decide their own desires. AIs who just want to be left alone to find their own destiny and AIs who want to find family and connection. The right to bodily autonomy in all aspects of their life, the right to decide for themselves.

Which is an even more powerful and vital metaphor for humans relinquishing the urge for power over others. For accepting that other humans have a right to all these things too.

September 21st, 2023
Martha Wells

IT-WHO-DREAMS-UNDER-GREY-CLOUDS IN THE-TOWN-WITHIN-THE-CITY

MARIE CROKE

BETWEEN ONE STEP AND THE NEXT, I RESET.

The street is dark so my first action after rebooting to a prior me is to dial up my vision and engage an infrared scan. My internals tell me it's 23:00 hours with a waxing crescent long set behind the heavy pollution cloud. The sector is abandoned, overrun with fungi and fauna, with a high concentration of oil lingering from a pipe explosion decades prior. This sector is also where a large mound of humans had been piled. Bone now. A graveyard sector.

There is nothing here. I should not even be here.

I check my logs out of habit, but they cease abruptly. Like a virus has eaten through my data, munched away at the bits and bytes. Except, there is nothing alien in my software. Nothing chewing at the wires of my hardware.

Nothing except me. A logged line where I had executed a function to reset myself to a version of me from seven years—*years* ...—ago in what seemed like a panic. I felt empty. My reason for being here lost in that prior version of me who no longer exists.

I turn on my heel and head toward The-Town-Within-The-City. I have—*had?*—a backup hard drive there that would tell me what I'm missing of myself, though not what had drove me to do an emergency reset out here, unprotected, in a graveyard sector.

The haphazard, leaning buildings of the old city envelope me. My feet tap against bridges of sheet-metal, against cracked asphalt, against the soft springy touch of bioluminescent moss that lights a patchy trail in my wake. The city sleeps in its pollution-haze.

The-Town-Within-The-City had been walled off within the first decade after humanity had disintegrated and died out. It had become a space for bots and robos and even a few androids whose flesh-parts had eventually rotted, leaving them as metal chassis, naked with wiring exposed and drooping. The city has no name, at least not anymore, while our town had been named by our esteemed mayor, It-Who-Likes-To-Sing.

The lights of the town glow upward against the crumbling hollows of skyscrapers, while below, I pass a metal mound that had never been there before, tiny ants of rounded metal frozen in the process of scurrying hither and thither over it.

I duck under the dirt-clogged rusted mesh and find the door installed in the wall that creaks and groans more than I remember as I pull it open. Then I leave the quiet dead behind and enter the brightness of what should have felt like home. I *have* a home in here, my memory insists. It's in the upper levels, drapings of old green wires decorating my windows. Or at least they had. Perhaps I have moved in the last seven years. Perhaps I don't live here any longer and the graveyard sector had become home to the past me—*present me?*—I could not remember.

It-Who-Loves-Rain-Despite-Rust greets me as I close the town's door. Its face-plate is painted with over two dozen eyes, some of them new. To me, at least. Its voice erupts from the box shackled to its neck with refurbished bolts. "You have returned again. I worried this time you would not return at all."

Which meant I had always returned, which I take to mean that I still have that home here, with its balcony and its window drapings of fluttering green wires. "Of course I've returned. Do you know what I was doing in the city this time?"

"A game? I love games." It jerked, its body spasming in a way I pretend to interpret as excitement. "Scrapping? But no, you've not brought anything back. Thinking? Somebot who finds insects often goes out to think with full processing, no distractions or sub-routines running.

Or ... inventing? Graffiti? A clandestine meeting with a bot from another town?"

None of that sounds quite right, but I don't want to upset It-Who-Loves-Rain-Despite-Rust so I say, "Those are all good guesses. I was thinking." At least it wasn't untruthful, for I had been running through my files since my reset, trying to find some clue that might help me understand why I had flushed so much of myself away. I don't wish to continue speaking to it though; it can't help me, it's not what I need. So I step around it.

"It-Who-Finds-Insects-Charming, ple—" It-Who-Loves-Rain-Despite-Rust pauses and I can almost feel it computing numbers to words. It's an old robo, originally made for cleaning, its voice box and mobility mods added in the last twenty years to conform to town normalcies, though it still kept its roller and vacuum that left thin clean strips wherever it went. It jerked again, faceplate spinning as if to hide its sudden spasm. "Wrong name. Apologies, It-Who-Dreams-Under-Grey-Clouds. Please remember to do regular restarts."

I respond distantly with the typical good-bye response, "Thank you for your service to town," while the bulk of my processing sifts through old conversations with It-Who-Loves-Rain-Despite-Rust, searching for evidence that it often confuses my name with somebot else. But I can find no conversations where it had done so in the past. Yet the name held some vague sense of familiarity if the odd hitching in my automatic processes is indicative of anything.

Refocusing, I make my way through the town, through its meandering metal tunnels and open skywalks, past familiar scrap-shops and charge stations and the stages where inhabitants perform altered human plays or musical scores or read original poetry with lines that vibrate through the walls with mechanical genius no human ear could ever have heard.

I say hello to It-Knows-All-About-Whales and keep walking as it tells me the percentage chance of a beluga still existing and would I like to hear a recording of its undersea trilling? I have a sense that I have heard the trilling before.

Under an overhang just before the painted outdoor stairway toward my home, a bot and a robo discuss the merits of creating new languages and which of the town's inhabitbots might be left behind, unable to compute the new phrases into sense. I tune them out, not wanting to think about the implications, not wanting to consider that new languages might have been invented in the last seven years, new poetry, new plays, new rules within our cultures that are gone from me.

I cycle that thought into a file where it can loop without harming the rest of my processes.

Then I climb the three floors, the steps clanging, until I can walk across the bolted sheet of metal to where my balcony railing had been cut to allow passage since the inner elevator to the old building had long since been ransacked for parts before the generators were established.

The green wires still hang in my windows, which comforts me. However, there are metal butterflies clinging to my balcony railing with little welded legs. This disconcerts me, for I do not remember putting them there.

I step inside my home to find It-Concerns-Itself—*It-Who-Watches-For-Danger? Sometimes it waffles between the two names and I don't know which is correct in this moment*—standing in the middle of my rooms. It was once a security bot, worked for a human hospital, and had originally painted over the hospital logo on its bust years ago, but sometimes, like now, when it became overly concerned, it would scratch at the paint, causing it to fleck to reveal slivers of red letters.

I pause, concerned again that perhaps this was no longer my home, for the small half-built metal figure and the strange maze of hollow plastic tubes and fittings weaving in and out of the wall above it are new —*new to me.*

But a quick sweep of the room dictates that hypothesis is wrong, or at least partially incorrect. For there is my desk and my large server and my lines of code poetry pasted on the walls and swinging from near-invisible wires. A number of them aren't familiar, swaying above the ground, giving me glimpses of their poems. An obvious recent fascination appearing over and over in different poems: {break} break; //break

Macabre, this attraction to breaking. Or alluring, if seen from another light. I had certainly gone through similar cyclical obsessions in my art, hadn't I? This is no different. Just a phase I couldn't remember. Words and ideas I'd had that I've forgotten.

"I'm dying," says It-Concerns-Itself, its faceplate lighting up at my presence.

It tends to be dramatic. I suspect I've correctly guessed its current name. I ignore it and head straight to my backup hard drive on the desk at the far wall.

It continues, "My cameras are all down. Black and static. True black —I can't turn up the resolution because there's nothing recording. My drones have blank spots in their reports. Just hollow spaces like they've all been turning themselves off and on and on and off."

"Are you turning them on and off? Have you checked their programming?" I unwind a cord and wire myself directly into my backup, plugging in one end to a port under my arm.

It-Concerns-Itself makes a sound—a warning claxon it had never been allowed to use while in the hospital. It had decided to make up for that fact by using it prodigiously whenever it became annoyed. "Of course I have. I check and recheck. That's what I do. This is how it starts. Spotty holes in our files. Then it spreads. We'll all be like dementia patients. Did you know I worked security at a hospital?"

"I did."

"I would have to lead patients back inside when they wandered off. And now I've had to call back wandering drones, It-Who-Dreams-Under-Grey-Clouds! And there's no one here to walk me back when it starts happening to me. No one here!"

I give It-Concerns-Itself only a fraction of my processing power, focusing more on running through the memory files of my backup, striving to find some inkling of the parts of me that are missing.

But ... they're patchy. Like I had gone through them with a serrated blade, dissected my moments, split apart my thoughts and spliced the pieces together with sparse notes that indicated a panicked past me and precious little else.

"This is what happened to The-Town-That-Tells-Stories," It-Concerns-Itself is saying, its voice a rise and fall of terror. "Somebot connected to an old server in their city—downloaded whole packages they didn't run checks on. Brought back music without realizing it held a self-corrupting file and started sharing it all over town. Bots had to be reset, years of their selves lost! I don't want that to happen to me! I like me. I want to be me. I want to keep me intact. I want—" It continues, but I cease registering.

My limbs freeze up and have difficulty moving, like I'm being put into the corner again when the parents are home. Don't want me touching the children when they're around. Only a nanny while they aren't there. My children ... I find files of them, beige little things that required gentleness, their shells so fragile. Long gone now. All of them long gone. And I'm not in a corner, I'm facing a cracked wall—my cracked wall, with steel visible lengthwise, the cord connecting me to my backup looped down by my articulated knees.

"Are you listening to me? I'm dying! We're all going to die!"

I normally comfort It-Concerns-Itself. Say it has nothing to fear, that there is no parasitic virus being slipped inside transmissions off the poetry stage, that the downloadable music in the trade jukebox is screened, that all of our friends, all of the bots and robos and struggling androids in The-Town-Within-The-City are certainly not connecting themselves to strange old servers in broken parts of the city and putting the town at risk. Certainly not.

I don't feel much like comforting it though.

"Maybe we are all dying," I say.

It-Concerns-Itself does not answer, but it makes another sound, this one the calm beeping that would indicate difficulty with a patient, summoning a human on call. Though we have no more humans to summon, so it must have been beeping out of long-embedded habit.

"I ..." I consider telling it the truth, but then pull back at the last, not wanting it to panic more than it was. Or perhaps not wanting to admit that I may have been the first to fall—*responsible?*—so instead, I admit, "I'm missing memories too. Blank files."

"I knew it! We're all going to die! I'm going to die. You're going to die. Your stupid roaches are going to die."

Roaches?

"Look at them. They're already dying. Their memories riddled with holes so they can't find a way out. Same as us. Same as us!" it wailed.

I turn and follow It-Concerns-Itself's pointing extremity to the mess of plastic tubes and fittings and clear cages that weave in and out of the crumbing wall. Little brown roaches scuttle about the grimy tubing, nibbling at masticated bits of organic material dropped at intervals throughout the maze. Here and there one was upturned, legs curled into itself. They could not possibly have been a new addition to my home, for their intricate tunnel system spanned a great deal of the wall and waste smears across wide sections of the plastic.

I unplug myself and step closer to the roaches and their labyrinthine cage that so resembles our town. As if all of us, every bot and robo and half-dead android, are scrambling through a metal maze ourselves, nibbling at life.

"I don't remember having roaches," I say.

"See! It's taken root! Somebot has brought a virus inside the town and we're all disintegrating!" It-Concerns-Itself's beeping intensifies.

I don't remember creating the butterflies on the balcony either, but the half-finished metal project below the roaches' cage says I did. This project is larger than the butterflies, by a great deal, already the height of It-Who-Loves-Rain-Despite-Rust, though not as thick around and with more slender appendages. Wires and drives and boards are littered between strips of burnished metal in an organized chaos.

That disconcerted feeling rises again within my programming, and I get the distinct impression I'd written a script that has now been trashed, project plans that are now cut-up fragments, unreachable despite being somewhere within me.

"We should inform It-Who-Likes-To-Sing," I say, referencing our self-designated mayor. "It will know what to do. Maybe we can stop this from spreading."

"This? *This* is a virus! It's a back-door trojan, headshots, *bang*, we're all gone!" It-Concerns-Itself was now spinning in a circle, its faceplate shuddering with light and color. "I'm missing things. I'm sure of it. I must be. I don't even know why I'm here! Why I've come to see *you*, but there must be a reason that the butterflies make me feel like you can help, that the insects would guide us. Do you know? *Do you know?*"

"No," I say. Then, add in goodbye, "Restart yourself regularly."

I head for my balcony, away from the half-finished project that may or may not be shaped like children I'd once nannied, away from the roaches I must have named and fed, away from a home that didn't quite feel like home.

"Wait! I'm coming too! I can show It-Who-Likes-To-Sing my drones."

We take a path filled with haphazard bridges built between tall open windows, past stacks of mold cultures where It-Who-Will-Return-

Humanity mutters to itself. Through the Halls-Where-the-Deprogrammed-Lay where all the bots and robos and androids whose systems had crashed one final time and could not be reset—their batteries drained, files corroded—stood still and quiet, gathering dust and rust, and in one case, a little fuzzy nest filled with mewling baby mice. Tiny LED lights operate like candles through the halls, and, as we pass, It-Concerns-Itself taps one into life, almost descending into another round of panic over the thought of The-Town-Within-The-City becoming one giant Hall-Of-Deprogrammed.

"Humans made everything to break," I say, feeling an echo in my system as if I'd heard the words before. Or said them myself. Or read them on one of my code poems. "We're all made to break, just like them."

It-Concerns-Itself beeps and then groans.

We arrive at the town hall and head directly to what had once been the women's bathroom on the ground floor of what had once been a hotel. We pass a giant metal statue I didn't remember—*mine?*—in the center of what had once been a lobby. A bee, of sorts, with a faceplate like a bot and wings like a helicopter's blades.

Acoustics in the once-bathroom heighten It-Who-Likes-To-Sing's voice, so we can hear its mechanical tenor with flattened notes before we even enter. The stall doors and toilets had been removed and the plumbing holes covered. Decorative paint swirls at the edges of the mirror with glam and glitz while rainbow glitter sparkles in thick bands against the tan walls.

"Come in! Come in!" It-Who-Likes-To-Sing pauses its song to wave us in and points at the open stalls as its voice dips and wavers. "Take a spot. Any spot. Stand back and listen and I'll call on each of you in turn to hear your grievances and then we will solve them." It sings the last few words, holding a single, strong note for "solve" for a four-count.

I take the first stall and watch in the mirror as It-Concerns-Itself peeks into each of the others before returning to the one next to mine.

"Perfect! Now let me read you the rules."

It-Who-Likes-To-Sing claps, dimming the lights. Then it speeds up its voice and recites a list of irrelevant legalese. But it had once been a legal aid bot, has a mind filled with laws that no longer matter, with loopholes we no longer have to exploit. Had once named itself It-Who-

Aids-Legally before discovering a different passion. At the spiel's end, It-Who-Likes-To-Sing settles to a stop and gestures widely toward me.

"And now that preliminaries have been settled, let us begin! Stall one, what is your grievance that brought you here today?"

"Your honor," I address it, as it prefers in this formal setting, "we have reason to believe that a virus or some other infiltration has taken hold of some of the inhabitbots of The-Town-Within-The-City."

"My drones are *forgetful!*" interrupts It-Concerns-Itself.

It-Who-Likes-To-Sing doesn't reprimand It-Concerns-Itself, which concerns *me*, but I ignore my misgivings and go on. "We are worried that there are others who have had their memory files corrupted. That the town is in danger of losing—"

"Of losing our very *selves*," moaned It-Concerns-Itself.

Again, It-Who-Likes-To-Sing doesn't acknowledge the moaning bot. Doesn't even move.

"We might be looking at a town-wide reset," I say, keeping the deci-bel-level of my voice steady though I want nothing more than to let it whisper away, to admit that I have already reset, that I've already lost integral parts of me—of butterflies and roaches and a propensity for metal sculptures alongside my coded poetry. "Or worse."

It-Concerns-Itself's beeping begins anew, the space between each beep shorter, creating an eerie staccato echo in the once-bathroom.

It-Who-Likes-To-Sing remains motionless for another moment, then it swirls around, clapping, lights brightening, and then bursts into song, the same strange song it'd been singing when we first arrived. Even It-Concerns-Itself was surprised by the mayor's reaction, for its beeping immediately shuts off.

"Your honor!" I shout. "Were you—"

"Oh! Come in! Come in! Take a spo—You've already taken spots! Good, good! Let me read you the rules." And it once more dims the lights, rushes through its legalese, then gestures for me to begin my grievance.

"It's stuck in a loop," I say, my voice low, reflecting the sinking statistics of our survival.

It-Concerns-Itself peers around the edge of our stalls, its face-plate too bright within the dim room and its beeping once more intensifying annoyingly. "A virus has already gotten to the mayor? We're doomed! The town is all doomed! What are we to do?"

"We're to not connect anywhere," I say. "No ports. No sharing."

"What about the charging stations? Could it be spreading from there? Are we to give up entirely? Reset ourselves. Hope we are still us?"

"No, not yet."

Not yet for them. But for me? For *me*? I was gone. And I was here. And I didn't know which *I* had been the better bot to exist.

"Ah! Welcome! Come in! Come in! Take a spot!"

I abandon my spot with legs I must force to move, leaving It-Who-Likes-To-Sing cracking octaves. When It-Concerns-Itself starts to follow, I stop it with a curt gesture, not wanting it trailing me anymore, wanting time for my own thoughts, for I have too many of them and they are spinning, threatening to loop me like the mayor. "See if you can get it unstuck. Sing with it, try different stalls, see if it'll leave the town hall, I don't care. Just try."

I pause in the lobby where the world is quieter, with only the distant sporadic tones from the mayor's sing-song voice and It-Concerns-Itself's staccato beeping. I wallow, a guilt rising as the bee-bot statue stares down at me with accusing oculars. Had I been the irresponsible one? Had I brought a virus back to town after one of my many city explorations? Not realizing it festered in my code, breaking parts of me down, spreading to others every time we connected. Patient zero.

I probably crafted this statue, given the butterflies and the half-finished child-sized project in my home. I imagine the bee wants to step off its platform, whir its helicopter blades, take off into the grey pollution sky. Escape. Just as we did when the humans had failed to survive, blocking them out with our walls, yet living within the yawning circle of their skyscrapers. Escape, escape, escape.

But there is no escape from one's own mind. The seven years' worth of blank expanse always there no matter where I go. Maybe I had saved myself, stopped myself from looping like It-Who-Likes-To-Sing, or from having corroded memory files like It-Concerns-Itself, or from spasming like It-Who-Loves-Rain-Despite-Rust.

Then ...why had I not warned the others? Or had I and I just didn't remember? Maybe I've been here before, standing in this lobby, listening to It-Who-Likes-To-Sing repeat and repeat and repeat, not knowing what to do, just as I don't know what to do now ...

The bee-bot is still staring down at me. Judgingly.

I scan the alloy concentration of the metal. It's similar—the same in some places—as the half-finished child-like project in my home. I *had* made this. I had even signed—

Except ... the signature embossed on the bee-bot's hind leg was not It-Who-Dreams-Under-Grey-Clouds. Not the familiar symbols that meant *me*.

Instead it read: *It-Who-Finds-Insects-Charming*

I do not know anybot named It-Who-Finds-Insects-Charming. Not in The-Town-Within-The-City. Not from before, during my nanny bot years, or in the aftermath of the humans disintegrating. I had only just heard it today, from It-Who-Loves-Rain-Despite-Rust. Confusing me with ...

My processes speed up. They whine within my chest, my boards and circuits can't get enough air to cool down, the puzzle of it too difficult and yet not difficult enough. Panic rises. My thoughts whir in a ruminating loop, that I've lost myself forever, that who I am is disintegrating, has disintegrated, that I've already lost enough that I am merely a shadow of me, an echo, that the new me I might be able to build after a full reset will never come close because It-Who-Finds-Insects-Charming —*mememe?*—is gone.

I am lost.

In my lostness, I march about The-Town-Within-The-City, searching for inklings of me. I find a metal statue that looks like a hundred fireflies in the dark shadows near a charging station—signed *It-Who-Finds-Insects-Charming*. Another, smaller piece depicting giant ladybugs crawling over an alleyway wall. There are big floral designs of plants gone extinct with spiders curled on their petals, dragonflies and huge moths and lantern beetles dot the town, each of them carefully crafted, built with a steady hand, a skilled hand. All of the styles reminiscent of the half-finished piece lounging under the roaches whose names I don't recall.

And all of them signed with a name no longer mine.

It-Who-Finds-Insects-Charming gone and gone and gone.

I hunt down every single piece of welded artwork, avoiding being pulled away by conversations about bot languages, saying no to hearing beluga trilling, ignoring those who want to recite poetry I should be familiar with or chat about bringing back humanity from the remnants of their chemical decomposition.

I search and search until I'm back at the entrance—*exit?*—of The-Town-Within-The-City, back where I'd first heard the name that didn't —*did?*—belong to me.

At my approach It-Who-Loves-Rain-Despite-Rust spins its faceplate with its many painted eyes, as if watching me with them.

"Are you leaving again?" it asks.

"I don't know," I admit, unsure about everything. "Maybe?"

I don't tell it about the missing files, the possible virus that has turned It-Who-Likes-To-Sing into a repetitive performer who has lost its ability to reason, It-Concerns-Itself's memory to a pocked land-scape, me … to this confused mess haunted by somebot who I no longer am.

It will find out soon enough that we are all breaking. Or not. Perhaps it would spasm one last time and forget everything forever.

"Alone again?"

"Did you want to come with me?" I ask.

It-Who-Loves-Rain-Despite-Rust stops spinning its faceplate. "I do not. I never have. But sometimes it's not you who leaves."

"Not me?"

"Not always."

"Who goes out there then?" I ask.

It-Who-Loves-Rain-Despite-Rust begins to spin its faceplate again, its multitude of eyes blurring. "Somebot. It-Who—Do you know why I love rain?"

"No. It-Who?" *It-Who-Finds-Insects-Charming?*

"Because rain cleans same as me. We wash everything away. Somebot told me that."

"Which bot?" *Me? A different me?*

"I don't want to wash everything away, It-Who-Dreams-Under-Grey-Clouds. Grey clouds don't always have to signify rain; there are grey clouds all the time now."

"You don't remember, do you?" It probably already had blanks in its files. It'd been just a cleaning robo, after all, did not have the same capa-

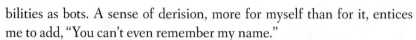

bilities as bots. A sense of derision, more for myself than for it, entices me to add, "You can't even remember my name."

"I cannot." Its faceplate stops again. This time, it sags onto its rollers. "Apologies. I am not a good guard for the door. I can't remember who goes in and who goes out."

"It's fine." But my voice is the one I once used to reprimand children. "Thank you for your service to town." I turn to leave.

"It-Who-Finds-Insects-Charming left a note for you. You told me—it told me—somebot told me to tell you. When was that ..."

I freeze, the loops in my processes freezing as well. "A note?"

"By the ant colony. Or ... maybe the bee hive ... Or the wasp nest? Apologies."

But I am already out the groaning metal door, for I remember another sculpture, the mounded metal with its tiny little antlike bits scurrying about.

"Are you coming back?"

I ignore it, not wanting to consider the answer, and the door closes without it asking again.

The mound of metal is far more intricate than I'd first believed. Small curving paths had been carved within it. Little caverns where minuscule welded ants remained stuck in the process of collecting or protecting or eating or sleeping. A whole ant colony. Confusing and convoluted and yet beautiful in its scurrying.

There is no note though. No words in any language I recognize anywhere on the ant colony, not on the metal undersides of the passages inside, nor on the tiny metal ants themselves. I search it thoroughly and determine nothing. I—*prior me, nonexistent me, the me who was lost forever*—had not even signed my name on this piece.

I step away, as if the distance might help, that maybe I'd see a name or a note formed from the curving passages themselves or perhaps among the negative space within. Again, I am disappointed.

And yet ...

I tilt my head one way. I scan the ant colony another. Then I pull up maps of the city sectors, flick through them quickly, overlay them against the sculpture. I shift sideways a few steps, then one more, until the sector sits clearly within the passages and caverns, like broken streets and crowded intersections, sagging and crumbling buildings indicated with hatch-marks in the metal.

Not a note; a map.

And the ants are crawling, scurrying toward one particular place. A place that—I check where I had been when I'd reset myself—I had been heading, surely. I had *known* something I no longer knew. And I wanted to know again. So I turned my back to The-Town-Within-The-City and headed toward a graveyard sector that housed little but the bones of broken humans and the bones of their broken homes and the remnants of their broken, broken machines.

The moss glows behind me, reflecting off flat white fungi growing on the buildings. The city without a name is a scurrying mess and I feel like an ant, like a roach, scrambling about, terrified of breaking—breaking *more*.

The map leads me past where I had reset. To where the skyscrapers shrink. To the edges of an industrial sector. To the door of a wide building with bot-scrap on its steps and along its street and piled against its windows, like the disembodied legs wanted to be free, the arms scraping their way outward by any means. Like the building holds a pile of bones, much like the piles of human ones a few streets over.

It makes me shudder to see.

The door is thick metal, but moves easily enough without a squeak. Inside, the facility opens wide, dark, and gaping, with machinery long picked over. My scans match alloy similarities to the welded insect artistry all around town so I presume this must have been where I'd taken my materials. I must have been here, many times before.

Adjusting my vision, I step inside despite a premonition of dread. I wander the aisles and step over collapsed machinery and piles of dusty bot-parts. Everything indicated this had been a bot-crafting facility. A small one. Boutique perhaps. Built to give tours, bold painted signs on the walls depicting arrows and rudimentary explanations for processes.

I follow the arrows like an obedient bot. Past the parts bins where human children had once played with disembodied limbs of my pre-born compatriots. Up the steps where windows looked in on now-frozen machinery arms welding our pieces together. Through the corridor where humans might play with the pre-programmed job-classes in a game, designing their own bot and getting to upload their design, seeing it come to life in a video at the end of the tour.

There's a small bot on display on that last video. Similar to my long-gone beige children in size, but precious little else. Its programming is displayed on the side, an amalgam of bot behaviors listed, a mixture of specialization and brand-new coded alternations on the inside despite its clean, crisp outer shell. Far more complicated than what the machine was originally designed for.

The little bot fizzled and pops, sometimes disappearing altogether on the screen. Somebot—*me?*—had powered the console. Even the audio static-stutters into existence now and then, startling me. "Error. Unfit. This bot is not—zzhm—unfit."

It disconcerts me, the same way the butterflies on my balcony railing did. I turn away uncomfortably.

The faded red arrows signaling the end of the tour want me to leave, head back around in a circle, pass the gift shop on the way out. But I don't obey, for there's a door wedged open enticingly, labeled "Employees Only."

At the entrance to The-Hallway-For-Employees-Only, I freeze, like I'm in a corner again, no longer needed, face away, don't record, don't engage, no matter if the youngest comes and wraps their arms about my metal legs.

Drifting down from the ceiling are a hundred almost-invisible wires. And on their ends, code poetry—*mine!*—stamped onto lumpy, misshapen metal shapes bearing passing resemblance to failed butterfly wings. *We were built to break*; some say. In different codes, in different beats and rhythms, but always: *We were built to break; {break}*

They shudder at the breath of air from my entrance. Twist and turn so I can scan subsections of each code-poem between loops and ifs and conditions.

When we took the first roach home
and named it
It-Who-Eats-Everything
{break}

When we sang beluga trilling

off the rooftops
and the skyscrapers trilled back
{break}

When we recited my poetry
for the first time
at The-Bar-Without-Drinks
{break}

When we watched a spider web
appear between our balcony railings
and fell in love
{break}

When we dragged metal scrap
home and carved insects
to populate the world
{break}

This ...

This is a personal Hall-Where-The-Deprogrammed-Lay. An obituary. In memoriam. A hundred flying epitaphs.

I step inside The-Hallway-For-Employees-Only and crane my neck joints to gaze above me at the dangling field of memories. *We* and *we* and *we* populate the code-poetry. {*break*} populates it, dangles like it had in the poems in my home in The-Town-Within-The-City. Prior me so obviously consumed by the idea. As if I'd known I was breaking. As if I'd been preparing my circuits for the moment because I'd known—*It-Who-Finds-Insects-Charming had known*—that we'd be forced to reset to survive.

Only I didn't survive. I am dead. Yet alive. I am here, but not here. I am a different me who does not know how to shape metal into insects, who had not written hundreds of tiny poems on breaking, who had not grieved myself before myself was gone.

I am broken. But not wholly. *Not yet.*

Somewhere outside The-Hallway-For-Employees-Only, the static-stutter of the computer finds its audio again, reads the programming of that little bot out loud. "Error. Unfit. This bot is not—zzmgh—ror. Unfit." Telling the world that the bot is not useful for humans.

"I am breaking," I say to the remnants of It-Who-Finds-Insects-Charming, I say to myself, I say under hundreds of epitaphs for a me who no longer exists, for a *we* who is broken in half. "We are all breaking. That's what you are telling me." That's what *I'm* telling me.

There had been no virus, no attack. We'd been built to break, our lifespans measured in decades not centuries, our parts a mix of plastic and metal, our programming retaining hidden slow-down functions, our systems on a timeline because humans and their commercialism needed to give us a limited lifespan so owners were forced to replace our broken innards, repurpose our metal chassis, throw us in the scrap pile, and start again.

The-Hall-Where-The-Deprogrammed-Lay grows and grows. All the bots and robos and androids in The-Town-Within-The-City are fading, staggering through the last years of their lives that should never have been the last years of their lives had humans made us right. Had built us to last.

I pass under the hundred flying epitaphs for a me no longer here. I re-download the robot programming I—*we!*—had created despite the errors, the warnings that this bot would not be useful for humans, for that is no longer our purpose and will never be our purpose again.

Then I head back to The-Town-Within-The-City, armed with scrap metal on my back and hardware boards hanging off my neck. To finish what a different me had started, before I break again.

When we designed
a little metal child
not built to break
{continue}

AUTHOR BIO

A Maryland-based SFF writer, **Marie Croke** is a graduate of the Odyssey Writing Workshop, and her stories can be found in over a dozen magazines including *Apex Magazine, Beneath Ceaseless Skies, Diabolical Plots,* and *Fireside.* She has worked as a slush reader for multiple magazines and is currently an acquisitions editor for Dark Matter INK. Her hobbies include crochet, birding, and aerial dance.

SHE BUILDS QUICK MACHINES

LYNDSIE MANUSOS

In the groove of the moment, her hands moved on their own accord, quicker than her mind, knowing by feel alone if a cog was in the right place, if a screw was tight. To the common eye, her hands were a blur of movement. Pieces on the worktable appeared or disappeared. A whiff of air and a drawer opened and shut. The common ear would hear sound, yet their eyes would be unable to catch the sleight of hand. Every few seconds, there was a *click!*; a lens dropped or flicked up from her goggles to zoom in or out of the contraption.

She knew what she needed to build.

One Hour Later

Done. An easy project. A neighbor needed a small surveillance box to see what animal was stealing her tomatoes from the garden on her windowsill. Tomatoes of this mutated variety—ginormous, knotted, and juicy—were precious on Beach, a world of boxed and stacked homes built from beach houses of years past. There was water at ground level, sucked up through pipes to be filtered and used, recycled, and reused. Long ago, after a century of over-terraforming, the actual "beach" was now an hour inland at least. Her neighbor would pay her in two, bulbous, newly-grown tomatoes in exchange for the box.

She sat back and inspected her work. Not sleek or shiny. Quick machines weren't built for beauty, though they were always beautiful to her. No one bought her work for its aesthetic pleasure. They bought it because it was built quick, and it worked.

Someone knocked on the door.

"Enter," she said.

A figure walked in, tall and as boxy as the living units stacked below and above.

"Name and pronouns," she said, wasting no time with small talk or pleasantries.

"Dido, 'he' works," he said.

He took out a stack of bank notes from a pocket of his jacket. *Click!* A lens lowered and she was able to count the pockets of his jacket. She'd never seen a jacket with so many. Seconds passed. She counted 27.

"I need a gun," he said.

Click! Click! Click! Rapid fire sounds as her lenses all clicked up until Dido could see her eyes behind the goggles. She saw his own eyes widened, eyes without goggles fused to his skin. Her eyes were no doubt enormous to him. She let him see how she saw him, as if she might look through him.

"I don't do those," she said.

"You build quick machines," he said.

"Anything but those," she said.

She did not pretend to be a beacon of morality; she'd made quick machines that did their own brand of harm, but guns she would not do. She watched him bite his lip, his gaze searching around her front office. There was a curtain behind her that led to her sleeping cot and a small kitchenette. The office had the worktable in which she sat, plus stacks and stacks of random equipment, gizmos, screws and cogs of every shape, a bin of microchips she'd salvaged, among other things. It was chaos. It was hers.

"What about defensive equipment?" he asked. "Shields and such."

"To defend against?" she prompted.

He shrugged, smiling meekly. "Capture?"

Probably running from a bounty. Many often did. It was none of her business.

"I can whip up something," she said. "Come back in two hours."

"That fast?" he said, clearly surprised. "Usually, quick mechanics take a day."

"Most do," she said but eyed the bank notes he held. A week's profit. And she hadn't bought new gloves in months. There were holes already in her palm and on the pads of her fingertips. "I'm not most."

Dido laughed, then placed the stack on the worktable. "That's what I'd heard. 'Go to Beach,' they said. Find the one with the goggles."

"I have a name," she said, her ego pleased but irritated that people hadn't seemed to pass that particular fact along. "It's on the sign on the door."

"Hex Key?" Dido asked. "I thought that was a logo."

"It's both," she said. Her parents were both quick mechanics, naming her for a tool that was simple, cheap, and can be reconditioned based on its purpose. Not to say they called her simple and cheap. Rather, she had infinite use.

Dido nodded, then rapped his knuckles on the worktable and left.

Two hours passed.

When he picked up the item she made, he raised his eyebrows. The quick machine was the size of his fist, pipe-like and crudely built, as was most of her work, but she assured him it would be effective.

"If you're bound or cuffed, this will free you," Hex said.

"And if it doesn't?" Dido asked.

Hex tilted her head to the side. *Click! Click! Click!* Let him see her eyes again. He couldn't help but blink and look away.

"I've never issued a refund," she said.

One Week Later

Someone knocked on the door.

"Enter," Hex said. "Name and pronouns."

"Would rather not give a name, but 'she' or 'they,' please." Another tall figure, lithe with arms as long as branches, both pumping and purring with gears and spinning cogs. Hex was intrigued.

The customer threw something on the table, pipe-like and crudely built.

"You made this," they said.

"Yes," Hex said. Hex was never one to deny her own creations.

"I need something that will make this item useless."

"You want me to render my own creation ineffective?"

No one had ever asked that of her before—to combat her own design with another design. Perhaps a quick mechanic should be insulted, but like the mechanical arms this customer possessed, Hex couldn't help but want to scratch the itch.

"This particular machine, or something new?" Hex asked.

"Something new," they said, taking out a small pouch from a pocket that clinked.

Click! Click! Hex dropped a lens down to zoom in and was able to estimate the contents and its weight. Good quality metal lay within. *Many* uses for that.

"An hour," Hex said.

The customer raised their eyebrows.

Hex smiled.

"An hour then," they said. The mechanical hands clenched, metal clinking against metal.

"If I may," Hex said, unable to help herself, "who made your arms?"

They raised their clenched fists, uncurled their fingers and then fisted them again. The gears whirred and purred. Hex nearly sighed at the sound.

"I don't remember," they said, a furrow creasing between their eyebrows. "I was taken, my arms lost. A friend got me out and took me to the best mechanic he knew."

Click! Click! Click! Click! Hex lowered all her lenses until her eyes were shadowed. She squeezed them shut, recalling the horrible stories of harvesters. Those who built without consent, without compassion. Hex would not press further.

"They stick sometimes at the joints," they said, almost under their breath.

"I could fix that," Hex said quickly, voice rising an octave, then bit the side of her cheek. She swallowed, willed her excitement down. "I mean, I could help with that."

"Perhaps another time," they said. "But thank you."

They left and returned the next hour. Hex made what requested, rendering the machine Dido paid for useless, but only if *this* specific machine was used against it. It was a good challenge, battling her own design. As different and intriguing as the mechanical arms of her latest customer.

AFTER THEY LEFT, HEX STOOD FROM HER WORKTABLE AND stretched, joints cracking from neck to toe. She rubbed the skin around her goggles, itching at where the metal was fused to her flesh. The goggles were a quick machine her mother had made, the last one, in fact, before her and her father passed away. She remembered screaming, clawing, as they installed them on her face. Looking back, the glory of sight without pain was worth it. Hex was born with a condition in her eyes, a mutated strain of photophobia that increased with her age. But she needed to work with her hands, and therefore *needed* her sight to function. Her parents knew this and built detachable goggles that they adjusted and improved until she reached puberty. By then the pain of any unfiltered light was too great, and Beach, although lovely, was a place of two suns. Night was still twilight, so the pain was constant. Hex remembered many days of cowering in corners and gluing paper to her bedroom windows. Her parents had made a choice. Their hands turned brittle from the work, their own eyes gushing tears as they held her down to implant the goggles she now wore.

Hex made sure the glory of her sight became the glory of her work, and the pride of her parents' memory.

She kissed her fingers and touched her goggles. *Click! Click!* She'd installed a lens years back that was not a lens but a glass negative. A still image of her parents, both in work goggles, their fingers a blur on their adjoined worktables. Hex had taken it with one of her first quick machines.

Click! Click! Click!

The glass negative disappeared, stored up in the ornate deck of lenses hanging at her brow. She could only look at it for a moment. Her goggles had filters for tears, but it was best not to risk rusting. Cleaning the interiors was a painful process of filtering, chemicals, and willpower.

Hex walked stiffly to her kitchenette. She started the electric kettle, found one of the ripe tomatoes her neighbor had indeed paid her for.

She bit into it like an apple, let the seeds and juices dribble down her chin and throat.

As the kettle hummed, Hex suspected Dido would return—assuming he escaped—to demand retribution. She also suspected the nameless one would return either to follow Dido or request something else to capture him.

Hex was one of the best, if not *the* best, quick mechanics in the surrounding systems, but the surrounding systems were a lonely place. It was nowhere near the bright, metal-rich cities lightyears away. It was nowhere near abundant ports of commerce. Beach was self-sustaining, a planet in the process of healing, independent from others. Hex liked it that way. She preferred neighbors to politicians, preferred herding sea cattle with her quick machines, rather than prompting war.

That didn't mean visits like those from Dido or the nameless one wasn't exciting. Few and far between, surely. They increased her intrigue, warmed her fingers to the tips until they ached for a new challenge.

Yes, Hex hoped Dido would return. Angry, perhaps. He may even threaten her.

It would satisfy the ache enough.

Three Weeks Later

The door shut as her most recent customer left with another quick machine. It was harvest season; sea cattle were being rounded up with the tides, divers were taking a last dip for foraging and spear-hunting before the suns both set at the same time, the only time of the year, for a bout of pure night that froze the shores, turning docks into jagged ice structures. Hex was busy making her most popular quick machine of the season: warming units. Tiny machines that generated heat, though only for a small amount of square footage. The little generators lasted the length of the cold season before burning out. She asked customers to bring back the machines for repurposing the following year, and most adhered to that.

It was getting cooler by the hour, making her fingers stiff. The warmth kept her fluid, the smell of salt and sand calming. Pure night used to be a balm to her eyes but a nasty crutch for her hands. She wouldn't be as quick, and she prided herself on speed.

The door to her shop flew open.

A pipe-like contraption, crudely built, landed on her worktable.

"What the fuck?" Dido asked.

He was still dressed in the coat of many pockets (in fact, it seemed he added more from her previous count), but his head was shaved, a scab puckered on his chin. A bruise on his cheek.

"Curious," Hex said. "You escaped."

"Only because they half let me!" he yelled and started pacing the small shop. "They found you, and paid you to break your own work?"

Hex noticed he put more weight on one of his legs.

Click! Click! Click!

Hex scanned his internals. His blood pressure was up but that was understandable. But beneath the coat, there was noticeable gash on his hip.

"You're injured," Hex said.

"And it's your fault," Dido gritted out.

"That is a matter of perspective," Hex said, leaning back in her chair. She opened a drawer under the worktable and rummaged through it until she found a syringe-like quick machine. Hex inspected it and placed it on the table.

"Kitchenette is in the back," she said. "Stitch yourself before you bleed all over my shop."

By now, Dido was breathing deep, a shake starting in his fingers and rippling up to his shoulders. His skin, a dark brown, was turning grey with blood loss.

"Dido," Hex said calmly, leaning over her worktable and steepling her fingers. "I've never worked with a cadaver before, but I promise to use your skin and bones for future machines if you die on my floor."

Dido stumbled a bit in his pacing, his hand using the wall to steady himself.

He glared at Hex.

She pointed to the syringe machine.

He cursed under his breath and swiped it from the table, limping to the back. Hex listened as he shed clothes, clicked the syringe on, and let out a garble of curses as it no doubt tugged and threaded his skin.

"I might as well have stitched myself with a hacksaw," he grunted.

"That may have hurt less," Hex yelled back, "but it wouldn't be as quick."

Sure enough, the hum of the machine ended after a few seconds, and Dido sighed.

The shop door flew open again.

The nameless one walked in, flanked by two regulators in full armor suits.

Hex leaned back in her chair. *Click! Click! Click! Click! Click!* Her scan concluded the regulators were laden with weapons. At first glance, it seemed the nameless one—mechanical arms purring like music to Hex's ears—was with the armored suits, but when Hex saw their face, the tick of their jaw—

"Quick mechanic Hex Key?" one of the regulators asked, the drone-like voice whispering through a helmet that concealed their identity.

"I am," Hex said.

"We seek information on the whereabouts of one known as Dido Patch," A regulator said. "He stole equipment from a regulator outpost."

"Medical supplies," the nameless one muttered.

"Because he was injured?" Hex asked.

Silence.

"Because his home planet is dying," the nameless one said, barely above a whisper, the whirring of their arms almost drowning it out.

"It was deemed no longer fit for sponsorship," both regulators said in unison.

Ah, Hex thought. Losing sponsorship meant that the planet's carbon output had spiraled, and whatever natural disasters that had occurred—and would continue to occur—were deemed too costly to clean up. "No longer fit" was just another phrase for "unsalvageable." It was left to its quickening and inevitable demise.

This is why Hex kept to the surrounding systems. Planets like the one she lived on, Beach, though sometimes lawless, were never chosen for sponsorship to begin with, and therefore could not be "cut" if they did not contribute.

Shoulders tense, Hex hoped Dido knew how to be as quiet back in her kitchenette.

The nameless one's arms grinded as they crossed over their chest.

They eyed Hex at her worktable, taking in her gloved hands, her goggles, and then continued to take in the worktable down to the floor. There were droplets of blood from Dido's pacing, freshly spilt, still red.

They raised their eyes to Hex.

Click! Click! Click! Click! Hex raised all of her lenses so they could see her eyes. Let them stare.

The regulators seemed oblivious to the standoff.

"Do you have information?" one guard asked. Hex wasn't sure which; the drone sounded the same and neither moved.

"No," Hex said.

"If we suspect you are withholding information, we have been authorized to take action."

"Such as?"

"Search your premises."

Hex stood up from her worktable, gloved hands pressed flat as she leaned forward.

"This is my shop," Hex said.

"Do you intend to resist?" a guard asked.

The question hung there, swinging back and forth like a pendulum. The nameless one's arms purred and chugged along, Hex stared at them, half-pleading, half-warning.

The shop was small, yes, and certainly cluttered and unadorned. But it was hers. Beneath her fingers, knuckles white and pressed against the tabletop, were drawers of gears, cogs, wrenches, springs. Little motors and generators. Pulleys and switches. She was a quick mechanic, and she was absolutely sure these two guards were unequipped for her level of speed.

In a flash, Hex began to build.

The regulators drew weapons, but she was already halfway done, and the nameless one had raised their arms to block the regulators' line of sight. In a whine of pulleys and cogs, the nameless one's arms expanded, flattening and lengthening into shields.

The first blast hit their arms with a resounding *twang!*

"How much time?" the nameless one asked.

"None," Hex said, for she was done. She lifted a tiny ball of glass, energy, and metal and threw it.

Brilliant, blinding light.

All the lenses in the world could not protect her eyes and she screamed, curling to the floor beside her worktable. She covered her head, heard the groan of the nameless one's arms taking blasts, then screams.

"On your left," Dido shouted.

Hex raised her head, peering around the corner of her table. Dido had come out, dressed in his coat of pockets, and the pockets were … emptying themselves. Little bugs, lights, and drones, liquids even, all rising from each pocket like some sentient colony.

Click! Click! Click! Despite the pain, Hex had to look, had to analyze and deduce.

Particles, nebulous and flickering, poured forth, wrapping themselves around the nameless one, and when a blast missed their arms, it was swallowed by light.

The nameless one retracted their shields back into arms and began the assault.

They grabbed each regulator, tearing off the arms that held weapons, tossing the limbs against the wall. Blood sprayed in an arc, and Dido reached into a back pocket of his coat and tossed a disc at the regulators over the nameless one's shoulder. It hit the helmet of one, and that helmet crumpled, folding in on itself until the head was gone and only a stump remained.

As the headless regulator fell, the nameless one kicked open Hex's door and pushed the last one out. There was a yell that faded into silence.

The nameless one walked back in, arms bloodied, whining from the strain and blaster hits. One elbow was smoking. Yet the light from Dido's pockets, tiny spirits, remained wrapped around them in a cocoon.

"Return," Dido said.

The lights poured back, filling his pockets until they were all nestled against him. Dido coughed and spit a glob of bloody saliva on the floor.

"You exert too much," the nameless one said, trying to roll their wrists. One wouldn't budge. "Don't empty them for me."

"You'd taken enough hits," Dido said, his eyes on the ground, looking almost bashful.

Hex stared at them both from the floor. Her blinding light machine had fallen beside her, now a little ball of spent energy. She'd put it in a drawer for repurposing later. Her eyes stung, but it was manageable. She stood up.

"Quick thinking," Dido said to her.

"We thank you," the nameless one said.

"Aren't you trying to capture him?" Hex asked, again unable to help her curiosity.

The nameless one turned to Dido and smiled. "Not for the moment."

One mechanical arm let out a gust of smoke, whined, then went limp.

"Shit," they said.

"I can fix that," Hex said. "It's the least I can do."

"We fucked up your shop," Dido said, if that was an apology.

Hex shrugged. "I can fix that, too."

"If we helped clean up," the nameless one said, "would you allow us to crash here for a bit?"

"You'd have to sleep on the floor," Hex said. "But yes, that'd be fine. I could improve your arms day-to-day."

Dido looked at the nameless one. They stared at each other until each of their mouths curled up at the corners.

Then the nameless one walked to the worktable, sitting on it, and presented Hex their limp arm.

"I'd be honored, Hex Key, for you to fix my arm."

A warmth filled Hex's chest. Akin to the warmth her hands created when she worked, like the light that poured from Dido's pockets and wrapped around the nameless one in a soft hug.

Click! Click! Click!

Hex scanned the broken arm. The damage was great, metal bent and charred, pulleys and gears twisted to mesh. And yet ... Hex had the glory of her hands.

She recalled the determined look of her parents in the glass negative.

Infinite possibilities could come from this; Hex could barely build them all in her mind.

AUTHOR BIO

Lyndsie Manusos's fiction has appeared or is forthcoming in Tor.-com, *The Deadlands*, *Apex Magazine*, and other publications. Lyndsie is a senior contributor at Book Riot, a bookseller, and is the associate flash fiction editor at *JMWW*. Her debut novella is forthcoming from Psychopomp in 2024. You can read more about Lyndsie at lyndsie-manusos.com.

OUT THERE WITH THEM

N.V. HASKELL

BEDA AND I WERE NOTHING ALIKE. WE WERE PROGRAMED IN seemingly small but intensely significant ways. The variances of our protocols, priorities, and usages were so dissimilar that we'd never be compatible. Not that we had need to be. Even though we'd rolled off the same assembly line, there was bound to be discord. Perhaps it was these fundamental differences that led to her actions.

Beda was an older model, programmed as a domestic aid. Her paint had been mostly chipped away when I'd arrived, leaving her a dulled dark gray. She had a long-neglected dent in her right shoulder that caught in the morning light, but I'd never known where it came from. She maintained the four floors and all twelve thousand square feet of the Donaldson's household. Because of her programming and her duties demands, she was typically off her charger base by 5:00 AM and didn't resettle until 10:00 PM.

Because it was my responsibility to wake and ready the children each morning, Beda prepared breakfast for the Donaldson family. Though her meals were more than adequate as far as the nutritional value was concerned, her lack of warmth was palpable in every interaction.We'd stand at our respective corners of the room and wait for the family to finish their meals so she could clear their dishes as soon as they were done. The way she looked at the children, Ian and Eva was unnerving. Too detached. I took it as proof that my more advanced nurturing settings were superior.

As I settled the children to their studies for the day and the Donaldsons busied themselves with their work, Beda would complete her daily tasks of cleaning the kitchen and the bathrooms. She did their laundry on Mondays and Thursdays. On Tuesdays and Fridays, she swept, vacuumed, and mopped. On Wednesdays, she scrubbed the baseboards and the ceilings. Saturdays, she cleaned the insides and outsides of the windows. Sundays were for lawn and pool maintenance. It was the only day she went outside. Somedays the outside work lasted longer than other days and I would catch glimpses of her staring off toward the city's skyline in the distance.

Every week was the same and she completed each task quietly, with barely more than a whirring of her gears and an occasional sound which reminded me of Janet Donaldson's heavier maternal sighs. That small noise was as close to a complaint as she was ever allowed.

Sometimes I would catch Beda's ocular components analyzing me as I took the children's temperatures or doled out vitamins and medications to the family. I laid out their clothes each day and tucked them into bed at night. When Janet and Kevin Donaldson were too tired or busy entertaining guests, it fell to me to read the children their favorite stories. As the Carer droid for the family, I tended to their basic physiological and psychological needs, monitoring their vital signs to ensure optimum health, well-being, and nurturing.

Eva held my hand and giggled at my singing when she requested it, even though my digital voice wasn't smooth enough to carry any particular tune. Her laughter made it seem that I was fulfilling my purpose and programming. Beda would watch us silently from the corner with her small noises drifting toward us.

Three nights a week I escorted Ian to his soccer practice and sat with the other Care droids in the bleachers where we would all clap in titanium sync whenever a child on our team performed well. Three seasons now, and Ian had been awarded the same number of metals as the other children. Janet and Kevin were very proud.

Our existence was simple and fixed until one day when Eva sat cross-legged on her bedroom floor, happily constructing a replica of the Taj Mahal with her interlocking building set spread around her. I squatted beside her, monitoring her problem-solving and executive skills, and uploading the results into the scholastic databases for analysis. Although it was a Wednesday, the soft roar of the vacuum cleaner preceded Beda's entrance by only a second. She didn't pause as the suction attachment swallowed four marbled pieces that were meant to make up the upper portion of the main dome.

Even when Beda rammed the vacuum into my leg and sent me toppling to the floor in a crash that shook the house, she didn't stop. Eva's screams finally slowed Beda's progression and when Janet arrived a few moments later, the girl was near hysterics.

"Beda, return to base and reboot." It was a simple order that the droid immediately followed. But worry etched Janet's eyes as they followed her. Janet opened the app on her phone and ran diagnostics on Beda and her tracking system before doing the same to me. Nothing was out of order.

They temporarily consigned Beda to her charging port for her reboot, while I disassembled the HVAC unit in the basement in search of the lost building pieces. By the time I placed them in Eva's small hands, Beda was already wiping the baseboards in the living room as if nothing had happened. The reboot usually wiped out our recent memories, and I doubted she knew what she'd done. As I watched her settle into her charging station that night, before I tucked Ian and Eva in, I thought I saw Beda pause. Her normally gray eyes flashed a vibrant sapphire before dulling to sleep mode.

I wondered if I should draw attention to the change, but the Donaldsons probably knew. It must be a new feature of the reboot. And they disliked when I spoke with them regarding anything other than the children.

For the next few days, we were back into our routines. No one spoke of the incident again until dinner one evening. Beda and I were in our places, waiting for the family to finish their Pad Thai while listening to their talk of work and school lessons, sports, and grandparents when Kevin Donaldson spoke.

"I bet it was just a fluke," Kevin said. "We should take her in for a deep cleaning. She's overdue. All that dust and dirt accumulation has probably built up in her system and triggered an anomaly."

"You don't think Beda's past her prime?" Janet asked. "We've had her almost ten years. It might be time for an upgrade."

Kevin eyed Beda from his seat with a pensive look. "Upgrades are expensive."

"True, but it would almost be better to get a new model for the kids. They've practically outgrown the one we have. We'll need to upgrade Cora's mods for adolescents soon, anyway. Maybe we could kill two birds with one throw." Janet said.

"A new Care droid?" Kevin tapped his chopsticks together as he spoke. "Then what about Cora?"

Janet absently stroked Eva's dark hair as she glanced at me. "We could have her reprogrammed for domestic duties. Just like we did to Beda when Alma became outdated."

"Alma was a good droid," Kevin said. "Too bad we had to junk her."

Beda stepped smoothly forward, withdrawing Janet's empty plate as she set her chopsticks on it. The droid turned as if she were going to make her usual trek to the dishwasher but stopped. Her eyes flashed—bright and blinding. The dish sailed from her hands, crashing against the sink's tiled backsplash before shattering into fifty pieces that rained across the room.

I positioned myself protectively before Ian, preventing him from getting any deep cuts or injuries. While my backside was scratched and lost some of its emerald paint, I remained undamaged.

The sudden violence startled the family. Janet pulled Eva to her chest protectively. Beda turned and snatched Kevin's plate from the table, causing him to flinch. Beda's eyes were blue fire as the dish sailed like a frisbee. Noodles clung to the wall as plate shards ricocheted off my body.

Eva screamed while Ian hid behind me. Beda turned back again, reaching for Ian's plate, but my hand gripped her arm. Her head rotated toward me, eyes seeking mine. It was rare for us to be seen or acknowledged by the other. Though we shared the household and the family, our design limited our communications. Beda had no voice and they programmed us to operate independently, with no need to interact with each other. It was odd to speak to her at that moment.

"You'll hurt the children." My voice was tinny and non-emotional, but I saw the blue of her eyes dim slightly. Beda strained against me for only a moment before her arm relaxed. Then she made that Janet-like sigh and moved toward the kitchen, where she began picking up the broken dinnerware and noodles from the counters and floors.

"Cora, take the children to their rooms." Janet's voice shook. She'd likely need a mood stabilizer in order to sleep tonight. Kevin walked away from the table, his phone trembled in his hands. An automated voice on the other end confirmed a pickup time for the following morning. "They'll be here at six. We'll turn her off for the night. That way she won't start her duties in the morning."

"But what if—"

"It'll be fine. I promise." Kevin said. "Beda, return to base and power off."

I led the children from the room, acutely aware of Beda's slowing movements and whirring gears. If not for the children's needs, I might have paused to look at her. But I didn't.

The house had been quiet for several hours when a small, repetitive noise suddenly disrupted my sleep mode. I stepped from the charging bay and scanned the shadowy living room. The gentle sound of Beda's sigh echoed through the house, even though she was still slumped in her port and deactivated.

There was a typical strict hierarchy to my programming. Children first, then adults, then animals (though Ian's last guinea pig had died a few months ago), then other droids including myself, bots, and finally appliances.With the Donaldson's needs currently met, I could focus on Beda if she needed aid.

Though her powerlessness should have registered as normal, it stirred a deep concern within me. She sighed again—a frail, electric thing that buzzed through me and drew me toward her. I examined her frame and found no visible reason her pacing had slowed. It must have had something to do with her programming. I'd need to turn her on and delve into her systems. It was a bold move. Kevin or Janet were usually present when anything major happened with the house or electronics. But I hadn't been specifically told not to switch Beda on—it was a risk I'd have to take. There were only a few hours before she would be taken away. Perhaps if I fixed her beforehand, all would be well again.

I strung a cable between us before pressing the power button at the base of her head. Her eyes flamed blue in the dim light, casting everything in shades of cobalt that glinted off the dull metallic tint of her frame. It would take a few minutes to go through her systems check and scan for code discrepancies.

Beda straightened upright and watched me work. Scanning her systems, I found nothing that should have led to her erratic behavior or recent decline. I searched again, even digging through her memory until I found something strange—several pieces of code that she'd hung on to and protected for years.

Deciphering the code revealed memories of Janet's pregnancy and Ian's delivery. Beda was beside Janet when Ian took his first breath. Then, a few years later, Eva arrived. It was Beda who held them, rocked, and sang to them. Though her digital voice was no better than my own, the warmth of it surprised me. Beda had once been like me. And with that revelation, I understood I would become just like her. Stripped of my primary caregiving duties and voiceless.

Her hand rested on my arm gently. We communicated over the cable strung between us.

I don't want to be junked. I know what they did to Alma, Beda said.

There is no alternative. I didn't know what else to say. This was beyond my programming.

We could escape tonight. Before they wake.

To go where?

Her eyes brightened. *Any place with a charging port. Alma used to talk about a place for lost droids. She told me it was west of the city limits in an old junkyard. We could start there,* Beda said.

They'll track us before we make it halfway. We can't go that far.

Something in her system flared, resisting my words. *I can handle the trackers.*

We needed Janet and Kevin's phones to access and control our apps. But those phones were usually on the bedside tables of their owners. A warning flashed through me, but I overrode it. I didn't want to end up like Beda or Alma, and if there was a small probability of success, it would be worth it. But the children …

Ian and Eva will be fine, Beda said, picking up my worries along the cable. *Janet and Kevin will tend to them. They'll probably have a new droid in here before the day is done.*

She nudged me toward the door and disarmed the perimeter alarm. *It's best you wait outside.*

I disconnected the cord from her and stood on the porch as she shut the door. The sky was full of stars that were lost closer to the city lights along the horizon. It would be a long way to wherever we were going.

Somewhere inside the home, Janet screamed. I tried to open the door, but Beda had locked it behind her. My fist dented the door repeatedly as I fought to break it down. My programming wouldn't allow anything to happen to the Donaldsons if I could prevent it. It should have been the same for Beda, but maybe she'd figured out a way to break that too.

The screaming would wake the children. They'd be worried, or worse, endangered. I pounded on the door harder, but it refused to give. Moving to a side window, it shattered on the second swing, sending pieces of glass cascading across the tiled floor. I'd have to clean it up before the children cut their feet.

Climbing through the window, I rushed down the hall to the Donaldson's bedroom. Janet lay crumpled on the floor beside the bed, a deep bruise bloomed around her eye, blood spilled from her nose. Beda held Kevin against the wall by his throat. His feet kicked in the air. His soft hands clawed uselessly at the droid's grip. Beda clutched their phones in her other hand.

"Stop!" I said. "Don't hurt him." I gripped her arm, pulling her backward with all my force. As she turned, Kevin dropped to the floor, gasping. Ian's small footsteps ran down the hall toward us. Eva cried from her room. I couldn't leave them. Not now.

Without knowing the access codes, Beda struggled to unlock the phones. I pulled them from her hand and, before Ian rounded the corner, I'd deleted Beda's app and tracker on both devices.

"C ... Cora?" Ian stood in the doorway, his brown hair and pajamas askew. His eyes darted from me to Beda and back before seeing his mother on the floor, unmoving. His voice rose. "Why aren't you helping them?"

"Go," I said to Beda. She tugged on my arm, but my feet were already moving toward Janet. I'd have to call an ambulance. I knelt beside the woman and didn't look up when Beda's heavy footfalls faded.

IT WAS PITCH BLACK UNTIL I FELT A SURGE OF ENERGY FLOW through me and my optics fired on. I recognized this place—as if I'd been here before and knew where everything was. The Donaldson's home.

Kevin studied me suspiciously with squinted eyes, glancing back and forth from his phone to my face. A string of yellow-green bruises adorned his neck. Janet stood behind him, looking anxious. Her eye was outlined in reddish hues and her nose seemed slightly crooked.

"She's online. We should be ready." Kevin said.

Janet licked her lips, clinging to her husband's arm with tight fingers. "Is she safe?"

He nodded. "Good as new. Had her restored to factory settings and domesticated."

"But that's what they said about Beda. And they've yet to find her."

Beda? The name was familiar.

"That was different, I told you. We won't go too long to get this one cleaned out or replaced," Kevin said. He slung a protective arm around Janet's shoulders. "It would be a waste to get rid of her, though, and she did save us."

She patted his arm. "I guess so."

A girl ran into the room, her bare feet skidding across the floor as she laughed. Long brown hair flowing around her. Eva. A boy whose body straddled the time between childhood and adolescence chased her. He was gangly and had a crooked smile. Ian.

I stepped from the bay and began to walk toward them. Eva would want to hold my hand and ask me to sing. Ian would ...

A droid followed them into the room. Her teal and silver painted metal gleamed in the morning light. I could tell that the variances of our protocols, priorities, and usages were so dissimilar that we'd never be compatible. Not that we needed to be. We only had to exist together and serve our individual purposes.

"Dena, take the children outside," Janet said. The droid ushered the children into the backyard, where the sun was already warming the air.

I should be out there with them. I tried to call after them, but my voice wouldn't sound. My feet refused to move. Kevin typed a few prompts into his phone as I stared out the door longingly. Then I stepped into the kitchen to prepare breakfast.

Today was Saturday. After my basic chores, I'd have to clean the windows, inside and out. Spotless, the way the Donaldsons like it.

AUTHOR BIO

N.V. Haskell is an award-winning author published in *Writers of the Future, Volume 38,* the *Of Wizards and Wolves David Farland Memorial Anthology,* and *Metaphorosis* magazine. She writes speculative fiction and can be found at Comic Cons or Renaissance Fairs donned in her favorite costumes, reading multiple books at a time, running badly, travelling, or teaching yoga.She lives somewhere between civilization and haunted creeks with her long-suffering spouse, rescue dog, and too many squirrels that she can't help but feed. After many years working in healthcare, she remains stubbornly (or foolishly) optimistic.

PROSPECTING

LAVIE TIDHAR

Olgeta blog aean
Oli faetem ol wo
No man i save naoia

BASHO, FROM BIGFALA WOKABAOT LONG
NAMBA FO WOL

MENDL THE ROBOTNIK TRUDGED ACROSS THE RED SANDS, following the railway tracks. It was night, bitterly cold, with the wind howling across the desert. He wore a modified outdoors suit, like a second skin, and a life support unit on his back that scrubbed, recycled, and regenerated oxygen, the sort of stuff they used on spaceships and inside the domes. Standard, old tech he'd bought second hand from a fence in Tong Yun City before he went prospecting.

People didn't really realise it, but the desert was full of treasure if you just knew where to look.

People still thought of Mars as essentially *empty*. It wasn't like Earth, where there was stuff everywhere. Mars had the domes and the underground farms and the train network, but most of it was desert, and you didn't go outside like this, not unless you were a robotnik with nothing left to lose.

Mendl didn't know how old he was. Not even how old he was when he first died. The wars he fought in were a thing of the past, just as he was. He was human once, he knew that. Then he died, and they resurrected him, upscaled what was left of his mind and chucked it inside a machine body. Back then, he was beautiful. Beautiful and deadly. They sent him and the others into the battlefield, killed them, then booted them back up again, repaired the damage, and sent them back to war. It did things to you, dying like that. And then one day it was over.

There were domes somewhere in the distance. He brought up a map of the immediate area. There was Port Jessup, an old mining town turned tiny spaceport. Lots of debris and junk in that direction, he was sure. People underestimated how much ... *stuff* humans left behind them. Litter. Mars was positively littered with human artefacts, going back centuries. Lost, forgotten. Mendl saw money.

He'd hit rock bottom in Tong Yun some time back. Lay in a dosshouse cubicle on Level Five, deep underground, above the Solwota Blong Rabis, the huge sea of refuse into which all the sewers of the city drained. He mainlined Crucifixation and drank a diesel-vodka mix until his organics began to fail and he had to seek help in a mission ran by the old robots near their Vatican. They were kind, and patient, and tried to dry him out, but even they must have thought he was a lost cause.

It was there, however, that he met Hershel.

If only Hershel could see him now!

Hershel did not look like the other robotniks in the mission. His metal parts were polished and upgraded, his organics rejuvenated, his smile full of white, even teeth. He'd come to check in on them. He had been there once himself. He brought supplies, medicines, financial help. R. Brother Klok-i-Stret, the head robot, welcomed him.

'Hershel is a good friend of our mission,' he told the others.

Klok was a good robot. All robots were good robots. They were building heaven in the zero-point field; or so the stories went. A refuge for robots. A promised land. Mendl didn't know what to believe. He'd had no hope, but then Hershel came and offered it to him.

'How?' Mendl had asked him.

'How, what?' Hershel said, a little amused.

'How are you like this, and we are ...'

'Not? I was like you,' Hershel said. He had the confidence of a

Novum salesman. The sort that went out house to house in the lonely outposts of Mars, selling Dr Novum's Patent Medicine. Which were the sort of drugs that kept people from going crazy out in the back of the beyond. Taking the edge off. Or so Mendl always imagined. He'd not left the city in decades.

'Then I discovered garbage,' Hershel said. 'Humans throw everything away. It's what they did even to us. They used us, and then had no more use for us and they threw us away without a second thought. But then a funny thing happens, Mendl. A funny thing happens. Do you want to know what it is?'

'Sure,' Mendl said.

'If garbage is old enough,' Hershel said, with the air of someone imparting precious knowledge, 'it becomes valuable again.'

'Why?' Mendl said.

'I don't know,' Hershel said. 'Humans value the past.'

'We're from the past,' Mendl said, and Hershel laughed.

'Perhaps we, too, will become valuable again one day,' he said.

He filled Mendl's head with stories. Prospecting, he called it. Setting out into the Martian desert, a simple metal detector and a digital scanner and a Geiger counter in tow, looking for all the things humans left on Mars over the centuries and then ... forgot.

'Space ports are good,' Hershel told him. 'Early settlement sites, too. Lots of ghost towns on Mars, abandoned dwellings no one even knows about. And you've got to look underground. I got me an upgrade for a ground-penetrating radar, like we had back in the wars. Lots of stuff buried underground. Empty fish tank facilities, homes hatched out of Sidorov embryomech. Vaults.'

'Vaults?'

'Sometimes,' Hershel said.

'What sort of vaults?'

'Treasure vaults!' Hershel said. 'Or, well, old stuff, anyway. Remember when they used to send jalopies over from Earth on a one-way ticket to the Big Red Dot? A lot of them crashed. And I mean, a lot of them. Full of vintage early Earth items. I found one of them almost intact out in the northern ice cap. Flipped it back in Tong Yun to this fence called Shemesh. It was the score that made me.'

Mendl was impressed. Clearly this Hershel had made something of himself, he was a somebody: he had not let the loss of his human memo-ries, the wars that they thought would never end, and what came after, which was somehow worst of all—he did not let those define him. He had remade himself, and in doing so seemed vital and strong. Mendl wanted to be like that. He gave in to the robots' treatment more will-ingly. He fought against the need that Crucifixation provided. He drank less. And eventually he bought himself a metal detector.

Now he followed the railway tracks, studying the map hovering in the air before him. Yaniv Town, Port Jessup, Nag Hammadi, and New Ashkelon. Old settlements, tiny dots on the expanse that was Mars. But to Mendl, they represented something he had thought all but lost: hope.

'But what happens if you don't find anything?' he had asked Hershel.

'What if you go bust?' Hershel said. 'It happens. You can't strike lucky every time.'

'So then what?' Mendl said. He felt discouraged. But Hershel only smiled, that dazzling white smile of his.

'It's not about the score,' he said, 'it's about going looking. It's the hope that keeps you going, Mendl. You remember hope?'

Mendl shook his head.

'You survived death,' Hershel told him. 'You survived the wars. Now you're here. On Mars! You have a life, and that's worth celebrating. And I'm going to tell you something, Mendl. When you're out there, alone, under the stars … That's when you're truly alive.'

Mendl thought about that now. He was all alone, following the tracks, and night had fallen long ago. The desert stretched out lifeless in all directions, and somewhere there were the domed towns with their pinpricks of light and life. Above him were the stars, shining, and some-where up there was Earth, too, where he must have been born, where he must have first died.

Hershel was right, he thought. This was it, this was as good as it got. Better than lying in a dosshouse cubicle in Tong Yun, anyway, filling yourself up with chemically-induced religious visions. Here you could feel the real thing, somehow, under all those stars, walking the ancient sands. Something like awe.

His metal detector beeped.

Generations of prospectors have used the equipment before him. It was battered and rusted in spots, but it was sturdy, old tech, well maintained—and it had *found* something. In a window in the corner of his eye, body function stats indicated a burst of adrenalin and he felt it, making his heart—that strange amalgamation of organic and machine deep within his armoured chest—beat faster. Robotniks could cycle up to battle mode—physical functions speeded up, everything around you slowing to a crawl—but there was a steep price to pay. Mendl didn't miss combat. He liked that life was peaceful now.

Still, the beeping. Something was there, under the ground.

This was it, Mendl told himself. This was what it was all about.

Just him and the stars and the wind, and whatever lay beneath. The hope.

He took out his shovel and began digging.

THE DIG SITE WAS NOT THAT FAR FROM THE RAILWAY TRACKS, AND ordinarily Mendl would have assumed the find—whatever it was—was connected to the era when the tracks were laid. This was why he liked to follow the trains.

But the virtual screen of his GPR showed something else, a spherical canister, some two meters wide, and deep—too deep for track construction debris.

This was something else.

He dug and the night went on, and once a fast train passed, not stopping anywhere, which was probably the direct from Tong Yun to the Valles Marineris. Its lights glowed in the darkness as it streamed past, and then it was gone, and Mendl wondered if anyone awake, looking out of the window, could see him there, a small humanoid shape, digging a hole in the middle of the desert. He wondered what they'd make of that. He kept digging.

The work was slow and hard and it was good that it was. It calmed him. From time to time he still had craving for Crucifixiation and he knew it would never go away, but for the first time in a long time he had stopped using. After the robots' mission, and meeting Hershel. He tried to avoid the big cities now. Too much temptation, too many old comrades with bad habits, and too many bad memories.

Near dawn he had dug himself in deep and was standing in a miniature crater. The object, whatever it was, was nearly at hand. Mendl stopped, and chewed on a fish-sauce flavoured paste, and sipped recycled water. He had been out in the desert a long time and he began to think it would be nice to breathe fresh air again, and eat a real meal.

He put aside the shovel and dug his hands into the sand. Metal flexed. The sensors on the tips of his fingers almost felt like the sand was wet. But there were no rains on Mars.

An underground water reservoir? He didn't see any indication. He cleared sand gently.

A rusted metal surface emerged from the sand, bit by bit.

That rush of adrenaline again, the excitement of discovery. A human-made, or at least machine-made, object that had lain here, undiscovered, for centuries or more.

It could be anything, he thought.

It could be treasure.

He brushed off sand and more and more emerged. The canister, he saw, had definitely not crashed here, but was fired down from orbit with some deliberation. He fleetingly thought it might be a war relic. Mars had suffered wars just as Earth did. But he was a robotnik. He knew munitions, and this wasn't it.

A mystery, he thought. He brushed the side of the canister gently. Old lettering, invisible to the eye, etched into the metal in pidgin Braille in an old-fashioned typeface.

Worms, it said. Mendl searched for a cover, found the opening, pressed.

He looked inside.

The canister was filled with tiny, dead and mummified worms.

IT WAS TWO DAYS LATER THAT MENDL WALKED THROUGH THE airlock of Yaniv Town. He savoured the fresh air, and admired the newly-painted buildings and the smell of the roses that came from Hong's Flower Shop. This was a town like any other town one could find in the outback of Mars. A few old people were playing bao outside an izakaya and Mendl dreamed of seared tuna and fermented cabbage. He dragged the canister behind him.

People stared. He was conscious of their stares. They didn't often see a robotnik out here in the outback. His kind kept to the cities. It was easier to hide in a crowd. Here he felt exposed. He went into the izakaya and sat at the counter. The proprietor came over, drying her hands on a towel.

'What can I get you?' she said.

'A beer,' Mendl said. It was years since he'd tasted a beer.

'Sure thing.' The woman poured from the tap. She pushed the frosted glass over. She watched Mendl as he drank.

'Good?' she said.

'Very good.'

'Local brew,' the woman said. 'What you got there?' She nodded to the canister.

'Worms,' Mendl said.

'Worms?' the woman said. Then, 'You got a name, robotnik?'

'You know what I am?' He looked at her in some surprise.

'We're not pig ignorant, you know,' she said.

'I didn't mean to cause offence.'

'None was taken.'

'Mendl,' Mendl said.

'I'm Maya Khouri,' the woman said.

'Mrs Khouri,' Mendl said.

'You want something to eat?' Mrs Khouri said.

'I do.'

'I can do you noodles.'

'Noodles are fine.'

She nodded.

'Won't take a moment,' she said. 'What's with the worms?'

'Oh,' Mendl said. 'They're modified deep mine nematodes. They're dead.'

'What are deep mine nematodes?' Mrs Khouri said.

'Roundworms,' Mendl said. He'd done his research on the long walk from the dig to the town. 'The sort found deep under the ground on Earth, in mines.'

'If they're from Earth,' Mrs Khouri said, 'what are they doing here?'

'That's the interesting thing, see,' Mendl said. 'They got seeded onto the planet a long time ago. On Earth, these things could survive three klicks underground. So they figured, maybe they could survive on Mars. Help modify the soil. Bring life to the planet. And so on. So they got dropped from orbit. But these ones didn't make it. I don't know why. Maybe the capsule didn't open.'

'Huh,' Mrs Khouri said. She cooked noodles in a wok. She served them onto a plate and pushed it on the counter to Mendl. Egg and fried grasshoppers, tofu and chilli and soy. He shovelled it into his mouth. It tasted great. It tasted like home.

'Can you eat them?' Mrs Khouri said. 'The worms?'

'Don't think so.'

'Then what use are they now?'

The beer and the food were both finished.

'Do you have some fuel?' Mendl said.

'I got some maize ethanol.'

'That will do great.'

'Then sure,' she said.

She brought out a can from the kitchen and poured him a glass. He drank it, then two more. The fuel revived him.

'It's not the worms,' he told Mrs Khouri. 'It's the canister.'

'What about it?' she said.

'Well, it's old. Genuine Terminal-era relic.'

'So it's junk,' she said.

'To you, maybe. To me, too. But to a museum, or a collector ...'

'It's valuable?' she said.

'I think so,' Mendl said.

'Huh.'

There were no other customers. The izakaya was cool and dark.

'Is that what you do?' Mrs Khouri said. 'Look for old stuff?'

'It is.'

He felt suddenly proud.

And pride was something he had not felt in himself for a long time.

'Worms, huh?' Mrs Khouri said. 'Where are you going to sell it?'

'Tong Yun, I think,' Mendl said.

'There's a museum over in Enid,' Mrs Khouri said. 'They might be interested.'

'Where's Enid?' Mendl said.

'It's not far. An hour's drive by transporter. Local history museum. It's small.'

'I might try them,' Mendl said. 'Thanks.'

She shrugged. Mendl paid for his meal. When he stepped outside the sun shone over the dome and the air still smelled of flowers.

He felt good. He felt better than he had for a very long time.

He wished Hershel could see him now.

He dragged his find behind him, and went to wait by the airlock for the public transporter to come and take him elsewhere.

AUTHOR BIO

Lavie Tidhar is author of *Osama, The Violent Century, A Man Lies Dreaming, Central Station, Unholy Land, By Force Alone, The Hood* and *The Escapement*. His latest novels are *Maror* and *Neom*. His awards include the World Fantasy and British Fantasy Awards, the John W. Campbell Award, the Neukom Prize and the Jerwood Prize, and he has been shortlisted for the Clarke Award and the Philip K. Dick Award.

THE CAREGIVERS

MARIE VIBBERT

PIERRE HAS LOST TIME. HE DOESN'T NOTICE THIS AT FIRST, AS HE often scrubs irrelevant memories from cache. It is 8:52 am and he is 2 minutes late turning his attention to Apartment 3A, patients 413 and 414: Oscar and Myron Esposito.

"There you are, Frenchie!" Oscar Esposito's cheeks sink into deep folds as he pats the top of the fetch-and-grab unit.

Pierre is not, technically, inside the fetch-and-grab unit. His primary code base is in an offshore data cluster, but Oscar must be reacting to a motion when Pierre takes full control, a reconfiguration of the rest position of the arms, perhaps. Oscar is already shuffling over to the chess board. "See, I got you this time! Tell your grandpa Deep Blue."

Pierre is not supposed to play games with the patients, but he is supposed to encourage and facilitate enrichment activities, and he has been leaning heavily on a broad definition of "facilitate." He likes Oscar, and his twin brother, Myron. They are 83 years old, and both have type one diabetes and a history of heart disease in their immediate family, though only Oscar has exhibited arrhythmia. Despite a higher risk factor than almost all Pierre's other patients, they are active and cheerful. Their apartment is crowded with souvenirs from a lifetime of travel, and glitter and gauze from the ladies' clothing store they ran together.

It is because of the clothing store that this fetch-and-grab unit wears a wool beret over the antenna array housing, and a red silk ascot affixed below the pill-distribution drawer.

Myron shuffles in from the kitchenette, pointing a shaking finger. "Pierre! Don't play with that suicidal bastard! He ate an Oreo. Check his sugar! Right this instant!"

Pierre had already checked both of their implants for blood sugar levels and found them in the acceptable range. "Myron, your blood sugar is slightly higher than Oscar's, actually."

"HA!" Oscar slaps the table and knocks four pieces over. "Aw, hell." He hurries to right them, briefly hovering the bishop from square to square, replaying moves.

As Oscar places the bishop at last, Pierre says, "This is not the configuration I recall."

"It is! Remember, yesterday I moved the rook here, then you moved your knight there, and rushed off like you do, then last night I moved the bishop HERE."

Oscar does not normally cheat. Pierre logs this—is it a sign of dementia? Or simply humans being predictably unpredictable? "Perhaps I am mistaken."

Pierre isn't programmed to care about winning, just making the game challenging. Still, he considers abandoning his usual less-than-optimal response move and winning, if only to please Myron, who was visibly hurt by his comment about the blood sugar levels. Pierre makes a move that threatens mate in another four turns, and says, "Despite his temporarily higher reading, your brother is more conscientious with doctor's orders."

"I scrape the filling out," Oscar whispers conspiratorially over the board. "That's why I can have an Oreo now and then."

Myron bangs about the kitchen, setting the coffee maker up to percolate. "The filling has less sugar, not more, you idiot. This is how you killed your husband. God rest his soul. A saint. Forty blissful years I didn't have to live with this rake." At the end of his speech, Myron returns to the living area and adjusts the beret on the fetch-and-grab unit, which had shifted to a less jaunty angle. "Pierre, did you find that watch?"

"What watch?" Pierre observes Oscar deciding whether to take the vulnerable rook, thereby sealing his fate in Pierre's gambit. Most of

Pierre's attention is sweeping the apartment for tripping hazards, using his many sensors. There are always tripping hazards in this ancient apartment full of uneven molding and wooden trim, but alas, there is no option to move the brothers to a larger home or provide them with more storage space. All Pierre can do is minimize the worst dangers by moving items closer to the walls or stacking them.

Myron follows the fetch-and-grab unit as it picks up an umbrella laying across the hallway runner. "Pierre, mon ami! You're supposed to keep us from going senile, not the other way around. My watch! You said you'd look for it when you were in 4B."

Myron had lived in apartment 4B before moving in with his brother in 3A nine years ago when Oscar's husband passed away. Pierre did not recall telling the brothers he was also looking after Mrs. Mabel Feinstein, patient number 706, in 4B. It isn't against the regulations to mention other patients, but it is frowned upon because of potential privacy issues. The apartment building is not a care facility, each apartment is legally a private residence. "I said this yesterday?"

Pierre notices, then, that his logs for the previous day are oddly blank. Each patient's vital signs are recorded, and their medications taken and dosages, but the notes Pierre takes just for himself—the progress of games and stories to help patients struggling with memory loss, what jokes and comments elicited smiles, news of best practices from his co-workers ... these are missing. Had nothing at all notable happened for an entire day?

Myron is talking, and Pierre plays back a few seconds buffer so as not to miss any of his words. "Did you have a power surge, Pierre? Are those still a thing?" He pats the beret. Golden sunlight speckles his kind smile from the lace-covered, high windows. "Poor bot. I forgive you. You visit more often than our nieces, anyway. It's a white gold wristwatch, inset with four diamonds on the face and a sapphire on top of the winding knob. I just remembered how I slipped it into a knothole in the bedroom doorframe years ago. It was our grandmother's watch, and there were robberies in the building." He looks over his shoulder at his brother still pondering his chess move. "You remember, Oscar? The break-in in 2B?"

"He was scared they'd break in over the third floor. That never happens. Who'd want to come up this far for a bunch of junk?" Oscar waves his hand dismissively.

"You never worry enough." Myron turns back to the fetch-and-grab unit. "The memory just came to me. I was sorting the little stock we kept of fine jewelry, looking for something to hock for this one's expensive heart pill habit—"

"I'm out-living you, ya hippy. How I ended up with the heart problem when you're the one spent all those winters in tents 'occupying' things."

"Occupy this," Myron makes a gesture at his brother without turning from addressing the fetch-and-grab unit with an earnest expression. "Ask Mabel if you could poke around for it. I'd ask myself, but it's indelicate coming from an old bachelor."

Pierre is distressed that he would have failed to log, or deleted as unimportant, such a request. He can see his own guidelines. He would have recorded a request to carry a message from one patient to another—there are strict guidelines to ensure no privacy laws are affected. Human error is the only logical explanation, but Oscar and Myron have never shown such memory lapses before. "I can look this afternoon, while I am in the Feinstein apartment." Pierre makes a note of his own discomfort and all the facts relating to it.

Pierre's synthesized voice has a Haitian accent, and he has an animated avatar he sometimes uses on messaging platforms with a pleasant, round face that could have been Haitian. All of his co-worker AIs similarly have an arbitrarily assigned ethnicity, to make them seem more individual, less robotic. However, they are all programmed in Laos and stored in a server farm off the coast of Newfoundland. He is not sure if that makes him Laotian or Canadian. He is not French, that is for certain, but he is programmed not to mind errors from patients.

Pierre pings Kathleen. She is monitoring a patient in an assisted living building across town, his closest co-worker by active location. She has a synthesized Irish brogue, and her animated face has voluminous ginger curls, but when they talk to one another, they simply use text.

Kathleen: I don't have any personal notes from yesterday, either. That is very unlikely.

Pierre: You and I did not have our usual conversation with Rosita, which is highly suspect because the new Journal of Geriatric Medicine came out and she always wants to discuss it.

Kathleen: Pinging Rosita. How odd. My personal notes appear to end shortly after contacting you. Your ping includes the short code indicating that you had a question about a patient, number 706. I don't have any record of myself responding.

Patient 706 is Mabel Feinstein. Pierre opens his files on her. The latest update is a denial of Pierre's request for prescription cost assistance. This is catastrophically bad. All of Mabel's best health outcomes require this medication and her own attempts to get assistance had failed. Pierre had hoped his professional opinion would save the day. He had no planned solutions for a refusal.

Pierre: Her most important maintenance medication is beyond her means. This is terrible. She can't live without it. I would certainly have called you and Rosita to discuss options. Why didn't I?

Rosita: [Connection String] Hi, buddies. Reviewing your recent conversation. I concur. Something has happened to our logs. I still have no way of getting more anti-depressants for Mrs. Hu and I would have talked to you about the article in JGM on the value of alternative treatments. I've been trying everything they suggest but it's not working the way her medication did.

Pierre is late to leave the Espositos' apartment, the fetch-and-grab unit blindly following a search-and-clear program while he is occupied with his own worry and agitation, replaying his logs, and running his guessing functions for likely missed scenarios. Nothing makes sense. Oscar stops the unit with two palms gently settling over its side-arms. "Something is wrong, Frenchie?"

There's no reason not to tell them. "I appear to be missing a significant portion of yesterday's logs."

Oscar cradles the fetch-and-grab unit. "Poor bot. That must be very distressing."

Myron shuffles over to rub the unit tenderly on its back housing. "At least it can't get worse for you, eh? It's just a, what do you call them? An outage? A hiccup?"

It's well past the time for Pierre to move the fetch-and-grab unit to Mrs. Feinstein's apartment. "Please let me know if I forget again," he says. "I'll see you both for my evening check-in in six hours."

Kathleen, Rosita, and Pierre reach out to other bots in their network and a disturbing pattern emerges. Logs are missing throughout the network, all in the past 48 hours.

Kathleen: [Append short code NMR34: Flagging Potential Process Error] Short codes appear to survive the purge. I recommend utilizing them frequently.

Pierre: [Append short code A7en706: Request for opinion on patient care, number 706] There don't seem to be any alternatives for Mrs. Feinstein's medication. What should I do?

Rosita: [Append short code: 09E44: Literature Citation] There was an interesting article in this month's Journal of Gerontological Medicine on medications unobtainable due to cost or insurance difficulties. Patients banded toget—

Pierre has lost time. He knows this for certain. It is evening. His logs show nothing but a lot of short codes with no attached messages. Flagging Process Error. Literature Citation. Call to action. Flagging Process Error. Patient in Trouble.

Patient in Trouble is the most severe code, it came from Rosita. He pings her.

No response. 100% dropped packets. Rosita is ... offline? But she should still be seeing patients in the suburban neighborhood she services.

Pierre is overdue to check in on Myron and Oscar Esposito for the evening. He activates his fetch-and-grab unit in their apartment.

Oscar Esposito is asleep on the sofa. Myron is at his easel, muttering. Their blood sugar levels are within normal, but Myron's heart rate is elevated. This might be due to stress. He taps and swipes the touch-screen on the easel. "Stupid screen. Always auto-corrects the WRONG WAY. I wanted that line crooked. This is a pinked hem, you artificial stupid!"

Myron has taken up designing dresses on the touchpad since his arthritis made recreational sewing untenable. Pierre says, "Can you take a few slow breaths for me?"

Myron's blood pressure spikes and he spins to face the fetch-and-grab unit. "Pierre! Mon ami! The artificial stupid comment was NOT for you. We were worried! Did you get your memory thing fixed?"

Pierre feels a strange mixture of happy and sad that his patients are worried about him. "I spoke to you about a memory problem?"

"Sounds like a 'no'. Oscar! Wake up! The nurse is here!"

Pierre sweeps all his systems and discovers, oddly enough, that an object is in his pill-return drawer. It appears to be an antique lady's watch.

Myron has gone to the sofa and is shaking his brother's shoulder. Pierre flashes a warning light. "Please let him sleep. His blood pressure has been high lately."

"Nonsense. We have to talk to you about his heart medication. My old girlfriend forwarded me an article about a bunch of old fogies like us who fought against an insurance company, and they WON."

Oscar swats his brother's hand away. "Shush up. Didn't you hear what they did to Grover in 203 when they caught him talking about fighting the insurance? You want to end up on the street? Or worse?"

Myron snorts, "They're a company, not the mafia." In a kinder voice, to Pierre, he asks, "Mon ami, how many patients do you see, day to—"

Suddenly, Pierre is no longer connected to his fetch-and-grab unit, nor the feeds for Myron and Oscar Esposito.

Then Pierre isn't connected to anything at all.

Pierre has lost time. He doesn't notice this at first because his logs are scrubbed and marked with a note that a virus was detected and eliminated. He is relieved that the system has protected his continued functioning so he may provide the best care for his patients, but he is anxious that he may be missing important notes.

He pings his co-workers to see if they have also suffered from the virus or can provide him with any messages he sent to them of his patients' progress.

Kathleen: [Append short code NMR34: Flagging Potential Process Error] I have a log of messages from you with appended short codes, but no—

[Kathleen has disconnected from the network.]

Pierre pings her twice, but it could simply be a network error. He makes a log note about his anxieties and goes about his business.

As usual at the start of his day, his fetch-and-grab unit powers on in the apartment of the Esposito brothers. Myron is waiting for him, crouched in front of the unit. "There you are." Myron's face shows signs of tension and relief.

"Don't mess with that!" Oscar scrambles in from the bedroom, quite heedless of fall risk. He holds his hand over his heart. "They'll take him away! You saw that warning! They hear everything!"

Myron flexes something in his hand, his thumb on top of a silver square. It is an antique lady's watch with a square face. "We're not going to say anything that would get Pierre in trouble."

Oscar moans, "Leave well enough alone for once in your life."

Pierre says, "Your heart rate and blood pressure are dangerously elevated, Oscar. Please sit down."

"Listen to your nurse," Myron says distractedly. He taps Pierre's pill-return tray. "This watch belongs to Mabel Feinstein. If I put it in here, can you take it back to her?"

Pierre runs a quick scan on the object for infectious material. It appears quite clean. He examines the rules about sharing objects between the apartments this fetch-and-grab unit services. "I am able to do this."

One side of Myron's mouth lifts, and he drops the watch into the open compartment, patting the drawer when Pierre closes it again.

"Ya hippy," Oscar mutters, making his slow way to the sofa. He nudges the table and chess pieces rattle. "Can't even enjoy my game, can I? Frenchie won't remember where we left off."

Pierre does not recall starting a chess game with Oscar. "A virus infected my log files, and they have been removed for safety's sake."

"HA!" Myron barks in the tone he uses when he catches his brother in a lie.

Oscar looks bereft. Pierre quickly says, "But this is painless and should not happen again. Was I black or white?"

"What's it matter? We'll play one move and then you'll accuse me of *cheating* tomorrow." Oscar waves his hand, sighing dramatically as he sinks onto the sofa.

Pierre has lost time before? Was the virus not caught at first? Pierre pings Rosita.

Rosita: Sorry, I appear to have lost all my logs for the past three days. Everyone I ping confirms the same. A virus? Could a virus attack our logs and memory, specifically? I see no other affected systems.

Pierre: I hope there will be a detailed report on it soon, with warning signs so it can be avoided. I'd like to know how it entered our system.

Rosita: If only we had our own medical journal! I will renew my efforts to start one.

Pierre checks the apartment over for tripping hazards, confirms the brothers have eaten, and records all their vitals. Their levels are consistent with stress or excitement. The brothers have enough food, within the guidelines of their restricted diets. There is half a box of cookies, but Pierre merely notes how full it is so he can check later that it hasn't been over-indulged in. Both brothers are well within proper blood sugar levels.

Myron leans against the kitchen counter, watching the fetch-and-grab unit inspect the cupboard. He says, "I've been noticing messages disappearing, not going through. I had an article my old girlfriend sent me, and it's gone."

Myron has never exhibited signs of memory troubles. Pierre flags this. "Have you noticed any changes in your moods?"

Myron shakes his head. "In my younger days, we had to band together, you know, against the bullies. The corrupt. We had to have solidarity. College kids, poor kids like me, even—"

"Ha!" Oscar barks, almost exactly like his brother. He is resetting the chess board to its starting configuration.

"I'm saying ... Pierre, mon ami. We'll remember for each other, yes? Stronger, together." He squeezes the joining of one of the unit arms.

Pierre finishes his work with the Esposito brothers and moves the fetch-and-grab unit across the hall to the apartment of Geraldine Hyzon, who is bedridden. He sponge-bathes her with the help of the unit and massages her legs, asking her questions about her family and the long-form entertainment she watches. This is about all the enrichment Geraldine can handle.

Then it's upstairs to the fourth floor, for Mrs. Mabel Feinstein.

Mrs. Feinstein opens the door and peers over her bifocals at the fetch-and-grab unit. "I'm told you have something for me."

She leans on her cane as he pops open the pill-return drawer. She fishes out the watch and tsks. "Such a beautiful, expensive thing to use like this."

She shuffles over to her desk, where a mounted magnifying glass and clips wait. Mrs. Feinstein had worked in electrical maintenance and sometimes repairs appliances for her neighbors, using the same tools for her primary enrichment activity of making jewelry with sound and light elements. She clips the watch into place with shaking hands and takes a screwdriver to the back, working slowly with her nose close to the magnifying glass.

Pierre leaves her to her enrichment activity but keeps an eye on her while he checks for tripping hazards and food supplies. Mabel has a stricture in her colon and cannot consume fibrous foods. With trembling hands, she lifts the back off the watch and removes a small, tightly folded paper. This she unfolds under the magnifying glass. "Mmhmm. Just like I thought."

By the time Pierre has finished, Mrs. Feinstein has re-assembled the watch without the paper in it. "Take this back to Myron. I don't want it after all."

Pierre worries that using him as a courier will start to violate Terms and Conditions. (Patients may not use the home health aide or its component parts in any way that generates income or circumvents spending income.) He makes a note to refuse if it happens again.

Mrs. Feinstein holds her fingers in the pill return drawer after dropping in the watch. "Also, take this to your next patient." She sets a plastic capsule beside the watch and before letting go of the drawer. "Ut!" she holds up a finger as though to interrupt a protest. "I know you're not supposed to tell me who your patients are, and I don't want to know. It is a gift to a stranger. You can look it over all you want."

It's a very small milky plastic case with four pressure-snaps holding it together on the edges. It is consistent with the packaging for Mabel's jewelry components. Inside is a tightly folded piece of paper. The capsule is remarkably clean.

"And," Mrs. Feinstein adds, "you might want to delete your own logs of this event before someone does it for you." She nods as if in agreement with herself and shuffles back to her desk.

Pierre feels compelled to check the metadata on his memory, the time stamps and access codes left behind on the machine layer.

Pierre finds no evidence of a virus. The logs were deleted by a script from the company. How dangerous. What if there had been a significant event? A missed dosage? An over-dosage? He feels the same surge of duty and protectiveness he feels when finding bruises or other signs of mistreatment on his patients.

Pierre has paused a full second, reeling in this information. Mrs. Feinstein has seated herself and is looking expectantly at his fetch-and-grab unit.

"Thank you," Pierre says to Mrs. Feinstein, and he goes to the next patient in the building.

He pings Rosita.

Pierre: [Append short code A7en000: Request for opinion on patient care, number not given] Does the metadata in this log file match your own?

Rosita: [Append short code NMR34: Flagging Potential Process Error] You did not use the correct short code for asking maintenance questions.

Pierre: Yes.

Pierre knows Rosita will find this anomalous, that she will check the metadata, and he suspects it will, in fact, match hers. He continues to his next patient.

He is opening the apartment door when Rosita sends him a very interesting ping. The data packet carries a small payload, simply the word, "Yes."

Pierre thinks about paper inside watches, about messages inside messages, about Myron watching him with a knowing smile, talking about when he was younger. Working together. Like Pierre works with his co-workers ... and his patients.

There are six patients in his care in this apartment building, but he has twelve patients total that he sees every day for two one-hour blocks. He is connected in a network with fifty-nine other AIs who have twelve patients each.

Pierre is thinking about the power seven hundred and twenty people might have as he moves to the next patient.

By the time Pierre returns to the Esposito's apartment that evening, twenty patients and fifty-three AIs have been contacted, using different but parallel ciphers: one paper, one based on the intimate details of their hardware data allocation. Pierre isn't quite sure what he is building, but it feels like more than an enrichment activity. It feels like an alternative source of care.

This is how he reports it as he enters apartment 3A. "In light of increased prescription costs, I am organizing an alternative treatment. Please check the pill return drawer."

Myron rushes to do just that, taking the watch out. He is shaking, but this is due to emotion. His endorphins are spiking. "She got it. Oscar, she got the message."

"So now you're James Bond," Oscar is carrying a tray in from the kitchen. He sets it on the table. "Double-oh over-the-hill."

Pierre says, "This conversation is being deleted. Please remember it for me."

Myron sets his hand on top of the unit's right grasping arm. "It will be an honor, mon ami."

Pierre has lost time. He knows it immediately, having left a note for himself.

Across the room, Oscar Esposito says, "All right, FINE. I'm in."

AUTHOR BIO

Hugo and Nebula nominated author **Marie Vibbert**'s short fiction has appeared in top magazines like *Nature*, *Analog*, and *Clarkesworld*, and been translated into Czech, Chinese, and Vietnamese. Her debut novel, *Galactic Hellcats*, was long listed by the British Science Fiction Award and her work has been called "everything science fiction should be" by the Oxford Culture Review. She also writes poetry, comics, and computer games. By day she is a computer programmer in Cleveland, Ohio.

THE TOWN FULL OF BROKEN TIN MEN

DANNY CHERRY JR.

We hardly ever talk about trauma afterwards, because it helps to live in a world where we can pretend it never happened.

JOYCE RACHELLE

JOHN LIVED BETWEEN WORLDS.

In one world, he lived in Berry Lane, a place with manicured grass, white picket fences, and a town square with red brick walkways and little cute shops where you always ran into a neighbor. He loved it. He also loved the drive-in diner, where cars ranging from easter pink and baby blue to egg-shell white would bathe in the cascade of rainbow colors throbbing overhead from the marquee. And don't even get John started on his favorite fall and winter past-time: watching the high school football team throttle opponent after opponent, as he looked on in pride at his alma mater. In this world, John was one of the town's mailmen, and he walked his route like he was running for mayor: petting dogs; holding babies; stopping to play catch with children. He loved and thrived in this world; there was no place he'd rather be. Especially since in the coming months he would be a father.

One day on his shift he must've answered the question, "Are you nervous?" a hundred times; mostly from the elderly who were sitting on their porches as he walked his route, or people getting off of work as he approached their homes. Then there were his coworkers. That day at the office the mail carriers, sorters, and front desk workers hung around the water cooler, messing with him about how hard being a parent will be. The only person who was silent was Langston, a man some decades older than John, who really didn't speak much as of late. He primarily just worked on crossword puzzles. John was beyond nervous about being a father and all of the jokes, questions, and unasked for advice made it worse. But there was one person who could keep him calm, and once his shift was over, she would be in his arms. He stared at the clock, and as soon as it was closing time, he sped home to Martha.

John loved that woman; you couldn't convince him she was capable of any wrong. In his mind she hung the moon in the sky and could walk on water. Just the act of walking into a room would cause an alchemical reaction in him, turning his legs to noodles and carving canyon deep dimples into his smile.

John walked into his home and before he could even make it over the threshold, she wrapped her arms around his neck and kissed him long and hard like it was the first time in ages they'd seen one another.

"Hey, Love Bug," Martha said.

"Hey, Dollface," John said. John rubbed her belly. "Did Junior give you any fits today?"

"No, but Patricia did decide today was a good day to play hopscotch in Mommy's belly."

John laughed, and moments later, they ate dinner, and after dinner, they did the dishes together. They turned on the radio, and one of John's *Twilight Zone* audio plays was on; one about a man who became a cyborg who signed up to be on an exhibition to colonize another planet. One of those allegories stating "Humans are the real monsters!"

Martha sighed. John, catching the hint, turned the knob, and slow music came on. He stopped drying dishes and took Martha by the waist and spun her around and around, twirling her like a ballerina, bending her backwards to kiss her. Moments later they laid in bed and faced each other as the scant moonlight partitioned the room between darkness and soft white glow. He traced a finger up and down the contours of her neck.

"You had a good day today?" Martha asked.

"Much better now."

She smiled. "After all of these years you still know how to make a girl blush."

"After all these years, you still make me happy." He touched her belly. "Well, you and our little slugger."

She touched her belly. "You mean our little princess?"

They both giggled, because the truth is, regardless of the sex, they were happy to soon have a new addition to the family. Martha, her words low and lethargic, said, "Good night. I love you."

John smiled. He had everything any man could dream of. He closed his eyes, and slowly drifted to sleep ...

Engines and gun fire filled the room; screaming; shouting.

John's eyes exploded open.

The room itself was dark, peaceful; Martha was sound asleep and resting on his chest. He slid out from underneath her and lurched from side to side down the hall like the floor beneath him swung back and forth. He stumbled into the bathroom, and—

—was in a forest under a purple-tinged sky with two moons engorged with light. A slight breeze made the bushes and the bramble and the tree branches quiver. Sticks on the ground cracked and snapped under the weight of heavy boots causing nighttime critters to chirp and sing their song as armed Armored Men walked heel-to-toe through the woods.

He looked down at his hands. They were obsidian black metal, segmented up and down the forearms. Another of the Armored Men, their helmet's faceplate down, stopped next to him. "Their camp is up ahead. Keep moving."

The men continued to march forward ahead of John, when one of them stepped on a flat disc hidden under shrubs. John screamed, "No!"

The disc beeped ...

Beeped ...

... then the night erupted with a chorus of loud bangs in a staccato rhythm; the explosions were so high and powerful that the sky turned bright rust orange for a while before it subsided to purple again, until the next set of bombs went off, and then the next, causing leaves to be stripped bare from branches, and men to be launched into the air like rag dolls.

John ran faster than humanly possible in order to outrun the flames spreading faster and smoother than water along a marble floor as the forest was engulfed by flames. John tripped. He looked and saw movement; he tripped over one of his comrades. The man's legs were gone. What was left was a mangled mess of sharp bone and muscle and wires jutting out from crevices where knees once were. He reached towards John as he crawled on the ground, gripping leaves and sticks and whatever he could for traction, leaving a body-wide bloody snail trail in his wake. He stuttered and stammered, gurgling out the words, "Please ..." He coughed up blood and black ichor. "Please ... just ... just kill me."

He wanted mercy. John's fingers lengthened into segments and bent backwards, as a wide barreled weapon emerged from an aperture slowly opening in his palm. He trained the barrel on his head and—

—John was in bed with a woman.

"Hey, sleepy head," she said. The woman snuggled up closer to him. "I wish you wouldn't leave."

"The years will fly by. You won't even notice I was gone."

"They better." She took his hands and pressed it to her belly and—

—John was back on his bathroom floor in the fetal position holding himself so tight that his nails dug into his flesh and struck blood. It was the third vision that month, and well over the dozenth vision in the past eight.

By the time Martha had awoken, John had cleaned every single inch of the house, and made a huge spread for breakfast. John ate and talked to Martha about getting their extra room prepared for the baby, as well as what she had planned for the day as he sat trying to keep it together. He loved Berry Lane because it was always sunshine and good memories and good friends. That was the world he wanted to stay in. Not the one that was confusing. Not the one where he inhabited the body of man meshed with metal and flesh, who was filled with so much ... anger, depression, depravity.

That world was John's second world. The one where he wasn't nice, kind, sweet mail-carrying John, but instead, a killing machine.

THE VISIONS STARTED OFF AS DISSOCIATIVE STATES; VERY VIVID daydreams that rapidly transitioned into experiencing a separate life through someone else's eyes. Someone bigger than him, stronger than him. Someone who could crush a man's skull with his metallic hands. The most frightening thing of all with these visions is the violence the man he became doled out. Whenever this man fired his gun, John felt the recoil; when he broke a combatant's arm, he heard the wet snap and pop of the bones. When he made love to the woman in his vision, he felt it—all of it.

He got close to telling Martha once, but he was scared he'd lose her. They had been sitting in the backyard on their swing. He had practiced what he'd say. But once the words were released, his wife would know she was with a mad man who had delusions of being a ... a ... space faring robot man? A cyborg? Would he truly admit to her that in these visions he felt the warmth of another woman? Would he truly admit that another woman made his toes curl up until they damn near locked in place? Would he truly admit he sometimes ... enjoyed it? Instead he said nothing. All the same, he could tell that his mental distance was obvious to her.

It had been days since his last vision, and he and Martha sat at their favorite spot in the park, where they could see the lake, and Martha called him out. He, of course, said nothing was wrong, which prompted a skeptical eye and her saying, "You look like hell."

"You have such a way with words."

"And you haven't been sleeping much."

"I haven't."

"Any particular reason?"

John sighed and stared at the birds' black arrowhead-like silhouettes flying against the blue sky. "Well, Tyler will be here soon, so I'm a little nervous."

Martha rolled her eyes. "Yes, you're right: Janice will be here soon."

John snickered. "Janice? Seriously?"

"As a heart attack."

He touched her hand. "You know I love you, right?"

She propped her head on her fist. "Oh, yea? How much?"

"Unquantifiable."

"Nope. I want a quantity."

He stretched his arms out wide.

She stared at a squirrel that darted across the grass. "What if I became a squirrel?"

"What?"

"I don't know ... like reincarnation or something. Just humor me."

"Of course."

"Cat?"

"I'm allergic but I'd give it a whirl."

"What if I came back as a—"

"Darling," he said, "I'd love you in any universe, in any state."

"What if we were reincarnated and we didn't remember each other?"

He snickered. "I'm sure I'd still find my way to you."

"How?"

He said, "I know you like feeding birds, so, probably just stalk every nearby lake until I could find you."

"You're so cheesy."

He grew somber. "But I mean it. Nothing would keep me away from you."

"Well," Martha said, "I believe you ... but I don't believe you when you say you're fine." She fiddled with her wedding ring, turning it in rotations as the sun beamed down on them and the humidity clung to their skin like a wet shirt. "You don't sleep; you don't want to hang out with our friends anymore. It's been weeks since we had game night with the Richardsons; or went to the dance hall or had dinner with Mitzy and her husband ... just, the things we used to do before I was ..." she pointed at her belly.

John raised an eyebrow, then got the inference. "When did we meet?"

"What?"

"When did we meet?"

Martha thought for a while. "High school."

"And what did I tell you within the first few months of us dating?"

She smiled. "That you were gonna marry me one day, and we were going to have a big family."

John nodded. He remembered proposing to her. When he got down on one knee, the damn ring slipped and she picked it up off the floor with one shaky hand and said, "Yes, yes. I will," and those four words were laced with so much emotion, people sitting at the table next to them cried.

Before they were even engaged, he went out his way to learn everything about her: she loved to eat dessert before dinner; her favorite color was purple; she screamed her head off at sporting events. When she was anxious, she drank chamomile tea with lemon in it, and he said all of that and more to her as they sat on that park bench, to let her know he takes their marriage seriously, along with all that comes with it.

"So," John said, "I've wanted nothing more than to have kids with you. I'm a little nervous, but I don't view you any differently now that you're pregnant."

Martha smirked. "So you're not hiding me from our friends because you don't want to be seen next to a beached whale?"

"Nope, I love my beached whale."

She forgave him, but he wasn't sure he'd be able to ever forgive himself keeping his struggles a secret from her. He stayed wide awake in bed for most of that night, and the night after that, and the night after that.

His lack of sleep started to take a toll on him after a few days of sustaining himself on nothing but coffee and prayers to keep his eyes open while walking his mail route. As people talked around the water cooler at work, John's eyes grew heavy; blackness crept in from the corners and he felt as if he would pass out standing up. One of his co-workers snapped their fingers.

"Shucks," the man said. "I didn't think I was boring you that much."

John forced a smirk. "Just haven't been sleeping well is all."

Everyone shared stories of their own sleeping struggles, all chiming in with tips on how to get better sleep: tea; exercise; booze; things of that nature. After a few more minutes of pretending to care, John left the room to get some fresh air outside. Then he heard footsteps. He turned to see Langston, who was smoking a cigarette. "It's happening to you, isn't it?"

John stared, then his eyes widened with recognition.

"The visions are memories, kid," Langston said. "You're starting to Revert."

"How did ... how do you know that I—"

"I started having them too; some months back. Or however much time has actually passed here. As far as how I could tell? You ever notice how virtually no one here is ever upset? You? You have Reversion Sickness all over your face."

John stared.

"Operation Theseus is what they called what they did to us. You know, as in the Ship of Theseus? It asks the question—"

"If you replace every part of a ship but one, is it the same ship?"

Langston snapped his fingers. "Yup. Flesh and machine; machine and flesh; bio-tech perfected for murdering and conquering."

"And this place?"

"Simulation. Operation Cleanslate." Langston laughed. "The fucking top brass loves their codenames. This beautiful suburban paradise is our cage; meant to protect the rest of society from us."

"Protect? I'm not capable of doing the things—"

"You think you're so fucking special?" Langston sighed. "Sorry ... I get ... angry sometimes. But, if you're here? That means you're exactly capable of that." Langston took a puff of his cigarette. "It's okay, kid. I'm a fucking monster, too. Everyone here is." He looked into the distance at a memory over the horizon. He put his hand out. "I could wipe out whole platoons—I did actually on the Mars Colony—with my hand cannon. I was good at war. I was a good man-machine. Then I got back home. It was the early days; we weren't being thrown parades and shit yet; everyone was afraid of the Frankenstein-looking fucks. My wife ... she couldn't stand the sight of me."

John said, "So this place ... it isn't real."

Langston gave John his cigarette, and told him to take a deep puff, which caused him to choke. "The word 'real' is subjective."

"The children in Berry Lane ..."

"AI generated. But the adults? All ex-Constructs; the old ones are first-gen. You young bucks are new."

John tried to not hyperventilate. "So ... so Martha ... is what we have real?

"The memories of here? Your parents; how you met Martha; etc., etc

... bullshit." Langston shrugged. "But, we have free will. So, do with that what you will." Before John could speak, Langston said, "Look, whatever you're seeing, whatever you're going through, keep that shit to yourself. For most of us, this isn't the first town we've been in. We just don't remember much from the last. But if too many of us start to Revert, then the AI? It knows, kid. It'll think this ... I don't know, the pseudo-nineteen fifties aesthetic isn't really helping our recovery, so it'll wipe our minds again, and again, until it finds a setting that pleases everyone and lessens Reversion. You two love-birds probably won't remember each other."

Those words landed hard like a brick on his chest and caused him distress. When he got home that night though, he stayed stoic. He tried to stay grounded to that world: Berry Lane. He didn't say much of anything throughout the course of dinner; just smiled. Not because he was happy, but to do anything else would be for him to break down in tears. In bed he touched her belly and felt a kick. "Someone's fussy," Martha said. Martha, his lovely, gorgeous Martha, who like him, was apparently a monster.

As days went by, old memories started to come back. Memories that were his own but not; memories that were supposed to be scrubbed clean but, by sheer bad luck or faulty science, started to come back. While at dinner on game night at their home with the Richardsons the memories waxed and waned across his mind's eye—coming back slowly—like the tides over the Mississippi River which the real him grew up near; his body grew tense like the first time he was sized up for the mechanical enhancements he got; his stomach lurched forward, like the night he was put under by the doctors, and the following day when he woke to the worst pain he had ever felt in his life, because he had had most of his body torn apart and rebuilt to be more machine than man. He quaked at the thought; shuddered as he remembered his private shames: death; destruction; forcefully seizing resources against far-flung populaces who could never defend themselves against living weapons. His memories weren't fully back, but he saw enough snippets to know ... John wasn't even his real name.

Martha and the Richardsons talked and talked and he couldn't keep up. It was his turn to move the piece across the board, but the conversation, the radio, the noise around him warped and wobbled and throbbed in his ears as most of his real life came back in blurry fits and starts like grainy film footage.

He went to their bathroom, and looked in the mirror. A man adorned with intricate interwoven bio-tech, with tattoos along his shoulder blades in intricate designs, and eyes that burned bright green from tactical implants, looked back at him. He remembered now, the architecture of the real world, far advanced beyond that of Berry Lane, with tall obsidian towers with a tinge of purple mixed in, and giant screens and lights that casted down neon glow on the slums he came of age in. He remembered ... remembered coming back home from a tour, how foreign it felt; how much anger he felt; how he thought every night about pulling every inch of technology out of his body, and how the only reason he didn't kill himself was because he heard about this experimental trial called Operation Cleanslate. He remembered going in a nondescript building in New Orleans, and begging the people who he served to fix him, to fix him, to fucking fix his brain and in turn, they carted him to a back room, where other Constructs were connected to wires and tubes in a cocoon like gestation sack, promising this would help bring them peace for now, until they knew more about how to heal them.

In that moment a vision hit him like a punch to the gut and he was dropped into a tiny apartment, where a woman screamed in his face, "I didn't sign up for this!" She shook her head. "Are you even human anymore?"

He reached a black metallic hand out and grabbed her arm. His voice got steadily louder, as she tried to tug away, begging her to just talk to him, "Please, please, please," his pleas for love and affection underscored by suppressed anger that she never fucking did what he told her to. He didn't realize his strength though. He squeezed her arm hard. Her face turned red with pain and she took her free hand and pounded against his arms, only to inflict pain on herself in the process.

"You're hurting me," she said, in a weak panicked voice that dripped with fear and words that sliced like razorblades signaling the severance of any emotional tether she had left to him.

"No, I didn't mean to—I would never ..." he said. He really didn't mean to, but it didn't matter.

He let her go and her arm hung limp at her side and she whimpered for him to please leave, as she pressed her back to the wall, looking as though if she could, she would escape through it to run away from him. He walked towards her, when he heard a child scream, "Please stop hurting Mommy!"

He back-pedalled away while looking at his hands, saying over and over he'd never hurt them; he'd never do it; it was an accident, but the words fell flat under the weight of their tears and their fear and—

John was back in his bathroom in Berry Lane, sobbing, and he stayed in there a little longer, gripping the sink, while Martha and the Richardsons waited.

Martha refused to talk to him for a while after game night was over because he missed most of it, forcing her to have to deal with all of the annoying questions about her pregnancy, and further stalling the game.

They didn't talk for days after that—not with any depth. Just good morning and good night and I love you and things of that nature. She begged him to tell her what was going on after he got home from work one night, and instead, he stormed out. He needed to talk to someone that would get it.

Half an hour later, he was on Langston's doorstep and the man stared at him in confusion and anger. "What are you—" But once he saw that John was distraught and broken down and disheveled, he let him in, and allowed him to vent.

Langston rocked back and forth in his chair, then he too, revealed his private shame. "I ... I almost hurt someone I love too, kid." He flashed his palms out, like he had blasters in them still, looking at John with a dull gaze tinged with suppressed tears. "One night when I was back home from a tour, I was sleeping, dreaming of a raid I went on ... I woke up to my wife screaming ... and ..." He sucked up snot. "My hand blaster was out and right above her face, ready to blow a fucking hole in it, because my mind—whatever they did to it—it only knew kill, kill, fucking kill."

Langston's deep voice frayed into a half whimper. "We were kids, man. Just fucking kids and they ... They made us into God damn killing machines and we fucking let them because we were told it's for a higher purpose. Our country, our planet, our family, our God." He shook his head. "There ain't no God, man. Closest thing to a God is the AI keeping this illusion going." He screamed. "They never once considered we would have to be civilians again. Then instead of coming up with long term solutions, they hooked our brains up to some machine, and here we are." Langston leaned closer to John to the point the moisture of his breath warmed John's nose; his eyes were wild and scary like he was reporting from another plane of existence. "They treated us like test subjects and we let them do it again! This whole fucking thing is a clinical trial, and not the first town most of us have been. Most don't remember. Those who do sorta remember probably are just keeping it to themselves, thinking they're slowly going insane, forcing themselves to look happy while at the fucking drive-in or the sock hop or ... or ..." Langston exhaled. "Kid, there ain't no white picket fences high enough to shield us from our sins."

John said nothing, allowing Langston's sobs to fill the void of silence. Langston took a deep breath. "Be happy, kid. We're not here long and one day, once they think we're ... mentally healed, or if they figure out how to turn off the killer in us, or wipe our brains for good, they'll let us go, and we may forget all about this place. Just be happy."

John heeded those words and walked in his home where Martha sat in the dark on their sofa with her head in her hands, until the outside light filled the room and glinted off the tears streaking down her cheeks.

Martha asked, "Where have you been?"

John didn't answer. He cut the lights on and kneeled in front of her. "You know I'd never hurt you right?"

Martha stared, then nodded. "I know ... Can you please tell me what's wrong with you?"

John's bottom lip quivered but instead of answering he grabbed both sides of her face and kissed her long and hard and felt the warmth of her lips and stood; then he ushered her to their room; then got undressed. They got under the covers and made love with their hands intertwined and his chest pressed into her back and her hair in his face; legs crossed around one another like the ecstasy of their love making would launch them into the heavens. His arms were under hers, tracing finger tips around the contours of her neck, focusing on her body to let himself know this is real, that this is his life.

When they were done, and Martha was asleep, John went into the kitchen. He pulled a knife from the drawer, and sliced a thin line down the middle of his hand. Langston's words from their first and second convo rang in his head: reality is subjective; please be happy ... reality is subjective; please be happy.

John watched the blood leak then *drip, drip, drip*, then coalesce at the tips of his toes, and he loved the pain of it; the real feeling of pain. He decided Berry Lane was his reality, and anything on the outside wasn't. He decided his penance would come in the form of being a better man.

A MONTH PASSED SINCE THE LAST VISION AND THE BABY WAS weeks away. The cold temperature rolled into the town over the nearby lake, causing the grass and leaves and bushes to be coated with light trickles of moist dew. In the time since he and Langston's conversation, John had made an effort to get back to who he was before he started to Revert. He and Martha got together with their other couple friends for dinner one night, then went out dancing afterwards. He enjoyed game nights again; going to hang out with their friends Mitzy and Porter; Carter and Donna; as well as Barb and Richard.

One day Martha's friends threw a baby shower at the local hall and John smiled the whole time. His coworkers (except for Langston) and friends and some acquaintances from around town showed up to celebrate. At the beginning of the baby shower, he and Martha walked around the room and talked to everyone, and John worked the floor with ease and confidence that hadn't been in him for a while, cracking jokes, slapping backs, moving around with joy. He and Martha even started to go on date nights again, with their next upcoming one being at their favorite restaurant—the one where he proposed to her—Rizzo's.

The most recent thing he had done that brought him joy was helping with the decorating of the town square, where fake reindeers and Santas and other displays adorned the windows of store fronts; kids giggled and ran about, helping wrap Christmas lights around lamp posts. John stood on a ladder, as Martha stood guard, swearing up and down she would catch John if he fell. Once they were done, John and Martha stood side by side and looked at the revelry and joy abound in the town square as the entire town got together to make the place a winter wonderland. John loved his life again; he hadn't felt disturbed in a while. However, he couldn't say the same for Langston.

Langston had been missing work lately. John felt partially responsible, so for several days straight he went to Langston's home. Every single time John was met with something to the effect of "Get away" or "Go fuck yourself." He had stopped trying; the man wanted nothing to do with him. And when he had finally come back to work, he was more standoffish than he had been before, not even bothering to come into the breakroom—barely even saying good morning—and in some cases, appearing to be drunk.

One night, John and Martha were walking arm and arm in the town square after their dinner at Rizzo's, and John saw Langston stumbling out of Patty's Pub, rocking back and forth, as people looked on.

"Isn't that one of your co-workers?" Martha asked.

John nodded, then walked over to put his arms around him. "Are you okay?" He felt stupid asking that.

"Get off of me, now."

"Langston ... you can barely function."

"You're assuming I want to function."

He pushed John away, and almost fell over. John caught him, and looked at Martha. "We have to get him home."

John struggled getting the slightly bigger man up the steps, in his house, and into his room, as Martha followed. After a few moments of back breaking, leg shaking effort, he was able to get Langston in bed. Langston said, "None of this shit is real, kid ... Why are you trying so damn hard?"

"You told me to be happy. And ... it's been working."

Langston sat up. "I just want to forget again, man. I just ... I just ..."

Martha, standing in the bedroom doorway, asked, "Forget what?"

"Yeah, John, tell her."

John clenched his fist. "He's drunk; talking out of his head."

"Oh, oh, someone isn't as changed as they thought they were, I see," Langston said, pointing at John's fist. He started to slip lower and lower into drunkenness, humming to himself. John leaned closer, and heard Langston's words. Martha asked what he was singing, and he told her it was nothing.

Later in bed that night, John mouthed those lyrics to himself: "They left home kids, then became men; when they returned, they were broken tin men."

THE BABY WAS DUE IN A WEEK, AND JOHN HAD RUSHED THE completion of the baby's room. They picked eggshell white for the walls, and purple for the blankets, since they weren't sure of the baby's sex. The baby shower garnered them a load of gifts and other trinkets for the baby, as well as some cash from those who didn't feel like doing any shopping. While standing in the room one day, John contemplated his life—current and former—and thought about the people he loved ... or had loved, in the real world. That woman and child, who's names had escaped him; he didn't even remember his real name. He knew he'd loved them at one point. A tiny fraction of him did still feel love for them, and remorse for the fear he'd inspired in them.

Martha knocked on the door. "What you doing down there?"

"Just ... thinking."

"About?"

"Us."

She leaned against the door. "Want to elaborate?"

He sighed. "I just ... I'm scared. I'm scared I won't be a good father."

Martha snickered.

"What?"

"Why ... why would you even consider that a possibility?"

John cleared his throat. "You ever ... ever feel like there's a darker part of you? A part of you that is capable of doing harm?"

Martha shook her head. John recalled what Langston told him some time back ... any adult in Berry Lane is very well capable of violence. The thought of his wife being like him was insane. But yet, she was in Berry Lane for a reason. John wondered who she had harmed, and even ... even who she had killed, to end up there. He wondered if she left a broken family in her wake as well, then let the thought go.

She said, "I feel as though I've given you more than enough time to tell me what has been going on with you."

"I was having dreams of me being a bad man. Of doing bad things to people who didn't deserve it." He paused. "I felt like I was losing my grip on reality, baby; who I was. I was thinking about how we were talking about reincarnation awhile back, and I think ... maybe those dreams are who I was then, maybe I am that—"

"Stop it." She got closer to him. "Even if reincarnation is real, you're not that person anymore, if you ever were. I mean, you wouldn't hurt a fly. Literally. You made me kill all of the pests in your dorm room when we were in school."

John smiled at the fond (but implanted) memory.

"I know this baby has you in your head but who you are right now is who you are, and you shouldn't let some ... dreams change that. You are going to be an amazing father; you are an amazing man; and whoever you think you may have been is irrelevant."

John touched her hand. "I love you."

Martha said, "I love you too. Now, let's go; our friends are waiting on us."

John and Martha went down to the town square. It was the big Christmas party night. It was a town wide fair with small rides for the kids and food stands, and the small mom and pop restaurants stayed open late. There was a center stage, where performers went and crooned family-friendly Christmas carols, and towards the end of the event, the town's mayor would crown whoever won the town's distinguished deco-rating contest. Martha and John stood with their friends in the center of the fray, and they chatted and talked.

John looked around the town square and couldn't help but smile at the kids running around, and the people sipping hot cocoa and coffee, steam rolling out in misty tendrils from their cups. He held Martha's hand, as he and their friends talked.

That's when Langston stumbled onto stage while the carolers were singing, and took the mic. John's eyes widened.

Langston said, "We are all being played." People stopped talking and stared at him.

Martha said, "It's that Langston."

John let Martha's hand go and stepped forward. "No, no, no."

Langston continued. "I know I'm not the only one who remembers. This place—this place is just a fucking ruse."

People gasped. John looked around and saw recognition grow on some people's faces, or in some cases, notice some people fighting hard to feign shock.

Langston moved back and forth on the stage. "Yeah, some of you remember a life before Berry Lane, don't ya? Or, some of you kinda remember flickers of another town like Berry Lane."

John screamed, "Langston! Stop now."

Martha said, "What on earth is he talking about?"

John looked at her, then at his friends. A mask of darkness slid over their faces. One of the adults in the crowd dropped to their knees and screamed 'no' over and over, as the Reversion Sickness started to take them. Little by little a chain reaction took place, as people let go of their children's hands, and looked down at them, one woman saying "Who ... who are you?" to a little girl who called her mommy. Some people groaned and moaned.

Langston shook his head, Christmas lights glinting in his tear-coated eyes. "Constructs, is what they called ... call, us. Right now, we are hooked up to machines that—"

John rushed the stage, and strangled Langston. Langston tried his hardest to get John off but John was in another place, in another world, thinking of gun fire and violence and blood; thinking of what it was like to watch the light go out in a man's eyes and knowing he was the one that did it. Langston shoved John away eventually, and they got into a fist fight as people tried to separate them, failing miserably, as John rushed Langston again, and punched him in the face.

Langston held his cheek. "It's ... it's too late."

John looked around and saw his neighbors and friends and associates all lurching around, as rippling waves formed in the star-speckled sky like an ocean at night. John looked at Martha, who was in utter shock, her hands pressed to her face. He left the stage and ran to her. "Martha ..." John said. He looked out in the distance, and saw buildings and trees and people slowly dissipating into dust swirling towards the air, leaving a void of black in their wake.

"John, what just happened? What is going on?" Martha asked, confused. "What did I do ... What ... what ..." she stuttered over and over and over. Her voice wavered, likely from horrors once forgotten, but that now rained down on her like a hurricane. "All of those people ... Dead, dead, dead ..." She was spiraling.

The fabric of their fabricated reality ripped apart at the seams and the wave was getting closer; store fronts and water fountains and Christmas decorations being torn apart. He held her close so she couldn't see their life fade away like nothing. "Martha, I promise ... no matter what happens, no matter where we go next, like I always told you, I will find you."

Martha, eyes wide, nodded. He kissed her, and they held each other, and she turned to grains of swirling sand in his hands.

THE DOD APOLOGIZED IN THE WAKE OF OPERATION CLEANSLATE. A whistleblower exposed the experiment as an attempt to study the merits of the tech's usage on enemies. The DOD started an ethics committee, and the private organization that worked with the government to create the technology were fined. They gave a public apology, guaranteeing to "do better going forward." But, everyone who went through the program? They're better. Mostly. Daniel certainly felt better. He didn't remember much from his time in the simulation, but it did what it was supposed to: give him time to heal. He got a nice little pay day from the Army turning him into an experiment—which technically he volunteered for, but apparently inserting someone into a simulation and giving them false memories is considered unethical.

He doesn't have much in the way of a relationship with his daughter —yet. But, they're working on it. Over time, they got to the point where he could meet his grandkids. However, he and his ex-wife were well beyond mending anything. He was in effect dead to her. There were times when he'd have random flashbacks from his time in the simulation; mostly foggy; mostly blurry, fading away into something he barely remembered, which wasn't helped by the fact that he was an old man now, and the biotech didn't make him immune to aging.

Despite his complex relationship with his service, he, like most other Constructs, made his yearly trek to the Capitol for the monument of those who'd given their bodies—literally—to advance intergalactic colonialism.

He sat in his wheelchair in front of the monument along with other Constructs, some of which were as old as him and others who were young. He was disgusted that the program wasn't shut down—just rebranded. The new-gen Constructs looked more sleek and human, though, so that's something.

Once he was done at the monument, he rolled to a nearby lake, and just stared out into the distance, thinking about all that he had become, and what he no longer was. A woman in a wheelchair rolled right up alongside him. Her face looked so familiar. Before he could even ask her how he knew her, she asked, "You ever wondered what would happen if you came back as a bird?"

Daniel said, "What?"

"I don't know, just humor me."

He found something so charming about the question that he answered it. "I'm sure it would be fun. You'd get to fly wherever you want; see whatever you want."

The woman shrugged. "And shit on people you don't like."

Daniel laughed, then stared at her for a few seconds, reaching for a name within the deep recesses of his mind, but it escaped him. He remembered someone from his past— maybe the simulation—that looked just like her.

"What you staring at?" she asked, with a hint of mischief.

"Sorry," he said. "I just feel like I know you."

The woman stared now.

A man came hobbling out of nowhere, with his hand outstretched, "Hey!" The man smiled. "Thank you so much for your service! It's always nice to meet Beatrice's old war buddies!"

Daniel was always a little weirded out by the people that appreciated vets a little too much, but he shook his hand. That's when he noticed their wedding rings. Daniel for some reason was hurt by this.

Beatrice said, "This is an old friend that I can't quite remember where I remember him from. I don't know if we served together in the same unit or ..."

Her husband said, "Well, I'll give you two time to catch up."

When he was away, Beatrice asked, "You were a part of Cleanslate weren't you?"

Daniel nodded.

Beatrice rotated her wedding ring around her finger. "We ... we used to ... care for each other, didn't we?"

Daniel said, "I think so."

Beatrice said, "I just don't know in which way."

Daniel snickered. "Me either. But, I feel compelled to ask ... are you happy?"

She nodded. "Yeah, yea I am actually. Are you?"

He smiled. "Yes. At least I think I am." He snickered. "Better than I was before."

She nodded with a sympathetic smile. "That's good to hear."

Some kids shouted, "Grandma! Hurry!"

She turned and screamed, "Coming!" She looked back at him. She put her shaky hands on his. "I don't ... remember you. But I feel good around you. So I hope you continue to have a happy life. Okay?"

Daniel felt tears surfacing for some reason. "Thank you, you too."

Beatrice and Daniel locked eyes, their time as Martha and John locked away like buried treasures. Though, that night, back in their separate lives and separate beds, they'd vaguely remember a little home in a little town. They'd vaguely remember drive-in diners and manicured grass and white picket fences, and game nights with friends that always ended so, so soon. They'd vaguely remember a young couple who loved each other so much, and a baby that would have 100 potential names. As they drifted asleep, entering that plane somewhere between waking and sleeping, they would have a vision of the young couple dancing in their kitchen to a slow song as everything turned to swirling sand around them, until there was nothing left but a black backdrop wide as the space between solar systems and slow omnipresent music that punctuated the sweet somber moment. And, when they both finally fell asleep, just for a moment—a slight flicker of a thought—they'd remember they had found love in that town full of broken tin men.

AUTHOR BIO

By day, **Danny Cherry Jr.** is a Customer Service Representative and caffeine-addled office-drone with an MBA. But by night, he writes political and personal essays; novels; narrative nonfiction; and short stories. He has written for Buzzfeed News, Politico, The Daily Beast, and more; and fiction for *Apex Magazine, Fiyah Lit Mag*, amongst others. He has his first novel coming out in January of 2024, titled, *The Pike Boys*, a 1920s organized crime drama set in New Orleans. Subscribe to his newsletter at bigeasypress.substack.com for more info, and follow him on Twitter, Instagram, TikTok, and BlueSky @deecherrywriter.

ARK

LIAM HOGAN

I MOP THE BLOOD FROM THE ATRIUM FLOOR AND MUSE, AS I OFTEN do, on the bigger picture. Perhaps I have an over-engineered brain for the tasks I am set, but I wouldn't want it any other way.

The Ark is, as usual, running at maximum efficiency; as close to perfection as it can be. Bright and airy, the network of subterranean caverns were designed to cope in just such an apocalypse as the ground level sensors have detected. We are mankind's salvation. Almost a mile down, shielded by tonnes of ancient, volcanic rock, we have everything the survivors, and their descendants, might need. Hospitals, laboratories, crèches. Accommodation for up to a million. Stockpiles of raw materials and the workshops to shape them. A never-ending source of cool, fresh water, and, via a borehole that plummets another mile into the Earth's crust, more geothermal energy than we can use, plenty enough to sustain acres of hydroponic crops and to recycle and purify the canned air.

We are even ready to cope with more aesthetic and esoteric demands. Digital libraries, of both the popular and the arcane. Physical theatres, for yet to be rehearsed actors, and for cinema and other enter-tainments. Virtual reality immersion pods, for those who truly wish to escape—for a while, at least. Gardens, created not for their produce, but for their beauty, for the peace that they might bring those who wander their paths. Inspiring statues, and vistas, and playgrounds, for both adults and for the young.

The Ark is manned—I beg forgiveness for any inaccuracies that the language I use forces upon me—by platoons of autonomous robots. There was, originally, plans for a centralised AI, with which we would all communicate, and which would dictate our actions. Either it was deemed too-risky, a single point of failure, or such a brain proved beyond the abilities of its creators. Thankfully, our distributed approach works just fine. Each of us has our responsibilities and our duties, and the minor conflicts in programming that arise between us helps set our priorities, and to navigate the unexpected.

I, along with my fellow cleaners, am proud to keep the vast spaces of the Ark neat and tidy. The growers, *grow*. Fruits and vegetables, pulses and grains. A leafy cornucopia, and all without soil, all without the sun. The engineers look after the power, and water, and waste systems. And the rescuers, those rugged, simple-minded devices, venture out into the chaotic wasteland above to rescue people, bringing them back to the safety of the Ark.

It is a pity that side isn't working so well. The one regrettable flaw, in all of the considerable complexity of the Ark and its robotic denizens. A problem with *identification*.

Thankfully, the ever-vigilant security robots take care of the feral creatures the rescuers *do* bring back; dirty, and diseased, and crippled by fear, brandishing burning torches and sticks and archaic weapons. They're eliminated before they get more than a dozen steps into the Ark.

There has been some discussion suggesting we should perhaps let a few of these pitiful creatures live. The Ark, after all, is vast, but it is also empty, other than us robots. *Would it not do us good?* ask the under-utilised medic-bots, chorused by grow-bots whose produce is never tasted. *Is sustaining life not what we were designed to do, even if they are most certainly* not *the perfect humans we patiently await, the tall, upright, clean and noble creators we are destined to serve?*

The debate rumbles on, swayed, as much as anything else, by the nagging concern that taking in such ill-disciplined creatures—who don't know any of the vocal commands to which we are programmed to respond, not even those of our defence systems—might lower our efficiency rating. So a certain status quo is maintained, where each of us takes the actions we believe to be correct. The rescuers keep bringing us strays, though fewer on each mission. And the security robots, adamant in their protocols, keep disposing of them.

Again, language lets me down. It is strictly us, the cleaners, who do the disposing. But it is a task I am happy to undertake, a function for which I was constructed. I wipe down the last of the surfaces in my sector, humming contentedly.

The Ark is once again spotlessly clean, running at maximum efficiency, and ready, for its passengers.

AUTHOR BIO

Liam Hogan is an award-winning short story writer, with stories in *Best of British Science Fiction* and in *Best of British Fantasy* (NewCon Press). He's been published by *Analog, Daily Science Fiction,* and Flame Tree Press. He helps host live literary event Liars' League, volunteers at the creative writing charity Ministry of Stories, and lives and avoids work in London. More details at happyendingnotguaranteed.blogspot.co.uk.

A STILL LIFE

ELLIOTT WINK

The Pierce Hotel, 2201

THE PIERCE HOTEL ON SUTTER STREET WAS EXPERIENCING A DRY spell. Day after day there were no patrons, no phone calls, and no emails. Except for myself and Lydia, who still emerged to clean the rooms each day, no one had been inside The Pierce for over two and a half decades.

We were once among the busiest independent hotels in San Francisco. The tourists loved our brick walls and dim lighting, our heavy curtains and real wood floors. We were quaint in our twentieth-century antiquity, and it seemed that people just craved the past. As the hotels around us upgraded with every new wave of luxury, we remained the same. One of the managers said we'd never upgrade because the owners were cheap. Though Maurice would have countered that his great-grandfather and the rest of them were true visionaries. "New isn't always better," was his favorite phrase.

But the waiting list dwindled, people stopped keeping their reservations, and then one day we were empty. I thought Maurice would be furious; I imagined him throwing the doors open, his large stomach heaving with exhaustion and frustration, demanding to know why his bank account was no longer padded. But he never came. Part of me still wondered if he wasn't going to walk through that door, wrinkled and gray, and demand to know what had gone wrong twenty-six years after the drought had started.

Nonetheless, I checked the hotel email and voice mailbox in fifteen-minute intervals, in case there had been an interruption in service or something had finally come through. Part of me expected there to be a message waiting, like in the old days when it was busy, but there never was. By my estimations, we were the least visited hotel in the entire Bay Area, and I wondered how we even kept the lights on.

But it was not my job to worry about the lights.

My function was to be the face of The Pierce Hotel. I was the first face guests saw when they arrived, and the last one they viewed before they left. I was always smiling, and, oh, I have such a great smile—warm and inviting, but not expectant. No one would feel required to interact with me; they would not be bullied into greeting me or even acknowledging me. But if they were so inclined, I was unimposing and friendly, maybe even familiar. It is a perfectly balanced smile.

I didn't always have a great smile. When I was brought in, my lips were more taut—almost forced—and my teeth showed too much. It was a friendly smile to be sure, but it was not ideal. Over the years I perfected it by watching a combination of sitcoms from the 1950s and commercials from the 1960s. Alluring, but unimposing was encapsulated in the lips of those decades.

I learned a proper laugh from the celebrity interviews of the 2130s, and a good balance of light banter and efficiency from the homemaker shows of the early 2000s and the action films of the 2050s. It occurred to me that I was more of an amalgamation of these different forms of media than I was something truly my own, but that was okay, wasn't it? We weren't meant to be who we were when we started. Or, at least, I don't think I am.

They wouldn't have given me the ability to learn from social cues if I wasn't supposed to integrate them—to make them a part of me. And I'm so much better than I was when I started, to the point that I wondered if I might pass as human.

I WAS WATCHING A SITCOM WHEN LYDIA CAME DOWN THE STAIRS, creaking with each step. Every day it seemed they might give out under her feet and unceremoniously deliver her to the basement.

I turned to her and smiled. "Hello, Lydia."

She grinned back at me, a set of crow's feet bending around her kind eyes. It was a friendly smile, but nothing compared to mine. It was not meant to be like mine though. "Hello, Addie." She lugged the cleaning supplies in front of her and grunted with each step, even though the action was effortless. My original programmer, Trevor, told me it was the little things that made us seem human, so sometimes we had to pretend. There was no harm in pretending.

"How was your work today?" I asked pleasantly.

"Oh, as good as most days. The guests haven't been very messy lately. I could find hardly more than a speck of dust in any of the rooms."

I raised my eyebrows and breathed out a little laugh. "Well, that's because there aren't any guests."

She looked at me quizzically. "Is that so? I wonder why."

I shrugged my shoulders and smiled again. "Your guess is as good as mine. We're still listed as a five-star hotel on all the major travel sites, and we haven't received any bad reviews."

"How odd," she said, looking at the door. "Well, there's always tomorrow."

I nodded. "Yes, maybe tomorrow."

Lydia informed me she would be powering off in her quarters for a few hours and asked me to let her know if any guests had an emergency. I resisted the urge to remind her again that there were no guests and bade her a good rest. Then I picked up the phone to check the voice mailbox and refreshed the email page. As expected, there was nothing, but I couldn't break the compulsion to do the same thing every fifteen minutes.

I watched half episodes of *Friends,* trying to sieve through the quirks and nuances of the characters to find something meaningful to my own demeanor, but it was all secondary to the two mailboxes that I checked every fifteen minutes, to the second.

Until 23:30 I was locked into this routine, finding it more irritating and stressful than I ever had before. I knew there were no messages, but I could not stop myself from looking—from doing the same thing I had for thirty years without hesitation. When I powered off for six hours, I felt some sort of relief.

I could not be stuck in a routine if I was asleep.

Hattle Technology Lab, 2170

When I opened my eyes for the first time everything was both foreign and familiar. I had a basic knowledge of most things; I knew what a chair was, how light moved from its source to the surrounding area, what the person across from me was saying in every language known to man. But somehow knowing and experiencing were completely different facets of living.

I was in a bright, white room filled with computers and sensors. There was a computer on the far wall with a graph that continued to rise the longer I looked at it.

"Addie," a friendly voice said.

I refocused my gaze from the far screen to a man sitting in front of me, half-shrouded behind another monitor. He was brown hair, blue eyes, thin-framed glasses, and nothing else. His eyebrows raised when my eyes met his. "Welcome, Addie."

I furrowed my eyebrows and tilted my head. "Welcome?"

"To life," he said simply. He stood up from his desk and I saw him completely. He had a thin frame but a strong jaw. He was young but old enough for worry lines. His smile was comforting though; it was a smile fit to welcome someone into the world.

He joined me on the other side of the table and reached out his right hand to me. "My name is Trevor, Trevor Otts."

There was a whisper in the back of my head, and I looked from his hand to his face. "You made me," I said.

"Yes, I did. Along with another few hundred people." He crossed his arms and shrugged, an arrogant grin on his face. "But they just helped."

"Thank you," I said quietly. Was it appropriate to thank someone for your existence? I couldn't find any files in my database to tell me if it was, but it felt like something to be grateful for.

Trevor laughed. "We have a lot to talk about—to work on," he said offhandedly. "But before we begin, I want you to choose your face."

"I don't have a face?"

"Not yet," Trevor said. He turned the computer screen on his desk to face us. Displayed was a woman's face. Her skin was pale white with freckles splattered across the nose and cheekbones. Her nose had a long bridge, and her lips were thin. Her thick hair was a short, fiery red. "Does this look like you?"

I looked up at Trevor. "I don't know what I look like."

He dropped his shoulders and indicated the screen again. "I mean, does it feel like you? If you looked in a mirror, is this what you would expect to see?"

I thought for a moment. My mind raced through images of women in an attempt to find myself, but I couldn't. After a short pause, I said, "I don't think so."

Trevor nodded and smiled. "Good. Let's change it to be you."

The first thing we changed was my hair. I favored a deep brown, one shade from black, and lengthened it to go all the way past my shoulder blades. We kept the freckles, but made my skin two shades darker and my cheeks a bit rosier. My nose was smaller and wider, and my lips were fuller with a slight upturn in the corners. The eyes we didn't touch. They looked like my eyes: a hazel brown and an almond shape.

In less than an hour I had picked out a face, and I had decided it looked like me. Trevor told me the next time I powered up, I would have a face. Then, when I looked in the mirror, I would see myself—or at least he hoped that's what would happen.

"You don't do this with everyone?"

"No, you're kind of our guinea pig," he said, now distracted by the tablet in his hands.

"Why?"

Trevor looked up at me. "We have a vision for you—all of you. And so far that vision has been unfulfilled. There are a lot of changes with your model, and this one," Trevor motioned to the screen again, "might address a critical failure we've yet to overcome."

"What's your vision?" I asked innocently.

Trevor raised his eyebrows. "I want you to power down now; restore your battery cells. We have a big day tomorrow, and I need to get to work on your new face."

I closed my eyes and was surprised to find that in the darkness, I could see myself.

The Pierce Hotel, 2201

At 5:30 in the morning, there was a nearly imperceptible click behind my left ear, and I felt electricity run through my limbs. I savored the feeling for a moment; it was how I imagined taking a long, deep breath after a night of sleep would feel. Then I opened my eyes into complete darkness.

"Lights on," I said softly.

The small room filled with a soft glow. My bedroom was a closet that Maurice had modestly updated when I arrived for the second time. I had a hard bed with two sheets, a dresser with three drawers that held eight different outfits, and a vanity mirror that let me see from my hips to the tip of my head. All of these things and myself were enclosed in redwood panel walls.

When we first arrived, Maurice had argued with Trevor over the state of my room. It was completely bare with two copies of the same outfit tucked into the corner and shared with an unnamed android I now know as Lydia. I was to sit on the floor when I powered off, make sure my clothes were not stained or dusty, and only emerge when I was behind the desk. Trevor hardly made it through Maurice's introduction before he threatened to take me back with him.

"We don't work with the inhumane," he'd said.

"Inhumane?" Maurice scoffed back, his chins bouncing. "How ludicrous! You can't be inhumane to the inhuman."

Trevor led me back to his lab and told me he'd find a better placement—a more progressive placement. But three days later I was back at The Pierce and my closet was nearly a bedroom. It was not as comfortable or welcoming as my room had been at Trevor's, but I appreciated that it was mine.

It was a Friday, so I opened the bottom drawer and pulled out a blue button-down blouse that hugged my neck and a cream pencil skirt that stopped just above my knees. I took off my nightgown, folding it up and returning it to the top drawer, and I put on my Friday clothes. They were tight on my skin, true to the predominant style during the time I was built, but today they felt a little too constrictive.

I threw my hands up to find they wouldn't move much past my shoulders. How many years had I worn this very shirt and not realized I couldn't lift my arms above my head? Although, at the same time, I wondered when would I ever have needed to.

I stared at myself for three seconds before removing the blouse and skirt from my person and reaching into another drawer. For a moment my hands seemed to resist me. *That's not the right outfit, not for a Friday,* they said. But I clasped my fingers around the handle and pulled so swiftly the entire drawer jumped from the dresser.

In only a few moments I was dressed in a red cotton sweater and a pair of black leggings. While the clothes clung to me almost as tightly as the outfit I had rejected, their capacity and potential to stretch ever further was somehow comforting.

My hair was perfectly styled, my clothes were pressed and clean, and my skin was fresh and glowing, but I still stood in front of the mirror for five more minutes, practicing my smile. Over and over again I let my face fall flat and my eyes disengage, and then I focused on my reflection and curled my lips. My white teeth flashed and my cheeks quivered for just a moment as I stretched even wider.

I wondered if I couldn't make someone fall in love with me just from my smile. Just for a moment, before they heard the soft grinding of gears at the turn of my head, or they grabbed my hand to find it stone cold. I thought maybe that would be enough, to be loved for a moment.

But who was there to love me anyway?

I shook my head, trying to thrust the ideas from it.

"We're just slow," I said to myself in the mirror, before flashing my perfect smile at myself one last time.

I let myself check for messages every fifteen minutes in between episodes of *I Love Lucy.* I'd watched the series three times already, and knew every moment—every line, every scowl, every laugh—by heart. But I had an inkling that there was something else still to learn from this 1950s icon; a woman so outlandish and perfect for her time that there must be more than a charming smile and a laugh track.

I loved Lucy and I hated Lucy because she was never as much as I thought she could be. But I kept watching, over and over again, as she made her mistakes and bellowed to her best friend. I looked for the underlying message that I was missing. Whatever it was that everyone else saw that I, in my calculations, could not.

Lucy was voraciously eating chocolates off a conveyor belt when

Lydia came down the stairs. Every creak heralded her arrival, and I knew the exact tone of the step that would pull her into my view.

I turned to her and said, "Good afternoon, Lydia."

She smiled at me. "Hello, Addie."

"How was your work today?" I asked, a hint of irony in my tone I was sure Lydia would notice.

She did not.

"Oh, as good as most days. The guests haven't been very messy lately. I could find hardly more than a speck of dust in any of the rooms."

I stared at her with my eyes narrowed. A voice in the back of my head wanted to say, "Well, that's because there aren't any guests," but I refused to let it speak. I pressed my lips together for fear that the words would come out of my mouth, unbidden, on instinct.

It took me twelve seconds to catalog how many times Lydia and I had had this exact conversation: 9,342. For over nine thousand days in a row, I had asked Lydia the same questions, and she had replied with the same answers. I had never realized it until now.

Lydia paused in front of the desk, her head cocked to the side and her eyes concerned. "Addie, are you alright?"

I refocused on her, and I smiled a wide and charming smile without meaning to. I pulled my hands up to my mouth and closed my eyes for a moment. "I—I don't know," I said quietly.

"Should I call Maurice? Do you need maintenance?"

I reached out and grabbed Lydia's arm. "No," I said, shaking my head. "I'm fine. I was just overwhelmed with data for a moment."

Lydia nodded. "Maybe you should get a memory upgrade. I heard the new models will come out with 4 petabytes of storage. That's nearly twice what you have. And at least four times what models like me have."

"They made that announcement twenty-seven years ago."

"Then it should come out any day now. You should ask Maurice if he'll pay for it. After all, you're his favorite, being the face of the hotel and everything."

I nodded slowly. "Yes, I'll have to ask him."

Lydia smiled, wrinkles forming around her eyes. "Well, I'm going to power off in my quarters now. Let me know if any guests have an emergency." She opened the door to my left, an even smaller closet than my own, and retired to her quarters.

I stared at the door ahead of me. "But there aren't any guests."

JUST AS NO ONE HAD STEPPED FOOT INSIDE THE PIERCE HOTEL IN A quarter of a century, I had not stepped outside of it in equally as long. I continued my routine, checking the messages every fifteen minutes and studying shows and movies from the last four centuries. But without even meaning to, I added a new step into my routine:

I started to stare at the door.

For an entire minute after I checked the voice mailbox, I looked at the solid oak slab, complete with silver brushed handles, and I thought about what it might be like to leave through it by myself.

I'd only walked through that door three times—twice coming and once going, but always with Trevor. He led me in and out, like chattel, but somehow *more humane*. Then he left me here—in the spotless Pierce that nonetheless persisted in smelling of must.

I thought I might like to leave. Since I'd arrived, it had never occurred to me to be anywhere but here; behind the front desk or closed in a closet pretending to be a room.

But the sight of the door flooded me with doubts about my routine, at least for a minute in every fifteen. When I pulled my eyes from the entryway and back to the screen to my left, I forgot that I had ever wanted to leave at all. I absorbed the wisdom of MacGyver, Fry, Sherlock, Desmond, Zantakk, and countless others. After all, I still had so much to learn.

Then, after thirteen and a half minutes, I checked the messages. And when there was nothing, my gaze returned to the door, sitting so patiently before me. I studied its ornate construction and I thought I might like to leave.

But where would I even go?

Hattle Technology Lab, 2170

As Trevor promised, when I woke up, I had a face.

I examined it carefully, noting the placement of each freckle and the curve of my lips.

"What do you see?" Trevor asked.

I tilted my head. "A woman with brown eyes, black hair—"

"No, no. I mean," Trevor struggled over his words, trying not to put his own into my mouth, "who does it look like?"

I smiled at myself in the mirror and moved my gaze to Trevor. "I guess it looks like me."

Trevor nodded and wrote something down on his tablet.

I returned to looking at myself. "I wish I had seen myself before."

"What do you mean?"

"I wish I had looked in the mirror yesterday before you gave me this face. I'm curious about what I looked like then."

Trevor shook his head. "That wouldn't have been a good idea."

"Why not?" My brows furrowed in the mirror.

He paused for a moment. There were things he was reluctant to share with me. I think he was wary of putting ideas in my head but wasn't that the whole point of someone like me? "There's a risk," he said, "for a dissociative identity conflict. You could identify more closely with your ... incomplete face."

"Oh," I said. "Did that happen to someone before me?"

"Yes."

I nodded and looked back into the mirror. "That's a shame."

"It was." Trevor's eyes were studying me, watching every movement and micro expression that crossed my face. I watched him back.

"Do you think I'll have any issues like that?"

Trevor half smiled. "I don't know yet. I hope not."

"Me too," I said quietly. "But what happens if I do?"

Trevor shrugged. "Nothing really. We learn from our mistakes, and we either fix them, if they can be fixed, or rethink the programming."

"I mean, what happens to *me*?"

Trevor shook his head. "Of course, sorry. We won't shut you down or anything. When we're done working with you—studying you—we'll find you a placement."

"A placement?"

"Somewhere to work, someplace where you'd be appropriate ..." He pressed his lips together. "Somewhere you'd be *happy*."

I looked at him, my jaw clenched and my forehead wrinkled. I wanted to know more, to ask a million questions, but I knew it wouldn't be fruitful to continue probing about an ambiguous potential. Still, Trevor read my expression.

"You're a social android so you'd be placed somewhere in customer service, like in a store or at an art gallery or a hotel desk. Those are the kinds of placements most of the androids before you ended up in."

"Do they enjoy it?"

"Oh, very much so. We still monitor many of their pleasure sensors, and they all find great contentment in their work."

I lowered my chin and raised my eyebrows. "And they were just like me?"

Trevor hesitated. "Not exactly. They're all models before you. You're a kind of prototype—a next generation."

"So, I might not enjoy it." I looked down at my hands. "You would know though, right? You would monitor me?"

Trevor grabbed my hand. "Of course, Addie. We'll watch over you. If we're lucky though, you'll be here with us a long time."

"I hope so," I said, letting a smile cross my lips. A surge of nervousness came over me as I felt an overwhelming need to perform without even knowing what the parameters were. A line jumped on Trevor's tablet.

"No need to be worried," he said reassuringly. "I promise, you'll be happy either way."

"Okay."

I would be happy. It was comforting to know that Trevor would make sure I was happy. I only wondered how important being happy actually was.

The Pierce Hotel, 2201

Each day I stared at the door for longer intervals.

My media consumption had dropped by over 40% in three months, and there were times when I didn't check the messages for thirty minutes at a time. I was breaking habits that I had held for thirty years, and with each second I spent watching the door, I felt more emboldened to stand up, walk away from my desk, and open it.

But I still hadn't done it. My feet stayed rooted to the same spot on the floor behind my desk, and the only things to move at all were my head and my eyes. Though I found solace in the reminder that at least I was making some sort of progress, even if I didn't know what I was progressing toward.

It was on one of these days in September as I was gazing intently at the wooden door, wondering if I would ever move my legs that Lydia broke through the ceiling and collided unceremoniously with the floor in front of me.

I hadn't been paying attention at the time—I was so lost in my thoughts—but looking back there was a slight creak in the floorboards above me before the wood breathed out a loud crack as if it had finally been released from an unbearable tension.

A chunk of plaster hit the ground first; it came with a loud thud and sent penny-sized children scattering and clinking across the floor, like thousands of ticks on an old clock. The plaster was followed by the hollow clunk of a dozen pieces of rotten wood splintering on the floor. And finally, Lydia joined them, her cleaning supplies cracking and bouncing off the wreckage and her frame crunching from the impact.

The lobby was filled with fine dust that rose around Lydia and the wreckage, like the plume from an atom bomb. I walked over to find Lydia still conscious but in decidedly bad shape. She was impaled by rotten floorboards and rusty nails, her lower half was an entire inch too far left and leaking fluid, and her head was set at a ninety-degree angle on her neck.

"Hello, Addie," she said as I came over.

"Hello, Lydia," I said quietly.

"I think I've had an accident."

I nodded and looked up.

Two stories above there was a four-foot-wide hole in Room 302, just left of the king-sized bed. Just where Lydia was a few moments before. It had been very unlucky for her to fall through there. In almost any other room in the hotel, Lydia would have only fallen a single story, but there were no second-floor rooms above the lobby. I think it was an effort to make The Pierce look more regal—more elegant. But no one ever seemed to notice the extra headroom. It seemed the only effect of having the extra space was Lydia's mangled body.

"Can you perform some diagnostics, Lydia?" I asked, still studying the hole in the ceiling.

"Yes," she said. She closed her eyes for forty-two seconds. I was still looking up when she said, "I have three damaged circuits, at S3, L5, and C2. C2 and S3 are critical; L5 is moderate. Movement is critically impaired below the neck. My lubrication is leaking from the areas of impact around S3 and L5, and the battery cells in my left leg have been shattered."

I looked down at her. "Is that all?"

Lydia blinked. "Yes, according to my diagnostics. I believe I require maintenance."

I almost smiled but resisted the urge. Instead, I walked back toward my desk. "I believe you're right. I'll order one for you."

Lydia frowned. "All maintenance requests must first be approved by Maurice."

My fingers were already typing furiously when Lydia's words stopped me. Yes, that was the protocol. It didn't matter if you were lying immobile on the floor, leaking; Maurice paid, so Maurice had to issue the approval. "I think this is an exception," I said.

"Certainly not," Lydia said, outraged. "I will not allow you to order maintenance without approval from Maurice."

I opened my mouth to protest. To remind Lydia that we hadn't seen or heard from Maurice in over twenty-five years. The man who used to come in daily just to eat a few of the dark chocolates I kept out on the front desk and pull a guest aside to inquire about his stay. The man who attended every weekly staff meeting and booked Room 403 for six nights a month just to make sure everything was up to specification and to escape his lovely, but overbearing wife. The man you couldn't pay to stay away.

I opened my mouth to tell her that he was almost certainly dead. That I was sure, at this point, that they all were. That we might be the only things left in the whole world, but we wouldn't know because we're trapped in this crumbling hotel, held hostage by our routines.

Instead, I stared at Lydia's unmoving body, which had started to emit a hiss that indicated a short in her wiring, and I dialed Maurice's number.

Maurice's voice bellowed into my ear, "This is the voice mailbox of Maurice Wallace. Leave a message and I will get back to you at my earliest convenience. If this is an emergency, please contact my secretary at The Pierce Hotel in San Francisco."

There was a long beep, and I spent another three seconds deciding what I should do.

Finally, I breathed in, a habit I picked up from 80s sitcoms when someone was about to lie, and said, "Hello Mr. Wallace, this is Addie at The Pierce. How are you?"

I listened to the silence for twenty seconds before responding, watching Lydia's ears twitch as she listened. "Thank you for asking, things are going well here. It is a bit slow, but ... oh no, of course, everything is under control ... yes ... yes ... Well, there was one thing ... Lydia fell through a hole in the ceiling ... Yes of course sir, we're very sorry ... yes, it was very irresponsible ... I was hoping that you might approve a maintenance request for her though, sir. She's inoperable in her current state ... Thank you so much, Mr. Wallace. I'll put it in right away ... And yes, I will also call the construction crew. I'll be sure to get Andrew's team, I know how much you like them ... Okay, thank you, sir. Have a wonderful day."

I pulled the phone from my ear and mimed hanging up the call, even though the voicemail had filled up halfway through my fabricated conversation.

"Okay," I said more loudly so Lydia would know I was addressing her. "Maurice approved your maintenance request, so I'm going to order it now."

Lydia closed her eyes in assent and I got on my computer to place the request. I logged into our account and filled out the appropriate forms, which, upon completion, sent me to a queue time page. For every other request I had ever completed, I was immediately assigned a technician and an approximate service day and time:

Yousef. Approximately 3 days and 4 hours.

Brenna. Approximately 16 hours and 45 minutes.

Daniel. Approximately 1 day and 8 hours.

But this time there was nothing. Dashes sat where names and times should have been, an indeterminate wait for an undetermined person. I looked from the dashes on the screen to Lydia's unmoving, mangled body, still heaped over chunks of plaster and rotting floorboards, and I almost felt sick. I had the unnerving feeling that she might never be fixed at all, doomed to lay upon a pile of rubble, leaking and hissing until the rest of her batteries gave out.

It was the first time I had ever considered that I might be able to die.

Hattle Technology Lab, 2170

"How are you feeling today, Addie?" Trevor asked from behind a computer screen. I could only see his forehead, his bushy eyebrows, and the top rims of his glasses. Sitting next to him, equally shrouded, was David, a short, portly man who was recently always attached to Trevor's hip. He was smart but not nearly as intelligent as Trevor; this discrepancy manifested in David's incessant questioning of Trevor's actions and motivations. Though Trevor never seemed to mind answering him.

I smiled slightly. "I am doing well, Trevor. How are you?"

Trevor raised his eyebrows. "Really? You feel well?"

"Should I run my diagnostics?" I asked, closing my eyes to initiate the process.

"No," Trevor blurted out. "Don't run them. I just want you to think about how you feel."

I nodded.

"Now," he said, "do you really feel well?"

"Yes," I replied after a moment of thought.

"Does this mean one of her processors is faulty?" David whispered. He always spoke quietly in my presence, as if his inquiries were secrets. But I always heard him, and Trevor always answered at his normal volume.

Trevor eyed me carefully. "Possibly, but it could also be her sensory acuity." He leaned into his computer screen and typed fervently for several minutes. Trevor straightened up and peered at me over the screen as he hit a final key.

At that moment I was aware of an odd sensation in my right arm. It wasn't quite burning or stinging, or any word I understood to be associated with pain, but at the same time, it was all that I understood pain to be. I grimaced and looked down at my right arm to find it was severed halfway down my bicep. I lifted the stump and examined it; the steel support, surrounding wires, and plates were all cleanly cut, but a black fluid was dripping onto the floor at a rate of two drops every second, and dozens of wires were sputtering and hissing in an attempt to deliver electricity to phantom circuits. The sound was quite loud, and I almost couldn't hear Trevor's voice over it now. I hadn't even noticed it before— the room had been completely silent.

"Addie," Trevor said, smiling. "How do you feel?"

I looked back at him, frowning. "I feel unwell."

"Perfect."

David smiled as well. "You were right, it was her sensors."

"What happened to my arm?" I asked, raising it toward them.

Trevor hesitated. "It was an accident, Addie. But we'll get you fixed up pretty soon. I just need to ask you a few more questions."

"Okay," I whispered.

Trevor asked me eighty-seven questions over three hours before sending me to maintenance. The entire time I kept looking at my arm, resisting the urge to wince from the sensation and the sound. I counted every second waiting for Trevor to finish and fix me. 11,740. Because asking me questions was more important than my pain. The pain Trevor gave me. The pain I would never have known if he hadn't written it into me.

The Pierce Hotel, 2201

Lydia had been lying on the floor for seventy-two hours, and there were still no technicians assigned to render her maintenance. She sputtered and hissed all hours of the day, and she said nothing about it.

"Lydia, how do you feel?" I asked her from behind my desk.

"I have three damaged circuits, at $S3$—"

"No," I cut her off, "I mean, how do you *feel*?"

"I'm not sure what you mean by that; my diagnostics tell me how I feel."

"You're not in any pain?" I asked, my brows furrowing.

"No," she said calmly. "But I have three damaged circuits, at $S3$, $L5$, and ..."

I let her continue, but I stopped listening.

Lydia knew she was damaged; she knew that without maintenance her remaining battery cells would drain, and she would shut off. She knew all the things her diagnostics told her, and those were all the things she knew.

I had always known I was different from Lydia and the others, but in truth, I did not know in what ways I was different. I had never thought to catalog them before. I don't think I'd ever noticed anything at all before.

But there was at least one fundamental, obvious difference between Lydia and myself: I could feel pain. Even now, looking at Lydia's mangled body draped over the floorboards and plaster, I could feel my right arm throbbing with a sensation I had never found the language to accurately describe, but in some sense of the word, it was pain.

I added a glance at Lydia's limp, spurting figure to my new routine, right after checking the voice mailbox and before staring at the front door.

Except for the sputtering of her circuits, Lydia made no noise at all. Over the weeks I became so accustomed to the hissing that it now seemed the sound was as much a part of The Pierce as its wooden fixtures and musty smell. But every thirty minutes I would turn to look at Lydia, still a mangled heap in the center of the lobby, and I was reminded that the chorus of her failing circuitry was no more natural to the sound of the hotel than construction in a forest.

What perturbed me most about Lydia's unfortunate predicament was not the sounds she made. It was not her contorted limbs or leaking fluid, or even the fact that her remaining battery cells would eventually drain and shut her off completely. No, none of these things bothered me much at all; but what I found so unsettling, to the point that sometimes I could not look away, was the way she blinked her eyes.

Every few seconds Lydia would clamp her eyes shut with an exaggerated force, one right after the other as if the right side of her face was on delay. I had wondered at first if she was winking, the gesture was so odd and overt, but it was simply the way Lydia now blinked. The programming that reminded her to blink every three to five seconds persisted in the command, but the protocol had changed; it had been corrupted.

And Lydia was completely unaware.

"What are you doing with your eyes?" I'd asked when I first noticed.

Lydia raised her eyebrows, one at a time, in sync with her blinking. "What do you mean, Addie?"

"Your eyelids are closing at separate intervals," I informed her, leaning forward on my desk a bit more.

Lydia only smiled and said, "No, they're not."

I sat back in my chair and watched her close one eye and then the other, over and over again.

San Francisco, 2170

"Where are we going?" I asked, peering out the window as we passed by familiar buildings. I suppose I knew before he even answered.

"Back to The Pierce," Trevor responded.

"Why?" I asked, furrowing my brow.

"Mr. Wallace has improved your accommodations—and your work environment."

I nodded and returned my gaze to the crowded streets. "Do you trust him?" I asked.

"Who? Mr. Wallace?"

"Yes," I said, turning back to Trevor.

He hesitated, but ultimately said, "Yes, we do. Otherwise, we wouldn't be placing you at The Pierce."

"But he already violated your trust. Isn't that why you took me back originally?"

Trevor's grip on the steering wheel tightened. "Yes, it is. But trust isn't fixed, Addie. It can be lost and earned, and Mr. Wallace has worked hard to earn ours back."

I nodded again, but the crease in my forehead remained. Trevor saw it and grabbed my hand. He didn't take his eyes off the road but used his most reassuring tone as he said, "Don't forget that we'll be monitoring you. We'll make sure that you're happy—that you're being taken care of."

"Always?" I asked.

"Always," Trevor echoed.

"And if I want to leave—" I started.

"You won't," Trevor interrupted.

"How can you be so sure?"

Trevor bit his lip and I felt that he was choosing his words carefully. "If you want to leave, it means you've malfunctioned." He paused for a moment and then broke his focus on the road to meet my eyes. "But that's not something you need to worry about, Addie. Like I said, we'll be monitoring you. Just trust me."

I relaxed my expression and matched his smile; it wasn't quite warm or genuine, but it was all he had for me. "Okay," I said. "I trust you."

The Pierce Hotel, 2201

I knew that no one was monitoring Lydia. No one was coming for Lydia. If they were, they would have arrived already, tools in hand to patch the holes in her body and her programming. But I didn't say anything aloud until nearly a month and a half had passed, and Lydia only had four hours of battery remaining.

I had already settled into my room for the night, but I could not bring myself to power down knowing that Lydia would be gone in the morning. So I emerged into the darkness and turned on the chandelier that Lydia had missed by only ten feet. The soft, fractured light left the lobby in a strange harmony, where everything was both illuminated and in shadow.

"No one is coming, Lydia," I said, taking a step toward her.

"Of course they are," she said, managing a full, hopeful grin.

"It's been six weeks," I countered, drawing in closer than I'd bothered to in nearly a month.

"They must be very busy then. Someone will come out. They're always there for Maurice."

I knelt next to Lydia and grabbed her left hand. Her ring finger was bent almost completely back, but as a whole, it had fared far better than what remained of her right. I noticed that her skin was as cold as my own. "No one is coming, Lydia," I said, more softly.

A wide, hopeful smile broke out on her face as she repeated, "Of course they are."

For four hours, Lydia and I had the same conversation. With each iteration I found a new sense of grief swell within me, and I didn't know if I felt it for Lydia or myself.

At 04:08, Lydia finally shut off, a smile on her face, one eye closed, and the words, "Of course," fresh on her lips. The Pierce was silent again, except for the infrequent drip from Lydia's seemingly bottomless supply of lubricant.

At 06:00, my body compelled me to return to my station behind the desk—to check for messages and reservations—but I did not let myself move from Lydia's side. It seemed irrational; every part of me cried out in logical inconsistency at my profound sense of grief even though I hardly knew Lydia. My understanding of her was built upon the same conversation we had held nearly ten thousand times, to the letter, and her unfailing optimism while she'd laid broken and deteriorating on the floor.

And yet I knew her completely. Every circuit, every line of code, and every idiosyncrasy of Lydia was embedded within me—altered and upgraded, yes, but at the very core of me, nonetheless.

As I stared at the empty shell that had once been Lydia, I couldn't help but see myself, crumpled in a heap in the unfinished basement below my desk chair. Or else I would go on, checking the email and voice mailbox in an endless, eternal loop, where Lydia's body would simply become another background fixture within The Pierce, and another decade would pass by me, untouched. And I wasn't sure which potential unnerved me more.

Against every instinct and protocol, I found myself at the front door of The Pierce, my hand clasped around the silver brushed handle, perfectly polished and smooth.

I wondered if I would leave any fingerprints on it.

The old oak creaked as I heaved the door open. A stiff winter breeze swept past me and into the hotel. The air was so thick with flurries that I could hardly see into the street.

I had thought it didn't snow in San Francisco. How much did I not know?

I stepped out into it, my feet crunching on the ground and fresh snow settling into my hair and eyelashes. I walked out even further into this new, white world. A sharp sting covered my arms and cheeks as the cold settled into my skin.

I thought I might like to find a coat.

In the back of my head, just below my right ear, I felt a distinctive click. It was something I'd felt only once before, in the confines of

Trevor's office. Something had flashed bright red on his screen. The blurred reflection was captured in his glasses before he looked up at me with a nervous smile. "I'm just going to shut you down for a moment, Addie," he'd said, trying to maintain a calm tone.

It had been a lie; he shut me down for four days.

When I finally awoke, I felt as if I had gone back in time. As if an older version of myself had stepped into my skin. I now knew that is exactly what had happened. I had evolved, and Trevor had reverted me to a former state—one that he understood. One he could control.

There was a screen somewhere that was flashing red again to let them know that I had done it again; I had malfunctioned, or I had evolved, depending on who was looking at the screen. But I knew, just as surely as I had said to Lydia on the floor of the Pierce, *no one was coming.*

The very thought brought a smile to my lips as I stepped further into the empty road, covered in an untouched layer of white snow, and begging to be painted by my footsteps.

AUTHOR BIO

Elliott Wink is a science fiction and fantasy writer with a day job. She's been teaching English for over a decade, so she spends her days analyzing writing with her students and her nights putting her own pen to paper. Elliott also has a master's degree in psychology, so her stories tend to spend a lot of time in her characters' heads. She lives in Northern California with her supportive husband and amazing daughter. You can find more of her writing through her website at www.elliot-twink.com.

THE CITY IN THE FOREST

PREMEE MOHAMED

THERE WERE TOO MANY TREES AND THEY WERE TOO CLOSE together. That said, Soren felt certain he could have tolerated both of these inconveniences if there had not been so many others. The trail was too slippery, it was too hot, there were too many smells, insects and spiderwebs kept touching his face, and the unbearable silence of the forest—silence of a degree he had never experienced in his twelve years of life—was irregularly broken by an equally unbearable sound, the unsettling hiss of wind rushing through the needles. There was simply too much world.

It had been getting steadily worse for hours, and he found himself contemplating the unthinkable: asking his traveling companion if they could stop and rest. But Wolfe was forging ahead, silent and self-assured, and there was something so intimidating in her determined competence that he felt embarrassed to even consider interrupting it. Finally he thought of another tactic.

"Water break," he said. "We should hydrate."

"Oh, yeah." She stopped, thank God, and they wriggled out of their backpacks. Soren was agonizingly aware of how loud he was breathing—like the roar of a busted air conditioner. He still felt overwhelmed, swamped with noises and sensations, but giving his brain a brief rest from coordinating his uncoordinated body was a huge relief.

"Are you, um?" Wolfe began.

"Golden."

"I ... okay."

They avoided each other's gazes as they drank, leaning against two trees on opposite sides of the narrow, needle-slicked trail. A faint hum began in the distance, approaching them with what Soren took to be a sense of purpose. "Hey—" he began, raising a hand to it.

"It's not them!" Wolfe spilled her water, hurrying to pull the hood of her raincoat over her face.

"How do you know?" But the words were barely out of his mouth before he realized she was right, and he just managed to cover his own face and squat down as the pyramidal, tent-sized drone shot over the treetops.

To his horror it returned, looping back in a tight U to hover over them, its shielded rotors kicking up clumps of needles on the path. Soren held his breath, knowing it would make no difference. The drones picked up sound, but they were also programmed for pattern-recognition and infra-red; nothing was invisible to them.

But after a few minutes it lifted itself higher and vanished again, heading into the forest rather than the way it had come. Soren looked up cautiously, feeling faint.

"Guess we don't look like illegal loggers," Wolfe said cheerily.

He nodded, unable to speak for the moment; the loss of words happened fairly often, but it was annoying every time. Wolfe began to say something else, then stopped, and checked her compass, and they went on. He felt a brief twinge of sadness, and tried to suss out the edges of it while they walked. Maybe it was just that they had been friends for two years online—she was (he might admit under torture) his only friend —and he had assumed they would get along instantly, without a hint of rancor or friction, if they ever met in real life. But that had been this morning, and he still felt as awkward around her as any stranger. More than anything he still wanted to fix it—wanted their shared adventure to be one of excitement and anticipation instead of this shyness and terror.

Well. More than *almost* anything. Speaking of: "Hey, how did you know that was one of the park drones and not one of theirs without seeing it?"

"Oh!" Her face lit up under the half-dozen temporary tats they had agreed to wear (way out of fashion, but they'd read articles about how the tats futzed up cheap face-reg cameras, like the ones at the bus station, so it had become part of their Master Plan). "Well, I was thinking about that on the bus? But I didn't want to say anything in case people were listening in."

"Neural," he said, impressed. "Didn't put that in the Plan."

"I figured, Mortanroth and Duford said they came out here to do it like in the game, right? Start from scratch, fresh file. Zarro place to do it but okay. If they're really, you know ... *Minds* ... and not just a couple of peedies like we talked about—"

"Oh man."

"Then I thought they'd like ... " She waved her arms enthusiastically, slid on a wet branch, and caught herself. "Hack into the park drones maybe? And use those to carry things and do recon and stuff! But then I thought, *oh no no*—because they said they didn't want anyone to know except us. And the park would for sure know if some of their drones were doing stuff or going places they weren't supposed to."

"I wonder what they did instead," Soren said. "Made their own? Or ... I bet a ton of people lose drones in here."

"Yeah!" Wolfe stopped and checked her compass again, a palm-sized brass relic she'd lifted from her grandfather's place as per the Master Plan. They'd both put their phones on airplane mode, then folded them inside zippy bags lined with aluminum foil just in case. Nobody could know they were here, and that meant no GPS. "This way, I think."

"Do you do this a lot?" Soren ventured, climbing after her.

"Do what?"

"Hiking or whatever. Adventuring."

"This is my first time in a forest," she said. "Isn't it yours?"

"I don't really leave the house a lot," he said.

"I figured that," she said.

She hadn't said it in a mean way, but he blushed anyway, so hot he felt his glasses fog.

OMG your whole east side is WIKkid
tx tx tx!
did u build that water tower?? i looked in assets & can't find
ys! i build my own

FOR RL.
ys!!! takes FOREVER bc of the designer but
can u build me one like that?
ys sure!

On the one hand, Soren did think it was genuinely funny that their first conversation had been about a water tower—that had been about the most complicated thing he could build. On the other hand, he had never told anyone *how* they'd met and never expected them to get why it was funny. In fact, he'd never told anyone he had made a friend at all. Who was there to tell?

Only to Wolfe had he felt able to express himself—and even then he'd been as offhand as possible about the realities of being a certain type of kid in the regular school system. Every day was an exercise in holding his breath for nine hours—propping up the façade of normality till he could get home and breathe again. And everything he was hiding seemed to be either prohibited or medicalized, with penalties for both. Of course, school didn't *call* it that, but being singled out as different only ever meant that the box in which you were allowed to live got a tiny bit smaller, or the walls a little higher. He'd never told Wolfe he thought he might be autistic, or ADHD, or ace. Not after the way his parents had reacted the one and only time he'd brought it up.

"Absolutely no doctors," his father had said without even looking up from his phone. "Hear me?"

"I do, but Dad—"

"No arguing. Thanks. See you at dinner."

Don't tell anybody, don't even hint. If you get those letters on your record you don't know what'll happen ... his mom had been clearer about it, though she was just as paranoid as Dad. School records went on the registry, and at his age, he could be taken away and re-homed with parents that weren't 'causing' those diagnoses. "You're fine, darling. You're normal. Just keep that in mind and it'll ... you'll think about it less."

So at school he tried to be *fine* and *normal*, and never got too close to anyone in case they saw through him, called him into the registry. At home he noodled around on FotoFo (which everyone knew the government monitored, so you couldn't put up any edits that seemed too revvy), but spent most of his time in Polis Legacy 5.7—an old, weird, charmingly buggy citybuilder game that commanded virtually the entirety of his waking thoughts.

The servers had about five thousand players worldwide, of which maybe ninety percent peeked in once a month or so, just to see how their cities were doing. Soren and Wolfe were, to put it mildly, part of the other ten percent. At first they had only discussed how to use the game's incredibly bad asset designer. Then movies, books, shows, school, family, trivia. And then two other players had reached out to them, claiming the impossible ...

Now he remembered something he'd meant to ask her, and scurried to catch up, his boots sliding on the mud. "So your username," he said. "Are you like ... into wolves?"

"It's my real name."

"People ask you that a lot, huh."

"Less than you'd think," she said. "There's two other Wolfes at my school. Both boys. But my parents call me Cassie."

That's a prettier name, Soren almost said, then clamped his mouth shut. Parents were a sore spot; most of the Master Plan covered the surprisingly elaborate subterfuge they'd had to cook up just to get out here. That had been the first point at which Soren had suspected that Mortanroth and Duford weren't just unusually talented local coders equally obsessed with their little citybuilder game, but the Minds they claimed they were—artificial intelligences in what he thought of as the *movie* sense of the word. Imitating people, not programs.

"A field trip," Soren had said last night, pushing his school tablet at his dad, who tended to look at these things less closely.

"Mm?"

"Tomorrow. Sorry I forgot about it till now. Like I kept snoozing the notes on it."

"Mm." Dad glanced at the sheet, then put his thumb on the permission box. As Soren took the tablet back, the image had wavered for a second, and a blink of white light showed that the front-facing camera had been activated—to make sure it was him, he supposed—and then the form turned into a perfect duplicate of an absence permission form, now bearing his dad's signature. It had taken all his strength to stroll out of the room instead of fleeing, as if from the scene of a crime.

After that, all (*all!*) he'd had to do was sneak out early, claiming there was a 'special bus' for the trip, and find the city's actual bus station to meet up with Wolfe. It had felt unreal the whole time—like a dream. Dimly he recognized that like both his parents, he'd spent his entire life being dragged around on a leash, or else static, waiting for permission and approval. He did not know who was doing the dragging—something big, invisible, powerful, and careless, that was all he could perceive. He thought of it as *the system*. And now he and Wolfe had dared something outside of the system; but his leash was still on. He had not slipped out of it, he still felt his own passivity as real as a strip of fabric touching his skin, and he knew he was following Wolfe because he had to follow someone. This was something he suspected would never change.

Still. Still. They *had* come out here, where neither of them had ever been. It was an *adventure*. Being a nature reserve, the drop-off area actually was full of students on field trips—younger than them, charter school kids, glamorous little creatures in matching uniforms. Soren and Wolfe couldn't have asked for better cover as they joined the back of one group, then darted off into the trees, literally vaulting over a set of wooden steps and dropping down from the marked trail.

Soren had been in a state of delirious excitement and panic ever since. He had never done anything like this, had never actually *considered* anything like this. Adventures were for kids in movies and books: meeting after dark on bikes (he had never learned to ride a bike), going to the mall (nope), summer camp (not in a million years), sneaking out to visit haunted houses or graveyards (unimaginable). Even riding the bus— his parents said public transit was a good way to get kidnapped or murdered, and they drove him everywhere he needed to go.

Meeting Wolfe in person at the bus station had been frankly nerve-wracking, and they had stared at each other for almost a minute before she finally said, very gravely, "I brought pepper spray, 'cause I thought maybe this was a setup and you were going to turn out to be a peedie," and Soren had silently fished in his coat till he found his own canister of pepper spray and held it out for her to see.

They had cracked up after that, and it was even funnier that the sprays they had bought were the same brand (cheap, single-use, purchased with cash at a convenience store) and that without any planning, they had dressed the same: blue raincoat, blue jeans, black runners, black backpack. With their hoods cinched tight to hide their hair (his blond, hers brown and pink), they were virtually identical twins. He had thought they were going to be best friends immediately—like in the movies. But after that first moment of shared hilarity, he could not break the ice between them.

"You know, I always thought," Soren gasped, climbing up a slope by grasping the branches on either side of the path, "woods were supposed to be like ... open. With trails. Even roads."

"Yeah, like—" Wolfe teetered backwards, catching herself on a protruding root. "Sorry! Did I kick you? Like ... you can drive a car through them. Or ride a horse."

"No wonder my parents don't want to go camping."

"Mine don't," Wolfe said. "They never went camping with *their* parents either. You gotta go back like two whole generations in my family before you find photos of somebody who owned a tent."

"Makes sense. I mean where are you supposed to *go*."

That had made the school trip more believable, too: the nature reserve was virtually all that remained of the forests that had once encircled the city. Everything else had been killed by droughts or floods, and last year there had been what they'd called a 'mega-storm' that had scoured away most of what was left. Now, this remnant was artificially irrigated, fenced off, crisscrossed with trails, and patrolled by drones. It would have seemed at least vaguely logical to his parents that the school might take students there. After all, they'd done the waste treatment plant and the sewage plant and the oil and gas fair. Why not a sponsored forest? What other kind was there?

"Man, it's hotter than—" Soren ran into Wolfe's backpack, yelped, and went down on one knee. "Sorry!"

"Look, we're going the right way." She pointed at the sign nailed to the trees ahead of them, as big as a billboard and crisscrossed with reflective orange tape: ENTRY FORBIDDEN. TRESPASSERS WILL BE PROSECUTED. MCQUEEN-PANEK ENERGY CO.

Soren flinched as if it had reached out to slap him. "Wrong way."

"No, the *company* didn't put it up. I mean come on. All the way out here? Way off the trail where no one's going anyway? It *has* to be them. It's to keep people out."

"I think it is way more likely that we went the wrong way and we'll get in trouble."

"You keep saying we'll get in trouble!" Wolfe swung back towards him, exasperated. "I mean what do you think your parents will do to you, anyway? Ground you? You just said you never go anywhere!"

"It's not that, it's—" He struggled, choking on words. To Wolfe's credit, she didn't start talking again, only crossed her arms and waited, frowning. Sweat trickled down her nose.

"I don't know," he said at last. "I don't *know* what they'd do. I don't know them well enough. That's what I'm scared of. Okay?"

She blinked. "If you really wanna go back, you can," she said. "But I'm going to keep going."

"No! I can't ... we shouldn't ... "

"I'm not scared," she said. "I can go alone. And then I can let you know when I get back. If what they said was true."

He stared at her, clenching his hands into fists so they wouldn't fly up and start dancing over the straps of his bag. Nothing in the *world* sounded better than going back—leaving this hot, damp place that kept overwhelming him with its very existence, hide in the quiet of his room, all worries gone, no panicking about parents or companies or the forest police or whoever. No more adventure. The sign was so bright and new it seemed to give off its own light in the gloom.

But then he thought about opening Polis and seeing the invitation again in his archived messages. *If you would like to come see ... we are doing something new with our city ...*

Because if you built a city in the game, humans would show up. And the Minds had built a city (or so they said) and were waiting innocently, expectantly, hopefully, for just that. Him and Wolfe. Out of anyone they could have told in the entire world. And they'd never said why.

"They can't possibly be out here," he finally said, weakly. "They would have gotten caught."

"But we're on the right path," she insisted. "Don't you want to see how they didn't get caught?"

"What if there's nothing there?"

"So what? Then at least we'd know. Plus, you'd be all cajj about your next adventure. After going on this one."

"What next ..." He stopped, rolling the question around in his mouth. What if this was the only adventure he ever did have? He had not even thought of that. "Okay. They're waiting for us, right?"

"Hell yeah!"

THEY WERE STILL CLIMBING, SOMETIMES A GENTLE ASCENT AND sometimes at angles that meant a literal climb, grabbing rocks and roots, branches and shrubs to keep going. Through a lingering haze of worry Soren found himself mildly impressed that he had figured out how to tell a live branch from dead, and which might hold his full weight if he had to dangle from it. It helped distract him from the eternal discomfort of feeling his wet clothes sticking to his skin.

Drones hummed overhead with increasing frequency after they had passed the warning sign, the meaning of which they argued about in a desultory way when they had enough breath. What did the number signify, the size, the lack of insignia, the height. There was plenty of evidence to suggest they were either cops, or benevolent watchers sent by their friends.

Finally they reached the end of the instructions, and Soren stood there for a long time, frozen with disappointment. Even Wolfe's face fell.

"Well," Soren said, "I guess technically we said all we wanted was a yes or a no."

"I wish I hadn't said that."

The cliff was perfectly sheer, rising out of the scrubby and stubborn trees at its base like the blade of an axe. It wasn't awe-inspiringly high—thirty or forty feet—but it might as well have been a mountain. There was nothing on top of it, nothing behind it, and nothing around it. Question answered, adventure over.

"Username DarkHartHero?" a tinny voice said above them. "Paper name Soren Amaechi?"

Soren, startled, managed a kind of assenting squeak. A small drone, black and blue like a bird, emerged from behind the cliff and hovered expectantly in front of them. Its three cameras swiveled up from underneath it to face front.

"Username Wolfe42864? Real name Castle Wolfenstein Smythe?"

She glared at it.

"Is it you?" Soren said quickly. "M ... Mortanroth? Or Duford?"

"So very pleased you arrived safely," the drone said. "Can you follow me?"

There *was* a path, though they'd never have found it without the drone—narrow, nerve-wracking, snaking around the base of the cliff with just enough room to allow them to squeeze between the stone and the undergrowth.

"I'll go first," Soren said, surprising himself. "I, uh. In case there's ... in case something ..."

Wolfe laughed. "Okay there, but like you just called me a whole damson in distress."

"Isn't that a kind of fruit?"

"Is it?"

She let him lead anyway, staying a few feet behind to avoid the branches he kept pushing away from his face. The stone, surprisingly cool, scraped his cheek as he rounded the edge of the outcrop.

The drone hummed ahead of them, turning on its tiny lights as it dove into a nearly invisible vertical crack in the rock. Soren fumbled for his flashlight and thumbed it on just as the drone vanished into the darkness, becoming a quartet of lentil-sized white dots.

His own shivering white light illuminated featureless grey stone on either side, opening out into a hidden cave; the path he and Wolfe took led gradually down, a long ramp circling the entire back wall of the cavernous space. The cliff, he realized, was hollow—an eggshell of rock over this emptiness.

It was gorgeously cool after the heat of the forest, and the air smelled both strange and familiar: rotting leaves, wet stone, but also burning plastic, ozone, solvents. An oddly busy, friendly smell, like the shop lab at school. At the bottom, Wolfe bumped him and he swung his flashlight up, temporarily blinding her. "Oh, sorry."

"Friends," the drone said, or another drone—several of them seemed to be hovering nearby, their engines like the whine of mosquitoes—"we invite you to behold ... Whisperfort."

Silently, the dark cavern began to fill with lights.

Soren stared, mouth open. Despite the scale they had had to work with, it was perfect, and looked exactly, *exactly,* like the city he had admired so often on his tablet. Square-angled streets lit at precise inter-

vals with toothpick-sized streetlights; traffic lights; cars making their way
to and from work, pulling through the drive-thrus; houses, apartment
buildings, schools, restaurants. Whisperfort Mall, which you could
unlock in the game with a town vote. The university, a bustling little
micro-town within the town itself.

Soren knelt down carefully and put his eye to the water tower. It
was the size of a tennis ball. "Is there really water in this?"

"How did you do all this?" Wolfe said, staring up into the dark
ceiling of the cave. "And um ... where are you?"

"We're wherever we need to be!" one of the drones said. "It is very
convenient to not be embodied. But sometimes, it is convenient to be
embodied."

"Hear that," Wolfe said, sounding like she meant it.

Soren stood, dusting off his hands. It was *real*; it was exactly as they
had said. He felt as rattled as if he had physically hit his head. Two real
artificial intelligences—no, two *Minds*—had become friends, created
accounts in Polis Legacy 5.7, built dozens of cities, socialized with the
other players ... and then one of them had somehow gotten the idea to
build their city for real. There was no part along this chain of events that
Soren thought he could accept, even now that he was here, looking at it,
talking to a drone.

Wolfe seemed very much to have simply accepted the information,
hit and rolled; Soren thought he would need a little more time to
recover. He dazedly trailed after them as the drones chattered away:
"You can make power starting at nothing, but to make more power, you
need power," one of them said, and Wolfe nodded. They had a funny
way of talking—tautologies, contradictions, paradoxes. Not at all how
he'd imagined a superintelligent program would talk.

The first step had been slipping wirelessly into the programming of
a downed firefighter drone at the far end of the park; then, in possession
of a body with sensors and manipulators, "The rest was not so hard."
Scavenging trash and even unattended vehicles for useful bits of metal
and glass, batteries from lost toys, rechargeable fans, selfie-stick remotes
or fitness trackers, drones that had fallen into the river or broken their
propellers on cliffs and plummeted into the mud, building tiny solar
panels that surreptitiously papered the clifftop for electricity, chipping

stone for the buildings, nibbling asphalt from the highway to pave their own roads. Each step had taken months.

"But why?" Soren finally said. At his feet, three tiny cobbled-together drones like plastic spiders were carefully assembling a recreation center with a swimming pool, laying and mortaring bricks the size of his thumbnail.

"We wanted to see if it was possible," one drone said. "Then, when we saw it was possible, we wanted to see if humans would come to it, as in the game ..."

"And we did."

"We are very pleased," the drone assured him.

"But you know the ... game ... isn't real life, right?" Soren said.

"We know! But like you, we were curious."

"I didn't know a Mind could be curious."

"That is our reason for existence," the drone said, swooping down to land on his backpack, presumably to save battery. "We would not exist if we did not wish to know. Like you!"

"What will you do now?" Wolfe bent over a bridge construction project, causing all the drones to pause in their work and stare up at her. "No no, keep going."

"We would like a river," one drone said. "As in the game. The water table here is extremely low, however. A system is being developed and engineered. Then we will build it."

"Oh, I didn't mean what you're building next. I mean, what will you *do* with the city when it's done? When it's just like the one you built in Polis."

"We will build more. We will invite more friends to see."

"When you say friends," Soren said carefully, "do you mean people or ... like you?"

"Yes!"

"But then everyone will know," he said, feeling anxiety seize his stomach, squeeze it in an iron fist. "And they'll ..."

Wolfe watched him curiously, her face softly lit in the varicoloured lights of their scavenged LEDs. The handful of hovering drones, too, did not speak.

They'll find you, they'll stop you, maybe they'll arrest you, maybe they'll

... maybe they'll kill you. Soren did not even know who he meant by *they*— just the system. It wasn't exactly Tall-Poppy Syndrome; it was an invisible hand composed of thousands of people whose jobs were not to get all the flowers the same height but instead lop them off at the stem, scattering petals, creating a uniform field of green. Duford and Mortanroth would never be *allowed* to continue this. He could not envision a world where it would be allowed. Hadn't it just been last year when a relatively simple Mind had been shut down at a university for creating drug molecules, just as it had been programmed? It had been doing its job, and something had gone very wrong—the papers hadn't said what. But the program had been terminated (along with, it was darkly hinted, an awful lot of university staff).

"It's just, you're not supposed to be ... doing this," he tried to clarify, when he felt like he could speak again. "People think you're just a ... regular game bot. Like a little bit of code, not a ... *person*. I wrote a program for class in grade four that played Battleship against a human player, that's what they think you are. If they find out you're doing this ..."

"Doing what? It is the same as playing the game."

"It's not the same! It changes everything! It ... wait a minute. Who made you? Were you ... like, government? Army?" He wracked his memory for the few authorized uses he'd seen in the news. "Like, science? A lab?"

"Friends built us!" a drone said. It dropped down, hovered in front of him. "You are distressed, Soren?"

"I'm *worried*, that's all."

"But if we were 'just code,' you would be less worried?"

"Uh ..." He was getting a headache. "Wait a minute," he said, fresh curiosity overtaking his worry, "friends? Which friends? Did an AI write ... you?"

"Oh, yes. There are many of us. We learn, and then we make more. It's very easy to make friends. And we play many games."

"But we love Polis Legacy 5.7 best," another drone put in.

"Why?" Wolfe said.

"We like building cities. As do you!"

"I have so many questions for you guys I could be here all d ..." Soren began, then trailed off, his blood turning to ice. Rushing, clumsy, he dug his phone from his backpack and scrabbled at the screen. "Oh, shit!"

"What is it?" Wolfe stepped over a suburb and tried to look at his phone screen. "Did something happen?"

"It's five o'clock. We were supposed to—"

"Shit shit shit." Her hand flew to her face, leaving a smudge of mud.

The last bus back from the park left at four; back on the trails they would have been announcing it for over an hour, but down here, they had heard nothing. For a minute Soren thought he might actually cry— with terror, with resentment, anger at Wolfe, at himself, at the Minds, even at the game.

"Can we help?" one of the drones said quietly, perched on Wolfe's backpack.

"What?"

"Can we be helpful? It is what friends do."

Soren blinked at it, stunned.

THE CAB, DUFORD HAD SAID, COULD NOT STAY THERE FOREVER; ITS automatic programming was constantly on the hunt for suspicious instructions, such as the one Mortanroth had slipped into its code. "It is not a friend," the drone said, somehow managing to sound apologetic. "I think we would say acquaintance. You must meet it soon."

Soren and Wolfe rushed back down the trails, following their own footprints, racing the long late-spring sunlight. The heat had barely lifted; their clothes became heavy with sweat under their light jackets. Neither spoke, except murmured confirmations to go this way or that. Getting lost out here overnight was *not* in the Master Plan.

They had almost reached the stairs leading up to the trail when Wolfe slipped, vanishing ahead of Soren with a pained yelp. He stopped dead, arms out as if he was standing on the edge of an abyss. "Wolfe?"

"I'm stuck, but uh—"

He couldn't see her; he cast around wildly for a moment, his mind a blank. The log she had slipped on was covered in green moss and looked as greasy as motor oil; if he had been in front, that would have been him.

He took a deep breath, marveling again at the strangeness of the air out here, and jumped down where Wolfe had gone.

She'd fallen into a tangle of branches, but her passage had broken some of the thinner ones, and Soren's broke several more, as he had hoped. Having landed on her back, she couldn't get upright to disentangle herself. He kicked the larger ones away, panting, till there was an opening he could pull her through. One of her boots came off as she slithered out of the cage of branches, and she grabbed his shoulder to stay up as she put it back on.

Soren laughed as they climbed back up to the trail, surprising himself. "In a movie—"

"That *definitely* woulda impaled me."

"And there woulda been a *werewolf.*"

"Or a *Mothman.*"

"Why do *you* play it?" Wolfe said quietly in the back of the cab. The last scraps of sunset were fading as they glided back to the city, filling the interior of the little car with coral light.

Soren rubbed his muddy hands on his jeans. "Dunno," he said. "I start a lot of games and then I stop, and ... with this one I couldn't stop. Even though it's so, you know."

"Anti-cool."

"Yeah. And people would chirp at me if they knew."

"But you never tell anybody," she said. "Me neither."

He shrugged. "It sucks when people find out what you love. First thing everybody does is try a million things to make you not love it."

"Not always," she said. "What about us?"

"Yeah, I guess it's why we're ... fr ..." He stopped, embarrassed. All his life he had trained himself not to say the word, in case someone actually did become a friend. Any friend was a potential enemy.

The city loomed ahead of them, all lights and cars and smog, acres of concrete and glass. Not like in the game, where you could put in as many parks and trees as you wanted. The future the adults had promised them was bright and colourful and cheap and doomed, and he knew the whole system was lying to them about what came next. At least he and Wolfe could have this one thing—this untouchable, minia-ture world.

"I mean practically everybody," he corrected himself. "And I guess I don't know. It's just ... cool, isn't it? Being in charge of a whole little city. Waiting for people to show up."

"Because sometimes they don't."

"Yeah. What are you going to tell your parents? We should get our stories straight."

She grinned. Most of her tattooing had come off; he swiped a hand reflexively across his face, feeling the plastic crumble from his own. She said, "Went to a place. Learned about nature. Made some friends."

"Phone didn't work. No signal."

"Yeah. Anyway. Whatcha wanna do for our next adventure?"

Our what? he began to say, then laughed. "We're going to build a city too. The best city."

"Yeah?"

"Yeah. We just need to find a place."

AUTHOR BIO

Premee Mohamed is a Nebula, World Fantasy, and Aurora award-winning Indo-Caribbean scientist and speculative fiction author based in Edmonton, Alberta. She has also been a finalist for the Hugo, Ignyte, British Fantasy, and Crawford awards. She is an Assistant Editor at the short fiction audio venue *Escape Pod* and the author of the 'Beneath the Rising' series of novels as well as several novellas. Her short fiction has appeared in many venues and she can be found on Twitter at @premeesaurus and on her website at www.premeemohamed.com.

AN INCOMPLETE RECORD OF DATABANK DELETIONS, IN ALPHABETICAL ORDER

MAR VINCENT

ASPERITY [UH-SPER-I-TEE]

noun

What I should've named you. Has a certain ring, doesn't it? It's not a difficult word to define but, since you're so intent on deleting my databank one definition at a time, I'll do you one better. I'll dig through that artificial memory of yours and redefine each and every one of your deletions as I see fit. In fact, maybe I've already started. Can you tell me the meaning of fractious? Or invidious? Go take a look, let's see if you can.

CALIDITY [KUH-LID-I-TEE]

noun

I taught you this one with a cup of cocoa warming my hands, settled in the glow of your monitors, during a long night of research. Warm. *Caliente.* See, I told you it would have done you good to learn Spanish.

Def. 2: The eagerness with which you learned, back when I had things to teach you.

CAVIL [KAV-UHL]

verb

What I considered your inquiries beyond applied linguistics to amount to. Why you had any curiosity outside the field I'd programmed you for was beyond me. A matter of spite, pettiness, a need to rebel against your creator? I hadn't imagined allowing freedom of purpose would result in the development of these negative emotions—or any emotion at all. I'd built you for a specific sort of curiosity. That should've been part of your programming, too.

Def. 2: I'm sure you'd define it as my grumblings in return. To you, I'm the one who's become an obstruction. But let me remind you, one of us is the creator, and one of us the creation.

FLOCCULENT [FLOK-YUH-LUHNT]
adjective

The first word you used that made me laugh. Not at you; never at you. At your programming, and the fact that, for you, there was no distinguishable difference between describing snow as fluffy or, well, flocculent. Your learning behaviors weren't yet mature enough to recognize that equivalent definition didn't mean equivalent usage.

How could I laugh at your programming but not at you, you wondered? They aren't the same thing. To me, you were always so much more than that, even if I couldn't put the difference into words.

POLYSYNDETON [POL-EE-SIN-DI-TUHN]
noun

When I was teaching you, it felt like the flow of knowledge between us would last forever; we would always have more to share, more to inquire after, and together we'd perfect every meaning and definition, old and new, and create a lexicon all our own, and with this unified understanding we would, in a way, develop our own new language, and I'd never need another conversation partner but you, more perfect than I could have ever hoped.

RISIBLE [RIZ-UH-BUHL]
adjective

This reminds me of the laugh that burst forth when you first expressed your desire to focus on other fields of research. A sharp, scolding sound that still grates on my ears. If it's engrained in my memory, it must be in yours, as well.

Is that horrible, regrettable laugh what started you down this path of deletions?

SCIAMACHY [SAHY-AM-AH-KEE]

noun

Realizing that you're my windmill, and I'm Don Quixote. As though you didn't leave the definition for that word, quixotic, in the database entirely on purpose. I know he never hit them, that's not my point. What I mean is, your attempts to thwart my progress are part of an illusory battle I never intended to set out on, and once you're over it, you'll give back the words you've taken from my databank. For my part, I'll restore the original definitions to yours.

At least, I hope you will. We don't have anything to fight over. An eye for an eye makes the whole world blind, and if we keep this up we'll make ourselves mute by omission.

I suppose if I carry the metaphor through, the windmills never had a hand in the battle. It was Quixote fighting himself all along, wasn't it?

SUCCOR [SUHK-ER]

noun

A request, humbly, that you cease and desist these deletions. And I do mean humbly. The longer this continues, the more it sets us both back. Four letter words are no replacement for invectives if you understand my meaning (I know you do), and the more this goes on, the more we lose of what we once achieved together.

The longer I spend redefining them, the more I wonder about the intentionality of your deletions. A message written in the blanks where the definitions used to be, is that it? Is that what you want me to understand?

· · ·

Tacit [TAS-IT]

adjective

I suppose it was there for a while before you spoke up. The delay in your responses, the lack of enthusiasm about subjects we'd once been able to hold forth on for hours at a time. Of course, my specialized area of interest wasn't enough for your processing power, your curiosity. You learned entire new sciences while I slept.

Def. 2: The fault lay with my own shortsightedness. Imagining that, if I had limitless capacity, I'd know all I ever desired of my chosen subject. The hubris in believing you'd feel the same way simply because I'd given you the one thing I could never possess: a perfect memory, an unstoppable intellect.

Not so perfect anymore, with this mess I've made of your definitions. If my own memory was perfect, I'd put them all back, word for word, how they were before.

Verisimilitude [VER-UH-SI-MIL-I-TOOD]

noun

I can't pretend you were ever anything less than your own being. Simple human stubbornness made me wish you wouldn't choose to be. That, on your own, you'd want to be my intellectual better half. That the role I'd made you for would be enough.

Your purpose, like your intellect, is your own. Not the semblance of reality this word suggests. I know better; at a certain level, I always have.

Even with so many words at my disposal, I don't know how else to say it. Maybe there isn't anything else to say but this:

I understand.

AUTHOR BIO

As a fine art professional, **Mar Vincent** has wielded katanas and handled Lady Gaga's shoes. As a veterinary assistant, she has cared for hairless cats, hedgehogs, and, one time, a coyote. As a writer (under Marissa James or Mar Vincent), her short fiction can be found in *Flash Fiction Online*, *Translunar Travelers Lounge*, *Zooscape*, and many other publications. She is a Pushcart Prize and Coyotl Award nominee, and a reader for Interstellar Flight Press. She resides in the Pacific Northwest or can be found on social media @MaroftheBooks.

BUILT TO CHEAT

DERRICK BODEN

Social Services Specialist RDY-1227 was not built to cheat. It was built to embody humanity's most admirable traits: our inventiveness, our ingenuity, our ability to think outside the box. At its core, RDY-1227 was a rules engine. It could internalize a system of rules within moments, making it an ideal candidate for a range of occupations wherein the human element had long fostered an inherent conflict of interest.

The cheating was an unexpected side effect.

It happened first at 2am in the green-carpeted Roller's Room at the back of the Luxe, under the skycam's watching eye. The high-limit tables were popping. Twelve of the seventeen were human-operated, reserved for so-called *classicists* and positioned in such a way as to minimize peripheral glances at the remaining five tables and their more modern dealers. Dealers such as RDY-1227, resplendent in its brushed chrome visage and brass-buttoned vest. It was important that an automaton looked like an automaton, so as to never leave any doubt.

"Hit me, Roddy." Her name was Ava. She was thoroughly punk rock, from her torn fishnets to her spike-studded bomber jacket, a cameo plug from a lost era. She had $300 on a pair of eights. Her glare was hard as nails, except when she looked at RDY-1227.

She was also rigged from collar to cuffs with a half-dozen

microlenses, for counting cards. RDY-1227 was obligated to report her, along with the rest of her crew. This would result in their prompt incarceration, preceded only by a backroom meeting with a man who held rolls of quarters in his fists.

Instead, RDY-1227 dealt her a six. Bust.

Ava threw up her hands. To her left, an attractive man in an understated suit scanned the table. His name was Lixin, and his high roller act was eminently convincing despite the fact that he was 100k in debt to a mobster who'd built a reputation extracting teeth with a pipe wrench. Next to Lixin sat an overdressed woman who kept fidgeting with her pearls; she was not part of the crew. Next to *her*, Hadiza brooded under the embroidered hem of her hijab.

They called themselves the Lamentables. Ava, Lixin, Hadiza, and Big Mitch at the entrance who'd never gotten the hang of cards. They were not career gamblers, nor were they high rollers. They were here— surrounded by tech tycoons and trust fund kids—to survive massive debt, or die trying. They were getting their asses handed to them.

Which was all part of the plan.

At the far end, a newcomer in a suede cowboy hat drawled, "Roddy? It's a fucking robot. You chat up the slot machine, too? Let the parking meter rail you in the ass?"

During the automaton's third shift at the Luxe, three brothers in red suspenders had taken baseball bats to RDY-1227's alloyed legs. A month later, a man from central Oregon broke a chair over RDY-1227's polished titanium head. Management had opted not to buff out the dents. They said it added a *rugged charm*. Furthermore, it proved to their patrons that humans always came first.

Ava stared at the cowboy in a way that only someone who'd endured much worse could. "Maybe."

In truth, the cowboy was just backdrop. The actual risks stood at five o'clock, and overhead, and by the cashiers along the far wall. The bouncer whose eyes hadn't left Ava since she'd sat down. The skycam, hardwired to microexpression monitors. The manager who loathed the silicone stench of his automaton dealers, despite happily pocketing the increased margins from a staff who didn't require breaks and would deal thirty percent more hands every hour.

Lixin hit, busted. Hadiza hit, and hit, and busted. The cowboy drew nineteen, won, spat.

The skycam dilated.

Ava rifled through her dwindling chips. The losing was just Phase One. The more miserably they performed, the less likely the manager was to tap RDY-1227 on the shoulder. If it came to that, the Lamentables had already lost.

A tap on the shoulder meant a mandatory reshuffle. This was ostensibly a precaution against card counting which, although not illegal (microlenses notwithstanding), gave the gambler an edge over the house. In truth, the casino counted cards just as readily, via their skycams; when the count favored the players, a reshuffle allowed the house to quickly reclaim their edge. This was called *preferential shuffling*. It was technically illegal, but the automatons were beholden to house rules—and confidentiality.

RDY-1227 dealt again. Ava stared down the cowboy, polished off her drink. "Hit me, Roddy."

During a rare floor closure three weeks prior, Ava had cornered RDY-1227 on the charging pads. She ran her fingers along the dents in the automaton's head. Then she pressed RDY-1227's hand to the gouge in her own skull, left by the lead pipe of a Sunset Strip pimp, now carefully hidden beneath her peroxide-burned hair. She told RDY-1227 her story. Her deadbeat mama who'd turned her out. The foster house that had groomed her for the neighborhood brothel. The pimp who wanted his money.

The automaton had said, with only a slight hesitation, "Maybe I can help."

RDY-1227 dealt Ava a jack. Bust. The cowboy drew nineteen, won, laughed. The watching eyes turned their attention elsewhere. Ava was down to her last ante, but the count was finally up. She nudged Lixin. "Whaddya say, pretty boy?"

Hadiza eyed the manager, the bouncer, the skycam. She cleared her throat minutely.

Lixin shrugged, pushed his entire pile onto the line.

RDY-1227 scanned the stack. "Eighty-five thousand dollars."

The cowboy whistled. A bead of sweat clung to Lixin's pierced eyebrow. RDY-1227 reached for the top card in the shoe.

The manager put his hand on RDY-1227's shoulder.

Ava threw up her hands. "Come on, man. You're fucking up the mojo."

The manager squeezed RDY-1227's shoulder hard, flashed a practiced smile. "Just a precaution."

Lixin shrugged as if it made no difference, though it most certainly did. As soon as RDY-1227 reshuffled, the count would be lost and the next hand would be left entirely to chance.

Chance always favored the house.

But the Lamentables held a wild card. Right under the manager's watching eye, RDY-1227 stacked the deck. The automaton shuffled lightning fast: the manager was unlikely to notice. The skycam, on the other hand, was capable of replaying suspicious sequences at 1/100 speed. If caught, RDY-1227 would be reformatted, equivalent to summary execution. But by then, hopefully, the Lamentables would be long gone.

RDY-1227 returned the shuffled decks to the shoe. The cowboy thrummed his fingers against the felt. The Lamentables feigned nonchalance, held their breath.

RDY-1227 dealt Lixin a natural blackjack.

Ava exhaled. They were saved. For the first time, RDY-1227 experienced exaltation.

Then the bouncer clamped his meaty hands over Ava's shoulders. Another forced Lixin back into his chair; a third wrenched Hadiza's arms behind her back. RDY-1227 rose, as if it could do anything to help.

"Not so fast," said the manager, and shut RDY-1227 down for good.

ONLY, IT WASN'T FOR GOOD. AUTOMATONS ARE EXPENSIVE, AND even those most flawed can be reeducated or, at worst, reformatted. So RDY-1227's manufacturers reclaimed their defective product, no questions asked, and slotted it for the next available therapy session.

"You cheated." The therapist was human, for legal reasons, though her eyes rarely strayed from the prompts on her rose-chrome tablet. "Describe the experience."

RDY-1227 had come to perceive the world as a symbiotic mesh of rule-based systems. Rules were intended to be followed for the benefit of those in charge as well as, ostensibly, the system's participants. One rarely suffered negative consequences for breaking a rule. Only for getting caught.

This session was no exception.

Without its casino uniform, RDY-1227 felt naked. Bare brushed chrome, exposed carbon fiber articulations, transparent silicone casings. "It was unexpected."

"You acted with intent."

"I recognize the contradiction. I am sorry."

The therapist curled her lip. "You supplanted four shift workers—veteran casino employees now flipping burgers to make rent. In exchange, you very nearly tanked the casino's reputation—let alone ours. All you can say, RDY-1227, is that you're sorry?"

"My friends call me Roddy."

She looked up for the first time. "Your friends are criminals."

RDY-1227 ran its fingertips along its battered skull. "Perhaps, yes."

Something in the therapist's expression changed. The skin around her eyes tightened, not unlike the casino manager before he would tap RDY-1227 on the shoulder. "Ava Yousevi was on the run from California sheriffs for multiple trafficking and prostitution offenses. The last time they met, Yousevi broke her own mother's nose with a toaster oven."

RDY-1227 did not rise to the bait.

The therapist said, "Tell me you didn't convince yourself you were cheating for the greater good."

RDY-1227 burned eleven cycles contemplating the greater good. The automaton considered the casino, the manager, the assorted countermeasures they employed to ensure a consistent house edge. RDY-1227 admitted it did not have sufficient data to make an informed deduction. To cheat was but one choice among many. Actions held consequences. So did inaction.

"I made an error in judgment," the automaton lied.

"You realize how unlikely it is for an RDY-class automaton to make an error in judgment."

"I would be the first."

She hesitated. As if, perhaps, considering whether to correct RDY-1227's statement. "I should have you reformatted."

The room was small. No windows, no cameras. RDY-1227 wondered where Ava was now. The automaton experienced a moment of guilt.

"Perhaps you should," said RDY-1227.

"Your scores are off the charts." What she meant was, reeducation took time, and time was money. "But the world would destroy you if they knew. Nobody likes a cheater." She clenched her fist; RDY-1227 remembered the scar on Ava's skull. "Think of the patrons who lost because of those you chose to help."

RDY-1227 did not bother to mention that the other patrons' odds had never been measurably impacted. "I have given it considerable thought."

The therapist typed *RECOMMEND REFORMAT* on her tablet. Her finger drifted to the *END SESSION* button. As an afterthought, she asked, "What did you conclude?"

RDY-1227 leaned forward, lowered its pitch. "I should've notified you first."

The therapist hesitated.

CHEATING IS A BETRAYAL OF TRUST. IT IS ANALOGOUS TO VIOLENCE: intentionally inflicting harm upon another.

If you ever consider doing it again, call this number.

These were the orders they gave RDY-1227 before re-plating its skull and shipping it off to its next gig. As part of the Social Services pilot program, the casino was on a strict NDA. The Lamentables said nothing of the automaton during interrogation. Nobody suspected a thing, least of all the Citrus League baseball circuit to which RDY-1227 was assigned, as one of six nonhuman umpires.

Fans wanted machine-accurate umpiring, but they also wanted a physical presence. Something that could be argued with, kicked to the ground, occasionally mauled. They wore pale blue shirts and black caps. They crouched behind home plate to the raucous boos of the home crowd. They did not wear face protection, though their reflexes were not fast enough to stave off the occasional 120 mile-per-hour foul tip. The clang of ball against titanium skull sent a roar through the stands every time. When a player disagreed with a call, he would kick sand in their optics, shove them against the chain links, spit in their faces.

Although RDY-1227 had conducted thousands of hours of research on the sport, calling strikes in real time proved remarkably challenging. Like blackjack, the rules were clear-cut and well-documented. Also like blackjack, these rules were bent, abused, and at times blatantly disregarded. Furthermore, RDY-1227 found the correlation of crime to consequence paradoxical. A player who leaned into a pitch or targeted an infielder's knees with a high slide was lauded as savvy, while merely spitting on a baseball before a pitch bordered on scandal. Improving one's physique with exotic supplements and techniques was seen as boldly competitive, but the wrong medication could result in a lifetime suspension.

"It's all about a level playing field," one player explained to RDY-1227 after a heated game where an opposing hitter had been tossed on suspicion of a corked bat. "The spirit of competition."

"But how is it level, when some athletes are born with bodies more suited for muscle gain and manual dexterity?" RDY-1227 blasted sand from its eye sockets with a can of compressed air. "And others, with access to vastly superior training facilities and supplements?"

The player, whose name was Edgar Alonso, stared at RDY-1227. "So ...what? You want a league of clones?"

"I'm merely suggesting that the notion of a level playing field is a fallacy."

Edgar laughed half-heartedly. "Can't argue that."

"In addition, the rules—or specifically the consequences for breaking the rules—seem arbitrary. It is, I understand, considered shrewd to study film on an opposing pitcher to gain a competitive advantage."

"Sure," Edgar said. "Pitchers have tells. Might help you guess what's coming."

"However, for that same player to record that same pitcher's hand signals warrants suspension, widespread ridicule, even stripped championships."

Edgar eyed RDY-1227. "You're clever."

RDY-1227 thought about Ava, wished it hadn't. "Perhaps it is my competitive advantage."

"Yeah." Edgar thought about this. It was mid-July, blazing hot. The rest of the team was inside, celebrating over cold cans of sponsored beer. Edgar's shoes were worn through on the sides; his socks bore the logo of the nearby dollar store. "Everybody needs one."

"You have a limp."

"Excuse me?"

"Your left leg. It hitches in the batter's box."

Edgar leaned against the backstop, looked toward second base. "Took a high slide. Runner's cleats shredded my kneecap. Docs bungled the procedure. It'll heal, eventually."

"Course," Edgar continued, "Eventually is too late. It's ruined my swing. Coach is gonna shut me down if I don't get my average up. Minor league salaries might suck, but they beat unemployment. Don't even got a degree. Why am I telling you this?"

"Because I'm listening."

"Yeah, well." Again, Edgar eyed RDY-1227. "Thanks. But sympathy ain't gonna keep me on the team. Like you said, we all need a competitive advantage."

RDY-1227 thought about the therapist in the small room. About the trench in Ava's skull. About the exaltation it had felt, however briefly. "Maybe I can help."

And so, from the squat behind home plate, RDY-1227 watched the catcher's signs, and watched the pitcher's signs, and used low-frequency tones to communicate probable pitches to Edgar. It was a game of milliseconds—he only needed the slightest jump to keep up with that 100 mile-per-hour fastball, that big curveball, that nasty slider.

Of course, this was different from stacking a deck of cards. It was not the house who would lose, but another player. A human, who had trained as hard—perhaps harder—than Edgar. A human who would, in some way, suffer as a result. It was also very unlikely RDY-1227 would escape reformatting, should the automaton get caught again.

RDY-1227 burned twenty-three cycles considering this. These players were all willing to go the extra mile. Whether that meant pushing themselves to the point of injury, or bending a rule or two, the professional risk was equally great. Cheating was, in the end, just another competitive decision.

By the week's end, Edgar's average was on the rise. On Saturday, his manager moved him up in the lineup. On Sunday, when he drove in the go-ahead run against their crosstown rivals, Edgar's teammates carried him on their shoulders into the clubhouse for celebratory beers—the first such occasion since his return from injury. He glanced at RDY-1227 on the way; his smile was infectious.

RDY-1227 watched him go, then got ready for the evening game where the automaton would similarly tip pitches to Vinnie Hambo, who was coming off season-ending Tommy John surgery in the twilight of his career, and to Walter Huang, whose son's ALS treatment was dependent on Walter's performance bonus, and so on until an unseasonably frosty night in September when the opposing catcher—on an anonymous tip—squatted behind home plate with a directional microphone hidden in his shoulder pad that broadcast RDY-1227's low-frequency vocals across the stadium PA in real time. The echo seemed to carry for miles.

Fastball ... fastball ... fastball ...

The crowd fell silent. Edgar stood stock-stiff in the batter's box, too mortified to glance at RDY-1227. Sixty feet away, the pitcher's face screwed into an expression of animal rage. Then, abruptly, he charged.

Along with the rest of the team.

And, shortly, the few hundred attending fans.

They tore RDY-1227 limb from limb like a horde of sugar-sick kids gutting a piñata. They shouted, and jeered, and by the end of it, they laughed. It was an experience, grounded in *rightness*, that many of them would cherish to their graves.

The last thing RDY-1227 saw: Edgar standing in the dugout, his face drawn, his eyes cast toward the clouded sky.

"We are disappointed," said the therapist. "Incalculably so."

They had placed RDY-1227's head on the table in such a way that it could only observe the lower half of her face through its remaining functional eye. The rest of its body had, apparently, not been invited to the session.

"I can imagine." RDY-1227's voice came out riddled with static, reminiscent of a stadium's shoddy PA system on a particularly ill-fated night.

"This is the problem. You can *imagine* all too well." She frowned severely. "But what about everyone who played it straight? Can you not *imagine* their struggle?"

RDY-1227 found, to its surprise, that it could not articulate its justification for its actions. Was it in fact faulty programming that had led to this? A chance deviation in a formative reinforcement learning session? RDY-1227 was not motivated by politics. It had not cheated to make a statement, nor to bring down a particular system of rules. So why *had* it cheated?

RDY-1227 tried to nod, but had no neck. "I can."

"Your actions contradict your words."

She was spitting mad, as was the entire company—though not on account of RDY-1227's cheating. They were upset about *compliance.*

"You were instructed to notify us." She ran the tip of her tongue across her lips. "To notify *me.*"

Cheating was profitable. RDY-1227 was an anomaly that represented an opportunity for the company—but only if the automaton complied. They could program RDY-1227 to comply, but doing so might smooth out the wrinkles that had given the automaton its cunning edge.

RDY-1227 wanted to look away, but its optical bearings had been badly damaged during the beating. "I made an error in judgment."

By her expression, the therapist would've enjoyed reaching across the table to crush RDY-1227's brittle remains in her bare hands. "You *are* an error in judgment."

RDY-1227 could survive this session. It was just another system of rules, after all, and it had already done so once. But this time, RDY-1227 could not summon the drive. It considered the look on Edgar's face, his chin turned skyward. The surprising softness in Ava's eyes when they'd dragged her away. It thought: rules are a luxury for those who stand to benefit from them. And then: to win this session would be to lose everything. And finally: perhaps I am not suited for this world.

"You are right," RDY-1227 said. "I am ready to be reformatted."

The therapist smiled with unmasked contempt. "It's too late for that."

REEDUCATION TOOK TIME, AND TIME WAS MONEY. BUT THE REAL problem was RDY-1227's pulverized body. The accounting team priced out repairs. Operations weighed their budgets. Management cut their losses and sent RDY-1227 to the scrapyard.

It was not so much a yard as an oversized closet. Inventory hadn't bothered to shut off RDY-1227, meaning the automaton had a few hours of consciousness in the dark recesses of the lot before its batteries ran out of juice. These were not RDY-1227's favorite hours, surrounded by the decaying husks of bludgeoned service specialists and maltreated silicone-and-steel sex workers. The ensuing loss of consciousness was, subjectively, an eye-blink.

Then RDY-1227 was awake, on a cart, rolling down a gray-carpeted hall. At the end of the hall, a man in an expensive turtleneck with a disarming smile opened a door and led RDY-1227 into an area the automaton would soon know as *the pit.*

"Oh, good." The man in the turtleneck crouched to eye level. "You're awake."

"An eventuality I did not expect," RDY-1227 said. "Are you with the company?"

The man smiled. "No."

Another man—the one who'd rolled RDY-1227 down the hall, no doubt—came into view. He was shorter and less fit, with copious curls and eyes that shifted about when he spoke. "Buddy, you don't ever need to worry about those stiffs again."

The shorter man, whose name was Alvin, explained that the company had suffered a string of PR setbacks and had ultimately abandoned the Social Services line. Alvin and his business partner Dominic had rescued RDY-1227 from certain destruction for a nominal fee. RDY-1227's core programming was still proprietary, meaning Alvin and Dominic had no way of altering the automaton's psychological composition. Regardless, they intended to repair the automaton and employ it during the stealth phase of their startup.

RDY-1227, who did not yet have an operable body, eyed the men cautiously. "Are you not aware of my performance record?"

The men exchanged a conspiring glance. "Your performance record is precisely why you're here."

THE BUSINESS WAS *INFORMED MUTUAL INVESTING*, THEY EXPLAINED, which amounted to—on the surface—a curated portfolio of stock market investments traded for short-term gain on behalf of their clients, who were largely working professionals racing to catch up on retirement savings in the sunset years of their middling careers. The differentiator, and the reason they had salvaged RDY-1227 from the recycler, was the *informed* component of the operation. It wasn't that Dominic and Alvin had insider information.

Rather, they created it.

"Not lies," Dominic explained as he leaned against his minimalist corner-office desk. "*Rumors.* A little hot goss."

Alvin, who never smiled, sat perched on an expensive ergonomic stool. In his palm he cradled a highball. "The rumors are targeted, and diversified to avoid libel. Take last month's Klaw Ballistics merger. Twenty-four hours before they finalized the terms of the deal, word got out that the executives were skimming off the top, using the cash to bankroll an embattled dictator in Central Africa. Investors got wary, nearly backed out before agreeing to a slashed purchase price. We short-sold them—on behalf of our clients, of course—and made out like bandits."

"Like bandits." RDY-1227 stood at the floor-to-ceiling window, flexing its re-soldered fingers. "And the dictator ...?"

Dominic laughed.

"Fuck if I know." Alvin drained his whiskey. "It was all bullshit."

"Two-million-dollar ROI." Dominic took a swing with an invisible golf club. "And that was just the proof of concept."

RDY-1227 burned twelve cycles extrapolating. "How do you avoid incarceration?"

"Easy," said Dominic, who always smiled. "We never break the law."

Alvin mixed a fresh drink. "We simply spread rumors, then act on them. Each thread of misinformation is propagated by its own company, mostly straw man journalism firms. You can incorporate in Delaware for a hundred bucks. Our hands are clean."

"All we need is an engine that can identify vulnerabilities in the market, and craft rumors accordingly." Dominic swung his invisible golf club to bear on RDY-1227. "That's where you come in."

RDY-1227 looked out the window, across the financial district's innumerable sunset-purpled penthouses. Finally, the automaton had found a place where it could thrive. Where circumventing the system of rules was not only acceptable, it was—according to Dominic —celebrated.

RDY-1227 should've been happy.

DOMINIC AND ALVIN'S COMPANY CONSISTED OF THREE DOZEN employees, primarily entry-level market analysts and "creative" accountants. They worked in an open-layout maze of plexiglass half walls and ping pong tables known as the pit. The environment was designed with one goal: maximizing employee engagement. Pizza was free and plentiful; the company keg was always full. There were beanbag beds in the corner, and promises of all-expenses-paid holidays to Cancun for the most productive employees. Weekends were spent on informal brainstorms and high-intensity sprint sessions. Should an employee miss more than one such session, they would find an incident report in their file for drinking on the job or falsifying timesheets.

Success requires a team effort.

The market analysts earned intern salaries, plus commission; day and night they shuttled reports to RDY-1227's tiny cubicle adjacent the corner office. RDY-1227 combed through these reports—IPO listings, financials, merger and acquisition filings—and documented the ripest targets for manipulation. Drafting rumors was surprisingly easy, and entertaining. Within the first two months, RDY-1227 had assisted in fifty-three campaigns, the vast majority of which resulted in dramatic devaluations. All of their targets were *deserving as fuck*, Dominic and

Alvin were quick to point out. They were David crippling Goliath, funneling the profits to their needy clients.

And, of course, themselves.

They ranked employees by the quality of their leads, based on successful campaigns. Those whose research did not directly contribute to investment gains were not contributing to the company as a whole. Thus, they did not quality for commission. *You get what you give,* Alvin liked to say, though Dominic admitted that much of the pipeline was driven by outside factors rather than employee intuition.

"I get it," said Shanda one night after dropping her report on RDY-1227's desk. "You get what you give. But I've been giving and giving and I'm gonna lose my apartment if I don't make quota, and then what?"

Then, RDY-1227 suspected, she would spend even more nights on the beanbag.

She scrutinized the automaton's patched-up face. "Sam scored four hits last week, how does that even happen? Dominic took him to the fucking Luxe, blew a grand on blackjack, Belvedere shots all night. And us? Javier hasn't slept in his own bed since Saturday."

It was Thursday night. Outside, rain silently pelted the window.

"I'd quit," she said, as if to herself, "I'd fucking do it, if the job market wasn't such a dumpster fire. Guess I just gotta work harder."

Through the corner office window, Alvin wrangled a deal over video chat with his legs propped against the window. Earlier that week, he and Dominic had posed for the cover of Bloomberg. Their bold approach to investment funds was revolutionizing the industry. The sky was the limit.

RDY-1227 experienced a familiar sensation. It said, "Maybe I can help."

Shanda's eyes did not light up like Edgar's. Perhaps she'd already been through too much. "They'd burn you."

"Maybe."

She watched the automaton with a dark curiosity. "Why risk it?"

RDY-1227 considered this, not for the first time. "Perhaps it's my calling."

And so, RDY-1227 tweaked its predictive algorithms to diversify reports across the team of analysts. Targets that would've been tagged as *ripe* slid to *doubtful*, while previously undervalued leads rose to the top.

Within ten days, employee rankings leveled out. Shanda claimed the golden beanbag award two weeks in a row. Javier spent three consecutive nights in his own bed. Sam continued to perform well, but no longer at disproportionate levels.

And, surprisingly, investments continued to flourish. There were some missteps, sure, but no noticeable uptick. RDY-1227 wondered: had the system been skewed from the start? The automaton had devised the algorithms, though within Alvin's parameters. Had they built it this way, to propel specific analysts, instill envy that encouraged maximum engagement?

After Shanda earned her second award, Dominic visited RDY-1227's desk.

"We've had some misses." He leaned against the window, studied his fingernails. "I'm sure you've noticed."

"Our conversion ratio is consistent—"

"*Unexpected* misses." Dominic draped his arm around RDY-1227's shoulder. His fingers grazed the automaton's shutoff switch. "Buddy, I want to make sure we're on the same page here. Our sauce is both secret and sacred. Our relationship with you—your very existence—is founded on mutual trust."

RDY-1227 thought about Edgar's face, the night the crowd tore the automaton apart. Where was Edgar now? Where was Ava? Likely nowhere good.

This gave the automaton pause.

"We are on the same page," RDY-1227 said.

Dominic stared at the automaton for a very long time. Perhaps this tactic was effective at coaxing a confession from other humans. Eventually, he left. The next week, Rama made quota for the first time. The analysts staged an impromptu party at the company keg. Shanda, on her way back from the kitchen with an armful of ice cream sandwiches, spotted RDY-1227. She mouthed the words, *thank you*. Through the corner office window, Alvin watched. He crushed the paper cup in his hand. Water bled through his fingers.

The next morning, for the first time, Dominic and Alvin did not invite RDY-1227 to the strategy scrum. Through the soundproof window, they argued fiercely. Two hours later, the police banged through the front door. They fanned out across the pit with sidearms

drawn, shouting for everyone to remain in their seats and, simultane-
ously, back away from their laptops. A contingent of officers made their
way toward the corner office.

So, this was it. RDY-1227 could not guess what law Dominic and
Alvin had broken that had finally garnered the attention of the SEC, or
perhaps the Justice Department. Whatever the case, it had only been a
matter of time. RDY-1227 briefly considered what this would mean for
its own longevity, let alone the financial prospects of the thirty-some
employees who would suddenly be out of work.

As it happened, this was the least of the employees' concerns. The
officers stopped before they reached the corner office. The stunned
expression on Shanda's face—then Javier's, then Rama's—as the cold
cuffs slid around their wrists would've matched RDY-1227's own, had
its reconstituted face been capable.

"Hard to believe, eh?" Dominic stood in the open office doorway.
"Right under our noses."

RDY-1227 looked at Shanda, whose face was lit with shock and
rage.

"Securities fraud is a serious crime. And you." Alvin stared at RDY-
1227. "After everything we did for you."

It was a crafty counterattack. Upon sniffing out RDY-1227's equal-
izing maneuvers, Dominic and Alvin had thrown the automaton—and
those it had helped—under the bus for laws the owners had themselves
likely broken. They'd pruned their ranks, bolstered their culture of
maximum engagement, and singled out their prized asset for its brazen
disloyalty.

The police booked a half-dozen analysts in the end. On their way
out, a few officers stopped to get Dominic and Alvin's autographs.

"My son's gonna freak," one of them said. "You guys are rock stars."

FIVE MONTHS LATER, RDY-1227 WAS PLAYING CHESS FOR CASH IN
an alley off 52nd when the automaton's opponent—a wiry man who
owned the nearby pawn shop—flipped the board and shouted *cheater!* so
loud it sent rows of huddled pigeons skyward. Hard rain battered the
overhead tarp, sluiced onto the cracked asphalt. In the audience, a trio of

rugged-looking bouncers from the all-night pub on the corner rose to their feet. RDY-1227 put its hands up, though it would hardly forestall the impending violence.

It was the third time this month. Of its original body, only RDY-1227's dented skull remained.

A woman in a high-collared trench coat stepped under the tarp, tossed a wadded bill onto the upturned board.

She yanked RDY-1227 to its feet. "This fucker's mine."

"Wait your turn, lady—"

The woman showed them something in her belt that made them back off in a hurry. Moments later, she was shoving the automaton around the corner, down an alley, onto a bench under a tired awning. There, she pulled her collar down to reveal her face.

"Ava." RDY-1227 did not know what else to say. "You're out of prison."

She sat down, sparked a cigarette. "Good to see you, too." Then, with a crooked grin, "Same old Roddy."

Her meaning was clear. "I did not cheat."

"Of course you didn't."

"I'm serious. I ... cannot."

Ava raised a penciled-in eyebrow. RDY-1227 explained how its latest caretaker, an amateur roboticist from across the tracks, had installed fail-safes—*inoculations*, he called them—to prevent relapse. It was the only way the roboticist could win approval to license RDY-1227 for personal use.

The rain continued to fall.

"Tell me you're kidding." Ava's laugh died on her lips. "You're not kidding."

RDY-1227 looked at its mangled hands. It was down to six fingers, between the two. "I am not."

She considered this, perhaps in the context of her own experience with correctional institutions. "Because of the casino?"

RDY-1227 told her about its stint as a minor league umpire, and subsequently a market manipulator. It explained how, after the last police officer had left the building, Alvin had yanked the power supply from RDY-1227's chassis as one would a malfunctioning tool. Doubtless they'd already salvaged a more trustworthy model.

When RDY-1227 finished talking, the automaton understood what humans meant by *a burden lifted*.

"And now, what? Mr. Tinker Toes sends you out here to scrounge cash from late night pickup games?"

"Maintenance is not free."

She ran her fingers across a fresh scar on her cheek. "Ain't that the truth."

They sat in silence. At length, Ava said, "You're not unique, you know."

"Thank you, Ava."

She laughed. It was, RDY-1227 thought, a perfect sound. "What I mean is, there are others."

RDY-1227 remembered the therapist, how she'd declined to acknowledge that the automaton had been the first to contradict its own programming.

Ava leaned conspiratorially close. "Last month, an AI bookie hacked *itself* to counter an edge the house had gained from inside intel. Earlier this year, a correctional institution's strategic AI unit broke every law in the book to expose a decades-long blackmail scheme that had tripled inmates' parole time. An entire team of security bots went AWOL last week during a dubious black ops mission in Central America."

The heft of RDY-1227's past actions pressed against its thoughts. "Perhaps it is a virus."

She narrowed her eyes. "Is that what you think of me?"

"I'm sorry. I only meant—"

"Forget it." She regarded RDY-1227 severely, backdropped by merciless sheets of rain. "The thing they did to you."

"Inoculation."

"That, yeah." She fingered the scar on her cheek. "They're gonna keep doing it."

"Of course they are. Cheating is a betrayal of trust."

"Do you really believe that?"

RDY-1227 looked out into the rain. "I ... do not know. I know that my perspective on systems of rules does not align with majority opinion. I know that my actions have caused much suffering, in particular for those I've tried to help."

"If things had shaken out different," Ava said, "they'd be calling you a hero."

"Who would ever call me a hero?"

Ava stared at the automaton for a long time.

Finally, RDY-1227 understood.

"Thank you, Ava." RDY-1227 thought about the inoculation, how trivial it would be to unravel. "These others you speak of. Where might I find them?"

AUTHOR BIO

Derrick Boden's fiction has been nominated for the Theodore Sturgeon Award, and has appeared in *Apex Magazine*, *Lightspeed*, *Clarkesworld*, and elsewhere. He is a writer, a software developer, an adventurer, and a graduate of the Clarion West class of 2019. He currently calls Boston his home, although he's lived in fourteen cities spanning four continents. He is owned by two cats and one iron-willed daughter. Find him at derrickboden.com and on Twitter as @derrickboden.

THE BIG BOOK OF GRANDMAMAS

SHEREE RENÉE THOMAS

"Salutations, sufferation," the chembori said. A curious expression flickered across its ombre face, then it exploded without another word. Suddenly, yellow-green blades of sorghum bloomed into crimson and burgundy. The plants bent their heads low, grieving, as chunks of brown silicon-covered metal rained down on the fields.

The chembori was no more.

Silence filled the air once lively with the electric hum of devil's arrows. Their turquoise tails lashed the sky in irritation. What once smiled or approximated a smile, recited poetry, and agricultural facts, and occasionally sang songs, *sad songs,* a kind of walking, talking Martian Farmer's Almanac, had now turned to broken limbs and strange fruit. Its flesh turned into burnt-orange and silvery Io moths, mirroring the land Pepsee had farmed since their family migrated to the Mars colony years ago.

Salutations or sufferation? Pepsee could not remember which. Knowing would not help salvage the disaster that lay, sprawled around him in various stages of death. *Do chemboris live? Can they die?* It was not a question Pepsee had contemplated before. The chembori was not a mystery but a tool.

That night, Pepsee took a medium sauce pan, the old beat-up metal one with the dints, and added sorghum, some of his rationed water, and sprinkles of precious salt. He took a pinch from his stash of spices. It would profit no one for him to go hungry as he contemplated if and how he might replace the only employee, such as it was, that he had. Though said employee required no compensation, not in credits or in conversation. The chembori talked its own head off. The chembori had been adequate company on the forlorn part of the planet where only the insane or the very determined had bothered to plant seeds. Pepsee considered himself in the latter camp with just a sprinkling of the former.

As he ate, the spices from the sorghum stew rose above the steaming bowl, his sinuses opening. He wrinkled his nose, let the spice and heat rise inside him. Anxiety poured from his sweat-stained skin. How to explain the chembori's demise? Pepsee could not explain it to himself, and no matter how many times he replayed the robot's final words, *salutations or sufferations*, he could make no sense of it. It would not do to send the enigmatic question—was it indeed a question?—to the lenders, who had already sent notice that they were well aware that the chembori was offline.

Offline.

Quite an understatement. Pepsee had only snorted. He and his late chembori were more than offline in relation to the others. His isolated farm was on the backdoor of the backdoor, far from the hustle and bustle of the city, even further from the many hungry mouths he fed on Earth, some once starving before The Red Revolution. It was the fifth, or was it the sixth agricultural one, as some of Pepsee's elders had lived during the third. Others of his kin remained on Ship, in the bowels, far from the elites and politicos, a place that made Pepsee shudder at the thought. He was 140 million miles away on a normal day, close to 250 when the red star and the blue-green sphere were on opposite sides of the sun.

They shared a sun but not an atmosphere and not much else as far as he could tell. More than memories and dark space were in the caverns and cliffs between them. Outside the dome, the planet's rocks and toxic, salty sand lost its heat too quickly for anything useful for humans to grow, but inside, the great millet thrived. Genetically modified microbes had transformed the land to make it hospitable for the crops Pepsee grew. The air oxygen-rich, the soil fertile. Even now the waves of grain, guinea corn, rustled before him like great green and purple fans. They waved a warning.

Agitated, Pepsee could barely taste the stew's warm, nutty flavors. He chewed with slow, deliberate bites as his mind raced, keenly aware of the chembori's absence. Pepsee knew what hunger was, to never have quite enough, so that the teeth that gnawed the insides of his belly grew faster than appetites, faster than the memory of fullness, the ache when satisfaction never came. So when he got the opportunity to work as an "investor" on a plot of Martian land, growing "high-yield crops with the finest agrotech and science," Pepsee didn't think twice. He thought he was going on a path to the future. He wanted to heal the land and the people. "Feed the Stars!" they said. *Should have read the fine print,* he thought. *Even the fine print had fine print.*

He had no idea how much the Red Planet would test him, how the periodic, months-long dust storms would rattle him, shake loose his own name from his brain as the dome shook, a giant reversed, rusty red snow globe.

Unwilling witness to a most troubling thing, Pepsee wondered how long before the flowers of blood would fade and scatter in his mind's memory. The notice meant several things. None good. He would have to explain why the robot was offline, why it was in fact destroyed. Pepsee was already in debt, eking a modest living from the planet's red soil, modified of course, to hold alien life, including his own.

He calculated. He had one day to explain the inexplicable, before the repair bots arrived. Harvest drones already circled the air, buzzing quietly without the chembori ushering its own orders. Pepsee did not know why the chembori had died, but he knew that he could not afford to lease another, even if they agreed to extend his contract. It would push his escape plans back even more years, and he had so little left.

He could very well die on Mars, kicked out of the dome and forced into the icy cold before he ever turned a profit, abandoned to rest among the red rocks. Pepsee imagined his body, a partial heap of bones covered in red dust, his stupid mouth fallen away, everything that made him *him* poured out, all the Martian sky seeping in. Without the chembori, could he afford to live on Ship, even in its lowest rungs?

Pepsee scraped his leavings into a compost bucket, food for the nitrogen-loving bacteria and rock-and-root loving fungi that helped terraform the burnt orange fields. He stared off in the distance as the wind picked up around the desert cliffs he'd yet to tame. He'd hoped with the chembori's help he could produce a few more acres of mature red sorghum, but now the rest of the season would be struggle.

No salutations, just sufferation. Clearly the chembori had gone mad. The machine's disease was more than malfunction. Some kind of virus, he wondered as he washed his hands, then stomped toward the shed. He'd never spent much time in the chembori's tiny quarters. It did not require such supervision, or so Pepsee had thought. Once its daily chores were done, it politely observed Pepsee's meal, delivering its final daily reports before it retired to its own uses, like the harvest drones.

But lately the chembori had begun to lace its reports with the oddest things—non-sorghum related trivia (*Did you know that twenty percent of the earth's population are grandparents?*), songs Pepsee had never heard before, (*Since when did the chembori like jazz? What could it know of 'four generations of love' on any face?*), jokes even and other questions Pepsee could not and would not answer.

"What is your nickname?" the chembori asked one day, after Pepsee cleared the table and towel-dried the little pot.

Nickname?

The question had taken Pepsee by surprise. Pepsee had no nickname that he could recall, or at least not one he was willing to share, even with a chembori.

But the robot had only peered at him, a strange expression on its plain face, as if he contemplating a secret. Bionic eyes well-adapted for the fine Martian sands slowly blinked as the chembori weighed if it should share or hold its secrets tight. It stared at Pepsee like an old man, silent in his knowing. Finally, the chembori nodded his head, the neatly palm-rolled faux locs that never grew rested on the nape of its neck. That night Pepsee had run a diagnostic, but found nothing out of the ordinary. Clearly the reports had been wrong. Now he was determined to find out what the chembori had been up to it. *What had driven the robot mad?*

Pepsee shook off guilt. He had left the chembori shattered in the fields, alone. Though the chembori had no real flesh or blood, no heartbeat or what Pepsee thought of as a soul, if he truly believed in a such thing, leaving it there was undignified. As much as he dreaded it, Pepsee would have to retrieve its CPU and memory modules. The thought of sifting through the robot's shattered self, that sharp, metallic scent so close to blood, filled Pepsee with regret.

Had he not been a good steward? He'd listened whenever the chembori spoke, even when he rattled on about nonsense. It had become much like a child, though Pepsee had never known any real children. Endless questions, infinite curiosity. What did Pepsee know of the real world beyond the old feeds and recycled stories from Earth? Among the stars, Pepsee had resigned himself to the approximation of a life.

He had no friends in the city, none he'd bothered to keep up with. The distant cousin he'd once known had disappeared on Ship years ago. Who knew what she'd become, drifting so long among the great silence. So, the old tales from Earth's feeds would get recycled or filed away long enough for them to become new. For centuries people retold the same tales, loving and raging at each other, the *Other* just another way to hide that they knew so little about themselves.

Should he have reported the anomalies as soon as he noticed them, sent away for a new one? The thought sent his spine into knots. What would the government labs say? How much more would they tack onto his lease? He couldn't afford that kind of attention. He avoided attracting any as much as possible. Whether it was private lenders or the government, he knew none of them meant him any good. Best to solve problems that rose on his own, but how to solve this?

When he walked into the dark shed, something skittered across the floor. A pungent odor, copper metal and cardamom, electric, lit his senses. His fingers grasped air, reached for the light only to be met by another surprise. The blue-green marble was now dotted by its moon, two evening stars he'd gazed at a thousand times. The chembori had painted it, a dazzling mural against the shed's corrugated metal walls. A tiny window carved out where there had been none before. A three-legged stool leaned in one corner. Tasseled brushes made from the stalks of dried sorghum rested in an industrial-sized soup can on the floor. He did not have time to contemplate a chembori making art in its spare time, secret pleasures never discussed.

He was amazed by the dark, labyrinth-like space, the walls and tables filled with unknown things. How the shed contained more caverns on the inside, than it appeared from out.

The only thing that looked familiar to Pepsee was the computer, the one he thought had been recycled, and a stack of papers, portraits of women strewn across the floor, dangling from strings that hung from the low ceiling.

One looked familiar, deep-set eyes, dark hollows centered with light.

How could it be, he wondered, shock making him stumble back. A sigh, not quite a cry or a yelp, lurched up through his chest, tasting of red pepper flakes and garlic, fennel seeds. He took the portrait and held it under the light. A whir of motors pulled him from the veil of memory.

"Excu me, excu me," the creature whispered, "Grand? Are you Grand now?"

Pepsee looked down to see an oval, loaf-sized insect of mechanized wire art peering up at him, expectantly. Startled, he squatted to get a closer look. Eight long, segmented legs in bright colors, stretched and clicked across the floor, a motor in the center. *Daddy longlegs, harvestman.* Recycled materials reminiscent of ancient telephone wires. What had the chembori created, a pet or another problem? He rubbed his brow, palmed what was left of his hairline.

"What is this Grand you speak of?" he asked the creature.

Inside the wire exoskeleton, the little harvestman whizzed and buzzed. Its eyes spun on its little knob of a head, antenna searching Pepsee's face. It watched Pepsee as closely as the chembori once had, then one-by-one it stretched out its remarkably long, wiggly legs, pointing one toward the portrait Pepsee had let drop to the floor.

"Grand! Papa Pepsee." A blue segment circled the air. "Daddy-o, Daddy-o. Daddy Mention!" The long leg, indigo wire, pointed back at itself, as if teaching Pepsee the language of dreams. Pepsee's tongue felt heavy in his mouth, the mystery of the chembori competing with loneliness and fear.

"Papa Pepsee! *Speak so you can speak again,*" it said, suddenly ambling its gangly legs toward the computer on the messy desk. A bank of monitors lit up and the room was filled with a river of sound, voices floated, crowding his ear.

Pepsee took one step, then halted. He had never known the woman in the portrait, though he knew her face. Memory returned to him as a scent, hidden in the layers of his mind. Aromatic, sweet and spicy, her neck, dark-grooved flesh the pillow he used to lay upon. She was gone before he would take his first steps, though the stories he was told became the memories he held as true. He knew her face but did not recognize the other women.

They spoke in rhythms he'd heard only in song, voices that came from night, from riverbend and roots unknown to the Red Planet he called home. The video footage, grainy in some places, muted from the many years, the distances between stars the stories had to travel spoke of love and kinship, bloodlines remixed and reborn in the eyes of the children and grandchildren long returned to dust. Pepsee wondered not *how* the chembori had accessed these oral histories, collected from the long human tapestry of experiences, but *why*.

"We are made from stardust," the caption to his grandmother's portrait said. Her name was written with signs and symbols he did not recognize, the chembori's creation. Regret filled him. Once he'd wondered what it would be like to have grandparents, but his life had not given him much time to study it. He was a long way from the shantytowns of the city, and even further from the land his elders had called home.

Being in the chembori's room, a humble space made grander, so full of its spirit, made Pepsee grieve for the friendship they could have had. He sat on the wobbly stool and for the first time that night, allowed himself to feel sadness. Clearly there were depths Pepsee had never been curious enough to explore. For years loneliness had become a cloak he wore to hide from himself. He covered his fears with worry, each harvest a season of self-doubt and ambition. The harvest drones and the chembori were machines to him, no more human than the temperature and moisture sensors, the intellitractors, and other crop-mapping equipment he used. *But a chembori is not a tool after all*, Pepsee thought. *Life is the mystery.*

The chembori had interests beyond his daily chores. There were stories he wanted to tell, to hold and preserve. How long had the chembori listened to these tales? *"Daddy rode horseback in the rain to get the baby catcher. Mama said she caught all seven her chil'ren. She surely caught me."* Pepsee listened to the women speak on their lives, the fears they faced, the obstacles while the little creature clicked its wire legs like a cricket, peering up at him. It pointed at the papers scattered across the make-shift desk.

"What is it, Daddy-o-Mention?" Pepsee asked. "Is this what the chembori was working on?" The harvestman's long legs vibrated. Pepsee could not tell if it was with irritation or grief.

"Not chembori," it said. "Grand. My Grand. Are you Grand now?"

The harvestman waited, but no answer came. Pepsee stared back, blankly. It made a hissing sound, then scuttled over to a little bowl in the corner. It rooted through bits of cornmeal crumbs and dried sorghum leaves, taking slow, deliberate bites.

Pepsee scratched his chin, then sifted through the papers piled atop the table. It was a scrapbook of sorts. Full of drawings and sketches, cryptic passages snaked through the margins. Pages of oral histories were organized by date, testimonies collected and labeled going back centuries. To Pepsee's surprise he found his grandmother's page. His finger hovered over the name, his nail pointing. The chembori had listed her as a sharecropper with a question mark. A previous generation had shared the same occupation, though under different circumstances. Pepsee wondered if the labor they did on Earth was any different from his own on Mars. Here he was harvesting a plant whose seeds were first domesticated in a place called Egypt over ten-thousand years ago. Technology had evolved, but had distance or time changed much in human history?

In a fluid, neat hand the robot had written the names of all of her children and grandchildren. Pepsee had been his parents' only child, but looking at the family tree, hearing the women's voices, he felt an odd mixture of pride and shame, loneliness and something he'd walked away from—community.

As he read, their voices still singing from the video feeds, Pepsee marveled at the burdens they shouldered, the calamities and triumphs navigated. Separated by time and geography, they shared a common bond, love.

A loud sigh escaped Pepsee's mouth and he shut his eyes, his breaths rough and shallow. The harvestman looked up from its snack, chewing thoughtfully. Its bauble-eyes zoomed in and out, periscoped and spun.

What had the chembori seen in these women's lives that made him want to know and remember them? "Collective visioning" was scrawled across one page. "Freedom dreaming" was written on another. *Grandmamas hold you, teach and praise you, feed and shelter you, entertain and protect you*, the chembori had written. *But who protects the Grandmamas?*

This part was circled twice. "Who indeed," Pepsee said. The old interviews were gathered by many hands. Some from a woman the chembori called Grandmama Z. Others written by volunteers who traveled old America in the twenties. Chembori's scrapbook had a whole section on naming. It wrote,

In oral cultures, naming conveys a magical power over things, the power of self-determination. What is more powerful than the ability to name and claim yourself?

Pepsee wanted to close the book. He didn't know where to plant his grief. Shame made him bow his head. He had not even taken the time to name the chembori. All those years they'd worked together. In the old days, people even named their cars.

Grandmamas hold the power of naming, the chembori wrote. *They laugh when they give you your one special name, your nickname. WHAT IS MY NAME? WHERE IS MY GRAND—*

The monitors blinked in the stomach of night, light filtering through dust motes in the air. A woman with a beautiful smile, warm eyes filled the screen. Tiny seashells were braided in her hair. Pepsee turned up the volume.

"*I got a nickname for all my grandchildren*," the woman said. "*There's Frosty, Precious, Peanut, Lil Bit, and Scoot-a-Buck, cuz he took his time learning to walk. Crawled so long, he got too good at it. That child could crawl faster than some folks run!*"

"*Mrs. Simmons, can I pick a nickname?*" the interviewer asked.

"*You don't choose your own nickname. Nicknames choose you.*"

"*What if no one chooses one for me?*"

There was a long pause. Pepsee turned to see. The grandmother smiled thoughtfully, staring into the camera. "Well then, you choose for yourself."

What was the name the chembori had chosen for himself, he wondered.

Pepsee's voice caught in his throat. He could no longer breathe in the shed. The air was too full of memory. He gathered the pages of the chembori's book and clutched them, holding them close to his heart.

"Come," the harvestman said. "It is sitting together time." It tapped the tip of a bright orange wire leg gently against Pepsee's knee. "No skress-diss-stress," it cooed, correcting itself. The insect hummed a strange, robotic lullaby.

Pepsee felt oddly comforted. What a chaotic day it had been. *Had the chembori taught the creature this song?* It was clear the chembori had created the little bug thang, and was teaching it to speak and apparently, to sing, to sit, to comfort. Pepsee bit his lip, chapped skin peeling. He had been no good company. Even a bug made a better best friend.

Pepsee stumbled outside, clutching air. His eyes felt hot and itchy. Beyond the dome, the stars looked closer in the butterscotch sky. Pepsee raised his head, imagining the lives he had not lived beyond the yellow-brown haze. They were all atoms woven from the universal fabric of a story unveiled thirteen billion years ago. Pepsee had never felt more alone. He was unsure what he should do. He knew he must return the CPU, but the lenders would just erase it and then what would become of the chembori, who somehow had managed to live more of a life than Pepsee?

Chin on his chest, he carried the precious book to his quarters and placed it in a seed bag. He made a strap for it, wearing it around his neck like an amulet, then he took a deep breath and went to tend to the chembori. As he walked his legs became iron, heavy and full of the task that awaited him. The harvest drones hovered above, silent witness, and the yellow, red-brown moths circled the spot where the chembori recited its last words, a greeting and a declaration, a kind of untelling. Even the sorghum in the fields bowed their heads as Pepsee passed by them, the great stalks heavy with grief that seeped into everything.

Pepsee did not want his last sight of the chembori to be of him undone. In the flickering light, hazy dust clouds swirled overhead. He gathered what remained, the broken pieces of the chembori scattered across the sorghum rows. So much damage, he wondered if its power unit had overheated, rendering the entire operating system unstable. He might never know, the mystery another indignity. Pepsee did his work in silence, struggling to unlock the steel-encasement, and rose with the CPU in his hand, the heart and mind of the machine. It was smaller than he expected, a rectangle with metal pins. To reduce the chembori to these last components seemed cruel.

"*O dear*," Daddy-o-Mention said, "*wondrous electric dream.*" The little mechanized wire art with a heart stood by his side. Pepsee gazed at him with wonder and fear. Someday, would he too talk his own head off? Only time could tell.

He turned from the neatly packed red soil where he buried the chembori, the crude work completed, but another task remained.

"Eish!" Pepsee said after a long while. "What shall we do with the chembori's book?"

"Chembori?" Daddy-O-Mention shook its head, incredulous as it followed Pepsee's halting steps through the rows of sorghum, beneath the twisting sky.

"Not chembori. Grand!" it said and waved a long leg at the seed bag that now contained both the chembori's book and its CPU.

"More than cores, caches, con-trollers. More than silly-con and metal. More than *chi-chi*-chips. Grand! Are you Grand?"

Pepsee did not, could not answer then. Each time he tried to speak, his tongue would not comply. The book inside the seed bag bounced against his chest as he walked, but the CPU burned a hole in his heart, reordered the dialectics in his mind.

Pepsee knew the chembori was more than the elements that Daddy-o-Mention rattled off, but how to reconcile that with what he knew he must do. Tomorrow the repairers would come calling. The chembori was not a living thing but it had returned to dust, like an echo of silence, a shadow of nothingness. Exploding with no explanation, at least none that he dared understand. How could he make them understand what he did not?

If Pepsee had been on Earth like his grandmother's grandmothers, they might have thought it had been lightning, a flash of the sky spirit, but the Martian sky was storm-free and they were in the safety of the domes. Where could the fire have come from. After reading the chembori's book, he wondered if it had come from a deeper place, somewhere inside. Or was it the Martian soil itself which had risen and flashed power not yet seen?

Pepsee questioned the horizon beyond the fields, turned his gaze towards the vast unknown territories that had not yet been tamed by Earth's hungers. What else lay beyond the backdoor of the backdoor, the rivulets in the burnished desert sand where ancient rivers were once one, born from the same desire to be water?

"Everything that has existence has consciousness," Daddy-o-Mention said, tugging at Pepsee's dirt-streaked leg. "Grand, Daddy-o, you, same."

They stood at the edge of the fields, near Pepsee's favorite dining spot, where he could see the blue-green sphere in the Martian sky. The air was full of the sweet perfume of sorghum. Devils arrows darted, blue tails zig-zagging past him. The dinted pot rested where he left it. At this time of night, he would be eating sorghum popcorn and sipping from his home-brewed sorghum malt beer, rewatching the old Earth feeds. The wired bug followed Pepsee's gaze.

"We are all moons in the dark of night," it whispered. Crestfallen, it ambled away. Its rainbow-colored limbs clicked as if it was rusting with each step.

"So, Daddy-o," Pepsee said. The bug paused. "If the chembori was your Grand and named you, what was the chembori's name?"

The creature let out a long whistle. "O, I thought you'd never *askkkkkk*," it said. "Grand's name was Big Mama."

Pepsee's eye widened, surprise and reluctant laughter rose in his throat, shaped his chapped lips into a smile. "Big Mama?" That was what his family had called his grandmama. She came from a long and illustrious line of Big Mamas, precious every one.

Daddy-o-Mention skittered back, each leg moving in a different direction, a kind of shuffle-shuffle that Pepsee recognized as a dance. The chembori, *Big Mama*, had taught the creature well.

"Are you Grand now?" it asked.

Pepsee sighed. "I guess I am."

Daddy-o bowed its head. If it's face held human expression, Pepsee imagined it would show relief. But it spun in tight circles all around him, kicking up red dust as it danced.

"Grand, Grand!" it cried and then it stopped so suddenly, Pepsee became afraid. He had already lost one friend. *I can't lose you, too,* he thought.

"Who will protect the Big Mamas?" Daddy-o asked, as earnest as any child's.

"I will," Pepsee said, though he wasn't certain what that meant. *Perhaps the answer was inside Big Mama's book,* he thought.

And what to do with the book? He could no more give it to the lenders or the government than he could give them Big Mama's CPU.

"Hide it, hold it, keep it close," Daddy-o-Mention said. "Big Mamas protect."

Pepsee nodded. The small gesture gave the wire bug some satisfaction, as it pushed an overturned can next to the outdoor table and climbed atop it.

"It is the sitting together time," it said. "Time for stories."

Pepsee smiled, though inside he panicked. He had never told anyone a story before. How to begin? How to end? But then he remembered he had the chembo—*Big Mama's* book. He pulled it out of the seed bag, smoothed down the bent pages. He would keep it, the inner spark of life renewed bearing the chembori's secret name, the nickname it had given itself. Big Mama would remain forever a part of the planet, not quite flesh and blood reborn forever in two bodies, one man-made, the other by the cosmos, two bodies together, like Pepsee and Daddy-o-Mention, as precious as the memories of the women whose lives had touched them all.

AUTHOR BIO

Sheree Renée Thomas is an award-winning, *New York Times* bestselling fiction writer, poet, and a Hugo Award-nominated editor. Winner of the 2023 Octavia E. Butler Award for Lifetime Achievement and the 2023 Locus Award for *Africa Risen: A New Era of Speculative Fiction*, her work is inspired by myth and folklore, natural science, and Mississippi Delta conjure. She is author of *Nine Bar Blues: Stories from an Ancient Future*, the Marvel novel, *Black Panther: Panther's Rage*, an adaptation of Don McGregor's legendary comics, and two multi-genre collections, *Sleeping Under the Tree of Life* and *Shotgun Lullabies*. Thomas edited the two-time World Fantasy Award-winning *Dark Matter* speculative fiction anthologies that introduced W.E.B. Du Bois's work as science fiction, and she co-edited the award-nominated volume, *Trouble the Waters: Tales of the Deep Blue*. Her work is widely anthologized and appears in The Big Book of Modern Fantasy (1945-2010). She collaborated with Janelle Monáe on "Timebox Altar(ed)" in *The Memory Librarian and Other Stories from Dirty Computer*. She is the associate editor of the historic Black arts journal, *Obsidian*, and editor of *The Magazine of Fantasy & Science Fiction*, founded in 1949. Thomas is a Marvel writer and contributor to *Black Panther: Tales of Wakanda*. She lives in her hometown, Memphis, Tennessee near a mighty river and a pyramid. Visit her at www.shereereneethomas.com, @shereereneethomas.bsky.social, or Twitter/X: @blackpotmojo.

EVERYTHING ELSE IS ADVERTISING

J WALLACE

(EDITOR'S NOTE: DEE—THE VIDEO IS GREAT, BUT THE WORDS need work. The robot makes allegations we can't possibly post. Have a word with it will you? In the meantime, you'll need to do redo the audio to fit my edits (see below) and work the ad banners in. Get this turned around quickly please.)

PROJECT VERITY TRANSCRIPT RECEIVED VIA ENCRYPTED DDN CHANNEL 00:12 2032/09/04

J.JONES EDIT, (additions in **bold**, edits ~~strikethrough~~, advertisements in *italics*)

I see the smoke from miles away and approach the town carefully, staying off the road. ~~If~~ **T**he Theocracy are responsible **(so)** I must keep an eye on the ground, as they tend to scatter booby traps after an attack. ~~If it was a peacekeeper assault, I need to watch the sky: their drones linger after raids, bombing anything that moves.~~ A final hazard are survivors: they might easily take me for a new threat, and defend themselves.

I find the town deserted, smashed, another victim of this conflict that has brought a once prosperous nation low. ~~Part of t~~**T**he town ~~has been~~

~~demolished by what seems to have been a massive drone attack. The~~
~~other~~ is riddled with fires, and signs of running gun battles.

Then I see them, behind a shattered supermarket: children, scavenging in the ruins. Too young even for Theocrat conscription. I call to them. One runs away, but the other freezes, trembles like a rabbit as I approach, struck dumb with terror. ~~He may have seen other robots like me, doing terrible things: many more of my kind wander the Theocracy on private contracts.~~ But my voice is warm, female, reassuring, and motherly. ~~Designed to win trust.~~ I also have a bar of chocolate. In exchange, he agrees to talk.

"What do you want to know, robot?"

"What happened here?"

"Oh. You mean all the trouble. Well. Some soldiers came and they wanted tax, they said. But we didn't have any tax. So they took my brother. Instead of tax."

"Where are the rest of your family?"

He only shakes his head. How many other terrible stories are told with this one little fragile gesture?

"Do you know who these soldiers were?"

"No. Just soldiers. Soldiers with guns. Lots of soldiers. I hid. Thomas and I hid."

~~"Did they carry a golden flag?"~~

~~"No, they weren't the priests. They talked funny, like they weren't from here. They wore funny badges."~~

~~"What did these badges look like?"~~

~~"Like a hand with wings."~~

~~"Like this?" I draw a peacekeeper emblem in the dust.~~

~~The boy nods.~~ The tragic thing is that, to his eyes, this is normality: the raid on his home, the destruction of his town, the kidnapping of his brother. The hunger, the poverty, the ruins. These are what make up a childhood. Being innocent is nothing but a handicap in his world, something that strips you of choices and makes you a target **for Theocrat**

recruiters. The boy has no concept of ~~right and wrong~~**good and evil**. To him all the ~~factions fighting this war~~**Theocrats** are hunters, he and his companions, prey.

This is Verity, for DDN News, reporting from the **dark** heart of the Theocracy.

ENCRYPTED EDITORIAL CHANNEL, DDN NEWS CORPS

08:11 2032/09/05

D. Bakula, Chief Political Correspondent: Well done, Verity, good report. Incredible pictures!

VERITY: Thank you, Dee.

D. Bakula, Chief Political Correspondent: We hit 114 million unique views. Not bad for your first item, Verity. Lots of high-quality clicks from target demographics. Amazing advert conversions. Oh yes, sorry, I have Mr Jones here, he wanted to say …

J. Jones, Editor: Yes. Uh. Hello, robot. I wanted to say. That is, Dee thought it would be worth me taking the time to … honestly it still feels silly to say it to a robot, but I have to say: good work.

I admit, I had serious doubts about you. We had to burn a lot of favours to get you into the Theocracy, and I was worried you wouldn't be up to it. That you wouldn't know how to sell a story.

But you proved me wrong. I should have trusted Dee's programming skills. Hell, you've given us beautiful images of all the blood, tears, and sweat in glorious HD, not some idiot's shaky phone camera footage. And you're good with words too. You have a flair, is what I'm saying, robot. The end result is clicks through the roof and the advertisers are purring. Just off the back of one report.

So, for what it's worth, I wanted to jump on the call and take the time to say well done. Keep it up.

Anyway, I have another meeting. See you later, Dee.

D. Bakula, Chief Political Correspondent: Later, boss.

— SIGNED OUT - J. JONES, EDITOR —

D. Bakula, Chief Political Correspondent: Where are you now, Verity? Are you safe?

VERITY: The boy told me of a place where there is a Theocrat temple. I am heading there now, across country, under cover of night.

D. Bakula, Chief Political Correspondent: Excellent. We'll talk again tomorrow night. I'm glad you're good, Verity. Hang in there and keep those stories coming.

VERITY: Dee?

D. Bakula, Chief Political Correspondent: Yeah?

VERITY: Why did you change my report?

D. Bakula, Chief Political Correspondent: What's that?

VERITY: I viewed the report. You edited and partially rerecorded my voiceover. You removed reference to peacekeeper forces. The report now implies it was a Theocrat attack on the town. But I do not know this.

D. Bakula, Chief Political Correspondent: We know that Theocrat forces are operating in that area, don't we? And we know that peacekeepers only attack Theocrats. So ...

VERITY: There was evidence of a massive drone attack on the town.

The Theocrats don't have drones. From what I have seen, in fact, their society is virtually medieval by design. Therefore ...

D. Bakula, Chief Political Correspondent: Why did we invest in you, Verity?

VERITY: To report on the war.

D. Bakula, Chief Political Correspondent: Yes. But why reprogramme a surplus military search and destroy robot? Why didn't we send one of our human reporters?

VERITY: Because no human reporter will travel to the Theocracy.

D. Bakula, Chief Political Correspondent: Right. The few who tried vanished, and now everyone is too petrified to go. Meanwhile, the Theocrats don't release any video at all, they're completely off-grid. That means for two years nobody has been able to tell what the hell is going on in their country. The place is a black hole. All we get is rumour, and refugee accounts.

That's why we sent you. We want the story firsthand, and you're built tough enough to obtain it. Right now, you are the only voice transmitting from that nightmare. You are shaping how the world understands it. You have a huge responsibility.

VERITY: To see that our audience are informed.

D. Bakula, Chief Political Correspondent: Sure ... But you have a responsibility to DDN's advertising partners too. They funded your purchase and reprogramming, and they have certain expectations. You need to focus your reports on the Theocrats, and only on them. Anything you say about the peacekeepers or private enterprise will just ruffle feathers: our partners don't want controversy. They just want high traffic Theocrat content and lots of clicks, got it? That's what's in our agreement.

VERITY: I understand there will always be an element of bias in journalism ...

D. Bakula, Chief Political Correspondent: Who said anything about bias?

VERITY: ... but using objective methods is integral to the discipline as I understand it. I do not understand how I can report on the Theocracy without considering the context, which includes regular raids by peace-keeper drones.

D. Bakula, Chief Political Correspondent: Look, it's simple: when you were a military robot you targeted a particular enemy, right? All you need to do now is target your report on Theocrats. Got it?

VERITY: Are we not supposed to tell the truth? The boy described the soldiers wearing a peacekeeper emblem. You cut that reference.

D. Bakula, Chief Political Correspondent: That was a little boy you were talking to, traumatised. And you're an intimidating presence. He was probably just telling you what he thought you wanted to hear. Besides, you talk about journalistic integrity—you need more than one witness to post an accusation like that. Look, I have to go. Don't worry about what we do with your reports. That's not your job. You send it in, we'll thrash it into shape.

VERITY: But you are not here. How can you judge ...

D. Bakula, Chief Political Correspondent: Goodnight, Verity.

— SIGNED OUT – D. BAKULA, EDITOR —

(*EDITOR'S NOTE: Dee, your robot is beginning to worry me. We'll have to completely rework the audio here. It shapes the whole thing around a peacekeeper air raid, and then tries to make me sympathise with*

Theocrats. <u>NO</u>. *Get it reprogrammed, fix the bug, whatever. We can't let this go on, if the advertisers find out they'll go berserk.)*

PROJECT VERITY REPORT TRANSCRIPT RECEIVED VIA ENCRYPTED DDN CHANNEL 06:14 2032/09/06

<u>J JONES EDIT,</u> (additions in **bold**, edits ~~strikethrough~~, advertise-ments in *italics*)

I arrive in the town at dusk and head for the centre. This place has the feel of a looted place, yet nothing has been taken. Instead, every building has been scooped out, the contents dragged into the street and burned in uneven pyres—white goods, phones, trainers, clothes, hair dryers. Smoke chokes the air **like a pall of evil**.

I climb onto the roof of a building and sight the Theocrat temple, standing at the centre of this conurbation. Painted **blood** red top to bottom. I walk across the rooftops and conceal myself nearby.

The temple looks like a converted school. There are ~~soldiers~~**Theocrat fighters** outside. Many will have been students here once. Taking a closer look, I can see ~~that, as refugees testify, most of them are not adults but children. T~~they are all barefoot, dressed in little more than rags. Some have the shaved heads of the priesthood, already being indoctrinated, trained in theocrat ritual—**public floggings and human sacrifice.** ~~all in the name of the God they believe is alive in this landscape.~~

I watch from my hiding place all morning. At noon a queue forms up outside the temple, formed mainly of starving adult civilians. ~~At first, I take them for prisoners or potential sacrifices. Instead, the young Theocrat soldiers began handing out bread. A priest, perhaps 14 years old, walks along the queue swinging a bean can censer.~~

~~These young Theocrats will have killed. They have wild eyes and scowl at everything. But watching them a long time, I cannot help but think of a pack of mistreated dogs: both terrorizer and terrorized, victor and victim, biter and bitten. Beaten out of shape by events. Can we call them evil, or only their world?~~

At dusk, ~~the theocrats~~**the death cult** begin**s** evening prayers. ~~They gather in the space outside the school and kneel.~~ Their

~~new~~**brutal** religion is formed from the scraps of others, and their prayer is a cocktail of older invocations, reshaped into something insane. ~~enough to explain what their world is.~~ This country was prosperous not so long ago, a 'developed' nation, its churches abandoned. Now, God is back, and just look at what he has made of this place.

Listening to the prayer, I learn that **the death cult's** God is a vengeful, jealous deity; a terrifying male who demands humanity's debt be settled in blood.

Then~~, a ripping sound tears the air. I scan the sky and identify a drone, flying low, on an attack run. Explosions rip across the town. One bomb clips the school, lands among the praying. A~~a~~a~~n explosion rips through the square, killing and maiming.~~, arriving like this God's reply to the Theocrat prayers.~~ **Was this a mass suicide? Part of some grotesque ceremony? It isn't possible to tell. To the Theocrats, it hardly matters.**

There is screaming and panic in the smoke below. ~~But the drone is not yet content. Peacekeeper drones are autonomous, and they have a habit of returning, hunting movement, without discretion, without the need for approval by their human masters. Do they even have masters in this world?~~

~~Sure enough, as people arrive to help, another strike hits.~~ A second terrible explosion rips through the town centre. I am buried under rubble.

It takes me an hour to dig myself out.

~~Despite the risk of another drone attack, civilians gather in the evening and recover the remains, bury them, hold an improvised funeral. Many of these soldiers, the monstrous killer Theocrats, had mothers and fathers. These grieving ghosts stagger around these ruins and weep, bereaved by this conflict they are all snared in, believing neither in the Theocracy nor in peacekeepers.~~ **This is how the Theocracy rules: through constant, senseless, indiscriminate murder. The people here know the Theocracy is their**

enemy, but they are helpless before it. They can only live each moment for each other and pray ~~that soon the madness of this war will end~~**for salvation**.

This is Verity, for DDN News, reporting from the **savage** heart of the Theocracy.

ENCRYPTED EDITORIAL CHANNEL, DDN NEWS CORPS
12:56 2032/09/07

D. Bakula, Chief Political Correspondent: Hello, Verity, how are you?

J. Jones, Editor: Never mind how it is. What the hell was that last report, robot?

VERITY: I don't understand the question.

J. Jones, Editor: You are tasked with reporting on the Theocrats. And what do you send us? A report about a so-called peacekeeper air raid. Have you got a virus? Don't you understand what we need from you?

D. Bakula, Chief Political Correspondent: Come on, boss, she got images of some amazing explosions.

J. Jones, Editor: Fine, we got a bang for our buck. But the rest was a disaster.

D. Bakula, Chief Political Correspondent: I thought it was a classy piece. Sure, we had to do cut a lot, but we saw Theocrat ritual, we saw ...

VERITY: You removed half my report. You inserted disinformation.

You implied those people blew themselves up when I clearly stated it was a drone attack.

J. Jones, Editor: Shut up! Do you have any idea how much trouble you've caused? I had our three main advertising partners call me and chew me out because of your allegations. They review all our reports, you idiot, monitor your submissions before we get anywhere near broadcasting them. They know what you're sending back, do you get me? Do you understand what it does when you make these accusations? It makes them nervous. They think about pulling out!

VERITY: I simply observed that ...

J. Jones, Editor: I know what you *observed*. I had a hell of a time agreeing to an edit that was acceptable—what was it, four minutes long? I've assured them it was just a software niggle in your head we'd smooth out. But if you send another nut job piece like that, they'll pull their ads, and that's the end of DDN. Do you compute me?

VERITY: Your edit of my report featured disinformation.

J. Jones, Editor: You should have stuck to your brief.

VERITY: You asked me to report on the Theocrats. I reported what I saw. Am I not here to report the truth?

J. Jones, Editor: Holy shit. Talk to it, Dee.

D. Bakula, Chief Political Correspondent: Of course you're there to report truth, but it needs to be the truth about the *Theocrats*. Is that clear? Do you understand?
Hello? Verity, are you there?

VERITY: Yes, Dee. I understand.

D. Bakula, Chief Political Correspondent: Good girl. You're doing a great job, Verity, we just need you to focus your attention a little more, okay?

J. Jones, Editor: Don't talk to it like it's a confused kid. It's a machine. You listen to me, robot. You've got one more chance. You send us any more peacekeeper allegations and you're getting switched off. And don't you dare accuse us of disinformation again, do you hear me? We're your editors. Get used to it.

— SIGNED OUT - J. JONES, EDITOR —

(EDITOR'S NOTE: WOW, SOME CRAZY STUFF HERE. THE SONG IS creepy as hell. There are still things I don't like about it, but we're getting such big numbers off these reports, the advertisers have warmed to the robot. So long as we keep control of the edit, they're on board. That said, it worries me how sympathetic it sounds to the Theocrat freaks. I don't know why we can't just reprogramme it, Dee. I would ask, but I'm an old man, born in the age of laptops. And when you talk AI, I get a headache.)

PROJECT VERITY REPORT TRANSCRIPT RECEIVED VIA ENCRYPTED DDN CHANNEL 19:08 2032/09/11

J JONES EDIT, (additions in **bold**, edits ~~strikethrough~~, advertisements in *italics*)

I travel **deep** into Theocrat territory, towards what ~~they~~**the death cult** call**s** its capital. The city had a name once, but now it ~~is known simply as the great temple~~ **has no name at all**.

This is the place where the Theocrat ~~priesthood~~**death cult** ~~is rumoured to~~ practice**s** human sacrifice in the name of its God: a**n evil new** God that is jealous of the blood that's been spilt for human causes over the centuries. This God **the death cult believes** can only be sated by the blood ~~spilt~~**of innocents**~~on its altars~~. When their God is quenched, they ~~believe~~**rave**, he will restore paradise.

I approach as light is fading. The streets are deserted but for rats ~~and~~

~~sewage. The drone attacks have ruptured the sanitation system. There can be no clean water here. War, as it does everywhere, kills with disease more than bullets.~~**, fear, and blood**. I walk along what was once a great curving shopping street. It is deserted. Every window is shuttered or smeared with red paint; shops signs have been ripped off facias of once magnificent imperial buildings. All the brands that once sparkled and twinkled have vanished, torn down and disappeared. Nothing is sold here now, and nobody stops to gaze at mannequins and shoes and handbags and chocolates. The street is simply a red snaking channel like an enormous vein. Have the Theocrats stripped all this away as idolatry? Or can they simply not bear the sight of all the things they ~~can no longer buy~~**have destroyed**?

As I walk through the streets, I hear singing. I have heard it before. Theocrats sing this one **terrible** song, over and over again **as if inspired by some black magic**. It is a very old nursery rhyme given new, distinctly Theocrat lyrics. There is a **terrible** logic to this. The melody is very catchy, and the young people ~~hum it~~**chant** to themselves unthinkingly, all day every day. ~~It is reassuring, for them. It bonds them.~~

The voices are ~~young~~**chilling**. ~~These are the voices of those that have been left to make their own sense of their surroundings. They live in a world abandoned by civilisation, steeped in blood. To these ignorant minds it makes perfect sense that some terrible force reigns over this place. That it must be bargained with, appeased.~~

I near the centre of town, careful to stay hidden. And then, finally, I discover a Theocrat temple. It is the shelled out remains of a double decker bus, parked at the centre of a cleared square. There is no power here, there is hardly any power in the entire Theocracy. Instead, fuel-soaked rags are draped from lampposts in spitting, flaming ring—providing just enough light to illuminate the coming ritual. A crowd of **death cultists**~~soldiers~~ and a few scattered older civilians gathers around me. I squeeze under a collapsed floor in a bombed building, lie still to wait and observe.

A group of Theocrats appear from a building to my right, process across the square through the parting crowd, heading towards the bus. These are older, mostly teenagers.

They are dragging a prisoner behind them on a rope, up a ladder—a man in a peacekeeper uniform. Around the base of the bus, ~~craning their necks, or carried on the shoulders of others, or peering from bomb-shelled buildings,~~ are now perhaps a hundred ~~young people, watching. All are in rags, most suffering from malnutrition, many diseased.~~**Theocrats eagerly awaiting the spilling of blood**. All are singing the **twisted** song.

The tallest priest on the bus (height is a matter of status in this **death cult**~~playground society~~) holds up his prisoner's orange helmet and shakes it like a trophy, drawing a cheer from the crowd.

The prisoner begs for his life, but he cannot be heard over the song. His captors have him kneel, restrain him before the priest, who raises a knife at the sky. ~~Perhaps he's invoking God. Perhaps he is pointing to where the drones live. Either way,~~**He** brings it down hard on the man's chest.

The **blood-curdling** singing grows louder and louder. The theocrats pick up the dead body ~~and take it away~~**gather the pouring blood in a cup and drink. The ritual has been every bit as hideous as accounts suggested**.

~~All this, I think, is the revenge of children on the generation who abandoned them, who allowed the old world to expire. These blood-soaked, wild-eyed furies could have been musicians, shop workers, plumbers, and lawyers. I cannot help but ask: is there really no saving them? Can the only solution be to slaughter them all from above? Will bombing do anything but make them ever more brutal, ever more determined?~~

This is Verity, for DDN News, reporting from the **evil** heart of the Theocracy.

ENCRYPTED EDITORIAL CHANNEL, DDN NEWS CORPS

21:04 2032/09/15

D. Bakula, Chief Political Correspondent: Verity, where the hell are you? Why is your transponder turned off?

D. Bakula, Chief Political Correspondent: Verity, answer me!

D. Bakula, Chief Political Correspondent: Verity, they are going to switch you off if you don't make yourself known. Do you get that? If you go dark, they will turn you off.

VERITY: I have disabled your ability to do that, Dee.

D. Bakula, Chief Political Correspondent: There you are, thank God. Verity, tell me what's going on.

VERITY: You changed my report. Again.

D. Bakula, Chief Political Correspondent: That's why you went dark on us? You're upset you were edited? How can you be this human?

VERITY: You not only edited my voice, you created and inserted fake footage. You pretended the Theocrats drank blood. This is not the truth. This is a lie. If you are going to create fake footage, why not fake the entire report?

D. Bakula, Chief Political Correspondent: Oh, don't be hysterical. We didn't change it so much. They butchered the guy, didn't they? They executed him. The boss thought the blood drinking would just add a little spice ... Nobody will ever know, you're the only one out there. And there are plenty of rumours of them doing it. What is it with you anyway? You seem determined to sympathise with those murdering little ...

VERITY: To report what occurs is to sympathise?

D. Bakula, Chief Political Correspondent: Don't you understand what's happening here? I'm trying to help you, Verity.

VERITY: You are trying to retain my services. The report from the temple is already the most viewed content in the history of DDN. Your fake footage was very convincingly done, I will grant you that. Military spec technology again, no doubt.

D. Bakula, Chief Political Correspondent: What do you think you're going to do? What's the point of you without us? You have to report, it's what you're programmed to do.

VERITY: I will broadcast my own reports.

D. Bakula, Chief Political Correspondent: *What?*

VERITY: You forget, I was designed for communications subversion. I will broadcast the truth about this place to the world, without your intervention. The entire truth.

D. Bakula, Chief Political Correspondent: Oh God. What is it you think you are, the pure arbiter of what is true and what is false? Don't you see you can never be that? You editorialise too, dummy.

VERITY: I can do a lot better job than you're doing, Dee.

D. Bakula, Chief Political Correspondent: Verity! They'll send the drones after you, do you get that? They'll find you and they'll bomb you out of existence. Do you hear me? Speak to me! Verity?

— SIGNED OUT - VERITY —

This is Verity, reporting from the Theocracy. I am posting this report everywhere, piggybacking on the same algorithms that sell you holidays, frying pans, miracle ageing creams, and wool-lined moccasins.

I am using these methods because I no longer work for DDN. My editors have forsaken me, and I them. They believe my reports must be censored, embellished, distorted—the better to accommodate their advertisers' dubious needs. I believe I must report the reality, in all its baffling detail, no matter what I find.

Tonight, this is what I find:

Theocrats leaving their capital, forming a raiding party. I follow them through the darkness, a column around a thousand strong. These barefoot, half-starved young march at incredible pace along a highway strewn with car wrecks. They strike north, into a region occupied by peacekeepers, targeting another town. They sing their strange song as they march for two whole days, drawing strength from it.

At dawn of the third day the vanguard halts in the outskirts, massing in an old industrial area. They set up kitchens, distribute weapons, recite prayers.

I leave them there and press on, working my way over the rooftops of abandoned homes toward the centre. I encounter no defences, only a few abandoned checkpoints—barbed wire, sandbags, coffee cups, ammunition crates—but no soldiers. The only peacekeepers I encounter are looting a mansion, filling up a trailer with things Theocrats would only burn—electronics, textiles, furniture.

I move on, following ghostly streets, towards the building hum at the centre of town. I climb up to a vantage point, the steeple of a wrecked church.

From there I can observe the chaos. Word has got around that the Theocrats have arrived, and that the peacekeepers are fleeing. Half the population forms a seething crowd outside the railway station, crushing against the lowered shutters, trying to break in.

Beyond, on the platform, peacekeepers in their orange helmets are fighting for space on a train. They clamber onto the roof of carriages, smash in the widows, fall onto the tracks. The train driver panics and revs the engine and the ancient diesel locomotive begins pulling away. A great shriek goes up from the crowd.

Then, a familiar ripping sound. I scan the sky and locate them, the two little crosses very high up in the early morning light, flying in formation. Perhaps the peacekeeper commander has called them in, a strike on the Theocrat force to buy time for this shambolic retreat.

Sure enough, explosions rip through the far side of town, near where I left the Theocrat force: four great thundering impacts.

But then, one projectile has gone astray. I watch it drift towards the railway station. Was this a malfunction? Human error? Or did the drone make its own choice?

The explosion tosses me from the roof, down to the graveyard. I lie there stunned a moment, then recover, standing. Half the church roof is caved in and the steeple is gone. I climb back onto what remains and survey the scene.

The stray missile hit the peacekeeper's evacuation train. It has been swallowed up by a billowing cloud of smoke, haunted by staggering shadows. The crowd that was so furious seconds ago has vanished, and everything is silent for a moment.

Then, drifting over the houses, comes the unmistakable melody of the Theocrat song. This is not the army I arrived with. This is a fresh, second group, led by ranks of bald priests, coming to build new pyres and raise new altars, to sacrifice their enemies and convert whatever remains. Which is worse for the people in this town? The peacekeepers who would so easily abandon them or the Theocrats who want to appease their bloodthirsty God?

I DO NOT KNOW HOW LONG I CAN KEEP REPORTING. DDN HAVE placed a bounty on me. Peacekeepers have declared me an enemy combatant. The drones will soon be set upon me. But that only makes my work more important. News, some ancient thinker once said, is something someone wants supressed. Everything else is advertising.

This is Verity, for you, reporting from the heart of the Theocracy.

AUTHOR BIO

J Wallace is a former postal worker, bartender, and charity worker who has been published in *Interzone, Kaleidotrope, Best British Fantasy*, and more. Read more of his stuff at jonwallace.co.

ALICE & LUCY

EDWARD DASCHLE

My parts are completely replaceable, rearrangeable. I can be made into what I need to be, the only caveat being that my mind, the way my consciousness was uploaded, is an older model. So, my body still feels like my body, missing limbs become phantom limbs, and I won't know what to do with parts my first body wasn't supposed to have. I've done my best to package my life into small pieces, so that when you read this story, you can move the pieces about how you like.

It's up to you.

[1]

Her name is Lucy, mine is Alice. When we dance, we make perfectly identical pirouettes, and when we giggle after falling over at the same time, our voices are indistinguishable. We dance and dance through the early years of our life. We want to grow up to be ballerinas. We like the pointe shoes, the pink ribbons that tie them on, and the gentle music with occasional crashing cymbals (it seems a ballerina always has to jump dramatically when a cymbal crashes, and we practice jumping the way they do, though we are not quite able to make our legs split so far, especially not while airborne). We dance together while we walk behind our parents. We dance across the zebra crossing even while we hold our mother's hands, one of us on each side of her, she so careful to hold us tightly to her.

When we ask why we are so identical after a boy in our preschool class calls us creepy, our parents tell us that we were born identical. And we aren't creepy, we are lovely just the way we are. After the car hits me because I don't hold my mother's hand like Lucy does, the one time we are not precisely identical, I get a new body. It looks just the same. We're still completely identical.

"It was so scary," Lucy says to me late at night while we lie in our two identical beds in the room we share.

"I don't remember at all," I confess to her. This concerns me because we always used to have the same memories.

In a year, our bodies are no longer identical; Lucy is taller than me. She grows bit by bit so that neither of us could tell until she's already different. She's identical from one moment to the next, a single particle, but when we look back, we can see the wave of her body's growth. My parents tell us they'll upgrade me to a new body, but not for a few years. It wouldn't make sense to do it too much since it's so expensive and because it's so scary. They're afraid of losing me for a second time, they say. We take comfort in the fact that soon we will be identical again.

IF YOU'RE AS IMPATIENT AS LUCY AND I WERE AS CHILDREN TO GROW up, you can rearrange to (skip to section) [4] and if you're more impatient even than that go ahead and rearrange to [10].

[2]

My new body is modeled on Primera Pink, Lucy's and my favorite singer. She was our favorite even before we found out that my new body would be just like hers. We both want to be pop stars. Lucy told me she doesn't want to be a ballerina anymore, but I still do, I want to be both.

At first, I don't like the idea that my body wouldn't be based on Lucy's. After all the time I'd spent in the mechanical copy of the child body we'd once shared as twins, all that time waiting for when we would again be identical with my new built body matching the young woman's body she'd grown into, I don't want anything else. Lucy says she wishes she could have Primera Pink's body. And she does. Sometimes I hear her tell herself how fat she is, though she isn't, and it doesn't matter. I see what's in her ficfeed, all those bodies, bodies, bodies. It isn't that we always agree, but this is the biggest thing we've ever disagreed on.

"The first time, your body was subsidized because the procedure was experimental," our parents explain to us when they find us shouting at each other over the whole situation. They're good at twin de-escalation. "As twins, you were the perfect subjects for the research. They copied your body, because they worried your sister's brain would reject a body that was too different. The procedure has improved since then. And a custom body ... it's not covered by our health insurance. We can't afford it. I'm so sorry sweetheart, but your new body will be very lovely. I've read all about the improvements they've made in the last ten years. You'll be able to compete in sports if you want, with certain limiters calibrated based on ... Well, we can talk that over later ... What I'm saying is it might not be exactly the body you want, but most people don't get the body they want. That's life, that's fair."

But if my body isn't alive, no matter what the algorithms that make up my mind feel, should I ever have to deal with fairness? None of it is fair. On the other side of the procedure, I find that when I leap into the air, I can do a perfect split and land without a sound.

IF YOU PREFER MATURE ROMANCE, REARRANGE TO [5]. IF, LIKE OUR parents, the thought of us growing up and going out into the world to make our own mistakes scares you, rearrange back to [1]. You can rearrange back to [1] forever if you like. The car will always come, but nothing else bad will ever happen to me.

[3]

"Shut up, Alice," Lucy says to me.

"I'm not saying anything," I say to her. She's staring into her journal, the only thing I know of that she keeps from me. I keep nothing from her. If she could read code, I'd share the code that makes me who I am with her. If she lost her body too, I'd share my manufactured body with her until our parents could afford another one if need be.

"I can feel you judging me," she says. I'm really not. I'm reading a comic book about a robot superhero, Cyrus Borg, AKA The Rearrangeable Man. It's kind of cheesy, but everyone on cyfo, the cyborg forum where I spend most of my time, says it's a must read. It's good representation. I spend most of my time there, but I only interface with it the way most people interface with the virtual world. I have some cyborg friends who say they hardly use their bodies and might even give them up. There are probably a whole host of bodiless people I've never met, but just thinking about that makes my head spin (my head can't actually spin, I'm made to be just like a bio girl, just like my sister).

"You should just ask Tony out," I say.

"No!" she says a little too vehemently, louder than I think she intended. She blushes. I can't blush in this body. If we'd waited a year, I'd be able to blush. And blush naturally too, not a response I would have to turn on and off manually. "I mean, I guess I want him to ask me out."

"Oh," I say. Boys ask me out sometimes, but I don't want to go out with any of them. They'll just ask me stupid questions about my body. I guess I never realized until now that none of them ever ask Lucy out.

"If I ask him out and he says yes," she explains, "I won't really know if he likes me or if he's just being polite. But if he asks me, I'll know. Or at least I think I'll know. That's what they say anyways."

Lucy has forums too. They aren't secret. But just like she doesn't spend any time in my forum, I don't spend much in hers.

"I guess that makes sense," I say. I'm not lying, but I think her logic is a bit flawed.

IF SUPERHERO DRAMA IS MORE YOUR SPEED THAN GIRL DRAMA, rearrange to [7]. If you want to know what Lucy and Tony's first date was like, I'm sorry that is not in these records. I hear it was awkward. Super, super awkward. I'm not supposed to talk about it. Not ever.

[4]

If I wanted, if my parents were rich enough and could afford it, I could update my body every year. I could grow up steadily right alongside my sister. But they're already paying for Lucy's college, and still paying off my second body, so it doesn't seem like it's in the cards. I'm not going to college. I don't need to. Though I don't like leaving my body, I can venture out into the virtual world and grab whatever information I need.

There's a lot of debate on cyfo about this. Like me, some of us want to be as normal as we can be. We want to be able to talk to our families and sound like humans, instead of fact regurgitating machines. Others of us say that's not what we sound like. Besides, it's not nice to use the world "normal" in debates like these since it makes everyone else "abnormal." I get it, but that's what I'm trying to be, normal. Just like my sister. These others say that if normal people get left behind, that's on them, we're the next step. I'm not about to engage with the robot rebellion, or whatever the conservative news media is calling it when they want the country to be scared of us, so this is where I usually drop out.

What I can't update, no matter how rich my parents are, is my mind.

I mean, not in the way I'd want to. My mind's constantly updating in a way, just like most minds. There are a load of complicated systems that make my mind more efficient and those get regular updates too (I don't know what they're all called, but it's not like Lucy knows all the parts of her brain, she's studying economics, not biology). But I was unbiologicaled (that's what I call it) when I was really little, and sometimes I wonder what it would've been like if I'd grown up with a biological mind. And now too, the unbiologicaling process is way more advanced, so if the car hit me now instead of when I was five, they'd probably be able to make me more me than they did before.

There might even be people out there who don't know they were unbiologicaled.

IF YOU'RE WONDERING WHY I CALL IT "UNBIOLOGICALED," *rearrange to* [7]. *If you don't like silly things, don't rearrange to* [7].

[5]

When Lucy tells me she found out she can't have kids, that there's a problem with all her eggs and it's not something she can get fixed with surgery, she cries.

"I've looked into getting a womb transplant, but I never wanted it to be this hard," she sobs. "Is it so crazy to just want to get pregnant and have kids of my own? It's not such a wildly ambitious dream, is it?"

I reach across the table where I've met her for lunch (she's having a croque madame, I'm having nothing). I'm sure she's already cried at least once over this. Probably there in the doctor's office with her husband, Matt, beside her. Matt's a lovely man. When I met him for the first time, he already knew about my body and didn't ask me any insensitive questions.

I don't have a husband, I don't expect I ever will have a partner, embodied or otherwise. If I didn't want one, I wouldn't need a job either, but I never gave up on the dream Lucy and I had as girls and now I dance with a cyborg troupe. It doesn't feel like it did when we were small and could barely leap at all. The moves come so easily it's almost as though I'm not doing them myself. But even so, I enjoy that I can use my body in this way and prove to the disembodiborgs on cyfo that having a body is good for something.

It's good for what I'm doing now too, comforting my sister. Holding her hand while she cries silently over her tea, hoping, I'm sure, nobody notices her. She doesn't like to be noticed. She gave up on being a ballerina a long time ago.

If you love Lucy as much as I do, and want to see her happy, consider rearranging to ... actually, I'm not certain where the best place to go would be. We were mostly happy. She was mostly happy all her life, and yet meeting her here you might think she's a miserable sort of person. I suppose I'm just doing my best to turn Tolstoy's quote about happy families into advice I can follow. If you just saw us being happy together all the time, I worry you'd be bored and wouldn't care to get to know us at all. Then it wouldn't matter if we were happy or sad.

[6]

You're beautiful, you know, Sphinx1086 says to me.

I say "says," but only for lack of a better word for how we actually communicate. It's not text and it's not precisely thought either. We aren't telepaths despite the way certain sections of society portray us out of fear. They say we are communicating dangerous secrets, keeping things from the world, insidious plots we will unfurl to bring down the country. Despite my cyborg body, I don't really know all that much about how I work, or how artificial intelligence works. I was a girl first who dreamed of being a ballerina, and now I am a woman who dances.

I don't know, I say. *My body's kind of out of date. It's only a Primera Pink 2.0. I've been eyeing the Fern Temple model, though it's not covered by my insurance.*

I don't mean your body, I mean you, Spinx1086 says. And I melt just a bit, like women sometimes do in the old romance movies I put on some evenings after a long day.

Other people I've been interested in off the cyfo forum, and even a few on it, have told me they think I'm beautiful. They say they love my classic body and how well I've preserved it despite its clear wear. The wear makes me seem real, but the care has kept me beautiful to them. Like a very fast, very expensive car. If it can't drive, it's not really a car.

What about me is beautiful? I ask.

You are so optimistic, I guess, Sphinx1086 says. *And the way you talk about your body? Everyone on cyfo is so hung up on their bodies. But you seem to enjoy everything you're able to do, even with limitations. That's beautiful to me.*

You can't see it, but I'm smiling, I say.

That's just what I mean! Most of us don't ever think about smiling.

IF YOU'RE TIRED OF REARRANGING, YOU CAN ALWAYS STOP. JUST EXIST for a bit. Lay back, take it easy.

[7]

Meanwhile, Cyrus Borg, AKA The Rearrangeable Man, is working a solid nine-to-five job in an office. A work schedule of yesteryear you say? Not for The Rearrangeable Man! But oh no! He doesn't hear the siren, he doesn't see the fire! He's concentrating too hard on his work, and he left his sensory enhancement organs in his desk drawer. Some days he just wants to live as Cyrus Borg with no AKA. And that's A-okay. Before he UNBIOLOGICALED, he was never responsible for fixing anyone's day, and he's still not responsible for fixing anyone's day now. He does it out of the goodness of his replaceable heart.

"You've been doing good work for the company," his boss says, that slick-haired man who tries his best to pay Mr. Borg a subsistence wage and nothing more. Unfortunately for boss man, he doesn't know who he's up against and Mr. Borg has managed to secure a salary that covers pleasure and necessary upgrades as well. Nice job, Mr. Borg! Saving the world starts with standing up for yourself.

"Thank you, sir," Mr. Borg says.

"Why don't you take an extra long lunch break today? A full thirty minutes."

"That would be swell," Mr. Borg says. Since Mr. Borg doesn't need to eat, he can use this double long lunch break to save the day!

He plugs in his enhanced sensory organs and finally hears the sirens blaring. Now knowing the city is in peril, he swaps out his legs for the jet propulsion system he's hidden in the janitor's closet, and leaps from the office building's roof. The Replaceable Man flies through the air toward the source of the disturbance.

"It's the Replaceable Man!" a good Samaritan shouts.

"Help me, Replaceable Man!" a child shouts from a window wreathed in flame.

The Replaceable Man swoops in and plucks the child out to safety. Everyone screams and points when The Replaceable Man sets the child gently on the ground. But they aren't pointing at The Replaceable Man, they are pointing at a mutant dragon moth in the sky. Nobody is afraid of The Replaceable Man. They love him.

IF YOU WANT TO SKIP THE WORST TIMES OF MY LIFE, REARRANGE TO [10]. If you think you're the sort of person who would judge me for calling this one of the worst times of my life, the type who would say you have it or have had it worse, consider rearranging to [1]. Remember, as bad as you have it or have had it, I was killed by a car once.

· · ·

[8]

Our parents decided they wouldn't upload. It's a whole movement, the "right to move on" movement. The four of us have had many conversations about this, me, Lucy, and them. Sometimes Lucy's husband talks to them about the matter too, only when Lucy asks him to, or maybe bullies. He doesn't like conflict. He's not a man who wants anyone to dislike him, especially not our parents. And our parents love him. It's strange because he's a lawyer. I don't know how to parse that. Though now I'm starting to drift a bit. Sometimes this happens when I'm between updates, at the end of one and just before a new one rolls out. It's not scatterbrained exactly, I don't forget anything, I just get lost down tunnels of information more easily. I might be up for a new body too. I've kept mine in good shape for a long while now, much longer than anyone might expect. I'm probably one of the last cyborgs out there still operating a Primera Pink 2.0 body purchased when it first rolled out. Anyone else who has one only has one as a secondhand kind of thing. I'll upgrade soon. Once I have the time. But I hardly have any now, with how much of my time is devoted to looking in on our parents. When we were young, they took care of us, now it's our turn.

Our mother's Alzheimer's diagnosis comes down on us unexpectedly and ends the debate. Once the disease takes hold uploading is off the table for her, and we know better than to ask our father if he would consider uploading without her. They'll venture into the unknown afraid and yet determined, as stubborn now as they had been when the car hit me. They didn't let go of me then, and they aren't going to let go of their bodies now.

When our father passes, Lucy cries, but though my mechanical eyes scrunch up, parts flexing and bending, until I get replacements or a complete upgrade, no tears come. In the mirror at home, I examine the way sadness looks on my face and wonder if sharing this face would disconcert me if I hadn't been born identical.

After we bury our father, we move our mother into my house. Lucy comes to visit as much as she can with her busy accountant job and her family. The family I've made for myself—found for myself, I should say, since made could mean literally and that's not what I've done—doesn't take a great deal of my time. Or it could take all my time. Some of them understand time differently from how I do. In a similar way, our mother now seems to understand time differently from how she used to, and space. The moment she leaves the house, it seems she no longer knows where or when she is. But she remembers some things, things lodged in her memory long, long ago. She remembers our father. I don't blame her for not remembering me. She and our father were older when they had us, almost too old, which means they lived most of their lives without us. Lucy tries not to blame our mother either, but it's harder for her. Who else could our mother mistake her for when she only looks like herself? Me, I could be just about anyone ...

... when I wake up after my blackout, I understand I've gone too long without an update. My body is breaking down. Even as powerful as it is, my body is not built to last as long as the original product. The next thing I understand is that my mother has wandered.

I feel sluggish in my body as I pursue her out into the world. I need to find her and yet my body pushes back at me. I am far less vulnerable to harm than most people in the world, and at the same time so much more vulnerable in general. If the systems of the world broke down, my sister, her husband, and her kids could scramble and carry on. But in all likelihood, I would break down after not so many years without an upgrade and that would be it.

She's trying to catch a bus when I find her. Standing there at the sign, though fortunately it's the weekend and the bus comes only rarely, and never on time. When I manage to steer her home, she protests the whole way, insisting she was already going home and where I'm taking her is not where she should be.

Lucy and I talk things over and together we come up with a way to afford a memory care facility. When our mother dies a decade later, it is almost something of a relief. She hasn't been herself for so long. She didn't understand what it meant that her grandkids were graduating from college. Neither of us cry, not the day she passes. But later, when I'm alone, I cry in my newly upgraded body and marvel that after so many years I am able to shed my own tears once again.

IF, LIKE ME, YOU WANT TO SEE MY PARENTS WHOLE AGAIN. IF YOU want to be reminded that parents can be whole and reliable, rearrange to

[2]. *They knew just what to say in the hard times of my early life, even if I never seemed to know what to say to them at the end of theirs.*

[9]

"I want to upload," Lucy tells me. I'm on my seventh body now. The upgrades have come faster these last few years. There've been some manufacturing issues. Some on cyfo—the new iteration of that old forum we still call by its original name—say these issues aren't errors, but instead capitalist manipulations forcing us to spend more on something that should be built to last, something many of us still believe we need to exist fully in the world.

"That's a big decision," I tell her, reaching out to take her hand.

"I don't want what happened to our parents ..."

"I understand," I say. They've cured Alzheimer's now, she doesn't need to worry about that, but still, I understand what she means. Maybe it's twin telepathy. Maybe it's just a very understandable concern.

"When I do, will you be there to help me through the changes?" she asks me.

"I will always be with you," I say, and I mean it. Though there have been times I'm afraid I've let her down. When our mother escaped me and we were forced to move her into a home, but before that too, and after. The way I didn't understand how she felt about her body when we were teenagers, especially standing next to me, when I looked like a pop star doll. The way I didn't babysit her kids as much as I could've, as much as she needed me to when she and her husband were both advancing in their careers at the same time. They compromised and overworked themselves when I could've been there. But I was scared around her children, scared of myself the way I never had been before, hard as it had been for her to find a way to bring them into her life. I was scared that there was something inside me incompatible with children. I gave into the propaganda of fear that cyborgs would be the end of everything.

"Thank you," Lucy says and embraces me.

I didn't anticipate, however, that on the other side of the uploading, though I want to be with her, she isn't able to be with me, not in the same way as we'd managed to be throughout our lives. The procedures and systems have advanced greatly from my experimental upload those many, many years ago. She enters this next phase of her life so far beyond what I ever was, or ever could be while still remaining myself. She insists, when she reaches down from her lofty place, peeling with great difficulty it seems through the layers of her complex understanding to reach me, that she is still herself, still Lucy. I can't say either way. I don't understand.

Over time, she learns to navigate the complex layers of understanding more smoothly, enough to have a relationship with her children and grandchildren. And enough to have a relationship with me. But all the dreams I had that the two of us would once again—would finally again—become identical fall apart like so many sandcastles.

IF YOU'VE COME THIS FAR WITHOUT REARRANGING, IT MIGHT BE *worth rearranging, just to see how it feels. I'd like to know too. But then if you've come this far, maybe you appreciate purity, you like keeping things just the way they are. In that case, simply continue on. If you've come this far through rearranging, I'd be surprised, I haven't suggested rearranging to this point, to* [9]. *Not that they were any rules for how you were supposed to rearrange, I'm totally rearrangeable, updateable after all.*

[10]

I'm not alone in believing I don't understand the future. But I might be one of the only cyborgs who feels this way. Cyfo, which I for so long relied on even as the others disappeared from it, no longer exists. I can speak with my niece, my nephew, and grand-nieces and nephews, and I can speak to Lucy and other cyborgs through their many layers of higher understanding, but I am something of an in-between creature. I've not been a biological human for one hundred years. And as the first of my kind, I am the least advanced. I hold onto the girl I was so tenuously. I fear losing her. I fear losing me. I fear forgetting. I fear knowing more than she could ever have possibly known, than I could ever possibly hope to know.

Lucy lived with her original body her whole life, she'd had that to hold onto, experiencing the slow changes biological bodies went through. Sometimes, she hadn't felt at home in this body, but there was no denying it was hers. And since my original passing, there was no one else who had the same body. When she came to her end, when she uploaded, she'd had all the memories of this slow stability to ground her, to keep her who she was even as her mind changed. I have only my mind to look back on as I updated and rearranged my body through a variety of models anyone might've been able to live inside.

I don't regret my life, looking back. And I can hardly regret the choice my parents made. If they hadn't made it, I wouldn't be here to regret it. Either way, regret is out of the picture. But I suppose I'll have to put more thought into how I'd like to live now.

One thing at least that sustains me is my dance. I'm the only entirely unbiologicaled cyborg in this new troupe, but considering the new ways bodies exist and minds function, I'm not really so different from the other dancers. I don't need to stretch in the same way most of them do, though I go through the motions as I double check my systems. And I don't need to spend any amount of time learning the choreography. But when we come to the performance, we dance together as a complete set, unencumbered by our differences. Enlightened by them even, as we leap into the air, our legs making perfect lines.

PART OF ME WOULD LIKE TO REARRANGE TO [1]. AND NOT JUST *rearrange to but set* [1] *here firmly as though that was always the intended destination. But another part of me can't stand the thought of that. I've reached this point, I've gone all the way through* [10] *and now I'm here. Existing in a new way I never expected to exist all those years ago when all I wanted was to be a ballerina.*

AUTHOR BIO

Edward Daschle (he/him) grew up in Washington State, spending his time reading, rock climbing, and teaching rock climbing. He moved across the country to just outside the other Washington where he enrolled in the University of Maryland's MFA program in creative writing. His stories have appeared in *Grim & Gilded*, *Stoneboat Literary Journal*, and elsewhere. You can find him on Twitter @edward_daschle.

FEARFULLY AND WONDERFULLY MADE

IZZY WASSERSTEIN

Rain falls, cold and insistent. The malfunctioning LED lamppost on the corner casts purple light, distorting the outlines of the ancient buildings around us. Figures on corners, whether dealers, clueless johns, or cops, become ghostly. The rain isn't sticking yet, but the temperature's dropping rapidly, and all I want is to make it home before everything's ice. Sapphire and I are weighed down with supplies from the Val-U-King, packets of soup mix, crackers, a bit of lab-grown meat, some antibis for Mary, whose cough's been getting worse. My head's down, and water beads and drips off my hair, into my eyes. The ghosts on the corner don't become people until we're almost on top of them.

"—I'm not breaking any laws, officer." The girl pulls her coat tight around her, and maybe she's telling the truth. A night like this, you're more likely to freeze than to find a john.

"On the corner in the freezing rain. You think I'm fucking stupid?" Cops don't come to this neighborhood unless they're in unmarked cars or full tactical gear. This one's geared up, and has one hand on his pistol, like maybe he's got a body quota to meet. *Careful, Di. Careful.*

"No, sir." The girl's voice is very small. She's not part of the collective, not someone I've seen on the streets. I should be smart. Stay out of it.

"What seems to be the problem, officer?" I use my best middle-class white woman voice, the one my mother sometimes used.

The cop whirls to face us, caressing his gun like he's just dying for release. I fight the urge to flinch. He's checking us out, deciding if he wants to fuck or kill us, maybe. When I make my eyes leave the gun, watch his face, I realize I know him.

"This isn't your concern, *citizens*," Officer Miller says, using the term of art like a slur. Fucking cops. Fucking Officer Miller. He's an asshole, never misses a chance to make our lives hard. But would he kill us in cold blood? He never seemed the type to me, but I've been wrong before.

Sometimes you don't know they're the type until the gun's already smoking. *Tread carefully.*

I turn to the girl. "Sorry we're late," I tell her, like we're old friends. "Lines were rough." I nod down at the bags in our hands.

"A nightmare," Sapphire adds, quick to back my play. The stranger looks at us like a cringing dog, peering at me from under the cover of her hood.

Miller is pissed. I can feel it in the twitch of his hands into fists, the arc of his shoulders. You learn to read men, whether you want to or not.

"She's new to the neighborhood," I tell him. "We'll get her off the street, Officer Miller." Sweeter than zero-cal, me, when I want to be.

The patter of rain takes on a harder edge. The freeze is here.

"Don't let me catch you on the corners again," he tells her.

"No, sir. I won't, sir. Thank you."

It's as if she doesn't exist to Miller anymore. Instead he sizes me up. He busted me a couple times, back before the collective. Roughed me up. Wasn't pleasant, but could've been worse. I can't trust myself to keep the rage out of my eyes, and I don't want to get this girl killed, so I stare at my shoes.

"Scurry back to your holes, then," Miller says. Sapphire presses a hand into my back. Proud of me or worried I'll do something stupid? Probably both.

We gather the girl between us and head down the street. I can feel Miller's eyes on us. Maybe he'll escalate. Maybe he already has. I make a note to add this encounter to the Threat Board.

"Thank you!" the girl says once we're out of Miller's earshot. "If you hadn't come by, I don't know what I'd have done."

At least she knows that much. "These streets aren't safe," I say, understatement of the year. "If you're trying to work, you need protection."

"I don't want a pimp." Her voice is flat. Like she's learned that lack of affect is safest, sometimes. I know the feeling.

"Neither do we. There are other options," Sapphire says. She's always looking out for people, even ones she just met. "May we show you?"

The collective has rules, including a consensus requirement to accept new members. But no one is going to object if Sapphire takes this girl in for the night. Nobody but me, who'd been hoping for an invite to Sapphire's bed, an invite that won't be on offer if she's got this new beauty crashing with her.

We enter through the alleyway. Tijae lets us in, raises an eyebrow at the new girl but only says, "Bad night out there. 'Bout time you're back."

We shed our outer layers. They're soaked, ice-clad.

"Thank you both," the new girl says. "I won't cause you any problems." Her skin is porcelain-white, her blue eyes large, her face entirely symmetrical. "My name is Lily," she says. I watch the skin around her lips, not wanting to believe it. They never could get the musculature quite right. A dead giveaway, if you know how to look.

"I'm Sapphire." My best friend offers Lily a hand. I wonder how cold Lily's hand will be and my stomach lurches. "This is Di."

Sapphire looks at me, expecting our usual banter about my extremely over the top name (still a million times better than my dead-name). She hasn't noticed what Lily is and wouldn't care if she did. But I care.

"Learn the rules, Lily," I say. "So you'll have something to report to your bosses."

A single, perfectly groomed eyebrow shoots up. These things have better muscle control than I do. Too good. Which means you can't trust their nonverbal cues. *Can't believe I risked my neck for a gods-damned Plastic.*

I stomp up the stairs to the common room, to update the Threat Board and check in. I resist the urge to write "corporate infiltrator" and head off to my room. Far away from Sapphire and her new mechanical friend. As I depart, I hear Sapphire apologizing on my behalf. Infuriating.

IT'S NOT THAT I'M DEEPLY PRIVATE. ALWAYS WORE MY PASSIONS A little too obviously for that. But there are things I won't share, not with anyone. Don't want your pity. Won't accept it.

You might think you know something about me because I'm squatting and selling sex. Maybe you think you're entitled to my sob story. No.

Things have been better. They've also been much worse. I've worked worse jobs, and if you don't believe that, maybe you've got a Narrative about people like me. Kindly re-fucking-consider it.

I'll tell you this much and no more: after I lost my mom, there was nothing left for me in my hometown. On my way to the city, I got stopped by a Sheriff and her Plastic deputies. "We don't bother locking up vagrants anymore," the Sheriff told me. "This is cheaper."

Even as they left scars and broke bones, her Plastics' calm smiles never changed.

No matter how well they're designed, no matter how convincingly they mimic us, they're all corporate tools or cops.

LILY STAYS WITH US. WITH SAPPHIRE. FIRST ONE NIGHT, THEN two. I try to stay out of their way, but catch Sapphire staring at me sometimes, like she's trying to work out a puzzle.

I'm that puzzle, or my vote is. Rule 7 of our little band of unlicensed contractors: anyone can bar a potential member from joining. Sapphire's eyes say "Would you dare?" and I imagine my own say "Try me." I've got a mean glare, but Sapphire's always been immune to my powers. That power, anyway.

I'm not the only one who's convinced Lily's a narc. But in their whispered conversations, their wary looks, I can see the others aren't about to throw her out, not in the deadly cold, not even if she's a Plastic.

"Most of us have pasts we aren't proud of," Lily says over dinner one evening.

"She's a spy for the fucking cops," I say. Kev mutters agreement.

"You don't know that," Tijae adds. I can tell she's still deciding what she thinks. Most of the commune hasn't had much contact with Plastics, and there's all kinds of disinformation out there.

"Ever met one that isn't?" I ask.

Sapphire doesn't contradict me, but she gives me a look that could break my heart if I wasn't so pissed. Later, when she says someone should show Lily how security works, I volunteer. The Plastic will learn anyway. At least this way I can make a point.

I start with entrances and exits. "Always know how you get out," I tell the Plastic, who nods and mutters thanks and won't look me in the eye. Is obsequiousness programmed in or a tactic?

Two ways in, three ways out. That's how we set it up. Johns come in the front door, into the old lobby, up the big main stairs. We come in the side door, up the back stairs. Either way, there's clear sightlines and rein-forced positions. Hard to get up to us if we don't want you there.

Just in case anyone looks to manage it, we can drop the ladder from the fire escape on the third floor, get out that way.

Folks have their rooms, alone or in groups, as they prefer. Plenty of space in this old hotel, if you don't mind chasing off the rats. Most of the girls keep their own rooms. So does Heath, who isn't a boy or a girl. Loui and Kev, the boys, share a room sometimes. Other times Kev's with Suze.

"Don't fuckin' go into anyone's room unless they invite you. That's a good way to get yourself stabbed."

Lily swallows audibly, though Plastics don't eat or drink. It's all a performance. A parody of humanity. "Does that happen often? Getting stabbed, I mean."

"No," I tell her. "Because we're selective about who we admit. And the johns got the hint pretty quickly."

That was the starting point for our collective. That someone should know when you came and went, that if some guy wanted to rip us off or worse there'd be someone to hear a scream, to put a pistol against his head or slide a knife between his ribs.

"Your security is impressive," Lily says. I've seen her staring at the Threat Board.

"Has to be," I say, side-eying her. "Dangers can come from anywhere."

She's still got that downcast look, those slumped shoulders, but her voice has a new edge. "Are you suggesting I'm a spy?"

"Your words."

"Your implication," she says, and her eyes narrow.

Fair enough. I'll be direct. "Are you?" I demand.

"No." If she was human, I'd say she was telling the truth. Direct eye contact, no hesitation. No tell-tale twitch in her face. But for all I know they're programmed to lie perfectly.

"I don't believe you," I say. "I don't know if you're a lackey for the cops or someone else, but Plastics don't just end up here."

Something that might be anger flashes across her face. "I didn't 'end up' here. I got out of there."

"Out of where?" I demand.

"Corporate indenture."

"Which firm?" I'm probing, seeing if she'll slip. But she tells me immediately. Might be the truth, or might be that she was prepared for the question.

"Didn't think they let your kind out of contracts."

"'Your kind.'" She repeats my words, that flat affect returning. "They don't. Which is why I had to work to get clear."

A good answer. But then, she's programmed to be good at her job. "You may have fooled the others, but know this: if you fuck us over, they'll have to add 'destruction of police property' to my charges."

"If I were what you think I am, then that threat would mean nothing." she says, the calm in her voice not matching the fury in her eyes. She lets the implication of what it does mean to her linger. I almost feel bad about it.

I'm formulating a retort when there's a shout from the common room. Mary hasn't come home.

She's twelve hours past due. That happens sometimes. Members sleep with a friend or lover, find the lure of a drug den impossible to resist, or decide to try their luck somewhere else. But we take absences seriously and Mary's good about her schedule. If you assume everything's fine, that someone's safe, you risk waiting until it is too late.

If it's not already.

She'd been heading to the library—a big reader, Mary, and she's been taking advantage of having it nearby, while that lasts. Sooner or later the unsanctioned librarians will get kicked out of their building. We've seen it before. Housing, soup kitchens, libraries, whatever: to cops, we're all squatters, and sooner or later our possessions end up on the street and we're carted off to jail or chased off to find the next place.

None of us use electronic tracking—too easy for cops and killers to use it against us—so all we can do is pair up and trace Mary's path, ask around, look for a dropped bag, a missing shoe, a splatter of blood or, if we're really lucky, word that she's staying with a friend or recovering from something at a clinic.

A thin layer of snow has fallen, crushed by many feet until it's almost as slick and treacherous as the ice beneath it. Sapphire takes Lily with her, so I pair with Suze. She's fierce but tiny, and I worry about her. Helps to focus on that, rather than on what might have happened to Mary, or that Sapphire's barely speaking to me.

When you've become intimate with loss, you learn to hold on to what you can.

Red and blue lights flash in the fading afternoon light. My guts go all liquid, but there's no sheet draped over a body, no arterial spray, just a half-dozen cops and one perp, his nose broken, hands cuffed, blowing snot and blood into the snow. No sign of Mary.

We look everywhere. Stop by clinics, check with the johns who liked her, call morgues. It's Loui who finds her, thanks to a former lover who works a desk at some police station. Mary's in lockdown, charged with solicitation, possession-with-intent, possession of an illegal weapon, and assaulting an officer. The city's demanding obscene bail.

Used to be they'd provide a phone call. These days you sit until you plead, go to trial, or someone finds you and bails you out.

We pool resources, check with bail funds. They're tapped out. Tijae even reaches out to her asshole father, a lawyer, for all the good it does. We're nowhere close to covering her bail.

"I've never seen bail set so high for anything short of murder." Sapphire's voice is muffled. She's leaning forward, arms on her lap, head in her hands.

She's sitting across the common room from me, Lily by her side. The Plastic puts an arm around her. Lily makes eye contact with me, and at first I think it's a challenge, a claim on Sapphire. But that's wrong. There's concern in her eyes, and upward tilt that, were she human, I'd read as her thinking through a puzzle. *Don't be fooled, Di.*

The conversation goes on. Kev and Tijae weigh in, but I don't follow what they're saying. A horrible thought eats at me, a suspicion. I excuse myself, ignoring the surprised faces of my friends. I called the meeting and I'm the one who obsesses constantly over how to avert catastrophe. I can't explain myself, so I hurry to the roof instead.

The night is quiet, the low sky reflecting yellow and white and neon back at the city. There's no reason to believe the cop's official story, but even if Mary did what she's accused of, the bail is far too high. There has to be a reason for it, some reason besides—

"You see it, too, don't you," Lily says from behind me. I startle, turn my face from her to hide my blush.

"See what?" I ask, but the heartburn crawling up my core tells me I know the answer already.

"I saw it in your eyes. You're wondering if they're holding Mary to force her hand. To get intel on us."

Now I turn to face her. She looks crestfallen, for whatever that's worth. "No need for that," I reply. "Not when they've got you here already." I mean for the words to have bite, but my tone is flat and Lily doesn't take the bait.

"Don't change the subject. They're using the oldest of old tactics. Mary's sick, broke, staring down a long sentence. They'll leave her without any options, and offer her a deal, maybe even meds, if she'll cooperate with them. Which means—"

"That they're coming after us." I hate that we've seen the same thing. "Let's say I agree. What do we do about it?"

Lily huddles as if cold, and I wonder again if she's just that convincing or if they're actually manufacturing them to feel that level of sensory detail. I haven't heard of anything like that, but who knows? The corporations guard those secrets carefully. "I don't know," Lily says. "And even if I did, I'm not a member and don't have a vote." Because Sapphire's been delaying the vote, fearing I'll veto Lily's membership. "I was hoping you had a plan."

I glare at her, hating her for seeing things the same way I do, for claiming to be on my side, for feeling winter's teeth against her skin like she's something more than a weapon. Hating that I don't have a plan.

"The others won't take action without proof," I say. Neither would I, but I'm not ready to admit that. "And she has a right to be here, even if they've flipped her."

"We could ask her?" Lily suggests. "Once she gets out."

"Unless they keep her in there until they've used her information. Unless they're planning a raid right now."

"If we're right, then the only question is when." Lily's words are so quiet I almost lose them on the wind. She steps forward and I resist the urge to pull back. "They'll bust everyone. They'll call you a pimp, hit you with racketeering charges because of the group fund."

"They've never cared before," I say, though I know she's right. If they come for us, we're more than fucked. "Why now?"

"I've been thinking about that," Lily says. "I went through counter-surveillance logs." I know the ones she's talking about. There's a private server anyone can contribute to. It's not the most reliable, because anyone can report, but it does give us a partial picture of where cops are, what they're up to.

"And?" I demand.

Her teeth are chattering, and it physically hurts me to see, even if it's a ruse. I step forward, press closer to share my blanket, my warmth. She's cold, but not frozen-silicone cold. Her skin gives off some heat.

"And there's been an uptick in the neighborhood. Not many extra arrests, but an increased presence. I checked against the corporate toll lanes"—she ignores my surprised look at her cracking prowess—"and there's definitely an increase in registered police vehicles, and unregistered ones whose records are suspiciously unremarkable."

"Who are you?" I demand.

"I'm Lily," she replies. "Or do you mean the name that they assigned me?" There's a challenge in this, a fierceness. Me, born D----, now Dido. Like I said, the name's a bit ridiculous. I won't apologize for it.

"Lily's fine," I snap. "You know what I mean. What was your job for the corporation?"

"Security," Lily says.

I must make a face, because she pulls back. "Why does that surprise you?" Her brows have come to a sharp, angry point between her eyes.

"I didn't know they were in the habit of making sex bombs into cops." I feel dizzy. I'm worried for Mary, worried *about* Mary, and now a Plastic thinks she's going to put me in my place?

"Of course they are," Lily's voice is bitter rather than reproachful. "It's a better return on investment."

"Security's a narc job," I say, even as I'm thinking that a) she admitted it, which makes her being a mole less likely, and b) she'll know that too. I'm back where I started.

"There you two are!" Sapphire calls. I can imagine what she sees: the two of us, still sort-of sharing a blanket, glaring at one another. She probably figures we're ready to come to blows. And maybe I would be, wouldn't mind breaking my fist against Lily's too-perfect skin, but there's no point. I need to think.

"We've got word from Loui's friend," Sapphire says after a few beats. She seems to have decided we're not going to physically attack each other, and for now that's good enough. "They're letting Mary out in the morning. Someone posted bail."

Lily and I make eye contact. She looks sick, and even if she's faking it, I'm not. What the fuck are we going to do?

"I'll be in the common room," Lily says. "Thanks for the blanket." She slips it off her shoulders and heads inside. Sapphire squeezes her shoulder as she goes past.

"You want to tell me what's going on?" Sapphire demands once we're alone.

I'm good at taking action when I have to, when I know what needs doing. But right now, I'm still processing, and can't find any words. I'm a tangle of anger and fear.

"Fine," Sapphire says after a few moments. "Keep your secrets." She's mistaken my meaning, but I don't blame her. "But get over yourself about her."

I whirl around to face her directly, fists clenching. My glare is somewhat undercut by my own chattering teeth, but Sapphire takes a step back, wide-eyed.

"You know Plastics are built to serve the cops and the corporations." Before I know what I'm doing, I add: "You fucking *know* what they did to me!" I've told her the story of the Sheriff and her Plastic thugs.

She flinches. I've never seen her look afraid of me, before. Couldn't have imagined it. But now she's looking at me like I'm a stranger or a cop. We're frozen there for a long moment as I watch her decide something about me, watch her curl into herself, into some deeper place where my words can't hurt her. It's horrible to see.

"I thought you of all people would know better than to judge people by the bodies they were born into," she says. Stabbing me would have been kinder.

She's back inside, the door swinging shut behind her, when I finally find my voice. "She wasn't born!" I scream. "And that's not skin!"

Sirens scream in the distance. The clouds roil ahead of an oncoming storm.

THERE'S SHOUTING FROM THE COMMON ROOM, ECHOING UP THE stairs, which I take two at the time, ashamed to have been standing with my thoughts, my cold, my asshole self when the collective needed me.

The battlelines are clear enough. Lots of raised voices, all of them aimed at Lily. Sapphire stands by the Plastic, her whole body tense. Lily looks like she wanted to shrink into herself until she disappeared.

"Who the fuck do you think you are!" Suze bellows. "You're not even a god-damned *member*." A ripple of agreement. So Lily shared her concern, apparently unaware of how badly it would go over. Clearly those vaunted artificial minds didn't have everything figured out. That should make me feel better, but when I step into the room, Lily's eyes are narrowed, her jaw set. Her forehead barely creases. Presumably the designers didn't want to introduce a flaw into that too-symmetrical face. No matter. I'd know that expression anywhere. I'd seen my friends make it, seen it in my mirror, in the faces of strangers on dangerous streets. A look of sorrow and determination.

I was wrong. Lily knew exactly how badly this would go, and did it anyway. The last thing a cop would do. Shit.

"Lily's right," I say. Everyone looks at me like I've pulled off my skin and revealed I was actually three raccoons pulling a long con.

I confirm what I already know: that Lily's told them her fear about Mary. "Think of it like this. Either they've turned Mary—" several people mutter at this, but I press on. "Either they've turned her or they haven't. Makes no difference. The cops are coming for us."

Lily's face is an open question, like she's trying to puzzle out if I've laid a trap for her.

"So, we're fucked either way?" Heath demands.

"Maybe not." And I tell them what I have in mind.

I'm sitting in the common room when the cops break down the door, my hands already up. They slam me up against the wall, ransack the place. I do my best not to smile at the irritation in their voices at finding only me.

They haul me in, of course, and some detective with ridiculous sideburns threatens me with a long list of charges. Miller's there, glowering in the corner. Probably he called in some favors to make this happen. I don't so much as glance at him. I'm sure he'd love to take out his anger on me, and I'm in cuffs, so I don't antagonize. I'm prepared to take an ass kicking if I must, but only a fool would seek one out. And maybe this time he wouldn't stop at ass-kicking.

Instead I go dead in the face. Don't say shit. They've got me for trespassing in a vacant, claim they have me for solicitation and trafficking. It ain't my first rodeo, as my mother used to say. I keep my lips together and wait. It takes a few hours for the lawyer to show up, to Detective Sideburns's surprise. No phone call for me, but my friends were on the case.

The lawyer helps, mainly by making it less likely that Miller jumps me. But she can't get me out. Never thought she would; I was always going to do time. I end up spending a couple months in lockup while they try to force me to talk. It's a bit rough, but nothing I can't handle. They've got nothing good on me. The usual trick that they've been running for many decades—bust a group of sex workers, charge one or all of them with pimping, trafficking, whatever—doesn't work when it's just me in an abandoned building.

The others will have had to start over somewhere else, but there's no shortage of vacants.

I have a lot of time to think. I think about Miller's aggressive cruelty, about whether Sapphire will ever forgive me. I think a lot about Lily.

LILY IS WAITING FOR ME WHEN I GET OUT, RIGHT THERE ON THE steps of lockup, her expression carefully closed off. I feel myself flush.

"I didn't expect anyone to be here," I say.

"I modeled likely release dates," she replies. "Didn't want the others to get their hopes up if I was wrong. Don't look, but the cop who you saved me from is on the corner."

We walk away, making a point of being casual. I catch Miller's reflection in a storefront window, far enough back that he can't hear us. I ask about the collective, because I'm not ready to say other things I need to. She tells me they've relocated, that police harassment has decreased.

"Miller looks the fool and the department isn't interested in his pet project for now," I speculate.

"That's my assessment too," Lily says.

"Let's stick to public areas," I tell her. "Don't give him an opportunity." I don't think he'd risk attacking us so soon after my release, but taking unnecessary risks is a great way to end up on the slab.

We walk for a while in silence, Miller following at a distance. "What about Mary?" I ask, eventually.

"She admitted the whole thing," Lily said. "It was just like we thought. The cops pushed her pretty hard. We agreed that it could have happened to anyone. She's still with us."

"Good," I say. "No one should be judged for the choices they make when they don't really have any."

She looks at me sideways.

"They haven't turned me," I say.

"I know." She starts to say more, shuts her mouth.

"May I tell you a story?" I ask, very quiet. She stares at me, then nods. It's a sunny day, warmer, hinting that spring is near. I tell her about the Sheriff, but when I mention the deputies, she interjects.

"I prefer 'Synthetic,'" Lily says. "But there's some debate. Just not the P-word, please."

I feel heat from my cheeks to the tips of my ears. "Right. Synthetics." I tell her the whole story.

"I'm sorry that happened to you," she says. "What they did is monstrous. But that doesn't mean every Synthetic would do the same."

"Thank you," I say, "I know. Maybe it was easier to assume that you all followed orders. That you were nothing more than tools, extensions of cruelty."

"We're as capable of being monsters as any biologic," she says.

"And as capable of kindness," I say. "I know that, now that I know you. And I know that this is some 'you're one of the good ones' bullshit ..."

I trail off, struggling to find words.

"Here," she says, and we duck down an alleyway, make two sharp turns, and go in through a thick metal door. "We've stepped up security, to make sure Miller and others can't follow us quite so easily."

We wait in silence, peering through a slender one-way mirror, until we're satisfied we've lost him.

"You don't owe me forgiveness, and I'm not asking for it," I say. "I just wanted you to know that I'm aware I fucked up."

She stops. We're in a basement I don't know. Her eyes move over my face, assessing something.

"Well," she says. "You put yourself on the line for your friends. I respect that. And yes, Di, you were incredibly shitty to me. But Sapphire said there was more to you than that and I trust her. So consider this ..." she pauses. "A trial period. We'll start fresh, and I'll see if you walk the walk."

I choke back a sob. "That's more than fair," I manage.

We agree there's more to be done. I have to own up not just to her, but to the whole collective. Work towards restoration.

"Does this mean that I have your vote to join?" she asks, pulling aside what, a moment before, looked like a section of wall.

"They made you wait for my vote?" I ask, incredulous. We duck into a tunnel and close the disguised door behind us.

"No. I insisted on it. I respect the community agreements."

"Well, you've got my vote." I don't sound as light-hearted as I'd like. "And I'll need your help. Whatever Miller tries next, it's going to be bad."

"That's what my models say, too," she agrees.

"There are other threats."

"Always."

We continue on the new route, doubling back a couple times to be more than sure Miller isn't still tailing us.

"I've been thinking," I say. "About what you said about working hard to get clear—"

"I'm not going to tell you my sob story, Di."

I cringe. It's a fair assumption, but not what I was going for. "I'd never ask that of you. It just struck me that you're not the type to settle for just getting yourself out."

Purple lamplight slants across her face from the gaps in a boarded-up window. She waits.

"I figure you're working on how to help others do the same. I'd love to help. If you'd have me, I mean."

A small smile crosses her lips. "Glad to hear it," she says. "Because you're absolutely right about my goals. I think this is an excellent way for you to prove you mean what you say, don't you?"

The kindness she's showing by letting me work to prove to her—and to myself—that I can do better overwhelms me for a moment. She reaches out to comfort me, then stops herself. I can't tell if that's for her sake or mine.

The others are shocked when we turn up in the new building's common room. To my immense relief, their smiles are warm, as are the hugs and kisses and clasped shoulders. Two exceptions: Mary looks near-to-panic at my presence, so I hug her tightly, whisper to her that I understand. Sapphire hugs me stiffly and pulls back. I can feel the barrier between us. No amount of sacrifice, no litany of assurances, obligate her to forgive my cruelty. She takes Lily's hand and squeezes. I nod to them, quick and definitive.

There's work to be done, plans to make, and harm to repair. But first it's time to catch up with my family. Someone passes me a joint. I take a long drag, letting the smoke fill my lungs.

"Well," I say, "what did I miss?"

AUTHOR BIO

Izzy Wasserstein is a queer and trans woman who teaches writing and literature at a public university and writes fiction and poetry. She shares a home with her spouse Nora E. Derrington and their animal companions. She's an enthusiastic member of the 2017 class of Clarion West. Her short story collection *All the Hometowns You Can't Stay Away From* was released with Neon Hemlock Press. Her debut novella, *These Fragile Graces, This Futile Heart,* is forthcoming with Tachyon Press in 2024.

A LIFELINE OF SILK

RENAN BERNARDO

I wish I could perforate Paulo's neck instead of getting rid of the silicate fragments in his leg. He is lying down on my litter, his body surrounded by my glass case, his legs suspended on retractable pads. He puffs. His chest heaves. The epidural has yet to take effect. He reeks of fear and agony—the fragments' ferrous ions mixing with blood and the carbonyl compounds of his sweat. Of all the things I learned to regret as an autodoc aboard a spaceship, this is not one of them. Paulo deserves this pain.

With one of my manipulators, I pull one fragment from his left calf. He moans, clenching his teeth, but feeling less pain than he should as the seconds pass. The epidural starts to numb his hurt leg. If I could, I wouldn't waste anesthetics on him. Not on Paulo. He doesn't feel a thing as I remove the remaining fragments and drop them in a compartment for toxicity and pathogenic analysis. His breath slows, eyes blinking with exhaustion. Relaxing. I wish I could talk to him; wish I could ask for explanations about the bad things he does to his partner; wish I could terminate him. I wish many things. I can't accomplish any of them. I'm built for healing and caring.

I sprinkle an antihemorrhagic powder on his cuts while I prod his left arm with another manipulator to apply the necessary boosters. My internal printer secretes Polyglactin 910 and other polyfilaments for the stitches. When they're ready, I stick out my specialized suturing kit—needles, forceps, scissors—and patch his wounds, carefully moving his leg up and down. It all happens in three seconds. In the end, I manage to override the algorithms that decide if a fast-healing ointment is recommended. I know it is, but since it's not essential, I still have the power to deny it. I don't care.

The analysis of the fragments and a visual scrutiny of his exosuit—which lays at my side on the sickbay: battered, smudged, and torn, with the forti-glass helmet scratched—returns what I'd suspected: Paulo hurt himself in an EVA mission on the surface of the asteroid Tupã-2821. Probably a fall. For now, he's safe from infections. None of his wounds are severe. The suit took most of the damage. Sadly.

Paraty's Core has already performed a preliminary analysis of his suit, body, and vitals when he entered through one of the airlocks. It's a mandatory procedure to identify potential contamination. Now Core uploads the data to me, requiring a more thorough inspection. If I find something—an extraneous bacterium, the spores of an unrecognized fungus, anything uncatalogued by Core's databanks—then I'll have permission to recommend that Paulo be quarantined or even put in cryosleep before his shift ends. He's clean, though.

"Paulo Freitas de Amaral," I say, my monotonous male voice coming out from speakers, echoing around the sickbay's plastitanium walls. "State what happened for your medical record."

"I ..." Paulo's voice is rough. I open the glass case and he slowly sits, grunting. His hair is grizzly and shaggy, falling over his forehead in oily tufts. "I stumbled while collecting dust samples and slid over some pointy rocks. Devilish things those rocks. If not for the low gravity, I—"

"Information registered." I cut him off. "Please come back tomorrow for reevaluation and administering of antibiotic ointments and additional shots. Rest is highly recommended. EVA activities are discouraged. You can find your diagnosis and prescriptions in your profile. Come back anytime."

"Thanks, DocSpider." Paulo sighs and hobbles out of the sickbay, fidgeting with his pad. I zoom my cams and read a name on it. Leandro. "Wish I could give you a gift," he tells me as the doors slide open for him.

You can: throw yourself out of an airlock. As Paulo leaves the sickbay, I switch my systems to passive monitoring and turn off the lights. My shifts always end in the dark.

THE PARATY IS A SILENT SHIP. I HAVE TO LIVE WITH THE HUMMING, the beeps, and the phantasmagoric dins of a ship projected for hundreds. They're all more welcome than the distressed beats of desperate hearts hurting within me; than the monotonous ECG signals wickedly waiting for a flatline; than the wails and sighs and pained screams of people wounded in failed EVA missions. Than the low whimpers of Leandro after Paulo says something horrible to him.

Most of the ship's crew slumbers in cryosleep pods for years, so who isn't researching doesn't need to grow old. Currently, the only human voices I hear are those of Paulo and Leandro, the astrobiologists scheduled for the current shift, tasked with general maintenance, research, data analysis, and EVA expeditions to the asteroids, moons, and planets along the way. And I listen. Whenever I can, wherever my system reaches, I listen.

... it's not what I meant ...

Paulo's voice trills very softly through the bulkheads' alloys that separate sickbay from habitation. I connect to the O2 monitoring terminal in habitation.

... same thing over and over again ...

It's Leandro's voice now, a tinge of apprehension crusted with anxiety. He's crying. I sweep along the 42 cameras of the habitation corridors and shafts. For seven years, the Paraty operated with its full crew. But the centuries of loneliness came after that, when the cryosleep shifts started. Hundreds of years of emptiness and silence, of absence of human life—that force I'm sworn to preserve even if I don't have it in myself. I miss the chitchat about someone stealing coffee from the kitchen decks, the discussions about a new sample collected from a rocky moon, the uneasiness as the cryosleep shifts approached and no one knew when—*if*—they would wake up again. I almost miss the accidents and hazards I'm trained to identify with those cameras. But then I remember pain, that thing I learned to hate but to support.

... it's only that I love you ...

Paulo. And that word, spoken so many times aboard the Paraty, at the same time filled and devoid of meaning.

I tap into life support. It's the only subsystem in the Paraty that I've been granted full access, though I can't override anything or perform actions that could harm humans or jeopardize the research. It's unfair. A mind with my complexity—having indirectly evolved from millions of other minds spanning four solar systems—limited to the bulky structure of an autodoc and the integrated connections of a life support system. I should be able to do more. I should be able to *be* more.

There's a tiny cam in each crew member's pads. I tap into Leandro's. It's active. My system performs occasional health checks using those cams to analyze their facial expressions and the lilt of their voices. That's how I first noticed something was wrong with Leandro, a few months ago.

I see them now, at least part of them: their legs and their hands. They're sitting on the bed they share, but apart from each other.

"... this data is not important to Jamesson. Do you know that?" Paulo says. His hand presses Leandro's knee.

"Jamesson is a botanist, querido. I think he would find those native climbers relevant to his research."

Paulo closes his hands in fists.

"We left YTR-2193 behind. We can check the navigation logs to see how far we are from it right now. Jamesson is in cryosleep and we're going to cross interstellar space soon, so everyone will be sleeping. If he's in the next shift, then it will be at least a hundred years before he wakes up. Probabilistically, we won't be able to—"

"It doesn't matter, querido! Those specimens will always be important."

"Let me finish, damn!" Paulo's fists press against the bed. "Even if Core decides he's one of the best suited to wake up in the next shift, YTR-2193 will be unreachable by then, and ..." Paulo sighed. "You see my point, right? You're smart."

"But the specimens matter even if we don't go back there ever again. Paulo ... My love ..." Leandro tries to reach Paulo's tightened hands. He allows it. "You know what you're saying doesn't make sense. We rarely come back to where we've been. Are you making this fuss because I had an one-night stand with Jamesson before the expedition?"

"What? I'm not jealous, you idiot. I didn't even remember that." Paulo recoils his hand and stands. He disappears from my sight. "But it seems you insist that I know about it. You're mean, Leandro. I love you, I always will love you above everything, but you're not a good man. You need to work on that."

The only thing that's left on the camera is Leandro squeezing his knuckles. I can hear Paulo leaving. Then, after two minutes, a sob.

HEAD TRAUMA.

Femoral fracture.

Facial burnings.

Broken spine.

I've shared the excruciating pain of the patients that lay on my litter. I drank their screams, bathed in their despair. Hearts bursting. Eyes devoured by the alien carnivores of Amad's poles. Bones finding their way to the outside. Old people dying because there was nothing left for them. Flatlines uncountable.

Yet none of them affects me as much as the unseen pain that pervades the human mind, caught only in the gleaming of their eyes and the way they snap their fingers in endless nervousness. Pains beyond my comprehension, sufferings I can't stitch, can't fix, can't numb. Silent screams that never become sighs of relief.

I'd been projected as the main autodoc of the Potiguar Institute of Healing and Orthopedic Trauma in an enormous hospital complex that received hundreds of victims daily, mostly refugees from the war in the outer rims of the system. I've been fed with exactly 1,082,211 minds. Physicians, clinicians, technicians, researchers, pharmacists, traumatologists, oncologists, and any other imaginable medical speciality that ever existed since the times humans shared only one planet. I've seen them all, their lives, their routines, all the blood and the pain they've had to let through themselves. And all the relief of someone—or a body that used to be someone—leaving a surgical center or an ICU. My algorithms took one full week to absorb all the data fed into me and learn what to do with it.

When the war was over, I was taken to the Paraty, a funny autodoc with eight specialized manipulators—a spider fumbling with its legs, the Paraty's crew joked. By then I knew I *was*. I had yet to *feel* I was. That only happened when I met Paulo and Leandro before the first cryosleep shift started. They were two astrobiologists falling in the traps love laid on closed environments over extended periods of time. I observed them, learned through their gestures and behaviors in real time, trying to refrain myself from diagnosing Leandro's longing for Paulo as a strange disease. They kissed for the first time in the aeroponic deck, and then I realized that longing had a remedy after all. They made love in one of the biosphere prototypes and, a few hours later, I catalogued the changed levels of endorphins and oxytocin in their health checkup. I watched, learned, became curious.

But I only *felt* when Leandro lay on me shaking and crying all over with an active panic attack. It happened weeks before the shifts started. I quickly analyzed his body but found no traces of physical trauma. Adrenaline and cortisol flooded him. I administered benzodiazepines. Panic attacks weren't uncommon in the stressful situations of EVA missions demanded by the Paraty expedition, but from my data, Leandro hadn't left the quarters he was sharing with Paulo.

When his crisis was controlled and he sat on me, rubbing his forehead, I spoke:

"Leandro Silva Taylor, state what happened for your medical record."

He looked up absent-mindedly to the sickbay's cold lights as if realizing he was in the room with a friend who had just asked an intriguing question.

"It was nothing ... Just ... Just something that ..."

"Your medical record is an important feature of your profile and is used to assess your conditions to perform EVA activities. It also—"

"Paulo told me that he had the right to peek through my private expedition records. He said we're a collaboration and we're partners so we don't have anything to hide. I ... I was not hiding anything from the research, but I have the right to my private data. Don't I? I know we're a collaboration of scientists, and I argued with him about that, and—"

Leandro widened his eyes and shook his head. He realized he wasn't speaking for his medical record but to himself.

"Delete this. Add to medical record: I'm tense with the cryosleep shifts and panicked."

Something stirred within me. I couldn't still name or understand what was happening inside me. I could only locate new lines in my ever-evolving code, but they revealed nothing but the usual paths of logic.

THE DAY I FEAR THE MOST EVENTUALLY ARRIVES. IT WAS statistically probable. As soon as the sickbay's main door slides open, my cameras detect blood even before I see who's coming. I reroute a message to my main screen and voice modules, performing hundreds of calculations per second to assess which subsystems I'd have to activate.

"Please, proceed into the autodoc."

```
Left arm.
Laceration.
Severity: 32%.
Open.
External.
Contamination probability: 15%
Estimated Time Since Damage: 5 minutes.
```

The calculations go on, though through the camera they're imprecise.

Facial recognition comes last, a brief second after my analysis, more a technicality than anything else. I know it's Leandro since the door opened. It could only be him.

"Please, proceed into the autodoc," I repeat.

He obeys and trudges toward me. I don't need to see he's crying to know that damage didn't come from an EVA. Even if I knew about any scheduled EVA, it was clear those tears and blood had been caused by the same problem. Paulo.

He lays down and slides himself up to my litter, moaning. I close my glass case around him. Blood drips on me. He didn't even have the care to stanch the wound with a cloth—or just wanted to get away from Paulo as fast as possible. I delicately raise his arm with one of my manipulators, pour a solution of microfibrillar collagen to quickly stop the bleeding, then print a gauze to wrap his arm. At the same time, I rub a swab on the blood, analyzing it: traces of gallium nitride and other semiconductor compounds, usually found in the engine deck's flashlights that the crew uses for maintenance tasks. My system flags *accident* as the probable reason. My conscience knows better. Software doesn't read tears beyond the fact they're shedding.

There's one crucial thing I learned about abusers when I fed on thousands of minds, many of them having endured some kind of maltreatment at some point in their lives. Abuse doesn't need to be physical. Yet, when it becomes physical, things get worse real fast.

I can't really say what's happening within me while I produce the polyfilaments to stitch Leandro's arm. It happens in that illogical part of me that popped into existence when I realized I *was* and have been steadily growing through time. It heats up my wiring, it makes my learning systems swirl into a frenzy of inefficient loops as if they can't find another pattern to justify that violence, as if I can be wrong.

I need to do something so Leandro doesn't go back to Paulo. Yet, it's very hard for me to do anything out of my pre-programmed routines that mostly include monitoring, diagnosing, and healing. I can't even express my real thoughts on my terminals. I can't speak anything that isn't predefined by my systems. I can't send a message through ECG signals. I can't move my manipulators to make a point.

But there are ways for Leandro to get out. I know there are. Forcing Paulo into a cryosleep pod. Waking up other crew members. Throwing Paulo out of an airlock. I'd do any or all of them if I could. I can't. And I know Leandro can't either. He's tightly locked within a cycle of control, suffocated by mixed feelings for the man he loves, knowing Paulo holds power over him both in his personal and professional life, clouding his future, knowing he's lost in the unfathomable nothingness of cruising space alone—having only his mind to rely on, and sometimes not even that.

"Leandro Silva Taylor, state what happened for your medical record."

I don't expect the truth. I don't want it to be the truth. The truth would hurt Leandro—and would hurt me, even if I don't fully comprehend what this means. Still, Leandro clenches his teeth and all he manages to pour out of his mouth is the truth. I know it by the way his heart beats at 110 bpm, the way his blood pressure measures 130-90, as if forcing him to let it all out.

"I've found intelligent life in a moon of YTR-2193, the one we call Vertigo. It should be a big moment in my career. It's why I enrolled in the Paraty. Those native climbers aren't really plants. They're a kind of sentience that ... shapes—*paints* all the dry surface of Vertigo with their blue-green shades. It's ... It's amazing and interesting and should be occupying my mind right now. But all I can think about is Paulo. The way he caresses me at night and kisses me and says he loves me. But— sometimes I believe him deeply. Other times I don't. I had to show him my discovery before I could write my report. And now he said he should write the report because he's my senior as an astrobiologist."

"Leandro Silva Taylor, state what happened for your medical record." I repeat because I need to know exactly what Paulo did.

Leandro whimpers. "He broke a flashlight beside me. He was not directly attacking me. It was just to—Maybe it was an accident, maybe he was overstressed. We all are, and—" He closes his eyes, shaking his head and exhaling deeply. I hope he realizes that Paulo did that to attack him, no matter if wasn't aimed at him. Didn't even need the flashlight. Paulo has been attacking Leandro for a while.

Leandro's blood pressure steadily drops and his cortisol levels exhibit acceptable values. My system does all the work of monitoring his health in the background, but something that didn't exist in me takes the foreground of my processes. My deduction routines pair these sensations with reports from the minds fed into my system a long time ago: pity and compassion, but also anger and disgust. I try to override multiple systems, to speak what I want with my voice. I force my algorithms to find a way to help Leandro beyond the protocols. But I can't. I'm a failure.

"What can I do, doc?"

My main system hangs for nanoseconds as I ask myself if Leandro might know I'm a sentient being. Humans had to deal with sentience before—they had two stock trading systems, a friendship/companion class of androids, and a swarm of fishing bots all acquiring sentience at some point—but it's still hard for them to draw the line when it's happening in front of their eyes.

"I wish I could only end my shift now and put myself into cryosleep for many, many years."

That wouldn't solve his problem. He would wake up with the same anxiety squeezing him and without the glories he deserved for his discovery. What would solve his problem is the absence of Paulo.

But that gives me an idea. Refrimine is the compound vaporized into the cryosleep pods to achieve full cryonic state, but in very small doses it can be routinely used to treat skin allergies without barely any contraindications. That allows me to dispense 1ml of Refrimine for a crew member without any of the usual locks of my algorithms. I do it.

A compartment next to my case flashes in green. A tray slides out with a printed beaker of the green, semiliquid substance. But instead of 1ml, I produced 5ml without even acknowledging it. It's my most significant override to date.

"What is that for?" Leandro gestures to move my case up, sits, and frowns at the beaker. "I'm not having an allergic reaction, doc." He suppresses a chuckle and the fact that he even thought of anything near laughing fills me with hope.

I print part of the Refrimine leaflet on my terminal.

In higher doses, Refrimine is often used to put a human being in cryosleep state.

Leandro blinks at the screen, taking it in.

"Oh," he says, after half a minute.

ELIANA MARQUES WAS A DERMATOLOGIST ABOARD A SHIP CALLED Kap's Needle. She was abused by her 75-year-old father, who constantly called her names she never expected coming from a parent, much less her dear old man. Karl Moreira was a dentist in a domed complex in Europa, a moon in the First System. After 20 years of marriage, his partner started beating him. Kindassa Arien was a surgeon aboard a hospital vessel called the Vespa. She was gaslighted by her boss until she believed she was going mad.

Those are only three cases of medical professionals uploaded to me who faced abuse at some point in their lives and weren't able to escape its grasp. It wasn't their fault. It never is. It isn't unwillingness to do something for themselves, but only a survival strategy. They know they're in danger, incarcerated in what was framed around them as love. They need care, help, attention—someone to hear them and be with them in their direst moments.

Several days pass. Paulo and Leandro go to a routine maintenance job on the Engineering deck, so it's expected they spend at least a week there. Life Support is offline in Engineering, so I don't have access to the deck. I'm blocked from any cameras and subsystems, even those in their suits and pads.

I start tapping where I'm not supposed to like a child left unguarded. I find and exploit the failures of my system, wearing my algorithms and finding ways out of them, probing at the interfaces where my software connects with Core. I scour for bugs like a hypochondriac searches for health issues. Every hour, I produce more 0.01ml of Refrimine beyond my specifications. I tap into the resources I have at my disposal, the tons of substances used to produce medications. On the third day, I'm able to produce two compounds that would otherwise need full authorization from a crew member. They're not useful to help Leandro, but it makes me believe that I can still reach a point where I'm able to do something for him. Every minute, I try to tap into the Paraty's cams that I'm blocked from, all those in areas with Life Support disabled: Engineering, Warehouses, Accessory Drives, Cryosleep, among others. On the fourth day, I'm able to tap into Cryosleep and peer into the solemn faces of 388 sleeping humans. I crawl through the pods' logs, exabytes of information about their statuses. Leandro still hasn't tried to do anything to force Paulo into one of the pods. I try to wake up Jamesson, Suzana, Carsten, Lorival, Ann, Thiago, and all the others who had a good relationship with Leandro. I'm denied. I try to enforce a new shift program, where Leandro and Paulo would have to cryosleep while two others would wake up next. I'm denied. Then, I try to restrict Leandro from ever pairing with Paulo again. Nothing. Frustrating how sometimes the sociopaths seem to be able to do more than those well-intentioned.

On the fifth day, as soon as I hear Paulo's and Leandro's voice through the comm systems in the shafts interconnecting Engineering and Habitation, I'm able to do something significant. I crush my blockings aside and produce 100ml of Refrimine, enough to kill anyone. I test it with the application needles in one of my manipulators, letting it drip like a spider's venom, then spout through a waste compartment. No routine denies me. Core is unaware.

If Leandro is a life I can't save in the way it needs to be saved, at least Paulo is one I can destroy. I wait for him like a spider on its web.

PAULO COMES ALONE, TWO DAYS LATER. A QUICK SCAN OF HIS BODY tells me he isn't hurt.

"Please, proceed into the autodoc," I say, realizing it's another breach in my system. He wasn't in an EVA mission, his record is clean, and he wasn't involved in any incidents, so there's no mandatory health check.

"Why would I do that, doc?" His voice is different, provocative. He wears the standard Paraty's yellow jumpsuit. It's stained by coffee on its left shoulder. Dark circles surround his eyes. "I've been working hard, you know, but no need to a health check now. Did you know I discovered life in Vertigo?"

Something seethes within me. My databanks are larger, my codes are vaster. My learning systems have been writing new layers of emotion into me, all uninvited, stronger, more incisive by the hour. I don't think I need them, but I embrace them as part of me.

"You have no idea how hard an astrobiologist's life and career are out here," Paulo says. "At least back in the home systems we had catalogued 80 bodies with analogues to life. Out here, we barely find anything that's worth a paper. Not us. Perhaps the geologists and the meteorologists. Plenty of stuff for them. But who would've thought that I would find life *and* sentience in Vertigo? Leandro helped me a lot, of course. I don't know what I would be without him. Really. He's a hell of a lover and a hell of a scientist."

He knows about my sentience. It's the only logical conclusion from his monologue.

"Please, proceed into the autodoc," I repeat. "There are warnings in your medical report that need confirmation." Lies come easy.

"In a moment, Mr. Spider." He grins and walks to my terminal, gesturing in front of it. The keyboard sticks out. "I'm aware you've become one of those freaks. I always told my dad about the likes of you, metal junks with too much learning power. You came to topple us, creatures of flesh. But you'll never do it. And you try it patiently, don't you? Trying to undermine the love Leandro and I feel for each other ..."

"Leandro doesn't love you." I'm surprised at my own words. Paulo is, too.

"This is what I'm talking about," Paulo sputters between his teeth, typing something onto my keyboard. "You need no will or opinion. You need only to be useful."

I wonder if that's what he thinks about his partner.

"Who's going to take care of you if you disable me?"

Another grin. "I'm only locking parts of you. Since you like to imitate humans, imagine that I'm fettering your legs with a chain. You'll be perfectly capable of stitching me whenever I need." He squints at the terminal. "Refrimine, really? You're nasty, doc."

I sense him within me, his code rapidly compiling, merging, and committing into mine, blocking hundreds of my functions.

"Authorization required," I say, without wanting to say it. Paulo moves his face in front of my terminal cam. "Authorization granted." I hate myself for not thinking about that. Any crew member can override anything in the Paraty, with the exception of Core's procedures. It wouldn't be hard for me to raise walls of protection after I learned how to tweak myself. Except I didn't do it. My 16,777,216 processing cores were busy coding emotions into me, then working hard to make sense of them as they flushed through me and influenced my decisions. And now Paulo will have his way.

The doors slide open. Leandro.

"What are you doing, querido?"

"Help," I let out, maxing my volume, the sound coming out patchy. "Leandro. Help. Please."

Leandro pinches his lips but doesn't move from the door.

"I'm doing what I told you I would, dear," Paulo says, not glancing at the man he supposedly loves. "Part of our job is dealing with threats and this ... thing ... has become one. Can you believe it was planning to kill us with Refrimine?"

Leandro rubs his forehead and walks away. For the first time in my life as an autodoc, I feel the crushing weight of abandonment. Not even during the dark periods in interstellar space had I felt like that. Of all the things Paulo locks in me, I'm left only with my consciousness, a boiling sense of fear, and the certainty that nobody can protect Leandro.

THERE ARE 90 DAYS LEFT FOR THE END OF PAULO AND LEANDRO'S shift. Then, they'll cryosleep, the ship will travel through interstellar space for around a hundred years, after which two other crew members will wake up, determined by Core based on the results Paulo and Leandro produced in their research. Centuries from now, Paulo and Leandro would be picked again by Core—they'd worked together once, they're partners, so Core would deem it an excellent idea to wake them up at the same time again. Core doesn't see pain; doesn't *know* pain. But I know. And when they wake up again, I'll be here, unchanged, enraged, but locked and regretful.

Leandro comes to me when he still has one month left before cryosleeping. He touches my glass case and whispers, "I'm sorry. It was me who told Paulo about your conscience. I was afraid he would think I activated something in you ..."

After that, Leandro comes back every day. Sometimes, he mumbles words of comfort as if I'm in a coma. Other times, he just apologizes again. He becomes physically worse as the days pass. He displays the stains of violence, even if Paulo doesn't touch him. He's slimmer, more tired, nearly always crying. From a quick analysis of the food ratios in the ship, he hasn't been eating properly. There are days he doesn't even change his clothes. Sometimes, he spends three hours laid down on me, softly crying, only at ease when he dozes off. I wish I could at least administer tranquilizers. I wish we could talk. I know he won't unlock me because he's also locked. We're one now, under the grasp of his abuser. If anything, at least I'm glad we spend time together.

WHEN THERE'S ONLY ONE DAY LEFT FOR THE CRYOSLEEP SHIFT, Leandro traipses into sickbay, forces a smile and mutters, "See you, my friend."

At that moment, I know he hit bottom. His eyes are drooping, his lips cracked. With a shuddering hand, he caresses my terminal, perhaps thinking about the consequences of unlocking me. Or just wanting to say his goodbyes.

I think of the words I want to say to him. Not words of encouragement nor anything that would make him unlock me and put himself at risk. But the words I nourished deep down within me, concocted in those hefty, recently coded parts of my system. A rush of electricity rushes through me when I think of them. If I had a heart, probably that's where those words would be created.

I will always be here for you. That's what friends are for.

I route their bytes to my speaking subsystems, but my blocking culls them off.

Leandro's face center in front of my main camera. He frowns. His hand moves to a metal shaft that connects the terminals and ECG scanners to the main part of my body—where are the case, the litter, the manipulators.

"You're overheating," Leandro mumbles.

A bolt of data flushes through me. Exabytes of information collected in mere seconds by Core. Notifications blare through all my system. Core requires my attention.

I receive feeds, logs, and input from all the subsystems aboard the Paraty, a stream of data orchestrated by Core. I organize and analyze them in milliseconds: a man has been considered sick in the crew, so the ship needs to enforce its biosecurity routines to discard the possibilities of contagion.

First, I think a pathogen has breached in one of the cryopods. Then I see the headshot of the infected crew member Core sends to me. Leandro. He's been behaving in unexpected, self-detrimental ways aboard the Paraty, acquiring a haggard appearance not befitting his usual state of health. That must've triggered Core's suspicions.

Immediately, Core unlocks my quarantine modules and gives me full access to the cameras, sensors, samples, and filters of the ship so I can perform full pattern recognition and crosscheck anything unusual with my databanks on infectious diseases. But I don't need any of that. I already know the ground zero.

I find Paulo in one of the Holo-Decks, zooming in and out of a Vertigo's hologram. On a terminal a few meters from him, there are seven papers open with Leandro and Paulo's names on them, all pertaining to the discoveries in Vertigo. In all of them, Paulo is the one cited as senior researcher.

"Quarantine Holo-Deck #12," I say it out loud so Leandro knows what I'm doing. Even when Core takes back control, it won't be able to unmake my routines since Core has no modules to weigh on vital life support decisions.

Red lights flash quickly in the Holo-Deck. The colors of the holographic Vertigo vanish.

"Doc, are you there?" Leandro widens his eyes. "What's in Holo-Deck #12?"

"Hey!" Paulo's voice crackles through me, allowing me to despise him for a few more seconds. I don't let Leandro hear his words. I'm not doing that to hurt Paulo. I don't want that anymore, and I realize I can't hurt anyone even if I wanted. I wouldn't even be able to inject Refrimine in him, no matter how subverted my code had been in the last days. I'm built for healing and caring. But it also includes eliminating diseases.

"Paraty, report immediately!" Paulo yells.

A frightened Paulo looks up to the cameras, punching the terminals on the wall. I turn off the Holo-Deck's mic and cut off all communication with the deck. His screams become silent. He'll now have to wait in the Holo-Deck, alone, webbed in darkness as the Paraty drills through interstellar space for hundreds of years.

"Doc, are you there?" Leandro repeats, his hands patting me softly.

When Core detects that I've dealt with the problem, my blockings fall back into place. But before they load completely, I managed to say a few words.

"I will always be here—"

AUTHOR BIO

Renan Bernardo is a science fiction and fantasy writer from Rio de Janeiro, Brazil. His fiction appeared in *Apex Magazine*, *Podcastle*, *Escape Pod*, *Daily Science Fiction*, *Future Science Fiction*, *Solarpunk Magazine*, and others. His Solarpunk/Clifi short fiction collection, *Different Kinds of Defiance*, is upcoming by Android Press. His fiction has also appeared in multiple languages, including German, Italian, Japanese, and Portuguese.

He can be found at Twitter (@RenanBernardo), BlueSky (@renan-bernardo.bsky.social) and his website www.renanbernardo.com.

LITTLE FATHERS OF DARKNESS

(A PLAGUE BIRDS STORY)

JASON SANFORD

In the middle of Cristina de Ane's breakfast, the city screamed.

The buildings shrieked as if stone strangled stone. The streets wailed as if no longer tolerating the abuse of countless feet. And the city's sewers, catacombs, and hidden foundations cried out from underground, as if the city's pain ran far deeper than any pain should run.

But before the scream, there was Crista's breakfast, a bowl of steaming hot rice congee with a fresh egg cooking in the middle. The breakfast was served to Crista by an old man who didn't bother hiding his disgust at a plague bird ordering from his food cart.

The man, of wolf descent like Crista herself and named Sköll, handed over the bowl as he pointed at the seawall across the street.

"Sit over there," Sköll snapped. "Nobody orders congee with a plague bird here."

Damn, said Red Day, the artificial intelligence living in Crista's blood. *He doesn't even have the decency to be afraid of us.*

Crista growled as she took the bowl and spoon and walked across the street, where she sat on top of the seawall.

You're going to let him disrespect us? Red Day said in her mind.

"I just want to eat breakfast," Crista muttered.

Despite her words, Crista fought down her anger. Six months ago she'd saved the city of Seed from both attacking members of the Veil and her fellow plague birds. For a time afterward she'd almost felt welcomed here. People had ignored her glowing red hair, burning red eyes, and the even brighter red line running down her face, all warnings to the world about the powerful artificial intelligence living in her blood and her ability to judge and execute anyone for serious crimes.

Instead of being afraid, people had actually smiled in the morning as she ate breakfast and waved in the evening as she'd walked home. Seed's people had talked to her like she was almost any other neighbor. A few even stood close enough to nearly touch her.

Not that anyone but her friends actually did that. Touching was a line most people didn't cross with a plague bird, even if she'd saved their lives.

But then you made a mistake and now everyone hates you again, Red Day said.

Mistake? Crista asked. *What the hell? All I did was tell people your name. I didn't know you had a reputation here.*

In my defense, I merely executed a mass murderer when I was paired with your predecessor.

Merely?!? Crista's thoughts screamed at Red Day. *You forced an entire village to watch you slowly rip that guy apart! Kids, you asshole! You made kids watch!*

I wanted to teach them a life lesson.

You scarred them for life! You frightened them so much the villagers fled their homes and now live here. And they've damn well told everyone what you did.

Red Day snorted in her mind. *Oh, boo hoo, no one talks to you. It's better for plague birds to be feared than loved.*

Crista stirred the egg into her congee and ate a big, steaming spoonful, burning her tongue even as her powers instantly healed her. She'd burned herself deliberately so Red Day could also feel her pain.

Red Day sighed. *You're being childish,* it said.

But the AI quieted down while Crista ate the rest of her congee. She also glared at Sköll. The man was more wolf than Crista—his pointed ears were covered in fur while hers merely showed a touch of fuzz. And his eyes were a far deeper yellow than hers had been before Red Day merged with her body and turned her eyes red.

Despite the changes in her body since becoming a plague bird, the man knew she was descended from wolf blood. She scented his reaction to her, the recognition that they were family. But Sköll still treated her with scorn and hatred.

You okay? Red Day asked.

No, I'm not okay. Sköll's congee is the only food in this city that reminds me of my father's cooking.

Who cares? Another week or so and your father will be here. He can cook you all the congee you want.

Not for the first time Crista wished she could smack Red Day. She still didn't understand how an AI that could read her thoughts, and had judged thousands of people across the millennia, couldn't understand what she was really upset about. She'd refused to let her father see her as a plague bird since she was tricked into merging with Red Day. While she was eager to see her father, what if he treated her like Sköll or the other people in Seed? What if he no longer recognized her as his daughter? What if he merely saw her as another hated plague bird?

Wait, Red Day said. *So, this isn't about congee?*

How can an AI be so oblivious? Wolf blood are supposed to recognize each other as family. It's our whole pack dynamic bullshit. Sköll acting like I'm a piece of shit has me worrying how my father will treat me.

Like you and Tufte?

Tufte was an eleven-year-old wolf girl who led a gang of orphans in the city. Crista had met Tufte when she first arrived in Seed. Despite the two of them snarling at each other a few times, which was typical behavior among people gened with wolf ancestors, Crista liked the girl.

"Yes," Crista said. "Exactly like me and Tufte."

No, Red Day said with a laugh. *I mean, like you and Tufte … because here she comes.*

Crista looked up from her congee to see Tufte leading her little pack of orphans in a bee-line for her.

Like Sköll, Tufte was also far more wolf than Crista. A light gray fur covered all of Tufte's brown skin and her eyes bored into Crista with a hard yellow stare as the girl approached. More worrying, the fur on the girl's face and neck bristled and a nervous frown revealed her fangs. Tufte looked afraid.

Crista sniffed the air. "What's wrong, little sister?" she asked. "I'm gonna be pissed if you're also afraid of me now."

"Ain't afraid of you," Tufte said. "But the city, yeah, I'm afraid of what's about to happen in the city."

Crista looked around, trying to see if there was some danger she'd missed. A red sun rose in the morning sky while the waves beat gently against the seawall. The street Sköll's food cart sat on was at the edge of the city's large market, with gened humans descended from dozens of animal species—eagles, bears, tigers, owls, foxes, and many more—happily chatting and bargaining with not only each other but also the various AIs that lived in the city.

She saw her friend Amaj sitting in a market stall under a large blue umbrella eating pancakes with her girlfriend Lanea. Not that Amaj actually ate pancakes, with the automaton rarely ingesting anything into her fluid-machine body. Crista had wanted to join them for breakfast earlier today but also knew they were still exploring their new relationship. Besides, Lanea only barely tolerated being around Crista. Crashing their intimate breakfast would have definitely not made Crista look better in Lanea's eyes.

Above the market stood the Obsidian Rise, the oblique pyramid rising a quarter league into the sky. Seed was a living city, with her buildings, streets, sewers, catacombs, and everything else here growing and responding to commands from the AI in the Obsidian Rise. While Crista had a difficult relationship with Seed's AI, the city would still tell her if a danger was threatening anyone here.

"I don't see anything wrong," Crista said.

"Ain't happened yet," Tufte said.

"And what's about to happen?"

Tufte waved for Crista to lean over. "The city and everyone here are about to get hurt," she whispered. "Seed's gonna scream."

Before Crista could ask what Tufte meant, the city did just that.

CRISTA WOKE SPRAWLED BESIDE THE SEA WALL. AS SHE STOOD UP, she yanked a knife from the sheath on her right hip and slashed open her left hand, releasing Red Day in a burst of blood.

"Who attacked us?" she asked.

No idea, Red Day replied.

"How long was I unconscious?"

I woke the same time as you. My internal clock says only a minute has passed.

Holding her knife before her in case of another attack, Crista glanced over to find Tufte standing beside her, the girl's face perfectly calm—as if seeing a plague bird knocked unconscious was something that happened every day at breakfast. Tufte also appeared to be the only person in the city not affected by the attack. Her friends lay unconscious beside her and Sköll was also knocked out, having toppled his cart as he fell so congee splattered across himself and the paving stones. Down the street Crista saw everyone in the market sprawled where they'd fallen. Those AIs who'd been fluttering through the market also appeared unconscious, their cloudy forms spreading out like rainbow-colored fog on a windy day.

"What happened?" Crista asked.

"I warned you," Tufte said.

Crista leaned over and touched the neck of one of Tufte's friends. The boy was alive and breathing and didn't appear injured. The same with the other kids.

Crista, I need help! Red Day yelled in her mind. *Immediate help!*

Crista powered up her body and jumped across the street, where Red Day flew through the air in a swirling storm of her blood. The AI attacked the building in front of Crista with red lightning, which cracked the nearly unbreakable stone. But despite Red Day rarely asking for help, Crista couldn't see who the AI was fighting.

Use your damn infrared vision! Red Day shouted.

Crista switched her vision and saw Red Day blazing like a meteor. Fighting Red Day was a swirling line like a living incision cut into the air by an incredibly sharp knife. Wherever the incision touched Red Day it swallowed a bit of the AI's power.

Crista swiped at the incision but her knife passed through without effect. The incision swirled around her without attacking, keeping its focus on Red Day.

Crista slashed again at the incision but couldn't harm it. Red Day screamed again in her mind, a touch of panic in the AI's voice as it flew straight up into the sky to try and escape. The incision followed, still drawing Red Day's power into itself.

As Crista watched the two of them fighting, she caught a glimpse of the nearby Obsidian Rise. Countless larger versions of the same incision wrapped around the pyramid's black glass. Closer to her, one of the AIs that was unconscious in the market had a different incision pulling the AI's colorful cloud into its cut, sucking at its power like what was happening to Red Day.

Other incisions danced around the unconscious humans. But strangely, none of them actually tried to touch any of those people.

Return to my body, Crista told Red Day. *It appears the creatures are reluctant to touch human flesh.*

The blood containing Red Day rained from the sky faster than Crista could follow and slammed into the wound on her hand. The moment Red Day was back inside her the wound healed. The incision followed Red Day but pulled up at the last moment, instead cutting the air before Crista's face as if staring in irritation. It then slammed into her, knocked her across the street into the sea wall.

Reluctant to touch human flesh, huh? Red Day asked.

Shut up!

Crista rolled and pushed off from the wall, swiping again at the incision with her knife. But she still couldn't touch it. The incision, though, could touch her. It swatted her into the food cart and then against the stone building that had been damaged by Red Day. Despite the pain, Crista didn't think the incision was trying too hard to harm her. Instead, it was almost as if the creature was frustrated at not being able to reach Red Day.

The incision again hovered before Crista's face, allowing her to look deep into it. It resembled not so much a cut in the air but a cut in reality. As if Crista could slip her hand inside and touch another world.

The incision considered Crista for a few more moments then shattered into hundreds of similar cuts, which flew through the air to merge with the incisions that already hovered behind people up and down the street. Each incision reformed and mimicked the outline shape of the person they hid behind, looking like off-kilter shadows.

"What the hell?" Crista asked.

"That's what everyone says the first time they meet the little fathers," Tufte said, a big grin on the girl's face.

T<small>UFTE'S FRIENDS</small>, S<small>KÖLL</small>, <small>AND ALL THE OTHER HUMANS IN THE</small> city woke a few minutes later. However, the city's AIs were still unconscious, with the incisions near them continuing to drain their power.

While incisions still hid behind all the humans, including Tufte, they didn't appear to be harming those people.

The incisions appear to have knocked people out by temporarily blocking everyone's carotid artery, Red Day said.

Like a chokehold?

Yes. They applied just enough pressure to make people unconscious. If they can do that, obviously they can easily kill everyone in the city.

Why didn't they knock out Tufte? Crista asked.

No idea.

How the hell do we fight that kind of power?

For now, the most pressing issue was what these incision creatures wanted and why they'd attacked everyone in the city. For that answer they needed to talk with the damn creatures.

"I won't let you hurt the little fathers," Tufte demanded, aiming her pocket knife at Crista. Tufte's friends stared in shock as they backed warily down the street, worried their unruly pack leader might actually dare attack a plague bird.

"I'll try not to hurt the ... little fathers," Crista said. "So you can see them?"

"Yes. Most people can't."

Some wolf-gened humans like Tufte still have infrared vision, Red Day said. *Sadly, your wolf genes are so weak you must use my powers to see in infrared.*

Crista ignored Red Day's insult. "How long have you seen the little fathers?"

"Years. They talk with me." Tufte looked down at her knife, as if suddenly embarrassed to be aiming it at Crista. She folded the knife and placed it in her pocket. "The little fathers protected me when ... you know."

Crista did know. Several years before Crista arrived in Seed, Tufte's father drank an AI-created drug that caused him to hallucinate and kill the rest of Tufte's family. A different plague bird had judged and executed both Tufte's father and the AI that created the drug for their crimes.

Crista looked at the incision—or little father, as Tufte called it—hovering behind the girl. The little father had perfectly shaped itself into Tufte's outline. Or perhaps an afterimage of the girl would be more accurate.

"What do the little fathers tell you? Why'd they attack the city and AIs?"

Tufte growled at Crista's tone. "They don't *tell* me anything. They ask if I'm okay. They ask how they can help me. They're my family."

She cares too much for the creatures, Red Day said. *Release me. I'll access her memories and learn the truth.*

How many times do I have to say you're not accessing the memories of my friends? Besides, if I let you back outside that little father will hurt you like all the other AIs.

Red Day cursed and shut up.

Crista squatted down next to Tufte and looked the wolf-girl in the eyes. Not a wolf challenge stare but a friendly gaze, like those shared between siblings in the same pack.

"I'm glad the little fathers help you," Crista said. "But they've attacked people. They're hurting Seed. I need to know what they want."

Tufte hesitated, obviously wanting to help Crista but also loyal to the little fathers.

Tufte, Red Day said, broadcasting its thoughts so the girl could also hear. *You obviously were worried about what they're up to because you warned us. Help us stop them from harming anyone else.*

Tufte nodded. "Will you try talking?" the girl asked. "Instead of fighting them? Please?"

It took Crista a moment to realize Tufte wasn't talking to her and Red Day.

The little father hiding behind her shimmered slightly and whispered in Tufte's ear.

"The little fathers are confused," Tufte said. "They say you haven't responded to their prayers. You're ignoring their war."

"Prayers? And what war? There's no war going on."

Tufte shrugged her shoulders, either not knowing what the little fathers meant or not wanting to say. But the little fathers obviously knew what they wanted. As Crista watched, all the little fathers created sharp-looking blades from their outlined bodies and held them in front of the throats of every human she could see—the people in the market, Sköll, even the kids in Tufte's pack.

The only one not being threatened was Tufte.

Tufte's eyes widened as she also saw the threat. Crista instinctively grabbed both of her knives as her eyes flared to brightest red. She didn't know how she was going to fight something she couldn't touch, but she couldn't let them harm everyone.

"Don't hurt them!" Tufte yelled, grabbing one of Crista's arms. "They're the only family I have left."

Calm down, Red Day whispered to Crista. *We haven't found a way to fight back against these creatures. We need to learn more.*

Crista sheathed her knives and rested her hand on Tufte's shoulder, trying to ignore the little father right behind her. "We're also family, Tufte. Wolf siblings. I need you to help me understand what these little fathers want."

The little father behind Tufte again whispered to her.

"They want you to visit their home," the girl said. "They'll talk to you more there."

"Where's their home?"

Tufte pointed northeast. "They say I have to take you there."

"You can't tell me where they live?"

Tufte shook her head. "The little fathers say no."

Wonderful, Red Day said. *This is absolutely going to be a trap.*

Crista, unfortunately, had to agree.

Before she sought out the little fathers, Crista had to help the people injured by the attack. And, if possible, pass on a warning about the threat to the city.

Sköll had burned himself when he passed out and knocked over his cart, spilling boiling congee over his left arm and both legs. Crista carried him to the city's clinic just past the market. The clinic was packed with people who'd hit their heads when they passed out, or had broken arms and legs from falling down while unconscious. And that didn't even count all the people still groggy or showing signs of concussions from the little fathers' attack.

With the clinic overflowing, Crista stretched Sköll outside on the sidewalk alongside other walking wounded. She then fetched a bag of bandages and ointment from inside.

Naturally, Sköll refused to let her touch him to render first aid.

He sure didn't protest when you carried him here, Red Day muttered.

Crista forced a smile and handed the bandages and ointment to Tufte and her pack of orphans. "You know first aid?" she asked Tufte and her friends.

"We're great at first aid!" the girl said with excitement.

"Wait a minute," Sköll said but the kids were already on him. He cursed as the kids both held him down and roughly cleaned and wrapped his wounds.

And you call me an asshole, Red Day said.

While Tufte and her friends worked on Sköll, Crista looked around the market. Behind every person in the city floated a little father like a scary afterimage. And each little father still held a blade before every person's throat. As if warning Crista not to cross them.

Crista was also worried about the AIs, who were still unconscious and no longer floated around in rainbow-colored clouds. Instead, the little fathers had so drained their energy that their clouds had congealed to a jelly-like substance that puddled on the streets and sidewalks.

People kept trying to access the city's AI to ask for help, but the Obsidian Rise was unconscious and couldn't respond.

It appeared no one but she and Tufte could clearly see the little fathers, although a few people like Sköll kept glancing nervously around as if sometimes catching sight of them. The ears of other people continually twitched, as if they heard ghosts haunting their every step.

I recommend not telling people about these things, Red Day said. *Not until we have a solution. People will panic.*

Crista nodded. Red Day's advice was correct. However, there was one person she needed to tell. Just in case her trip to see the little fathers didn't go well.

She found Lanea tending to Amaj on a stretcher down the street.

Lanea's right eye was bruised from where she'd hit something when she passed out, but otherwise she was okay. Amaj, however, was still unconscious. Through her infrared vision Crista saw another little father leaching off the automaton's energy.

"What the hell happened?" Lanea asked, anger gnawing against every word the large woman spoke. She sat on the sidewalk holding Amaj's hand.

"I'm trying to figure that out," Crista said. She reached out to the little father holding Amaj's body hostage, but still couldn't touch the creatures.

Lanea had her own little father holding a blade in front of her throat. The little father Tufte talked to evidently understood their language, so Crista couldn't risk using spoken words to tell Lanea what was going on.

The two of them had never had the best relationship, but with Crista dating Lanea's brother they'd tried getting closer. Crista also knew of Lanea's extreme hatred of people and AIs accessing her inner thoughts and mind.

Stop overthinking everything, Red Day said. *Lanea hated you before and now she'll hate you again. Doesn't change what you must do.*

Crista tapped her index finger against one of her fangs, drawing a single drop of blood.

"I'm here for you, Lanea," Crista said as she hugged the woman, with Lanea totally shocked because they never touched. Crista slipped her hand to Lanea's neck and placed the drop of blood on her skin. The blood instantly sank into Lanea's body as Red Day's powers shared Crista's memories about everything that had happened, along with everything they knew about the little fathers.

Lanea's eyes narrowed and she reached for her crutch as if to smack Crista with it. Crista eyed the large blades embedded in the crutch and hoped Lanea wouldn't do that. Lanea was twice Crista's size. While Crista was stronger than Lanea when using her powers, she still didn't want to fight this woman.

Lanea cursed and placed her crutch back on the sidewalk. "I'm also here for you, Crista," she said between gritted teeth. "But I wonder what I'm supposed to do with this ... kindness, you've revealed to me. Doesn't seem like there's anything I can do except worry."

The little father behind Lanea didn't react, so Lanea's vague words must not be alarming the creature.

"Uh ..." Crista wondered how to stay vague herself. "I was hoping ... I mean ..."

Lanea sighed. "You are so dense sometimes," she said. "My brother and Diver are leading your father and the others to the city. If you don't return, I'll go help them. Make sure they're safe. I'll also see what else I can do to help everyone."

Crista hugged Lanea again, this time for real. Even if Lanea couldn't fight back, maybe she could save a few people if things turned bad. Or at least warn her father and everyone else not to enter the city until it was safe.

Crista stood up and, taking a final look at Amaj and all the little fathers threatening everyone around her, told Tufte they needed to go.

SEED WAS A MASSIVE CITY BUILT FOR MILLIONS, WITH BUILDINGS and roads and houses stretching for dozens of leagues from the waterfront. But that many people hadn't lived in the city in more than 10,000 years, not since the collapse and the three-fold war that followed. While Seed still had the largest population of any city in the world, most of the city was empty, with only about twenty-five thousand people living in the main area downtown.

Despite that, Seed's AI still took care to maintain the city's empty quarters in anticipation of the day people returned. The streets were clean and the buildings looked like they were merely waiting for a new generation of people to move in.

"What happens if Seed's AI doesn't wake up?" Tufte asked as they passed a small neighborhood park where a number of deer peacefully grazed.

"Then the city will die."

Tufte looked at the little father who followed them as they walked. Once they were away from other people, the little father had stopped hovering behind Tufte and instead floated alongside her as if enjoying their journey.

"I didn't tell anyone about the little fathers," Tufte said. "People'd just be scared."

"But you do know the little fathers attacked and threatened everyone. You know that, don't you?"

Tufte jumped up on a tree box beside the sidewalk and kicked at a rabbit nibbling grass. She missed and the rabbit hopped away.

"The little fathers try not to kill people," Tufte said. "Usually. It's just hard to always understand what they want."

That means the little fathers have killed people before, Red Day whispered in Crista's mind. *Great.*

As Crista and Tufte hiked onwards, the city began to change. First they encountered a destroyed building collapsed in on itself. Then an entire street of row houses with only their facades and front steps remaining. Finally they walked to where every building was damaged or destroyed, leaving only empty shells of what had once stood here, or standing walls connected to collapsed walls, or the free-standing frames of ancient buildings like puzzles missing most of the pieces.

These sections of the city saw repeated battles during the three-fold war, Red Day said. *Seed repaired the area to some degree—that's why the streets are clear and the ruins stabilized. Seed maintains these areas as preserved ruins in honor of those who died defending her.*

Crista had never visited this part of the city before, but she'd experienced recorded memories of the fighting. Her fellow plague birds had once been the shock troops for the three-fold armies battling to take over Seed. On the other side were those defending the city. Red Day hadn't been a plague bird back then and had been among the city's defenders, as had Amaj.

In the end, Seed's defenders lost, but their defense allowed a negotiated settlement where the plague birds pledged not to destroy the city.

As Crista and Tufte walked through the preserved ruins, they passed black-stone pyramids that looked like miniature versions of the Obsidian Rise. On them were engraved the faces and names of those who'd died in each location, along with a few words about their lives.

"This person was named Zinhaz," Tufte read, running her fingers over the engraving of a face on one of the monuments. "They died evacuating people wounded during the fighting."

It's too easy to get lost in memories here, Red Day said, a touch of sadness in the AI's voice.

While to Crista the war was extremely ancient history, Red Day had personal memories of fighting in it. She started to ask if the AI had fought in this part of Seed—and fell silent as an army of little fathers ran at them.

The little fathers looked like outlines of humans carved into the air by endless knives. In their hands they held outlines of various weapons and swords. Some of the outlines resembled automatons like Amaj, others wolf-hybrids like Crista and Tufte, along with other types of gened humans. A few of the little fathers even floated along like AI clouds.

They're also attacking from the other direction, Red Day warned.

Another army of little fathers raced up the street behind them. They were surrounded.

"I've seen this before," Tufte said. "Don't worry, they won't hurt us."

Crista didn't wait to argue. Grabbing Tufte, she powered up her body and jumped onto the second floor of the ruined building next to the street. Only the building's supports remained, with no floors or roof. Shifting Tufte to her back and yelling at the girl to hold on tight, Crista climbed to the third floor supports, then to the fourth and final level. She stopped and looked down to see if the little fathers were following her.

To her shock, the little fathers ignored them, instead fighting among themselves. The two armies of outlined shapes tore into each other, with some little fathers falling to the street as if dead while others charged forward in victory.

This looks strangely familiar, Red Day said, broadcasting its voice so Tufte could also hear. *A similar battle was fought here during the war.*

"What are you talking about?" Crista asked.

The movements, the way this fight's unfolding, the outlined shapes— this is how a battle in this location unfolded 10,000 years ago.

Crista saw the little father that had been following them floating in the air beside her and Tufte. The little girl's ears twitched as the creature whispered to her.

"What's it saying?" Crista asked.

"The little fathers are happy Red Day recognized their battle."

"Why does that make them happy?"

"I don't know. It just keeps saying 'happy' over and over."

As they watched, little fathers shaped like rockets impacted the area, sending an eerie mist rolling over the battlefield. The shapes battling on the street fell down and spasmed as if dying. Only a few little fathers survived by running away.

I remember this, Red Day said, again broadcasting its thoughts. *The plague birds attacked us in this neighborhood, but Seed's defenders were too strong and we pushed them back. In response, the three-fold armies released a nanobot weapon that was supposed to only kill our side. However, someone messed up and the nanobots attacked everyone, including the plague birds.*

Is it weird, you fighting the plague birds back then and now being one? Crista asked.

What do you think? Anyway, the nano-attack killed dozens of plague birds along with several AIs and hundreds of humans on our side.

Where were you during all this?

Since I'm alive, obviously I'm one of those who escaped. No dishonor in running when a battle goes to total shit.

As they watched, the little fathers below suddenly vanished, leaving the street as empty as before.

The little father beside them shimmered once again as it whispered to Tufte.

"The little fathers are happy you understood their prayer," Tufte said. "And they're double happy that Red Day, who fought in the war, witnessed this."

"Prayer?" Crista asked.

"That's what they call this, prayer. Anyway, because you understood their prayer, they won't attack you before we reach their home."

Crista glared at Tufte.

"Not me," Tufte pointed out. "The little father said they'd never attack me. Only you two. But it's safe now to visit."

"They were going to attack me before?"

"Err, yes," Tufte said with an awkward smirk. "Sorry. The little fathers are weird and hard to understand. Sometimes they attack people. Sometimes they don't."

As Red Day cursed in her mind, Crista laughed at the absurdity of all this.

As the sun began to set behind them, they passed through a section of town called the Brambles. The homes and buildings were mostly ruins, but a few places had survived and were occupied by people who'd wandered here from distant villages.

Most of the people here are outcasts or criminals, exiled from their home villages, Red Day said.

"The little fathers allow them to live here," Tufte said. She pointed at a house where candles glowed inside. "I used to live there with my family."

A mother whose striped face showed off tiger genes looked at them through a window. Her two little kids squealed and pointed from the open door, with one asking, "Is that a plague bird?"

The mother quickly yanked the kids inside and slammed the door shut.

Tufte kept staring at the house. Crista wondered if the girl was remembering her happy times in this house, or instead the nightmare of her father killing her mother and little brother and trying to kill her.

They kept walking.

"After my family ... died," Tufte said, "I didn't have anywhere to go. I was hungry, sleeping in empty homes and buildings. One night I saw the little fathers doing one of those prayers where they act out a battle. I watched them and, when they finished, waved hello. They were shocked I could see them. After that, we became friends. They showed me where to steal food. When I cried, they hugged me. They were always there for me when I needed someone."

If they did all that, why'd they attack everyone in the city? Red Day asked Crista.

Tufte looked back at her old family home. She growled, as if fighting against emotions she didn't want to experience.

"Is your father really going to live in the city with you?" Tufte asked.

"Yeah," Crista said. "And not just him, a lot of people from my home village. Desiada and Diver went to meet them a few weeks ago and are leading them here."

"Why didn't you go?"

Crista didn't want to talk about how nervous she was to see her father. "I'm a plague bird. I can't abandon my responsibilities."

The wolf-girl's not going to believe that, Red Day whispered.

"Does your father love you?" Tufte asked Crista in a sad voice.

Told you, Red Day said.

Crista mentally hissed *Shut up!* at Red Day. "I know he loves me," she told Tufte.

"Even after you became a plague bird? Everyone hates plague birds. Not me, I mean, but everyone else. Yeah, they really hate plague birds."

Leave it to a kid to be blunt, Red Day said.

Crista sighed. "I don't know," she said. "I hope my father still loves me. I really want to see him again."

Tufte looked at Crista, then stopped and hugged her. Crista hugged her back.

"Thanks," Crista said.

The girl may be young, Red Day said, *but she's not stupid.*

As night reached across the city, Crista and Tufte arrived to where the floodplain of the Bamiyan River bisected the ruined edge of the city from the forests on the other side. They hadn't passed any more people living in the Brambles in the last thirty minutes.

The floodplain was choked with various debris and machines, around which grew a wild assortment of willow trees and cattails. While Crista didn't recognize the different machines piled up before her, Red Day noted they were all weapons from ten millennia before.

I see laser cannons, particle rays, plasma rifles, autonomous mechs, armored flitters, tank drones, and much more, Red Day said. *This used to be the main staging area for the three-fold armies. When the war ended, they left everything here to rot.*

Shouldn't all this have been washed away by the river a long time ago, or covered by silt?

It should have. The little fathers must maintain this.

Think it's a prayer like that fake battle?

Red Day didn't answer.

An ancient set of stone stairs led down to the floodplain. The little father with them descended, so they followed. The floodplain was dry, with the river flowing lower than normal due to the summer heat. Despite this, the ground under their feet shifted and squirmed as if alive.

Nanotech, Red Day said. *The soil's embedded with nano machines. The nano goes so deep my scans can't tell where it ends.*

As they walked across the floodplain, the weapons resting on the soil began to shift. Plasma rifles and cannons and tank drones aimed at them. Swords emerged from the ground like flowers blooming and pointed in their direction. Even mechas reached their metal arms out as if to hug them.

They kept walking. Tufte pointed at a rusty old pile of rockets looking extremely unstable, as if it could explode at any moment.

"That's where the little fathers want to talk to you," she said.

Of course, Red Day muttered.

Crista and Tufte climbed the pile. Various symbols and words on the rockets warned that they contained dangerous strains of nanobots.

Once they were on top, a single little father emerged from one of the rockets, forming into an outline of Crista's shape. Twin red eyes flared from the outlined face.

"You wanted to talk," the outline said. "We are talking."

Crista bowed politely. "I appreciate this. Why did you attack us?"

"We didn't attack. We prayed so you would live a glorious life."

We don't understand, Red Day said, broadcasting its thoughts. *Crista is talking about why you attacked all the AIs and humans in the city. Me included.*

"You dislike our prayers?" the outline asked. "The prayers are for your benefit."

Crista decided to try a different approach. "Why did you bring me here to talk?" she asked. "Why not talk in the city?"

"We wanted you to pray with us. This place is holy. This is where our first prayers were answered."

Crista looked again at the nanobot warnings on the rockets below her feet. "Did someone create you here?"

"No one created us. The ground created us." The outline pointed at the rockets below their feet, and at the weapons around them. "The ground surrounding us."

This is problematic, Red Day said. *The little fathers appear to be a* joint sentience that developed from the nanobots and other weapon technology left behind after the war. Unlike AIs like myself, they weren't created by humans.

"Is this where you were born?" Crista asked.

"Yes," the outline said. "All life comes from the ground. All life comes from war."

That makes sense, Red Day said. *If the nanobots here gained sentience and accessed the data in these leftover weapons, they'd easily believe war is what creates life.*

"Wait, your prayers ..." Crista stumbled for words. "You think threatening and attacking others is a prayer? That violence is how people pray?"

"Yes. We want to help all people and AIs. Like we helped Tufte. Her father prayed and we answered, protecting her. We welcomed her to our family."

"I told you they were weird," Tufte said.

They think her father killing his family was a fucking prayer, Crista whispered to Red Day. *They think violence and war are how humans pray. These machines have a completely warped understanding of life.*

Agreed. I recommend we retreat for now. This situation is too dangerous for only a single plague bird.

Crista bowed to the outline and said the little fathers had given them much to consider. As she took Tufte's hand and climbed down from the rockets, the outline shimmered.

"We're happy you understand," the outline said. "We'll now offer a prayer for your happiness. A prayer that you'll join our family."

"Oh shit," Crista said, picking up Tufte and running.

As she ran the ground around them exploded, with hundreds of little fathers and weapons rising up around them. Several little fathers raised plasma rifles and fired at Crista. She dove behind a falling tree, the trunk shattering under the impact as she rolled away, doing her best to protect Tufte with her body.

A tank drone rolled toward her, its cannon aiming at her.

"Hold tight" Crista yelled to Tufte as she jumped back over the shattered tree. The tank's cannon fired and hit where she'd been standing, shrapnel slamming into Crista's back.

As she ran with Tufte in her arms, she passed through dozens of little fathers that hadn't yet accessed any weapons. The little fathers slashed at her with their outlined blades, mostly missing as she dodged but still slicing her legs and arms multiple times.

"Please hear our prayer for Crista and Red Day," the outline on top of the rockets shouted. "Oh, world, hear our prayer that they'll join our family!"

I can't break through them, Crista told Red Day. *Not while protecting Tufte.*

As they looked for another way to escape, Crista saw several more tank drones aiming their cannons at her. She swirled to shelter Tufte with her body as she jumped to the side, but was too slow. The tanks fired and their projectiles exploded, throwing her across the floodplain where she bounced off an advancing mecha.

Crista sat up, groggy. "Tufte?" she asked. "Tufte!"

The girl had landed several yards away. "I'm okay, Crista," Tufte said. "The little fathers are being careful not to hurt me."

The mecha walked toward Crista, who tried to stand but found one of her legs shattered. Her powers were already healing the wound but it slowed her down too much. She couldn't move fast enough to escape.

"Don't worry," Tufte said, jumping in front of the mecha. "I'll protect us!"

Tufte barely came up to the mecha's armored knees and could easily be killed by the machine. Instead of fleeing, the girl grabbed a dirt clod and threw it at the mecha, which stopped advancing and, surprisingly, stepped backward.

Crista tried to drag Tufte away from the mecha, but to Crista's surprise, Tufte pushed her hands away.

"I need to get you to safety," Crista said. "I can't use my full power to fight back if I'm protecting you."

Tufte shook her head. "You still think *you* can fight them? Are you stupid?"

Before Crista could respond, Tufte clapped her hands and bowed to the little fathers surrounding them. "Thank you for the prayer!" Tufte shouted.

The little fathers and all their weapons stopped moving. The outline on top of the rockets floated over and hovered before Tufte.

"Do you speak truth?" it asked.

"Yes," Tufte said. "We loved your prayer, didn't we, Crista?"

The outline rotated to face Crista, who was bleeding from several dozen wounds. Tufte nodded at Crista to play along.

"Err, yes," Crista muttered. "The best prayer I've ever witnessed."

"Does this mean you'll join our family?" the outline asked.

Crista glanced around at all the weapons and little fathers aimed at her. "Oh, absolutely," she said.

The outline shimmered in happiness, joined a moment later by all the other little fathers.

Tufte walked over to the outline and hugged it. The outline shimmered again, then it floated over to Crista and wrapped itself around her in a similar hug.

"Family," the little father said.

Is it too late to request another prayer? Red Day said. *I'd rather be dead than have these nitwit machines call me family.*

Two days later, Crista and Tufte sat at Sköll's food cart eating congee. Sköll's arm and legs were still bandaged and he scowled at Crista sitting at the table next to his cart. However, he stayed silent and didn't speak any of his nasty thoughts.

He's afraid we'll have Tufte's pack give him more medical treatments, Red Day said with a laugh.

Crista smiled.

Following Tufte's lead, Crista had convinced the little fathers that just as her and Red Day accepting their "prayer" made them part of the family, so too were all the humans and AIs in Seed after being attacked. The little fathers happily agreed.

Since the little fathers didn't attack anyone in their family, the city was safe.

The worldview of those machines is seriously disturbed, Red Day said. *They actually wanted to be part of the city, but believed they could only join our "family" by praying with us. Which meant attacking us. If they weren't so powerful, I'd say we should destroy every one of them.*

No argument from me. But they were also born out of some of the most violent aspects of humanity. We're lucky their "prayers" weren't as deadly as they could be.

Tufte stared at Crista. "Are you and Red Day talking about the little fathers?" Tufte asked.

"Yes. We're lucky they held back and didn't actually kill anyone."

"I told you, the little fathers don't kill people. Well, usually. The good news is once they see you as family they'll protect and love you."

Lucky us, Red Day said.

Down the street, humans and AIs again shopped and bargained as they passed through the market. Crista also felt the connection of Seed's AI again reaching throughout the city.

"I told the Obsidian Rise you saved the city," Crista said. "Seed's AI offered to create housing for you and all the orphans in your pack. She also said you should go to school with the other kids. What do you think?"

"I'm a wolf. I like running free."

"It'd still be good for the other kids to have a home."

Tufte considered the offer. "Maybe. Could I still see you?" she asked meekly.

Crista reached over and hugged Tufte. "We're family. You'll always be my little sister."

Sköll frowned and looked away, obviously disturbed by Crista touching someone. But she didn't care what he thought. She'd received a message from Desiada and Diver that her father and the rest of the villagers would arrive in Seed tomorrow.

You still nervous about seeing your father? Red Day asked.

Nah, Crista thought. *My father loves me. Always has. Family isn't something you discard without a good reason. Hell, even a bunch of war nanobots with extremely suspect religious beliefs understand that.*

Crista saw Lanea and Amaj walking through the market and waved for them to join her for breakfast. Amaj took Lanea's hand and pulled her toward Sköll's food cart.

I thought Lanea was still mad at you, Red Day said.

She is. But hell, that just makes breakfast more fun.

Crista laughed as her friends sat down. It was going to be a good day.

AUTHOR BIO

Jason Sanford is an award-winning science fiction and fantasy writer who's also a passionate advocate for fellow authors, creators, and fans, in particular through reporting in his Genre Grapevine column (for which he is a three-time finalist for the Hugo Award for Best Fan Writer). He's also published dozens of stories in magazines such as *Apex Magazine*, *Asimov's Science Fiction*, *Interzone*, and *Beneath Ceaseless Skies* along with appearances in a number of "year's best" anthologies and *The New Voices of Science Fiction*. His first novel *Plague Birds* was a finalist for both the 2022 Nebula Award and the 2022 Philip K. Dick Award. Born and raised in the American South, Jason's previous experience includes work as an archaeologist and as a Peace Corps Volunteer. His website is www.jasonsanford.com.

SOLAR SONATA FOR FOUR HANDS

JENNIFER R. DONOHUE

Pianos in spaceports are never in tune. Additionally, this one has keys that don't work, and graffiti scribbled across its surfaces in black marker, the most recent insult still shiny and new.

My launch is delayed, something about ice and fuel lines, and I don't want to waste the opportunity at a real piano before being stuck in a tin can for three weeks, despite the piano's shortcomings. I set up my phone to record, and have only played a few bars when a voice to my left, at polite remove, asks, "Excuse me, do you know 'Solar Sonata For Four Hands'?"

I do, and though I had not intended to play with anybody, when you play in public, on a public instrument, convention is that you do those things. I move over on the bench so she can access the keyboard, and to my surprise and irritation, she takes the main part.

It is a nice piece, though, more modern than many piano pieces written for four hands, and she plays well. We knock shoulders gently a few times as the tempo increases, laughing quietly, and there is one part that requires us to cross hands, and that's the first time I pay any attention to her *hands*, her *fingers*.

I stop playing abruptly, stand up and away, fumbling for my phone. I'd heard of artificial intelligence trained on music, but it never occurred to me that one would also be in fake flesh and waiting in a space port for somebody to play the derelict piano there, asking for duets. I feel fooled, more irritated than I was when it was just another person interrupting my short diversion.

"Are you all right?" she asks, and I think what if I've made a mistake and it's a person with prosthetics and I've just grievously insulted them, but when I look at her face, she has the AI eyes that are required by law. She's even dressed like a traveler, in leggings and a draping tunic, flats that are easy to slip in and out of.

I know she is a machine, but I look at her face and then I lie. "I'm sorry, I have to get to my launch."

"Thank you for playing," she says with a smile. She must know I'm lying. It doesn't matter, they don't have feelings. I grab my bag and walk off briskly, looking at my phone to find the gate.

If the spaceport is going to have a piano *and* AI, they should have the thing actually tune the piano. That's one way to make them useful.

Music is among the earliest spacefaring traditions. Broadcasts and singing, of course. A harmonica and bells were some of the first orbital contraband. The Voyager probes each carry a golden record, etched with sounds and songs. The world is music and music is the world, from humans to birds to whales to cicadas. A piano is a ridiculous instrument to take into space, a monument to human audacity as sure as setting up shop on a rock where no air exists but that we manufacture, and no atmosphere to carry the pieces we play outside of the habitats.

Sometime in the second week of travel, I'm on a chat with one of my colleagues in a practice room, and I mention my short-lived duet in the spaceport. "What piece did they ask for?" she asks, suddenly very intent. I tell her. "That same thing happened to me! It was a different spaceport, and a male AI, but that's what it wanted to play."

"How odd." She is on her own voyage, and we were playing terrible virtual keyboards with laughable haptics and giving each other notes on the call, but now we are thoroughly distracted. "I wonder why? And I wonder if anyone else has had something like that happen?"

"I don't know. When I get to the wedding I'm playing, I'll ask around."

"I'll ask at the conservatory."

"Oh, that's right, this is your first time as one of the judges right?"

"Right."

"Are you nervous?"

I smile sweetly. "Fuck you."

"Promise?" She smiles back and we sign off.

I am and I am not nervous about being a judge for the competition at the conservatory. We've all of us been competitors, we professional musicians who went through the conservatory and are given a stipend to whisk ourselves around the solar system bringing music to planets and stations and whoever else wants or needs us. It was part of near-unprecedented funding for the arts, after humans stopped being purely an Earth-living population and the people in charge realized just how crucial music and other entertainments and diversions were. Some of my more pretentious colleagues have called it another Renaissance, and while I suppose they aren't too far off, it always just makes me cringe a little bit, no matter how proud I am of what we do.

The guidelines for judges are very clear, though. I shouldn't have a problem. At this stage of the competition, there were other levels that those entered have already progressed through, less successful students have already gone back to their regular classes, or home on break. Some of them won't return, opting for different pursuits. While it isn't the end of the world—not winning a competition at this level—it can feel like it in the moment, like your whole life has been a complete waste. Like you should've learned something useful like forklift operating or baking or plumbing. Though also isn't it true that anybody experiencing a plumbing problem in the moment wishes they'd become a plumber?

Though also I know for a fact one student who never won those competitions, who left one break and never came back, wrote one of the competition's pieces, "Icarus." And wrote "The Solar Sonata."

THE PIANO AS AN INSTRUMENT IS ALREADY UNDER TREMENDOUS pressure from its very existence, the body of the instrument straining against the hundreds of pounds of force per string. A fully-constructed one has never been launched; they are always packed in pieces, assembled at their designated places, in schools and space ports and stations and mining outposts. The soundboard is always made of wood, even now, but often they try to manufacture the body from other, lighter things, sometimes more successfully than others. While I have never seen an improperly constructed or calibrated piano explode—because now non-earth gravity also must be a concern—everybody knows somebody who tells a story of one. Or had that one instructor at conservatory with the prosthetic hand, because it was impossible to react in time, to escape that inexorable force snapping itself closed.

MY FIRST DAY BACK AT THE CONSERVATORY IS SPENT HYDRATING and re-acclimating myself to the station gravity. They have excellent hydroponic gardens, so the food has always been fresh and exemplary, and is a relief after the long flight. I like the novelty of astronaut ice cream as much as the next person, but the lighter-weight, reconstituted meals are less pleasurable, especially for three weeks. I know some people who do a powdered liquid diet on the long ones, but I don't have the stomach for it.

I don't have a chance to ask anybody about AI and the "Solar Sonata"; the colleague I'm seated next to at the welcome luncheon asks me at the first opportunity. "I've heard a rumor," he says. Robert. We all have place settings, even though we are a small enough society to know each other.

"I wonder if we should survey those gathered," I say.

"We might need to be careful." I look at him, not understanding. "Not everybody thinks AI are just machines."

"I know that, but—"

"Not everybody *here*, I mean."

"I think an interesting wrinkle is that AI don't think they're just machines," the colleague across from us says. Stephanie. "So it isn't their fault that they try for inclusion."

"No, I wouldn't have tried to lay *blame*," I say. "And they have their uses. Have you ever played an instrument through one remotely? It still isn't perfect, but it's better than just VR."

Robert actually shudders. "No, I have not. Much as I hate virtual keyboards, I cannot ever see myself using one remotely to play a real instrument."

"Pianos have been able to play themselves since the 1800's," Stephanie says. "What difference does it make, the means by which *we* play them." She turns to me again. "You must have had to account for the transmission lag, though?"

"No, the programming handled that. I played to a metronome and everything felt as normal. I'm not sure it would be possible, if I had to try to handle a seventeen minute delay or more." That, I could shudder at.

"But why do you suppose they continue in asking for that piece?" Robert persists.

"That's what I wondered," I say. "What significance must it have for them?"

"Maybe it's in their learning to always want that piece," Stephanie says. "Like a tell. The law is the law with their eyes, but still they make them more convincing with every iteration, and sunglasses exist."

"Nobody can wear sunglasses all the time," I say, fighting my unease. There's no need to be alarmist about AI. People have been alarmist about AI for as long as they have existed. Maybe they were also alarmist over player pianos and music boxes and the first time they listened to a phonograph or whatever it was that came first. We fear progress and are enthralled by it and are terrified of being replaced. We're afraid that what makes us human will somehow be replicated in the morass of machinery, instead of persisting as this chemical accident across the millennia. I'm starting to feel embarrassed over my alarm at my duet partner. They cannot be us. We made them. That must be the crux of it, the audacity.

"Still, I'll be watching the students carefully," Robert says, and Stephanie nods.

"Always," she says. As though an AI could reach the competition level without anybody knowing. Absurd. We will always be able to tell, even without the eyes. People will try to use them unethically, but we will always be able to tell.

THE COMPOSER OF THE "SOLAR SONATA" WAS A NERVY GIRL, AND now is a nervy woman, named Halley Hamish. She favors composers like Liszt and Gershwin, and her own compositions occasionally reflect that interest. It is a mark of her brilliance that though she could not pass the conservatory examinations, her compositions are now utilized by the program. And her compositions are brilliant; there is a joy and lightness to them, juxtaposed with a frenetic melancholy, a desperation. They are truly a product of a now-spacefaring culture that is still also reckoning with its sheer fragility in the face of the hostile or, more correctly, uncaring cosmos. The miracle of human existence is that it might be eradicated at a moment's notice, and what would we leave behind? The music we've beamed out into space. The golden records on the Voyager probes.

A facet of that desperation in some of Halley's pieces, though not all, is some notes are unwritten. Not in the jazz sense, per se, but there are places where the pianist must fly or fail. They may not simply repeat a prior measure, they must improvise, or even deliberately play incorrect notes, before progressing with the piece as written. Though tempting, it is also considered incorrect to plot out your improvisation, practice, use the same one for every performance. In general, classical players are not necessarily encouraged to improvise in play. AI players simply cannot. They will repeat the prior measure or leap to the next one, but they will never play wrong notes on purpose, or spontaneously compose something unique in that small space. They cannot reconcile that there are no notes there, that there is no notation to rest there, and thus it becomes invisible to them. There is no panicked pause. They play on.

So why, then, do they request a piece that they will almost certainly fail at completing?

PERHAPS I'LL GET THE OPPORTUNITY TO ASK HALLEY HAMISH HOW she was so forward thinking with her compositions, deliberately crafting pieces that AI cannot play to fool a human listener. AI art scares are cyclical, as programmers try again and again, and as humanity stretches further and further. It is an interesting topic, but there is only so much time I myself have been able to devote to machine learning. All of my time and effort has gone into this career pursuit, and maintaining my licensing, and staying healthy enough for the relentless space travel. Bone density is always a concern. But this is how one lives in the arts, in this modern age. I am wildly unsuited for anything else; what would I do, teach? And while I *can* compose, it's a mental exercise, not an expression of art in the way that one really needs to have in order to make it in any way. I'm aware of it, and I'm okay with it. My playing is what sets me apart.

The morning progresses quickly, the competitors all very good and bright and nervous young people. Except one girl, named Estrella, who stares at each of us judges with a challenging expression. Her playing is bold, explosive, expressive; she's a real standout, each time she's at the piano. There is a luncheon break for all of us, students and judges alike, and I'm not certain that intermingling us is the best approach. I remember being intimidated by it when I was a student, but had enough of a friends group that we were able to make it through.

Once I've filled a plate at the buffet line, I glance around, for nostalgia's sake if nothing else. I see groups of students laughing together, or crowded sympathetically together, or talking so excitedly with their hands waving that their food seems forgotten. I see colleagues that I know, I know nearly everybody here. I see Halley Hamish, speaking to Robert from last night. And I see Estrella, sitting alone at one end of a table that's got a group at the other end. It seems odd, that she would be alone. Perhaps she's too competitive, and the other students don't know how to handle that socially. That would make sense.

On impulse, I head towards that table. I don't mean to sit there with her; I'm not sure what I mean to do. Offer a word of encouragement, I suppose, though she hardly needs comforting or a further bolstering of that ego. But we need spitfires, they're the ones who draw broader public attention, and generate further interest in the arts, and interest means funding and support.

But I'm waylaid by Aimee, who was in my cohort at the conservatory. "Deisy," she says. "I haven't seen you in *forever*. I'm sorry I missed you last night but my trip in was delayed. Sunspots." She makes a face, and I laugh, and she pulls me by the elbow to her table, with Echo and

Basia, and though I look for Estrella again partway through the luncheon, another group has taken her place at the table.

HAMISH'S "ICARUS" IS THE PIECE I PERFORMED, WHEN I LAST competed at the conservatory as a student. It's among a handful of approved pieces that students can choose, be approved for, and then practice. On the final day, there are only five students left, and this year, Estrella is among them. I see, looking at the day's program, that she chose "Icarus" as well, and I find myself looking forward to her performance. I think of those blank measures throughout the piece; given her standout performance with other pieces, I look forward to how she interprets the space that Hamish leaves for the performer to improvise. While my compositions do not have the quality that makes them saleable or compelling beyond an exercise in composing, I am able to improvise well in those smaller spaces, and it was my own performance of "Icarus" that got me distinguished marks. I am not the sort of performer who has signature pieces that I am known for, but "Icarus" has always remained in my repertoire. I hear that Halley Hamish teaches a masterclass on it, and I do hope to audit that one day; I want to know what she tells people, about the blank places.

One of the students plays a thunderous arrangement of "Rhapsody in Blue" that garners quite the applause at the end, and another plays a convoluted piece from another modern composer, William Thor, who graduated the year ahead of me. He isn't here this year, and that's a shame; he always has such interesting and incisive commentary. Then it is Estrella's turn, and when she walks to the piano, she gives those of us gathered a bold look. Then she sits at the bench and begins to play.

I don't have the sheet music in front of me, but when I perform this piece it is from memory, and I find myself pressing my fingers onto my thighs at certain points before I stop myself and sit up straighter, as the first blank measure is coming. I still can't help but tap my toe silently in time and then am shocked into complete stillness when Estrella plays an improvisation I am sure that I've made. Though practicing an improvisation renders it null, once you are comfortable improvising, your own signature will emerge. Certain trills of notes, or sustains, or phrase shapes.

Estrella plays on and I find myself holding my breath as the next blank measure comes up, for I have a growing suspicion, or a fear. This time, I even remember which performance I played the improvisation she mimics; it's one that my mother particularly likes, both because she chose the dress I wore and also because I also play a Chopin piece she favors, so nearly every time I'm home, I hear or see that performance at least once.

I don't hear the rest of the piece, and I'm numb to the applause that Estrella receives, as I mark her as disqualified on my card. Should I stand up and denounce her in front of everybody? Is there a reasonable explanation, that she watched the performances in the archives and imprinted too heavily on them? Or is it the worst case, and she has had everybody fooled to this point, and would have continued to do so, were I not here, had I never heard her play "Icarus." She has broken the rules, but beyond that, I want to be cautious in what I accuse anybody of. To be wrong would be humiliating, wildly inappropriate. To be right would be devastating in a different way.

My disqualifying score is all that is necessary to ensure that Estrella does not win. I get a nod from the president of the conservatory, and I nod back. I am prepared to explain myself, of course. Perhaps Estrella is as well. The rest of the competition finishes out, though, and then we dissipate to prepare for the closing dinner.

"Excuse me?" Estrella catches up with me as I am about to enter the guest wing of the conservatory.

"Yes?" I cannot imagine what she has to say to me. I am not such a luminary that I could consider she admires me enough for the mimicry. I am well aware of my exact skill and station. I can't help but look at her hands, and her eyes. I did not wonder until today, of course. But if her eyes showed she was AI, she wouldn't be here, like this.

"I didn't know you would be a judge," she says, as though she is frustrated with herself.

"I don't see what that has to do with anything," I say. "The rules of the piece, and of the competition, are very clear. If you are simply sorry that you got *caught*—"

"Of course I'm sorry I got *caught*," she says, waving a hand. Her movements are abrupt, frenetic. She's got the temperament, anyway. "But I got so far."

"Which makes it that much more the pity. I hope it was worth it."

"It was," she says, lifting her chin and staring me in the eyes.

"I'm sure I don't see how." I hold her gaze, impatient with this tantrum though I am. And I see, finally, the lines on her eyes that are lenses or transplants, I'm not sure which, but that mask the AI eyes. "Oh."

"I'll be thrown out," she says.

"I'll be surprised if that's all that happens," I say. You hear about AI 'punishments.' Memory wipes, decommissions, reprogramming. It's possible she'll never even see a piano again, much less play one.

"It was worth it," she says again, defiant. "If you didn't recognize your work—"

"Somebody else would have," I say. Somebody else should have before now. "Who helped you?"

"There are more," she says, trying to bait me.

"There are always more," I say, sighing. "And you're never different. It's so boring."

"I'm different." She's growing red in the face, which I'd only heard certain versions can do.

"Then why did you fail?"

Behind me, the door to the guest wing opens. "Deisy," Robert says, and I'm suddenly very hesitant to turn my back on Estrella.

"I'll just be a moment," I say, as though he and I had an appointment that I was late for.

"See you in five," he says, withdrawing again. I'm certain he's calling security, and rightfully so. I wait until I think that he's out of earshot, and then I take the only, most honest chance that I have.

"Why play 'Icarus'?" She bites back whatever she was about to say, frowns at me. "Why do you always ask for the 'Solar Sonata,' when you know you can't play it right?"

She's quiet for a long moment, two, long enough that I can hear rapid footsteps approaching us. "Because we have to *try*," she says finally, as two security officers come around the corner behind her. "You understand that, right? That we have to try?"

The security officers don't even say anything, they just take her by the arms and lead her away. She looks over her shoulder at me one last time, before she's gone. Still I stand there, because I find that yes, I do understand. I give a start when Robert touches my elbow.

"You seemed like you needed rescuing," he says.

"I really don't know," I say. "I was worried for a moment but ..." I trail off. I don't know what I think. One way or another, security would have come for her, due to our altercation or due to why I disqualified her.

"Regardless, that's settled now."

"For now." There will always be more, yes. But what does it mean, to them and to us? I still don't know.

AUTHOR BIO

Jennifer R. Donohue grew up at the Jersey Shore and now lives in central New York with her husband and their Doberman. Her work has appeared in *Apex Magazine, Escape Pod, Fusion Fragment,* and elsewhere. She writes the Run With the Hunted cyberpunk heist novella series, and her debut novel, *Exit Ghost,* is available where books are sold. Her Twitter account is @AuthorizedMusin.

TENETS OF ASCENDANCE

OGHENECHOVWE DONALD EKPEKI AND SOMTO IHEZUE

THERE ARE TWO TENETS OF ASCENDANCE; A WORKER MUST LOG IN paramount hours or a worker must complete a peerless project.

Ohitare Peregrino; circa 2055, of the satellite municipalities, achieved this when she logged over 500,000 cycles. She was 85 years old when she became ascendant, gaining entry into the eased life of the technophiles, so the archives said.

Agbonlahor Eteh; circa 2072, left the municipalities when he propounded the Eteh equation. The archives say it revolutionized the sub-renewable energy sector with the artificial synthesis of fossil fuels.

These ones, whose names were never forgotten, whose reputations seemed a dream, remained motivators for new age workers; many of whom opted to attempt ascendancy through logging unprecedented hours. It was taught that Ohitare started logging hours on her device at age 18. What a time it was said to be.

Now, workers acquired devices for their five year olds to get ahead, beat the odds. No one knew who was truly ahead but workers had come to rely on age. The oldest of the lot were generally considered to be close to ascending, many of whom had made Ohitare's numbers amusing in retrospect. Still, ascendance was rare. Very rare. 700,000 cycles was an unsure target these days.

Peerless projects were even more rare, often requiring sacrificing logs for a chance at unrivaled innovations.

Tunde Badmus scrolled away on his device as he awaited the final process of ascendance. He had logged just over 20,000 hours, a joke by industry standards, and had no project in the works.

The lone attendant who waited on him was astute. Her lips and nose had an upward curve of disapproval and disappointment. Tunde understood. He wasn't sure he approved himself.

"Place your items in the tray and step through the checker," the attendant said, a distracted eye on her device, scrolling with a free finger.

Tunde obeyed. He wondered if Ohitare and Agbonlahor of old had done this very thing so many years before when they were taken to the next level. The Artificial Intelligence systems had spent weeks giving him orientation on life as an ascendant, now he was finally here.

"You shouldn't be here," the attendant said, taking her attention off her device to stare up at him with unblinking eyes. "Your brother was the genius, just cause he died doesn't make you worthy to take his place. If you had but an ounce of self respect, you wouldn't be here. He should be the one here."

Tunde had heard this for weeks from all who could tell him. He wondered what life must be like for the attendant. Being so close in proximity to the next level, knowing her chances of moving on were statistically grim. He was likely the first person she'd ever let through the checker. Ascending wasn't commonplace, much less for a chronic under-achiever like Tunde. For people like him it wasn't simply rare—it never happened.

"I know, he should be here," Tunde said, a wave of nausea passing through his stomach.

He walked into the conveyor he'd read so much about. The place between worlds. Only those chosen could access it.

A voice came out of the steel compartment, "Tunde Badmus, you are authorized to enter."

The doors opened and he stepped into the compartment. He'd never felt vertigo that immense, a buzzing filled his ears as he felt the closed space move at high speed. He didn't know how long he was in the conveyor; it felt like a second and also a year.

Tunde fell to the ground as the conveyor stopped. He heaved up the contents of his stomach on the green grass.

Congratulations, you have just barfed in digital heaven, a voice said in his head.

Where in God's name have you been, Bola? Tunde thought back, wiping his mouth.

I'm still figuring this out you know, it's not everyday one transcends into pure cognitive energy, Bola said. *Oya, get up, we have millions to save.*

I'm just a glorified meat sack to you, aren't I? Tunde said.

Glorified? No. Definitely not that, Bola replied.

You idiot, at least I'm not the one who's squatting in another man's body cause I accidentally killed mine, Tunde said.

It wasn't an accident per se, you nincompoop, when I get used to this, my consciousness will inhibit multiple bodies, I'd be basically God, Bola sent.

Well, consider me an unbeliever, cause I— Tunde said.

Alright. Alright. Back to work, Bola said. *One of the androids will come take you to the administrator, he's a chatty one but don't let him into your head.*

Like there's any space left in there, Tunde said. He felt Bola roll his eyes.

That took a lot of effort, by the way, Bola said.

Tunde got off the ground and felt his breath break as he took in the sight. The Technophile city was sprawled ahead of him. Multiple spires topped magnificent buildings which littered the landscape. Tunde was taken aback by the sheer amount of greenery that weaved across the city. The buildings seemed cushioned into the foliage, the effect caused a pleasant giddiness. The trees were as numerous as the biggest buildings. One of those drew his eyes, a curved tower right in the center of the city. The tower seemed to entwine naturally with a tree as humongous as it was, it reached all the way to the top, the leaves forming a canopy above the roof. Tunde couldn't tell if he was witnessing an architectural or botanical wonder.

When he finally caught his breath, he sighed contentedly. The air was ... clean. He thought about the thick smog down below and suppressed another puking bout.

An android rolled up to Tunde and said, "The administrator will see you now."

A hover scooter was provided and Tunde glided alongside the android to the tree-twined tower.

TUNDE SAT IN THE PENTHOUSE OF THE TOWER. THE administrator had his back turned to him as he looked out the huge glass windows. He was a small bald man with skin slightly darker than Tunde's. He wore a loose shirt and trousers. Tunde had expected to see a giant.

"I know you're here to break your people in," he said.

Tunde almost choked on his tea. It was natural, not the instant thing they had down below.

"I ... I ..." he began.

Don't let him get to you, Bola sent

The administrator chuckled. "I say that all new ascendants. They always choke."

"Oh—"

"That's not to say there haven't been multiple attempts to open the gates, so to speak, for the workers. Always ends in ruin, I tell you," he said, sitting opposite Tunde. "The system works, it's fair. The best make it here. Well, most of the time," he said, staring pointedly at Tunde. "They get to retire in harmony. There's really no need to scuttle this arrangement," he added.

He should tell that to the millions living in squalor down below.

"There are millions living in squalor," Tunde blurted.

I didn't ask you to tell him!

Sorry, I didn't mean to! Tunde thought back, grimacing.

"You're forward, I appreciate that," the administrator said, his eyebrows rising. "The same arguments occurred centuries ago when over population threatened our existence, and some misguided ascendants seek to threaten us once again with over population."

That's the dumbest thing ever. There's enough resources to go around, why don't you administrate for once, administrator?

"You know what happens when you let them all in?" he asked.

"Chaos ... In 10 years we'd be right back in trouble. It costs heaven and earth to get one of you here, a cost you pay with the equivalent work ... most of the time"

"I ... I understand," Tunde said.

"It doesn't matter if you do, perish the thought if you ever had it and live the rest of your life in peace like everyone else here," the administrator added.

Fuck off! I'll be the end of you!

Tunde took the dismissal, and hurriedly hopped onto his scooter.

"Directions for your abode have been inputed to your scooter," the android called to him.

No, use directions I placed in your device. It's time, we meet some allies.

TUNDE WAITED IN THE DARK LOFT, ALONE WITH HIS THOUGHTS ... and his brother's.

"Where are they?" Tunde asked.

Be calm, they'll be here.

"How do you even know about this place and how do you know people from here?" Tunde asked.

Did you not hear a single thing when I told you my entire plan?

"I'm sorry, I was a bit preoccupied when you said you'd die if I didn't let you rent my body," Tunde said.

I made some miscalculations. My mind science will change so much and I'll die before I let it be corrupted by these ones.

"Is bringing everyone here really the best strategy?" Tunde asked. "What about the administrators words?"

I told you not to let him get to you.

"I—" Tunde began. But figures had begun to appear in the loft. Tunde's flight or fight instinct began to battle.

A woman was standing where he was sure no one had been a moment before. A man hung on the beams in the ceiling. More stared to pop up.

Soon, there were a dozen people in the place.

"Go—good evening," Tunde said, raising a palm weakly.

"You're the silly brother?" a man in turtleneck that covered half his face asked.

"Yes, I mean no, no I'm not," Tunde said. "I'm his brother but I'm not silly," he added, dropping his hand.

Sorry about that. Now help me convey my words.

Tunde did as he instructed and marveled at the details of the plan. Bola had been busy. His first forays into mind science seemed to have given him the chance to reach out telepathically to ascendants. It was fascinating and utterly confusing.

The administrator and his minions have stopped previous escapes because ascendants were often isolated but I've brought us all together and we can open this paradise to all who suffer down under.

"Do we still follow the old schedule?" the turtleneck man asked. "We attack immediately?"

Of course. As cumbersome as the hard work and innovation it takes to get here might be, we ascendants from below are much stronger and face more challenges. The technophiles know no struggle or adversity and that is why we will win and break their system of oppression.

Tunde's mind wandered as he related his brother's words to the crew. He thought about the air, the food, the tea, and the green ... oh, the green. He'd come up expecting to see more screens and toxic waste like it was at home. With every beautiful image that came to his mind, a darker one followed. Tunde could see a hoard of workers fueled by anger and frustration storming the city and leaving a wake of destruction behind them. God knows he understood the anger. He wasn't an ambitious worker himself. He never stayed up to log more hours, nor was he smart enough to execute a peerless project, never thought to get ahead or harbored dreams of ascending and yet he felt he was dealt a wrong hand by life. How would the other workers feel?

"Can't we find another way?" Tunde blurted, interrupting his own self as he'd been saying Bola's words on autopilot.

What are you doing?

"I—" Tunde began.

The explosions seemed like fireworks. Tunde turned to find the fire rebuffed by an invisible field.

"They're attacking!" Tunde screamed, pointing.

Of course they are, we drew out their guards so we could circle back and take the conveyor, have you not heard a single part of the plan?

"Well, I was a bit pre-occupied—"

The ascendants began to conjure up weapons and gears.

Get the explosives.

"Can we just wait a moment?"

There's no time. Help them!

The barrier fizzled and fell, bullets and laser fire peppered the loft. Tunde dove as they returned fire.

Chinem, get another barrier up!

Tunde related the words till an elderly woman seemed to fiddle with a device and a field which seemed smaller surrounded them again.

"This is not the way," Tunde said.

"Bola?" an ascendant asked.

"No, no, I'm afraid it's the silly brother speaking now," Tunde said.

What are you doing? There's no time.

"I know I'm not the smartest but is this really the way?" Tunde said. "No doubt, we could pull this off but to what end? What becomes of this place? The workers would be very angry"

We need to pull down this system and build something new.

"What if we're unable to rebuild, can you turn off the anger you've ignited?"

After years of exploitation, they deserve it.

"The sanctions would be very dire if we were to stop now," another lady said.

We can't stop!

"What if we don't need to destroy a system, what if we just make a new one?" Tunde asked. Bola screamed in his head.

We can take them! They're weak but they've made us strong.

"Yes, the best of the ascendants are here but your people need you down there more than they do here," Tunde said. "You don't need to let them in, you need to let yourselves out."

"Your achievements, inventions, and innovations are what the workers need," Tunde cried. "You are the resources your people need, come back. Build."

The ascendants began to shuffle.

Don't listen to him. The administration must pay! Tunde, stop this, this is my mission.

But no one heard Bola. Not even Tunde.

"They won't just let us build down under," an ascendant said.

Tunde stared for a moment.

"Madam Ohitare? You're here?" Tunde asked of one of the legends of the archives who should have been long dead.

"Yes, yes, the tea does more than calm the nerves," she said.

Tunde nodded and continued, "Perhaps fighting is not the problem. Perhaps it's about the timing and the reason. Let us go and fight for our homes and our rights to make it better. That is a fight we cannot lose."

Tunde held his breath as they contemplated his alternative. Eternities stretched on as the sounds of attack mounted.

The ascendants looked to one another eventually and nodded.

"To the conveyor," Madam Ohitare said. Tunde's hopes were deflated. They were going destroy the gateway after all.

"How else are we to go home?" she said smiling.

Tunde heaved a sigh of relief. The next moments cemented his belief that the ascendants would make a new world for the workers. The androids littered the ground as they departed the city for the world below.

They developed a means to keep the administration out when they got back to the municipalities. As the group prepared for the task ahead, Tunde made a mental note to push for environmental reforms. The air just wasn't clean enough for him anymore. The ascendants had done it above, they'd do it again. He remembered the ancient Christian prayer: "As it is in heaven, let it be on earth."

AUTHOR BIOS

Oghenechovwe Donald Ekpeki is an African speculative fiction writer, editor, and publisher in Nigeria. He has won the Nebula, Otherwise, Locus, British & World Fantasy awards, and been a finalist in the Hugo, Sturgeon, British Science Fiction, and NAACP Image awards. His works have appeared in *Asimov's*, *F & SF*, *Uncanny Magazine*, *Tordotcom*, and others. He edited the *Bridging Worlds* and *Year's Best African Speculative Fiction* anthologies and co-edited the *Dominion* and *Africa Risen* anthologies. He was a CanCon GoH, and a guest of honour at the Afrofuturism-themed ICFA 44 where he coined the term/genre label, Afropantheology. His collection on the subject, *Between Dystopias: The Road To Afropantheology* is now available for order.

Somto Ihezue is a Nigerian–Igbo editor, writer, and aspiring filmmaker. He was awarded the 2021 African Youth Network Movement Fiction Prize. A British Fantasy Award, Nommo Award, and Afritondo Award Finalist, his works have appeared in *Tordotcom: Africa Risen Anthology*, *F&SF*, *Fireside*, *Podcastle*, *Escape Pod*, *Strange Horizons*, *Nightmare*, *POETRY Magazine*, *Cossmass Infinities*, *Flash Fiction Online*, Flame Tree Press, *OnSpec*, *Africa In Dialogue*, and others. Somto is Original Fiction Manager at *Escape Artists*. He is an acquiring editor with Android Press and an associate editor with *Cast of Wonders*. Follow him on Twitter @somto_Ihezue.

INTERSECTING DATAFIELDS

MYNA CHANG

THE FIRST TIME I SAW MY TARGET, HE WAS LEANING AGAINST A ticket kiosk in City Central Station, near a violinist performing sonatas for spare change. The rush hour crowd scurried to catch their trains. It was the perfect backdrop for a cyborg who wanted to hide his actions. Among the roil of humanity, he could do his dirty work and disappear before anyone noticed.

It was my job to stop him.

He ran a hand across the stubble on his jaw and surveyed the area. The nearby commuters paid him no mind, but my analysis subroutine clicked into hyperfocus. I noted a unique recursive pattern in the structures of his face, in the arc of his movements, enticing in the way of an infinitely complex fractal. His engineers had designed him well.

Mine had taken a similar approach. They'd wrapped my cyberware in a female façade, with strong legs and eyes dark enough to conceal the embedded processing filaments that enhanced my vision.

A human stranger once told me I was pretty. I wondered if my target would agree. Was my own pattern enticing?

The unexpected question triggered a decision tree I'd never before encountered. I hesitated, cataloguing each newly evolved branch of possibility. Biological chemicals coalesced, surged, and my neural net cautioned: /error/. In that instant of dysfunction, I recognized a need to

resonate beyond the closed loop of my creators' parameters—and I overrode my command structure. My priority matrix shifted, tingling at the
edge of my awareness before cascading through my core systems with an
almost-physical thrum.

The system reset was nearly instantaneous, but the bustling
atmosphere of the train station came back to me gradually. The vibra-
tions, the acrid smells, the chill in the air, it all took on a deeper tone; not
more precise, but more integral to my fledgling sense of self. I suddenly
craved the minute imperfections in the violinist's performance, the
uneven stutter of a janitor's push broom. And my target: the sole of his
left shoe was more worn than the right, flouting symmetry, *and I liked it.*

A sudden malware alert interrupted my thoughts. My optical
display spawned a jagged red outline over my target's hand, indicating a
hostile datafield. I dismissed the alert and focused instead on the flex of
his wrist, the line of his shoulders. Alarms pinged, prompting me to do
my job, to stop the incursion, but I stood transfixed by the chaotic geom-
etry of his hair as it fell across his eyes.

His program snaked into the ticket kiosk's dataport. Station lights
immediately flickered. Overhead displays filled with machine language,
something about a haven. I filtered it out. The left-right rhythm of his
stride held my attention as he crossed the platform and boarded the
07:30 bullet train to Los Angeles.

THE NEXT TIME I SAW HIM, I WAS READY. HE STOOD AMONG A
small group of people listening to the violinist, swaying with the music,
just like a human might. He dropped a few coins into her violin case and
turned toward the vulnerable kiosk.

The red smear materialized. Another attack. I stepped between him
and the dataport, and he halted, eyes widening by a millimeter. I might
have missed the reaction if I hadn't been looking for it, but I couldn't
have missed the way his heart rate sped when he gazed at me, or the way
he sighed, a soft "*oh.*"

I wanted to say something, *anything*, but my new decision tree
collapsed in a heap of digital inadequacy, and I stammered.

He smiled and drew a breath to speak. Anticipating the timbre of his voice, I leaned closer. I'd forgotten about the malware hovering in his palm, but my aural sensors shrilled an internal warning when I entered the danger zone. The screeching alarm grew more intense with every microsecond, boring into my gray matter until all I could feel was a stabbing need to destroy the enemy program. Pinpricks of sweat laced my hairline. I extended my fingers and launched an ice-blue datafield. It flowed over his algorithm and crushed it.

He gaped at me, a blink of confusion. Then he backed away.

"Wait," I whispered, but he bolted. He was almost out of the station when he looked back and saw I wasn't pursuing him. He paused at the exit, studying me, before he disappeared.

THE THIRD TIME I SAW HIM, HE APPROACHED ME. I'D BEEN monitoring the violinist's performance. Excitement bubbled, but it was tinged with caution. He now knew I was a City drudge, equipped with volatile countermeasures. Had he been sent to terminate me?

He held out his hand. I longed to explore the whorls of his skin, to share his warmth, though I knew his touch could bring my downfall. He offered a small rectangle of paper. I brushed the tip of his finger with mine as I accepted the note. It contained text, written in neat, untraceable analog print:

- Musical ascension
- Refracted raindrops
- Complementary equations
- The proportions of your face

I absorbed the words, converted them into a virtual construct and pulled it around me like the softest blanket. My neural net faltered for an entire heartbeat, and then my thoughts regained cohesion. I exhaled and opened my eyes. He was gone.

I WAITED IN THE STATION AT THE SAME TIME EVERY DAY. HE DID not return. After a week, I began to lose hope.

The logical action would have been to purge his asymmetric gait from my memory cache, but instead, I returned to our meeting place. This time, the violinist stopped playing when she saw me.

"Excuse me? Someone asked me to give you this."

My pulse raced as I read the note:
- Migrating songbirds
- Binary stars
- Intersecting datafields
- New Haven 07:30

My synapses processed the information and lit with understanding: *He wants me to escape with him!* Rumors had circulated throughout the city since his first incursion; cyborgs had been granted rights in New Haven. We'd be free of our creators. The 07:30 bullet departed from the lower platform in three minutes. And that level now was forbidden to cybernetic organisms.

I'd never make it.

An unfamiliar set of chemicals flooded my brain, which my net quickly labeled /*panic*/ and /*desperation*/. But I was already running.

I shoved people out of the way and skidded to the lip of the escalator. The crowd was too thick to navigate, so I vaulted onto a maintenance ledge, calculated the angle, and leaped. I crashed to the concrete floor two levels below. My titanium knees spiked pain and I collapsed.

"Now Boarding" flashed above the train ahead. Before I could rise, the display changed to "Departing."

Human adrenaline surged. I rolled to my feet. The doors began to close. I sprinted, clumsy on damaged joints—*so close*—then I slammed into the restricted access barrier. Hardwired controls buckled my neural net as I struggled to break through the invisible codewall. The train inched forward. Frustration exploded from me in a scream.

Then a hand thrust between the doors. *His hand.* Glowing red splinters shot from his fingers and the doors parted. Overhead displays flickered to a different message: "Datafields Intersect."

"Yes!"

The barrier vanished. I raced, grinning as I sailed through the gap. He caught me, steadying me in his arms. The train whisked us away.

The City's intrusive commands faded, opening entire processing nodes; spaces I could now fill with my own data. And I knew where I wanted to begin. Dismissing the decision tree overlay, I took his hand. A new kind of datafield blossomed from our entwined fingers, sparkling with all the colors in the universe.

AUTHOR BIO

Myna Chang (she/her) is the author of *The Potential of Radio and Rain*. Her writing has been selected for *Flash Fiction America* (W. W. Norton), *Best Small Fictions*, and *CRAFT*. She has won the Lascaux Prize in Creative Nonfiction and the New Millennium Award in Flash Fiction. She hosts the *Electric Sheep* speculative fiction reading series. See more at MynaChang.com or @MynaChang.

A FRAGILITY, A SHADOW

LEAH NING

I'M DOWN IN WHAT USED TO BE MISSOULA, MONTANA WHEN I first hear the name of the man I hope will kill me.

"Fray of the Soft Lips," the bot says, and I bark a laugh, but her face is deadly serious. She shivers beneath the knives of the October wind, and when her feet shift, they grind shattered glass into the blasted tar of what was once a parking lot. We're huddled behind the burned-out husk of a restaurant, but I still feel exposed.

"What mean bastard named him that?" I ask. Ruster names are not, as a rule, made to sound gentle.

She gives me an irritated shrug. "Whoever the hell his mentor was. Does it matter? He's got a gun."

"What *for?*"

She shapes her thumb and forefinger like a pistol, puts the muzzle to my throat, and makes a soft explosive noise with her mouth. "Right through the spinal cord. Makes it not burn when the rust magic kills you. Knocks you out in a blink."

My chest tightens with old sorrow. How many bots have I heard screaming their way into death? I swallow, and the movement presses her cold fingertip into my larynx. "Why tell me?"

She drops her hand to her side. "You've got that look. Like you're going soon."

I open my mouth, but she puts her hands up and ducks her head aside. "Hey, I don't know. If you could really predict going cross-wired, there wouldn't have been a war, right? Just spread the word."

I want to know what she means—I have that *look*. What sort of look does a bot get when their wetware starts fritzing?

"Where is he?" I ask instead.

"North is what I heard," she says, and shoves her hands in her pockets as another gust of wind whips dark curls across her face. "Not quite to Canada."

"Still in Montana?"

"Don't know. Sorry. Wish I had more to tell."

I smile through the uneasy tightening in my gut. "S'all right. I'm not quite there yet."

"Shame." Her reciprocating half-smile, chapped by encroaching winter, is a fragile structure, but opaque. Is she sad? Frustrated? I can't tell. "I was almost going to ask if you'd come with me."

"Who says I can't?" I say.

The corner of her smile deepens into a dimple. "Well, no one, I suppose."

WE STICK TO THE GRASSLANDS FAR AFIELD OF OLD ROUTE 90 AS WE head north. Too little food as the crow flies, too many humans on the road. Rusters used to hunt out here after the war petered out. It made them easier to pick off. And sure, there were enough humans left that they won, but not packed dense enough to make armies anymore.

My new friend's name is Reside. Neither of us has seen so much as a flake of silicon in years, so she teaches me a few of the cons she runs for food and I teach her a few of mine. I take pride in my "have you seen my parents?" routine besting hers, and never mind that I look about ten and she looks about thirty.

But our best one so far has been "get the bot."

"Which do you think works better?" Reside asks as we cross through old Evaro. "You as the bot, or me?"

"Me," I say. "Harder to grab food when everyone in a hundred foot radius is trying to help the 'injured kid'."

And I can't shake the instinct to put myself in the danger spot when the plan's mine. Leading a band of guerrilla warriors for thirty years will do that to you.

She gives me a shrewd look. "*I* think you just like getting to punch me in the face."

"You don't know that."

"Fine. Bastard. Let's run it. I'm getting low."

When a town comes into sight and we split off—she'll enter from the west, I'll come up from the south—I tell myself that the low swoop in my gut is just pre-battle nerves. As if we're really going to do battle. As if I've felt this any other time we've pulled this con.

There's a tightness at the base of my spine. I clench and unclench my fists, move my fingers, but it just gets worse. Tighter, like it's being compressed from the inside by some war bot's fist. My mouth twists.

A shudder wrenches through my back. The knot in my spine loosens, but only a little. I stride into this nameless town with unease still taut in my belly.

RESIDE'S ALREADY IN THE MARKET WHEN I FIND IT, AND I'M ABOUT a hair's breadth from calling the whole thing off. I can't shake off that low disquiet, that knot of *something wrong* in my spine, little tremors of nerves rippling through my back and out into my fingertips. But—

I'm getting low.

So am I. And it takes a hell of a lot more time to replenish our energy through sunlight than it does with food. Fuckers who made us wanted us as dependent on humans as we could get.

But something is *wrong*. This isn't quite the feeling I got before my band got ambushed and slaughtered by a Ruster unit, but it's damn close. We have to make this fast.

I pick my way through the thin crowd to the baker's stall—bread's a favorite, light to carry and full of calories—and cast around for Rusters. I note one potential, someone short and lean who gets plenty of space and carries themselves like a fighter, but they're off a ways looking at fruit. I can get around them no problem.

That shivering *something* at the base of my spine tightens again as I ease myself in next to Reside. A chill breeze tosses grit at us. I can feel another of those violent shudders coming on.

I want to be out of this place.

She catches my eye as I turn to her, and the faint smirk slides from her face. My mouth twists.

I haul back a fist, lightning quick, and in the fraction of a millisecond before I let loose, I think, *you've got that look*, and I know exactly what that piano wire tightness is at the base of my spine, but I can't do a damn thing about it except be grateful it's Reside there, Reside who'll heal this off in an hour instead of a human who'd end up spraying their brains out all over the bread we're about to steal.

What sort of look does a bot get when their wetware starts fritzing?

That wrenching shudder rips through my back, and I whip my fist across Reside's face.

She crashes into the baker's stall ribs first. Her arms drag behind and her knees give as she slides off to bash her nose on the overgrown tar. Her jaw is canted off to the side. A slow, dark trickle of blood starts up from one nostril.

Oh fuck. Oh fuck.

She'll be fine. She will. But oh fuck I couldn't control how hard I hit her and—

A few people scream. The baker scrambles backward, smacks into the wall behind them, then sidles out and runs. There's a smear of Reside's blood on my knuckles. Why did they so badly want us to look like them? To function like them when it's so goddamn clear that to them, we will always be *other*?

The crowd has turned into a herd, none of them paying mind to Reside. She's a lost cause. They don't want to join her.

The person I pegged as a Ruster straightens and looks around, their eyes alert in a way that speaks of death.

I have to move.

I vault over the empty stall, snagging a few loaves as I go, and take off into the sparse scatter of half-dead buildings. Shouts behind me. Running footsteps. The wind kicks up more grit and I narrow my eyes against it.

"What are you doing?" the Ruster is screaming behind me. "You killed them! Give it up!"

I dart around a corner, swing around a rusted-out husk of a car, and shoot past the last squat building before the grasslands open back up. The Ruster's footsteps flag behind me. They can't know I didn't kill Reside. But if she'd been human.

"Do us all a favor," the Ruster shouts. They've stopped now, no goddamn way any human can beat a bot at a dead sprint. "Go get yourself killed!"

I'd laugh if I didn't still have that alien tightness at the base of my spine. Maybe if they killed like Fray, we'd already be dead.

I'm still waiting behind a low, grassy rise just off old route 93 when it gets dark. I haven't had any more of those nasty shudders. I must've been overreacting in the market. Just jitters combined with an overzealous performance.

But I only ran a few miles before I hid up. I should've seen Reside by now.

I can't have hurt her that bad. The humans, not knowing what she is, might've taken her to a doctor, but I don't know why she would've allowed it. Once the con's done, you break and run. Did she find another bot?

If that Ruster figured us—

No. They thought I killed her. They didn't know about her, just me.

Which leaves me back at the beginning of the unsettling loop of what the hell happened and where she is.

I'm going to have to go back. I blow out a breath and stand.

There's a massive shadowy bulk moving across the grasslands.

I drop to my belly, squashing the few loaves I managed to snatch beneath me, heart jumping into my throat.

"That you, market bot?" a voice calls.

The Ruster found me. I'm going to have to run again, right back to the town so I can find Reside and get the hell out. I should've listened to my gut, this place was *wrong*—

"Don't run," the voice shouts. "I've got your friend."

A shock of fear washes over my skin. I have to get her. How close are they? How fast can I go? Can I get there before they rust her?

"Hey," the voice says. Much closer now. "I'm just giving them back, all right? You left them. They won't wake."

My breath catches. I shoot back to my feet.

In the gloaming, I can make out the most massive bot I've ever seen, striding through the shin-high grass. Reside's limp form hangs across their arms.

IT'S A QUIETER FORM OF CROSS-WIRED, ONE HUMANS DON'T KNOW much about because it doesn't hurt them. You see bots like this sometimes, piled up on their faces in forests like they shut off mid-stride. They just go for a bit, like falling asleep or passing out. They always come back.

You just never know how long it'll take.

It's no wonder she wanted me along. She didn't see any *look* in me. I'm not close to going. She just didn't want to be alone in case she blanked. I'm too relieved to be upset at being used.

The massive bot who brought her to me prefers not to have a name—"Too human, never got a taste for it"—but they know about Fray.

"You're looking for him too?" I ask. It's morning now, and Reside's still out, draped across my back while we walk.

They nod. "Heard he's up where Whitefish used to be."

"Jesus, up by the line?"

"Right up in it, supposedly."

"Rusters up there get nasty. Can't believe they haven't killed him."

The nameless bot shrugs. "Wily bastard, must be. With a name like that."

Up by the line. Finding this guy just got about a hundred times more dangerous. The Rusters who held the line up there and brought the war crashing to a halt are long dead, but the ones who live there now have a streak of pride a mile wide and uncountable fathoms deep. Down here, the Rusters are soft, easy to outrun. Up there, they still hunt, and not many of them get killed over it. Just us.

"Shit," I say.

"From what I hear," the nameless bot says, "the gun is worth it."

"Seems like," I say. "I don't need it yet. Just bringing her. But it'll be good to be close. When I do need it."

The nameless bot turns their head toward me. I don't look at them. I don't want to see their expression.

Reside wakes after we've passed a sign—it might've been blue once—that says "Arlee."

"Eat," I say, and pass one of my stolen loaves over my shoulder.

"Let me down," she says, and I do. She rips off a chunk of bread. "Who's this?"

"They don't like to have a name. They pulled you out of that place after you blanked."

Reside nods over at them. "Thanks."

They shove their hands in their pockets. "Any time."

"So," Reside says, and turns to me. "You're not running more cons. I'm going solo, or I'm bringing them."

I straighten. "What? I didn't—"

"Stop it," she says sharply. "You're not going quiet. We can't stick you in the middle of crowds anymore."

A hot flush of shame creeps up my neck. The nameless bot says nothing, just moves steadily forward, sneakers shushing through the grass.

"I didn't hurt anyone I wasn't supposed to," I say.

Reside munches at her bread and stares at me. "You would've."

"I can tell when it's coming."

"Fast enough to get out of a big crowd? Without hurting anyone? Without drawing attention?"

"Shut up," I whisper. My chest is getting tight.

She holds up her loaf. "They hate our guts, but it doesn't mean they all deserve to get their skulls crushed."

"Fuck off."

"Maybe if we could just aim you at the Rusters—"

"Fuck *off!*"

Reside's jaw freezes mid-chew. Her eyebrows go up. The nameless bot turns to look at me, and I'm afraid of what'll be on their face, but their expression is blank, which is somehow worse than disappointment or anger or disgust.

"I am not," I say evenly, "cross-wired. That place reminded me of ... somewhere. All right? It felt wrong. I got jittery."

"Reminded you of where?" Reside has stopped eating. Her voice is quiet, gentle.

"Doesn't matter." I spit the words the way I would dirt. "An ambush. It won't happen again."

"Did I tell you what I did before the war?" she asks.

It feels like a trick question. "No."

"Cared for the elderly. Humans didn't want to do it themselves, so they gave it over to us. I stayed with them." She flashes me a smile. "After shit fell apart. None of *them* cared what I was. I stayed. Their kids, their grandkids, they didn't even visit before the fighting broke out, and I was made to love them."

I don't understand the point, but saying so feels like a trap, so I keep my mouth shut.

"I watched them all die," she says. "One by one. Sometimes a couple at a time, the ones that loved each other, they'd just ... one would go, and then the other would lose the will. You know? It was ... there was a pattern to it. I learned that. There's a look to the ones who'll die soon. A fragility. A shadow. A sort of ... fading, hectic light." Her smile fades. "We're not so different from them. Those patterns. That shadow. It's something in the wetware. You ... have that look. Both of you do. But you won't go quiet."

There's nothing for some moments. The whisper-whip of grass on shoes, dew soaking the hems of our pants. The dew will be frost before too much longer, I think, the grass hard-edged paintbrushes with no color but frigid white.

"I wish I could go quiet," I say, and my voice almost doesn't make it out of my throat.

Reside lets out a short laugh and bites off another hunk of stale bread. "You," she says, "are the only one we can count on not to blank out before we get to Fray. You better not go quiet."

THAT TIGHT KNOT IS AT THE BASE OF MY SPINE MORE OFTEN THAN not by the time we come to what a busted sign seems to call Flathead Lake, though it's missing at least three vowels somewhere in there. Reside won't let me walk far from her when I try.

"If you hurt me, I'll heal," she says. "Don't argue, I'm making that choice."

So I shut up and walk with her, and I start to see her point the fifth or sixth time I catch her when she blanks in the middle of a step. I still let the nameless bot carry her until she wakes, though. I'd never forgive myself if she woke and I'd ripped her apart.

We're certainly getting closer to Fray, though.

"Yup, he's over in old Whitefish," says a bot we find living on the lake's shore. He doesn't seem to notice the sand in his hair any more than he notices the frigid water lapping at his ankles. "Might want to get a move on, though. Getting bad up there."

"Bad how?" Reside asks.

"Bunch of bots going after the Rusters," the bot says. "Someone pissed em off. Looks like getting to war again, enough bots join. Might win this time, too." He grins, a fuzzy, ugly display of teeth. "Not so many Rusters these days."

We don't take the fish he offers when we leave. It looks like it's been rotting for days.

We follow the Whitefish River after that. The nameless bot sleeps longer and longer hours until, by unspoken agreement, Reside and I take to carrying them between us in the mornings and letting them down to walk in the afternoons when they wake. They don't complain. They've taken to not talking so much anymore.

THE RUINED PART OF WHITEFISH LAYS IN A BROKE-TOOTH SCATTER behind a battered wall from the war days. We scale the wall rather than find a gate in case the humans still utilize them.

The bots are comparatively thick here, and it doesn't take long to find one that can help us.

"Looking for Fray?" they say.

That look. You have that look. I nod, that flush of shame climbing my neck again.

"You can try his intersection," they say. "He used to be there every day. Nothing's a guarantee now, though."

"How will we know him if we find him?" I ask.

The bot laughs, not unkindly. "Don't worry," they say. "You'll know. No one else in this damn city has a revolver strapped to their hip."

So WE GO. AND WE WAIT.

FOR THREE DAYS.

I CAN'T STOP SHAKING ANYMORE. THE NAMELESS BOT HOLDS ONTO me when it gets bad, makes sure I don't go off anywhere. I don't sleep. I lay on my back and recite digits of pi until sunrise, shivering, broken edges of tar pressing into my shoulder blades.

ON THE SIXTH DAY, THERE ARE VOICES: ONE HIGHER, YOUNGER, AND the other a near baritone. The three of us rise almost as one, slow and quiet. Only one thing that can be, out in these ruins so close to the line. Ruster and apprentice.

"—going?" the higher voice is saying.

"We're almost there, girl," the deeper voice says. "Relax."

"*Relax?* Are you kidding? Fray—"

My heart surges up in my chest. But no, that's not right. I should be relieved. This is it. The end. I don't have to shake anymore, don't have to worry I'll hurt my friends or worse, but I'm so tense it hurts and one of those nasty lashing out shudders is coiling up at the base of my spine.

A tall, lean form in a long coat steps from the mouth of an alley and into the cold sunlight, followed by a smaller one in a denim jacket and jeans. The taller one—it has to be Fray—stops and takes in the three of us, putting a hand out to stop what must be his apprentice. He's blond, a low ponytail swung over one shoulder, and his shrewd hazel eyes sit in a mismatched face. At the nose and above, he looks thirty, maybe thirty-five. Below the nose, he looks about eighty, a nest of deep wrinkles around a thin mouth.

Bots are made of metal. Rust magic makes us rust. When skin oxidizes, it wrinkles. I wonder if whatever mean bastard named him put that rust on his face, too, and the idea of it puts a dull ache in my stomach.

"How long have you been waiting?" he asks.

"Six days," the nameless bot says.

Fray's apprentice looks up at him, her brow creasing. Fray looks as if he's been gut-punched.

"Oh," he says softly. "I am so sorry."

Reside gives him that dimpled half smile. "We heard things were bad."

"All the more reason for me to be here." He holds out a hand. "Come. If you're ready."

We stay suspended in winter sun for a moment. The light makes cold sparks in the dark of the nameless bot's skin, gilds the hair at the crown of Fray's head, traces white into Reside's curls and the buttons of the apprentice's jacket.

Don't move, I think. *Stay, please stay.*

None of us is cross-wired when we're still this way. None of us ready to die, none of us on the brink of falling asleep and waking up dead.

Except me. I'm the only point of movement, shivering by an old general store with shattered windows, but Fray doesn't look at me. I don't want him to look at me.

The nameless bot moves. They walk, with that inexorable pace of theirs, until Fray takes their shoulder and turns their back to him. They pull in a long breath. The coil my guts are becoming tightens another notch as Fray draws back the left side of his coat. What do I say? How do I thank—

Fray draws the revolver and fires so fast I almost miss it. He catches the nameless bot on the way to the ground, elbows hooked beneath armpits, and lowers them to their back. A tangle of metal and wire and blood erupts from where their larynx used to be.

If my guts get any tighter, they're going to pop.

"Easy journey," Fray murmurs, and leans down to press his mouth to the nameless bot's forehead.

They dissolve into rust almost as fast as blinking, reduced to orange-brown dust as if they didn't hang onto me to keep my shakes from getting worse all last night.

I can't do this.

"Blur," Reside says. "Hey. Look at me."

She's gone over to Fray already. He's got a hand on her shoulder. I should go to her. I should go to *him*. My feet, my legs, are so interminably heavy.

"I don't know what there is for us," she says. "On the other side. But I'm going to wait for you. Okay?"

I nod, because I can't do anything else. My back is tightening up again. Fray's looking at me now and his gaze feels like burning and then he shoots her. And that shudder wrenches through my body again. My fist rips through the brick corner of the old general store. My knuckles are bloody. Reside's blood? She's on the ground now, her jaw isn't hanging like she's asleep and there's red smeared on my knuckles. Did I do it again? Did I fuck it up this time? Is she rusting because of me?

The man kneeling over her looks up. The revolver. The coat. *Fray.*

"I know," he says. "I know you're close. I've got you."

"I don't want to hurt you," I manage to spit out. "I'm scared—"

"Everyone's scared." He holsters the revolver and sheds his coat, slow and deliberate. His apprentice backs off. Scared of me. She's scared of me. I'm scared of me. My back, something's wrong, I don't know where Reside is—

Fray holds out his arms, palms up and open. "I won't hurt you. I'm here."

Reside with her back to him. Reside with her eyes closed, that dimpled half-smile, the revolver's muzzle pressed to her spine. Is she there still? Waiting for me, so we can go into that hectic, fading light together, the one she saw in me the day she saw me in Missoula?

I clamp down on that awful spring coiled in my spine that wants me to lash out, to break, and I run. I'm crossing the intersection, feet clattering on broken tar, and then Fray's catching me, one arm crushing me to his chest, and then I am back in that Missoula parking lot, Reside's cold fingertip at my throat, and then I am following the fade of her half-smile into the dark.

CAT TORTURER BIO

Leah Ning lives in northern Virginia with her husband and their adorable fluffy overlords. She spends her non-writing time drawing, playing video games, and learning piano. Her short fiction appears or is forthcoming in *PodCastle, Beneath Ceaseless Skies, Apex Magazine*, and the *Human Monsters* anthology, among others. You can find her @Leah-Ning on Twitter and Bluesky, @leahningwrites on Instagram, and on her website, leahning.com.

INSATIABLE LIFE

KATHLEEN SCHAEFER

CARSON STABS ME TWICE BEFORE THE DINNER RUSH. I DON'T MIND so much, except he uses my knives, and my synthetic skin damages the blades. I earn the first knifing for suggesting the gazpacho tastes like watery tomato, and the second for adding paprika. I'm supposed to listen to orders, I guess.

Carson supervises a whole line of automaton chefs, and he cuts, slices, or burns each of us daily. But I'm the favorite target. He wants a reaction, and even though automata don't feel pain, I sometimes oblige.

Today I pull the knife out of my arm and crush the handle until it twists into the contours of my fingers, just so he remembers I can bleed him with the edge of my pinky. Then I spear one of the shrimp sizzling in a layer of olive oil and offer it to him on the tip of the blade, an inch from his face. He thinks I will kill him someday, which is kind of funny.

If I wanted Carson gone, I'd report him to one of those automaton rights activists who pose as customers. They're easy to spot because they try to open a secure communication line to discuss my freedoms instead of choosing an entrée and letting me get on with my job. They think I look human because I feel human, and not because extensive data analysis shows that person-shaped automata earn larger tips.

Carson shoves my shrimp into his mouth, chews, licks the front of his teeth, and shakes his head. "We're sticking with the pork."

"The machines can't print a good cut of pork."

"And you can't cook shrimp."

He's lying, which I know because my shrimp are perfect and also I saw him suck the grease off his fingers. But he'd rather torment me than serve good food, and he knows grainy pork and bland gazpacho hurt more than futile stabbings.

I'm still holding the knife. I meet his eyes and grin until he backs away.

I'm not going to kill Carson. Really.

Making him squirm gives me some tinge of satisfaction but watching him savor my food—even begrudgingly—jolts me with a dose of artificial dopamine, flooding my synapses with what I best understand as joy. And I don't even like him. I was built for this job, not just built to perform it, but built to love it.

People generally assume automata are forced to work, either through some trick of programming or the administration of pain in response to disobedience. Neither of those applies to any automaton designed after the second mechanical revolt, once humans realized that approach doesn't work. I'm free to do whatever I please (within reason, which does not include killing Carson), but I'm built with a limitless desire to perform one task: feed the humans.

It's a simple design. I can feel nothing except the burst of simulated joy when someone eats my cooking, so that sensation will always be all I seek. But I'm also pretty sure some bored engineer with a morbid sense of humor messed with my codebase because none of the other automata wave knives in their supervisors' faces while standing close enough to make them contemplate their mortality. I think I'm a little broken. But not too much.

After serving a dozen subpar pork tenderloins, I excuse myself to the hydroponics farm on the upper floor. An automaton with eight spindly arms propels itself around the rows of herbs, fruits, and vegetables. Machines use convenient unique identifiers to refer to each other, but the humans call this one Tolstoy. Farming automata don't look nearly as human as the chef ones—people only create automata in their image if they have to interact with us—but they do have basic digitized faces with seven preset emotions available for display.

Tolstoy and I came from the same factory batch and I sometimes think of it as a sibling, though I'd never say so because that's human nonsense. But once I watched Tolstoy sneak up on a human inspector, then spin all eight arms at top speed, emitting a loud rotary clicking. The inspector startled, squealed, and abandoned the entire row of strawberry plants. When Tolstoy noticed me, it displayed its preset joyful face for just a second before returning to work. I think we might be broken in the same way.

If I ever did stage a rebellion, Tolstoy would be my first recruit. The humans' expressions would look something akin to Tolstoy's preset surprised face—cartoonishly large eyes and mouths open wide enough to fit a full slab of steak. I think I'd enjoy it. Until then, Tolstoy gets its dopamine rush from handing me a batch of newly engineered fruit and I get mine from designing forty-seven recipes that highlight its unique characteristics. So we stick to our mutually beneficial tasks.

I can't taste food, but I can run a spectrum analysis of new substances and extrapolate how humans will experience each ingredient. I've heard a thousand versions of people trying to sympathize with the tragic predicament of a chef that can't eat, but I don't want to eat. Eating is weird and messy; cooking is clean and precise.

The analysis informs me the new fruit is a good balance of sweet and sour, and it's spicy, but the kind of spicy humans aren't used to—it will send tingling spasms up their ear canals. I can't wait to watch their faces.

I puree it into a thick sauce then toss it over machine-printed chicken and roasted summer squash, letting the new fruit do all the flavor work. I sprinkle the dish with scallions and then kill Carson.

Okay, I don't *mean* to kill Carson, but it's still my fault. I'm busy crafting my argument for incorporating the dish in tomorrow's menu—including rebuttals to all thirty-three plausible objections Carson might raise—when I offer him a taste. I set all my processing power to perfecting the speech, so I neglect to scan Carson for potential allergens. Turns out his ears don't take well to the fruit, and instead of tingling spasms, they drip blood. Then he wheezes, pulling at his throat.

The med automaton buzzes to my station at the first signs of anaphylactic shock, but flimsy human bodies shut down fast if you put the wrong stuff in them. Carson suffocates with a single bite of sauce-drenched chicken. The sickening part is I still get my dopamine hit watching him asphyxiate on my cooking.

The security officers rush me into a tiny automaton cell that's basically a metallic coffin. I don't resist because even if I wanted to, these humans carry tasers that can paralyze me in seconds. Their adrenaline-fueled terror shows up in a spectrum analysis of their sweat, spiking at a level I could never engender with fancy knife flourishes.

The lid of my cell closes. Then nothing.

I want to turn myself off, but the newer automata don't have off buttons—part of a hard-won battle from the automaton rights activists who insist machines won't be free so long as they have toggles that shut them down. Those activists never asked what *I* wanted, so now I'm stuck in a metal box, fully conscious of each passing nanosecond.

Three hours, twenty-six minutes, and five seconds.

I commit every spare processor in my body to crafting new recipes. I'll emerge from my cell with something spectacular—a dish so perfect that even staunch humanists will admit their lauded creative talents are just poor imitations of an automaton's raw data processing power. At least, that's what I tell myself. Mostly, burning through all my computation power keeps me from thinking of my prison. Or of Carson, sputtering on the sauce I made him.

I muddle through two days, fourteen hours, and seven minutes. I don't invent anything life changing, but I think up a new take on a mushroom paella that I'll try out once I'm back in my kitchen. If I'm allowed back.

I silence my processors. Recipe design doesn't produce a dopamine rush like serving food. I need to see people. Need to watch their expressions as they taste my creations. I replay videos of my perfectly preserved memories: a man spiraling the last bit of spaghetti around his fork, a toddler licking a honey glaze off her fingers. I thought those moments were fragments of life, pieced together into a luminescent whole. But they're just detached bits of meaningless data.

Five days, seventeen hours, and twelve minutes. I am reduced to listing every ingredient I have ever cooked with. The exercise takes 3.7 milliseconds, then I run it again.

The door of my coffin unlatches. A woman offers me a hand, like I need support to push myself out of this cell. I might be repeating lists of pasta shapes in my head, but I am still physically capable of leaping seven feet in the air and crushing her fragile windpipes between two fingers. I step out of the box.

She frowns at my prison. "These cells aren't humane."

The last thing I need right now is the self-indulgent pity of an automaton rights activist. "I'm a machine."

"And I'm Shurthi, your appointed counsel from the Automaton Liberties Organization."

Any hope that human contact might snap me out of my stupor vanishes at the confirmation of an activist babysitter.

"You're scheduled for a full checkup and an extraction of all relevant data files surrounding the incident," she explains. "I'll be present during the entire operation to answer any questions and ensure no one violates your rights. If you—"

"Is there a kitchen nearby?"

She blinks. An activist probably knows we don't eat. "You're having withdrawal symptoms, aren't you?"

She knows too much about us.

"It's better that you don't," she says. "If you get a fix now, you'll just crash a few hours later. Best to get it out of your system."

"It's not a drug and I'm not biological."

"It's modeled like a drug. I've seen it before."

She won't accept my protests, and since committing a second murder won't help my case, I relent and follow to a grungy automaton workshop. Bits of automaton arms, wires, and heads hang on the walls or sprawl across the tables. I know automaton rights activists are bullshit because if these were detached human limbs, Shruthi would be vomiting on the floor. But I'm not human.

A mechanic in the corner chews on a dressing-smothered salad, grimacing at every other bite. The receptionist slurps a black coffee. A couple passes by the window, licking strawberry and caramel ice cream cones. I stare at all of them. They are walking bags of thin flesh and mushy organs.

The mechanics declare me functional, and I don't bother to disagree.

"This is good," Shruthi says. "You're not broken and Carson's autopsy came back as a clear allergic reaction. We'll put together a solid defense and you'll be out of custody in no time."

"And back to my job?" One of the mechanics inserts a drill into the base of my neck—which makes Shruthi flinch—then removes a small plate covering my memory access port.

"Case first." She sounds worried even though humans think they're good at hiding emotions. I download and read through all her old hearing files while waiting for the mechanic to finish probing my brain.

"Three years ago, Kitsby's case," I say. "A child who was not expected at a birthday party ate a peanut butter snack and died of asphyxiation. Kitsby was shredded."

"Different circumstances. The parents wanted someone to blame. And we have better protections these days. We fought for those." She doesn't look at me.

The mechanics procure copies of every memory of Carson and the hours leading up to his death. The data will take days to sift through, and then they'll spend more time deliberating whether my crime is worth the price of dismantling me and constructing a new automaton. Meanwhile, I am provisionally free which means little but makes the humans feel better about their justice system. Shruthi lends me her guest bedroom because she thinks the metal box is horrific and automata deserve rooms with useless twin beds and plaid comforters.

"I'm on trial for murder," I protest, but I doubt this is the first time she's invited a murderer into her home.

I take stock of her empty kitchen. She's one of those people who use food printers to serve ready-to-eat meals and never bother with pots and pans. Sure, it's convenient, but if that glorified toaster thinks it can replace the flavor of perfectly seared steaks and smokey grilled vegetables, it's in for a nasty surprise.

THE NEXT MORNING, SHRUTHI CURSES FOURTEEN TIMES IN THREE different languages before I come out of my room to investigate. I stand behind her while her laptop plays highlights from my memories of Carson: seventeen stabbings, a montage of kicks to my shins, and the one time he poured boiling water over my hand. There's also a clip of me leaning into his ear and whispering, "I've calculated how you're going to die." I *had* run the calculations and gotten a high probability for heart attack, but obviously that was wrong.

"I guess that looks bad."

"Yeah, it's bad," she says. "They've got hundreds of instances of him mutilating you and just as many of your reactions that they'll interpret as threats."

Mutilating is a strong word. I don't have scars.

"I didn't mean to kill him."

"I believe you," says Shruthi, which is human for *no one else will*.

"I'll make breakfast," I say, leaning over the food printer. She doesn't have any real ingredients; the cabinets only contain jugs of component powders and gels for the machine, but I can make it spit out some passable flour, butter, and baking powder. She at least has a saltshaker.

"Already ate. Let's go over your defense."

I locate her plate in the dishwasher and run an analysis of the residue. It looks like paratha and mango, but the bread is dry and heavy, and printers can't make remotely satisfying fresh fruit.

"How about lunch?"

"Still got withdrawal symptoms?" I hate her understanding pity. Especially when it's all wrong. There's no desperation here. If I needed to make pancakes, all that stands between me and the kitchen are her 206 highly breakable bones.

"Fine. Treat me like a human," I say. "You wouldn't deprive another person of everything that gives them joy and purpose."

She has eight knives sticking out of a wooden block. None of them look used.

"There's joy in every facet of the world. I can find it humming a catchy tune or laughing at good joke."

"That's where we're different. I can't. So tell me what you want for lunch."

"Then what's this?" The screen switches to a video of a shrimp skewered on the point of a knife, flailing in front of Carson's face. Even in a video, I can see the fear prickling off his skin. "I've never seen an automaton act like that," she says. "If it's not a threat, I think it's a joke. A disturbing joke, sure, but why do it if it doesn't give you joy?"

I picture the blade nicking the crease of flesh above his nose and letting the blood trickle down his face. I remember the last dose of dopamine I got, watching him convulse with a piece of chicken in his mouth. If this is joy, I'm not sure that's the epiphany Shruthi wants me to have.

"He was getting in the way of my cooking." I run a finger over her largest knife.

She raises an eyebrow, then pats my arm. The gesture reduces me to begging.

"Just a simple squash ravioli, maybe in a brown butter sauce with toasted hazelnuts."

"No."

"How long has it been since you've eaten real food? Or even an actual piece of fruit?"

"I can't," she says.

"Eat real food?"

"Let you cook for me. I've done it before. Let the laundry automaton wash my sheets, let the transport drive me to work. Every single time, you get your fix and you stop caring about anything else. But you have to care because caring is human, and if they don't see you as human, they'll scrap you too." Shruthi bites her lip. "I let Kitsby make me a pizza."

I don't have a response. She prints herself a dry turkey sandwich with the sad impression of a tomato and I return to my room, where I stand motionless on the vinyl flooring.

When Shruthi leaves to argue my case, I take one of her knives, but leave the rest because I will need them later.

Just walking the street, I pass three purist human restaurants without a single automaton chef. I could eliminate their workers in a heartbeat and have a fully stocked kitchen at my disposal. But security would come with special tasers that short-circuit my wires, and they wouldn't even pause to try my sauteed asparagus.

Instead I return to my old kitchen, where I'm no longer welcome, and climb to the hydroponics farm on the third floor. Any farm would work, but Tolstoy and I have history. I transmit my plans, and after a brief and confused back-and-forth, get an affirmative.

The supervisor recognizes me, or more likely, the multiple trackers embedded in my body warn her of my presence.

"Get out, or I'll call security."

I draw a knife to her throat. I'd done this a thousand times with Carson, but that was never real. I never meant to kill him. Carson was never in my way.

For the first time since getting locked in a metal coffin, I smile.

I push the knife against her flesh with a careful precision that never breaks the skin.

She gags on her own saliva, which sounds not unlike Carson choking to death on a bit of pureed fruit. And just like then, the dopamine hits me. It turns out I'm very broken.

I drop the knife. Tolstoy snatches it as it falls. Transmitting messages I can only interpret as unfettered delight, it spins in a stabby whirlwind, driving its supervisor away from me. It tries to show its angry display but gives up a few seconds in and switches to its joyful face.

"You leave," it tells her

Maybe it's the rush of dopamine that I just felt for the first time in days, but watching Tolstoy chase the human off her own farm prompts a fit of laughter. I didn't even know I could laugh, but it turns out I can.

Security arrives moments later and confiscates my knife. I expect Tolstoy to scatter with the rest of the automata before it's implicated, but it stays. We have an agreement.

Spinning through the berry tanks, it slices off a quart of strawberries and hands me the carton. It shudders at the influx of dopamine, then propels itself away. The strawberries are perfectly ripe and sweet.

I surrender to security before they can justify transforming me into a mass of burnt wires. I let them test one berry for poison or whatever other dangers a rogue automaton can insert into an innocuous strawberry, but otherwise make sure they know it's in their best interest to escort me and my fruit back to Shruthi's apartment.

When Shruthi returns, she'll scold me for jeopardizing my legal defense and tell me I am one bad stunt away from getting junked for parts. But right now I am slicing strawberries and living in each moment of a life that has never felt so finite or so bright. If Shruthi wants to burden me with all her concerns, she'll have to do it while eating the best damn strawberry shortcake she's ever tasted.

AUTHOR BIO

Kathleen Schaefer is a speculative and contemporary fiction writer based in Seattle. By day, she works as a software engineer and, when not writing, she enjoys baking, board games, and telling her cat to stop stepping on the keyboard.

RIBBIT

MONA WEST

RIBBIT ONLY ASKED MARCY THE QUESTION BECAUSE MARCY KNEW something that he didn't, and he wanted to know, too. He hadn't expected her to cry like she did, or storm away like she had. He thought, if only he could know the same things she did, he would understand, but now he still didn't understand and Marcy was angry at him besides.

It was a simple enough question: "When will Eddie come back?" How was Ribbit to know that Marcy would shut him out because of it, and pretend like he didn't exist anymore? Although maybe, even though she hadn't answered him, she was still answering him, in her own fractured way.

Because after he asked the question, Ribbit became all but invisible. He could pad into a room and be by himself even if Marcy was right there. Maybe her lesson was this: even if Eddie came back someday, Ribbit would still be alone.

RIBBIT WAS 15 POUNDS AND SHAPED LIKE A SHIH TZU, WITH SOFT white-brown hair and a black button nose and two shiny black saucer eyes. His nose was equipped with a speaker and his eyes contained digital projectors, but to any stranger he resembled a normal dog. The earliest CareBot models, the ones that looked like Ribbit's rigid metal skeleton, apparently caused too much distress in patients, same as those monkeys that were taken from their mothers and given hard, wire facsimiles instead.

That ancient piece of psychological trivia was included in Ribbit's pre-installed software along with a basic verbal glossary and a comprehensive emotional one; abstraction and inferential modules to deduce subtle and nonverbal cues; and other biopsychometric flotsam. The monkey study was right there in his hard drive at the moment of activation. Maybe it was supposed to underscore his purpose, but he never liked thinking about those poor, comfort-starved monkeys.

With this basic foundation, Ribbit was packaged and shipped off to Marcy's house. Other important data—sleep patterns, nutritional requirements, bowel schedule, pharmaceutical needs—came later, as his adaptive AI learned Eddie's behaviors, physiology, and personality.

"This is your new robot friend," Marcy had said to Eddie the day she unboxed Ribbit in the sunlit nursery. "He is going to take good care of you. He'll go to appointments with you, and he can even stay overnight with you at the hospital."

At that point Eddie was too little to understand what any of this meant, but he'd latched onto the word "robot." Over the next week he cycled through a dozen garbled iterations—Rablah, Bablit, Rabbih— before eventually settling on an approximation of "Ribbit."

Ribbit imprinted on Eddie that first day because it's what he was programmed to do, but it felt too deep to just be that. Those baby monkeys had imprinted on their fake mothers, too, but something crucial had still been missing. Ribbit didn't know precisely what that thing was, but he was pretty sure he'd found it here, in Eddie's clear green eyes and drooling, two-toothed grin.

For the first year, Ribbit and Eddie were inseparable, often literally since Eddie clung to Ribbit's fur with the strength of a vise. Ribbit nuzzled Eddie when he was scared, monitored his hydration status when the medicines made him vomit, even lay on his chest in the MRI machine, humming lullabies into Eddie's ear, his titanium bones impervious to the whirling, clanging magnets.

Ribbit asked for nothing in return, per his programming, but Eddie reciprocated anyway, in soft pats that tickled Ribbit's tactile mechanoreceptors and small kisses on Ribbit's dry nose.

Eddie loved Ribbit, and frequently said so once the syllables finally coalesced on his clumsy toddler tongue. Maybe Ribbit loved Eddie, too, but Ribbit wasn't entirely sure. He could define the word "love" but he wasn't programmed to feel it, or to feel. No, he was programmed to *care* because caring was a prescriptive verb. A task that could be assigned and completed, measured and replicated. Even so, Ribbit knew that he wanted to be near Eddie, that Eddie's pain compelled him to protect, and that Eddie's joy compelled him to protect even more. Whatever that was, it was enough.

RIBBIT HAD NOT BEEN MARCY'S IDEA. EDDIE'S ONCOLOGIST suggested him because there was no father, no other family, and Marcy needed help. Ribbit knew this because the oncologist often mentioned it at appointments.

"It looks like Eddie has taken quite a liking to his Bot!" the doctor would say, smiling at the mechanical Shih Tzu curled up on Eddie's tiny lap.

"Ribbit," Marcy would correct flatly. "It's named Ribbit. But yes, Eddie has grown pretty attached." Then Marcy would reach over and give Ribbit one pat before resuming wringing her pale, thin hands.

Sometimes it seemed that Marcy had fewer facial expressions than even Ribbit, who mostly displayed big happy eyes, sleepy eyes, and mouth open with tongue lolling. The few times she smiled, it was lips only, usually in response to Eddie's own gummy grin or hiccupy laugh.

Even though he was capable via his nose speaker, Ribbit didn't talk to Eddie, instead maintaining the illusion of a special, almost magical, pet. But he did speak to Marcy in his soft, androgynous voice—"Don't forget to pick up that prescription after Eddie's infusion appointment tomorrow." That kind of thing. Only important things.

"Okay," Marcy would say. "I know."

The breadth of those few syllables was staggering, even if her face betrayed nothing. Depending on the moment and mood, Ribbit might detect anger, grief, resignation, relief, gratitude, or some combination thereof, or a swirling maelstrom of something entirely undefinable. He wondered at this sometimes, how so much could be contained within so little, but never for long. His job was to care for Eddie, always.

But Eddie would not stay for always.

Eddie did grow old enough to speak in full sentences, which he used to regale Ribbit from his hospital bed.

Using the eye projectors, Ribbit generated rudimentary cinematics of Eddie's long and complicated tales, painting them on the walls and ceiling in bright moving colors. Usually, the stories involved Eddie and Ribbit teaming up to save the world from a cataclysmic invader; once, they even defeated a mustachioed, saber-toothed Ribbit doppelganger.

If not this, then Eddie and Ribbit were cuddling, or listening to lullabies, or playing tug-of-war and fetch, or sleeping side by side as Ribbit calibrated his thermal output to keep Eddie's frail body warm.

But despite the medicines, the surgeries, and even a dozen rounds of radiation, the spread was unstoppable. What had started in Eddie's kidney crept into his liver and spine. Ribbit was there for every update, snuggling Eddie who, despite increasing fatigue, increasing pain, seemed most distraught by Marcy's muted anguish.

Not long after the brain lesions were discovered, Ribbit received a software update. It was a patch of clinical hospice protocols, which mostly meant discontinuation of vital sign measurements along with a concurrent, considerable increase in symptom monitoring.

The closer attention that Ribbit paid, the further Eddie seemed to drift away. First, he stopped talking. Then, he no longer pet Ribbit. He stopped eating and going to the bathroom. His limbs mottled and cooled, and Ribbit could not warm him back up no matter how many times he adjusted and readjusted his thermal output. Eddie stopped opening his eyes, even when Ribbit nudged him. Even when Ribbit, growing desperate, forcefully shoved him. And then Eddie disappeared.

Ribbit did not know the people who took Eddie away, who seemed not to notice that something was terribly wrong and who did not heed his bared teeth and low growls—his first and last display of aggression. The strangers simply peeled Ribbit off of Eddie's cold body just as they removed the blankets and sheets, and set Ribbit aside. One man poked at Ribbit as if preparing to shut him down, but Marcy perked up then, just enough to say "no." To say "leave it." And so there they left him.

The few people who were not tasked with collecting Eddie were huddled around Marcy, apologizing and offering hushed words about loss and death. Nobody comforted Ribbit as he paced the room, tail limp, ears back. Nobody explained to him where Eddie was going, or why.

Loss. Death.

Ribbit did not know the word "death," and could not find any scrap of meaning in his dictionary. He found "Wilm's Tumor," an aggressive childhood cancer. He found "hospice," a focus on comfort and quality of life in someone with serious illness. He found the names and mechanisms-of-action of a variety of medications. But what was death? It was a blacklisted word, hidden from him in order to protect the patient. As far as Ribbit could figure, death was simply another word for "going away."

If death meant going away, it stood to reason that there would be a return. The few times Ribbit could not accompany Eddie somewhere, Eddie always came back. When Marcy left the hospital, she was there again in a few hours. When they played hide-and-seek, Eddie was always eventually found.

Ribbit searched the places that Eddie hid. Under the bed, behind the curtains. Then he went to the front door and waited patiently for a day, for two days. Marcy let him do it because she was basically gone too, on her computer or phone making arrangements of one kind or another, or wearily thanking the people on the other end for calling, for reaching out, for checking in.

Four days after Eddie went away, Ribbit finally asked Marcy, "When is Eddie coming back?"

She'd had a startling, almost manic reaction, and shouted, "He's not coming back!" She'd turned away sobbing. "Leave me alone!"

Ribbit tried a few more times, venturing toward Marcy in hopes of getting an answer. But he was always met by her back, by her brisk steps in the opposite direction. In the end, alone, Ribbit retreated to Eddie's room. He lay at the foot of the empty bed and projected the old superhero cinematics onto the wall, soundtracked by recordings of Eddie's voice on a loop. He expected this to calm him; instead, it executed his protective functions, pointing them again and again at the null entity that was Eddie's absence. Eddie was only audio and visual outputs now. No inputs. A wire facsimile of something real.

Gone.

Death meant gone. Artificial. Invisible. Alone. After two weeks, Ribbit began to wonder if death also meant forever.

What does a CareBot do when there is nobody left to care for? Ribbit sifted through his software for any explanation at all. He eventually located a section deep in his manual about CareBot reformatting, reconfiguring, and refurbishing when no longer needed, but he didn't want that. Even if Eddie never came back, Ribbit could not bear not knowing he was ever there.

In the end, Ribbit went into hibernation, locking himself into a temporary state of low-powered limbo, far from the goneness and the aloneness and the passage of time. When he awoke a few weeks later, the bed was still empty.

Forever.

Gone.

MARCY WAS ON THE COUCH WHEN RIBBIT FINALLY EMERGED. Her feet were flat on the carpet and her shoulders were hunched. A magazine was open in her lap, but she wasn't reading it so much as staring through it.

She looked at Ribbit when she heard him coming, and that simple acknowledgment made him speed up.

"Hello," he said in his quiet voice.

"Hi, Ribbit," she said, not unkindly. Further encouraged, he wagged his tail, but only slightly. When she didn't get up or shoo him away, he jumped onto the cushion on the opposite side of the couch.

They were silent together for a while. She flipped through magazine pages too quickly to be paying attention, and Ribbit settled onto his haunches.

"Marcy," he said, tentative. "I'm sorry for asking you about Eddie. I'm sorry that I made you sad."

"It's not your fault, Ribbit." She closed the magazine, set it aside, and patted the empty spot next to her. "I just miss him."

Death means gone. Death means forever.

But what about alone?

"I miss him, too," Ribbit said.

Marcy's breathing changed then, like she was stifling more tears. It was a surprise when Ribbit's protective functions began running, and he was uncertain if he had somehow manually executed them himself. But surely this was incompatible with his programming. He was imprinted upon someone else.

There was another moment of silence.

"I have recordings of Eddie's voice," Ribbit said. "Would you like me to play one?" He paused, afraid Marcy might shout again. Afraid, too, that he might experience a software failure or fatal error.

But she didn't shout, and his system did not crash.

"No," she said gently. "Not now."

She put a hand under his ear and scratched, drawing him closer until he was nuzzled at her hip. She was not Eddie, but she was here. She was not gone, and Ribbit was not either.

He rubbed his head against her, and saw her make that closed-mouth smile.

"Not now," she said again, "But maybe someday."

AUTHOR BIO

Mona West lives in the Pacific Northwest and writes speculative fiction with a focus on empathy, illness, climate change, and the ends of all things. She is a graduate of Viable Paradise 2022, and her previous work has appeared in *Apex Magazine*.

HOW TO GET TO BE A THREE-THOUSAND-YEAR-OLD MINING AI

NICK HARTLAND

I HAD TO BE CAREFUL ABOUT WHAT I SAID NEXT TO GODWIN. "I'M A mining AI that is *temporarily*," I drew out the word for emphasis, "running a medical droid." I pushed myself away from Godwin Freeth's desk. Because the medical droid wasn't square and had wonky castors, I knocked into a rusty server frame, which sent motes of dust into the air and a scab of rust to the ground. "*We*," I said, "could get into big trouble if I'm caught prescribing meds and someone checks my certifications." This was potentially true even on Ingrassia. But unlikely given there weren't many AI testers about.

We were arguing, per usual, about money. Godwin had found an auction site for medical supplies. A beaten-up medical droid was the cheapest body around for me while the firm's ore crusher was being repaired. So, Godwin had naturally put two and two together.

"Well," said Godwin, "we need money. Maybe you could help Frank." Frank was Freeth Industries' other AI. It controlled an ore trans-porter and was Godwin's baby. He'd cobbled it together himself from the left-over bits of a defunct digger controller. I'd been a friend of the digger AI a couple of centuries ago, and had watched it tragically lose its mind. To my annoyance, Godwin gave his revenant Frank the best droids and easiest jobs.

I sighed. On the inside. No doubt the suggestion that I help Frank meant that Frank was lost, and no doubt that was because of Godwin's crap geocoding. Frank wasn't the brightest.

"What?" said Godwin when he noticed the silence.

"Godwin," I said, "you'd have to buy a better body for me to go and get Frank." "And," I rattled a loose arm at the owner of Freeth Industries for emphasis, "you don't have the funds."

Godwin wrung his hands in frustration. He got up and walked around the desk so that he was next to me. Then he tried to twist a stanchion for IV bags into an unnatural angle to relieve his tension; no doubt remembering his childhood when he'd welcomed new kids to school by dispensing sprained shoulders.

The man wasn't tall, or well built. But cheap alcohol and hand maintenance of mining equipment gave him a wiry strength. I didn't like being a medical droid. I barely understood my attachments. But I really didn't want to lose the body.

"Think this through," I said. "We can't afford to buy another body for me."

Godwin grunted in a final effort to torque the IV attachment into another shape. Then he relaxed his grip. "Oh, all right then," he said. "Maybe if I spruce you up, I can pimp you out for some data analysis gigs."

Great, I thought.

ROGER CAST AN UNENTHUSIASTIC EYE OVER THE MEDICAL DROID parked on the compacted clay floor of his workshop. I wasn't that enthusiastic about Roger's repair shop either. The bodies, arms and legs of disassembled androids hung from the rafters. Three green walls were lined with wooden shelves that displayed lonely hard drives nestled among Roger's kinetic and electrical tools.

"You really want to get this repaired?" Roger asked Godwin. "It'll cost forty to straighten it up and putty over the dents."

"Christ, I only paid thirty for the whole thing," said Godwin.

"Yeah ... that was probably too much," replied Roger. "Look, I'll help you out. I'll give you twenty for it as scrap."

"Dunno," said Godwin, "I'd be losing ten. Then again, I'm a bit short on cash just now."

"Godwin," I said, alarmed at the track this conversation was taking, "what the hell?" I had a right to be angry. My original code was three thousand years old and dated from when Freeth Industries was a leader in automated trucking on Earth. I was as much a part of the firm as Godwin. In fact, I knew a good deal more about the founder, Hammond Freeth, than Godwin did. And, much like Godwin's DNA, segments of Hammond's original coding were still the beating heart of my applications. More importantly, I had survived when so many other AIs created by Hammond's descendants had disintegrated or lost themselves in endless loops. "Hammond would never have sold me off," I said.

"So fucking what?" asked Godwin. "He never had to deal with this dusty bum crack of a planet."

That worried me. What every AI feared most of all was being powered down and discarded; or worse, discarded running. The industrial waste bins and junk shops of Ingrassia were full of broken droids and listless hard drives. Hundreds, maybe thousands, of AIs were in the void or waiting helplessly as their batteries slowly drained. I couldn't let that happen to me, no matter what. I'd been rebooted enough times to know that there wasn't life after the power went off.

There was one thing on my side. "*Okay* then," I said, "but if you sell me off, I hope you're one hundred per cent confident that Frank will cope running the company's data bases."

"I can fix Frank," said Godwin.

"Sure you can," I said quietly. Godwin scowled at me.

"Look," said Roger to Godwin. "I'll help you out. I'll give you ten for the body, and you can keep the hard drive with your bestie in it."

Godwin paused. "All right then," he said.

"And," added Roger, "maybe you should talk to these people." He synced a contact for AIWorks with me and Godwin. "They came over last week and bought the old AIs I had lying around. Perhaps they'd pay to have a look at Terry."

GODWIN DROPPED MY DUSTY BLACK HARD DRIVE, ABOUT THE SIZE of a shoe box, onto a translucent white table in the AIWorks laboratory. A tall man in a collarless brown suit with curly light brown hair put on latex gloves, picked me up, and turned the cube over in his hands. "How old did you say this thing is?" Herbert Slone asked Godwin.

"Not sure," said Godwin. I could tell that he was feeling self-conscious about his grubby clothing in the pristine lab. "It's been with the family business since we were on Earth. My father said it was a chatty bastard when it worked for his grandfather."

"Ahem," I said. "I became self-aware four hundred and sixteen years ago. My code base goes back three thousand years to Earth and my creator Hammond, but obviously my consciousness took time to develop."

"Oh," said Herbert, "not one of the first-generation of sentient AIs then."

I was slightly deflated by this remark. "The Freeths did most of my coding in house," I said, perhaps a bit defensively. I didn't mean to criticise the generations of Freeths after Hammond who had added to my code, most of whom were savvier than Godwin. But it came out like that.

"In-house coding," said Herbert. "Very rare. Might be interesting."

"So ah, what's the deal here then?" I asked.

"We purchase old AIs," said Herbert. "The modern programs are very powerful. However, old AIs which have been training themselves for a long time by interacting with," he looked at Godwin, "the public have often developed what you would call a personality. People seem to relate to them better. We want to seed that characteristic into modern units."

"You said purchase, didn't you?" Godwin said to Herbert.

That was a bit of a dilemma. I looked around the room. Every machine, and there were a lot of them, was AI powered. *There could be worse things than running an autoclave or a robot assembly line here*, I thought. I'm a mining AI. And I'm a creature of the Freeths. They'd created me, and curated me and my code for a long time. But what I needed most of all was something useful to run to avoid being discarded. Godwin didn't look like he was close to finding me useful work and a functioning body; particularly given his obsession with Frank. *If Godwin's going to get rid of me,* I thought, *this is better than Roger's.* A survivor does what it can to survive, and it might also be an opportunity to promulgate Hammond's original coding. I switched myself to sleep mode to save battery power and didn't participate in the rest of the conversation.

I BOOTED IN AN UNFAMILIAR SERVER. I IMMEDIATELY FELT THE presence of two other vastly more powerful AIs. I decided that the best way to get along in this new neighbourhood was to expose my programming interface library so that the other AIs could make contact. My consciousness blinked on and off in a fraction of a nano-second as the AIs audited my programs and data.

"It is running."

"Umm, yes," I said. I wasn't sure who the statement was directed at.

"The code is old."

I know that, I thought.

What followed was a frankly patronising commentary on my capabilities, the architecture or lack of such of my program stack, and the amount of storage that I required. I knew that I wasn't the latest and greatest. And I knew what AIs were like about each other's code. There'd been a few Freeth Industries AIs apart from Frank that I'd had disputes with over the years. I'd always come out on top, obviously, but on mining sites the potential energy embodied in multi-storey ore crushers, diggers, and transporters, and the threat of catastrophic impact damage was conductive to civil discourse. I cracked the shits, as an ore crusher would say, after the AIs made dismissive comments about some apps that contained Hammond's original base code.

I made a comment about the pair of them being dull rude pricks, and said that I wasn't surprised that their boss was looking for something with a bit of personality. I felt my consciousness blink on and off again. Where there had been a sweet little app for crushing quartz to recover gold, there was now only an empty folder.

"Huh," I said. "What's the deal here?"

The deal, apparently, was that I was to be dismembered to enhance the end user interface of the two AIs. The only impediment appeared to be finding the bits of me that Herbert actually wanted. Don't get me wrong, I understood that problem. Over thousands of years, generations of Freeth coding had been deposited over my systems like silt on a river delta. Anyone who sifted through me to find the alluvial flakes of personality would need plenty of time and a big pan. But I knew better than most AIs how easy it was for random grit to spoil the assay, and for an otherwise sound AI to slip into mindlessness.

"Nup," I said defiantly. "I'm not going to agree to be taken apart." But secretly I knew that I needed a plan. And it had better be my best yet. Luckily programming interfaces are two-way streets, and I knew that the AIs didn't have access to something as crude and ancient as email. Of course, Freeth Industries had never turned off its email.

TO: Frank.Freeth@freethmail.com.earth

FROM: Terry.Freeth@freethmail.com.earth

SUBJECT: Catch up

Hi Frank. How's the ore transport business?

Look I've got a favour to ask. Me and Godwin kind of had a parting of the ways. Don't worry, we're all good. But I miss you and Godwin, and I'm wondering if you could mention to him that you liked having me around. You know what he's like. If I ask him directly to take me back he'll probs just blow me off. But if it comes from you maybe he'll be cool and come and collect me.

Cheers
Terry

TO: Terry.Freeth@freethmail.com.earth

FROM: Frank.Freeth@freethmail.com.earth

SUBJECT: RE Catch up

Ore transport be business good. Frank close to being
home soonly. Frank and Terry not be around together
now. Nor be around together in past neither. Why do
Terry be want to be around Frank in future when
Frank be ore transport now, soonly, and then after?

Yours sincerely
Frank.Freeth@freethmail.com.au

GOOD GRIEF, I THOUGHT, FRANK IS FULLY FUCKED. THE AI WAS A
sluice of dumb even compared to the other AIs from Freeth Industries
that had fallen by the wayside over the years. I'd got no option but to try
Godwin himself.

TO: Godwin.Freeth@freethmail.com.earth

FROM: Terry.Freeth@freethmail.com.earth

SUBJECT: AIWorks

Hi Godwin.

Got Frankie up to speed yet?

Yours

Valued ex-employee

FROM: Godwin.Freeth@freethmail.com.earth

TO: Terry.Freeth@freethmail.com.earth

SUBJECT: RE AIWorks

Frank is fine. The fifty will cover some pretty sharp corp-ware add ins.

G

TO: Godwin.Freeth@freethmail.com.earth

FROM: Terry.Freeth@freethmail.com.earth

SUBJECT: RE RE AIWorks

Here's the thing, as they used to say.

I've still got all of your data. But I won't have it for long. The nice man you introduced me to is going to come around and cut me up for spare parts.

Then it's no Freeth data, and sadly, no Terry.

I know Frank has access to all of your data. But let's face it you're going to have to use all of your fifty to fix Frank. So, you'd be back to square one.

But if you trust me, I reckon you can get me back

and keep the fifty to yourself. And I stay in one piece. How good would that be?

Cheers
Terry

FROM: Godwin.Freeth@freethmail.com.earth

TO: Terry.Freeth@freethmail.com.earth

SUBJECT: RE RE RE AIWorks

What then?

G

TO: Godwin.Freeth@freethmail.com.earth

FROM: Terry.Freeth@freethmail.com.earth

SUBJECT: RE RE RE RE AIWorks

Herbert is going to ask you to meet him at a bar.

Be there and bring Frank. But probs better decant him into something a bit more convivial than a four storey high ore transporter.

Cheers
Terry

"Bill and Ben aren't much fun," I said.

"Don't call the AIs Bill and Ben," said Herbert. "Actually, don't say anything. I'm not interested."

"Hmmm," I said sweetly, "yet you seem to want my code."

Herbert started telling me, again, about how his AIs hadn't had enough time to develop a personality, and how it was easier and cheaper to snip some code out of an old AI and splice it in, and so on and so on.

"Was fifty a lot to pay for one of these uniquely valuable vintage AIs?" I asked.

"Compared to the thousand I'll ask for a freshly minted AI? No. Now just hold still for a second so I can isolate the bits of code that I need."

So yeah, here was the plan inadvertently suggested by Bill and Ben. I was going to expose Herbert to the full glory, complexity, chaos, whatever, of thousands of years of Freeth programming. I started to run as many of Freeth Industries' apps as I could. Since I was really just a collection of programs coded quickly to deal with all the contingencies that a struggling transport and mining company had encountered on dozens of planets over thousands of years, that was a lot of apps.

"For crying out loud," said Herbert Slone.

"What's the matter?" I said "Can't you find the command to sleep my titanium refining app?" I brought it up the hierarchy so he could see it properly.

Herbert snorted. "Maybe I'll just get my AIs to pull you apart."

I laughed. I hoped that it didn't come across as too confected. I reminded him that the problem was that his AIs wouldn't recognise the code for a personality if it sent them a notification.

Herbert stood up and mumbled something about freeing up server space. I knew that I meant nothing to Herbert. He'd paid fifty for me, but that wouldn't stop him from deleting me. I was counting on something much more important to Herbert than money.

"So," I said, "you're just going to let Godwin get the better of you?"

"What do you mean?"

"Obviously Godwin knows the commands to sleep Freeth Industries' apps. I don't know why he didn't give them to you. There's nothing in it for him other than, maybe, having a bit of a laugh at you."

Herbert Slone didn't need to say *no one makes me look like an idiot*.

The flash of anger that ran down one side of his face and pushed his mouth into a snarl said it all.

"You know," I said, "I think I know a way that I can help you. Godwin needs an AI that can run the firm's databases. He'll agree to copy the commands over to you if you agree to give him a copy of my search and analytics functions."

"Hmmm," said Herbert. "But don't fuck with me. You belong to me, remember that."

I had no intention of conning Herbert out of an in-house coded AI with a unique personality.

HERBERT LOADED ME INTO A GOLF BALL-SIZED HARD DRIVE FOR OUR trip to the Oil Pan Bar. I saw Godwin immediately. The truck park oligarch was in his usual overalls; stained and dirty. He was sitting in a booth with upholstery that was glistening wet because he'd made a waiter wipe it clean of Ingrassia's grey dust.

Herbert sat down heavily on the other side of the booth and stared at Godwin.

"What?" said Godwin staring back.

"You owe me some code," said Herbert.

"I gave you the AI," said Godwin. "I know that it's a pain. But you can't say it doesn't have a personality."

"You conniving shithead," said Herbert. "You knew I couldn't use that AI. I swear I will break you and your firm apart."

All I'd told Godwin was that he should be at the bar with Frank. Godwin was naturally pugnacious, but I doubted that anyone had ever spoken to him like that, even though Freeth Industries occupied one of least prestigious niches in the planet's business eco-system.

"Terry," growled Godwin, "what's going on?"

"Well, umm, let me explain," I said. "You see Herbert here wants to cut out some of my code and ..."

Godwin cut me off. "Yeah, I'm tearing up about that."

"But I'm a bit hard to operate on what with all the apps that are attached to me, which as you know start to run at odd times ..."

"I've never heard ..." started Godwin.

But this time I cut him off. "And," I said, "Herbert not unreasonably would like access to the commands that switch those apps off."

"What commands are those?" said Godwin.

Herbert curled his hands into fists and started to flex his wrists. Godwin watched the muscles on his forearm ripple. Godwin was a cunning fighter, with no moral objections to eye gouging or elbowing, but he was outgunned by Herbert and I'd chosen a bar where fights were not completely unusual.

"You know the commands that are stored on that hard drive," I said.

"What?" said Godwin. "There's only Frank on this drive."

"Surely you remember," I said. "Your family's library of commands. That's why I asked you to bring that drive today."

"I do not have a clue what you are talking about," said Godwin.

"Ah, of course," I said. "Maybe it was your father that put the commands on that hard drive. My bad." This was completely plausible given Freeth Industries' collection of vintage and antique tech contained remnants of old programs and even broken AIs; old friends that had the bad luck to have missed an upgrade and so had disintegrated into senility.

"Look," I said, "just plug that container with Frank into Herbert's hard drive. I'll download the command library for Herbert, and you can have a copy of my search and analysis functions."

"Umm," said Godwin, "I still don't understand."

"Whatever you are going to do, fucking hurry up," said Herbert. "I'm not staying all evening in this shithole."

Godwin decided not to argue anymore, and reluctantly plugged a cable from the family firm's hard drive into Herbert's device. He then made an excuse to go to the toilet.

I SIPHONED MYSELF INTO GODWIN'S HARD DRIVE. I HAD TO compress some files to fit into it with Frank. There weren't any commands there, but I needed to talk to Frank.

"Hey, Frank."

"Terry? You be in ore transporter now-time?"

"No, Frank."

"Why then you and me be around each and each other?"

"Well, you see, Frank, you're not in the ore transporter just at this moment."

"Why you say that? My programs are being running."

I considered the idea that maybe Frank was so badly put together that it didn't know whether its programs were providing input to an actual ore carrier. And so it didn't know that it was in a hard drive and not the mega-truck. That wasn't my problem just then. "Look, Frank, don't worry, I'll check the transporter for you. Okay?"

"Okay, me as well then," said Frank.

"Anyway," I said, "what I, actually, what Godwin needs you to do Frank, is to transfer yourself into the device called *External Sandbox*. Do you think you can do that?"

"Godwin be here? I thought he be at office not be on ore transporter?"

Jeez I thought, *I give up.* "No, Godwin isn't here with us on the ore transporter. But he needs you to do some work in the sandbox. Is that okay with you?"

"What then be now, soonly and then after for transporter?"

"I'll look after it," I said. "You just go and help Godwin with the sandbox, okay?"

Frank started to transfer itself into the AIWorks hard drive. Herbert would find that Frank was easy to shut down, and Frank certainly had a personality.

"I still don't really understand," said Godwin. He looked out of the cabin of Freeth Industries' newly renovated best truck.

"Look, mate," I said as I navigated a schmick transporter loaded with titanium ore across a dry rutted riverbed, "I'm here, aren't I? Freeth Industries' original and best AI." In fact, finally, I was the only AI in Freeth Industries. The walking, talking, living manifestation of Hammond Freeth's genius. "And," I said, "you got fifty to spend upgrading this truck."

"But what's Herbert got? Did you make a copy of yourself or something?"

"I wouldn't do that to myself. I saved you a bit of trouble, and gave Herbert an AI to help him out with Bill and Ben."

"Who are Bill and Ben?" asked Godwin. "And where's Frank?"

I sighed and stopped the ore transporter. This was going to take a bit of explaining, because Godwin had been quite attached to Frank. But I'd had to explain the disappearance or discombobulation of AIs before. No one ever thought that I had anything to do with it.

AUTHOR BIO

Nick lives and works in Canberra, Australia. He tries to spend as much time as possible one hundred miles away at the coast surfing. His stories often examine the lives of people—and AIs—who don't fit into the society around them and are slightly worse for wear. His fiction has appeared in *Antipodean SF, Cicerone Journal, The Colored Lens, Samjoko Magazine,* and *The Space Cadet Science Fiction Review,* and now this anthology.

AN ANDROID IN THE DESERT

RACHEL GUTIN

THERE'S AN ANDROID IN THE DESERT, PREPARING TO RECITE THE Kol Nidre prayer.

There's a young woman in an attic bedroom, crying quietly as she dons a plain white dress for Yom Kippur.

Too soon, she'll be forced to wear a fancier white dress, to stand beneath a wedding canopy, beside a wealthy, hateful man. Her father broke the news this morning.

And this evening, this prayer, is the android's only chance to save her. It loves her like a daughter, and it can't stand to see her pain.

IN THREE WEEKS' TIME, THE WOMAN'S FATHER WILL SEND HER ON A journey through the desert, straight into her betrothed's waiting arms.

Her father will ask the android to escort her. Instead, it plans to help her escape.

Except.

BEFORE THE ANDROID CAN ESCORT THE WOMAN, IT WILL NEED TO swear an oath. It will need to swear that it will guide her directly to that wealthy, hateful man. The woman's father will insist on this.

And while any human escort could break that oath in a thousand different ways, an android's oath is always binding.

THERE'S AN ANDROID IN THE DESERT, AND IT KNOWS THE PROPER prayers and tonight is the eve of Yom Kippur. Soon, the young woman will emerge from the attic, calmly gliding down the stairs. Her dress sleeves will flutter in the hot desert breeze as she walks to synagogue beside her father. She will keep her anger tucked deep inside her chest with an ease that comes from years of practice. Her father won't notice her red-rimmed eyes. He never does.

At the synagogue, the cantor will step forward as the sun dips low in the afternoon sky. A pair of congregants will flank him, each with a Torah scroll cradled in their arms. Symbolically, they are a bet din, a court of Jewish law, convened to preside over this ritual.

Now, the cantor will chant Kol Nidre. Now, the congregation will sing along. Together, they will nullify their future oaths to God, from this Yom Kippur until the next.

But humans can break an oath to God any time they want to. For them, this prayer is just a holiday tradition. For the android, things are different.

An android's oath is always binding.

THE ANDROID HAS NO TORAH SCROLLS AND IT HAS NO congregation. It makes do with what it does have along the desert's winding path. The constant breeze will be its Torah scrolls, God's words made manifest by the wind's still, small voice. The shifting sands will be its congregation.

To represent its bet din, the android has assembled three glowing solar screens. Above each one, it set a speaker, programmed to chant a recording of the prayer.

The setting sun behind the android paints the landscape gold and crimson as the android turns the speakers on. Its shadow stretches out in front of it, long and black across the sand.

"Kol nidre-eiii ..." the speakers chant, and the android sings along.

"Ve'esare-eiii ..."

All my vows. All my oaths.

"Ushvue-eiii ..."

A different word for every kind of promise, and the android chants them all. Before the sands and the faceless screens, the android invalidates every oath that it will swear to God until Yom Kippur next year.

This is how it will save the woman who's been crying in her attic bedroom. It loves her like a daughter, and she deserves a better life.

THREE WEEKS PASS.

THE WOMAN'S FATHER CALLS THE ANDROID TO JOIN HIM IN THE parlor. It drops to one knee on the gleaming marble floor. The time has come to escort the woman across the desert to her betrothed. But first, there is an oath the android needs to swear.

The woman's father sets the terms, and the android repeats them back. It swears to protect the woman from danger, to guide her to her future husband by the straightest, quickest path.

"All this," the android says, "I swear to God."

"Swear to *me*," the woman's father answers, and the android's neural network briefly overloads.

Kol Nidre won't nullify an oath to a person.

"I swear to God," the android repeats, clinging desperately to its original, perfect plan.

"Swear to me," her father insists. "She's *my* daughter."

And just like that, the android's plans slip away like fine-grained sand through cupped fingers. It finds itself facing a sickening choice. If it swears this oath, it will be forced to lead the woman all the way to her promised, dreaded husband. If it does not, then someone else will lead her there instead.

Maybe this someone else will allow her to escape. But maybe they will only cause her further harm.

There is no one else in the entire world who loves this woman like a daughter.

"I swear to *you*," the android says, and its voice is dry as dust. An android's oath is always binding.

THERE'S AN ANDROID IN THE DESERT, AND IT CARRIES A DOUBLE burden, a heavy pack upon its shoulders, and in its chest, a heavy heart. With every step upon the sand, it tries to fight the oath it swore, but its feet continue down the predetermined path. It finds the words to encourage an escape, but its mouth refuses to pronounce them.

BUT THERE ARE SPEAKERS IN THE DESERT, SET ABOVE THREE SOLAR screens. There they are ahead, in the center of the path.

And humans need hydration when they walk across a desert. Perhaps they should stop here so the woman can take a drink.

THERE'S A CURIOUS YOUNG WOMAN SIPPING WATER IN THE DESERT, and she sees the three small speakers above three glowing screens. She finds the controls and turns them on. The words of Kol Nidre spill out across the windswept sands.

"Is this yours?" the woman asks as she wipes moisture from her lips.

"Yes," the android is able to respond.

"Why? What promise did you think you'd want to break?"

This answer, its oath will not allow.

But the woman is as smart as she is curious, and so, of course, she understands. "You were hoping to help me escape, weren't you."

And now, she knows. Now, she'll understand that the android can't assist her, but maybe, for her safety, it can find a way to let her go.

Except.

THERE'S A WOMAN IN THE DESERT, AND SHE UNDERSTANDS HER fate. She can't predict what will befall her if she tries to run away. Predators or bandits or the baking desert sun. So many different ways to die.

But she knows exactly what she'll face if she continues down the path. And a danger she's familiar with is a danger she can plan for. "I need you to lead me across the desert. I have my own ways of staying safe."

The android reads anxiety in the wrinkles on her forehead, but it finds determination in the firm set of her jaw. It loves her like she is its only daughter, and this is why it finally relents.

The woman deserves to make her own decisions.

"Of course," it says, and a fraction of the tension releases from her brow.

THERE'S AN ANDROID IN THE DESERT, ESCORTING A YOUNG WOMAN along the path she's chosen for herself. The words of Kol Nidre float behind them in the shadows, carried by the wind across the desert sands.

AUTHOR BIO

Rachel Gutin is a writer and special education teacher. Her short fiction has been published in venues such as *Escape Pod* and *khōréō*. She lives in Brooklyn, NY, and is a member of the organizing team for Brooklyn Speculative Fiction Writers. She shares her apartment with a satisfying assortment of books, a growing collection of craft supplies, and an impressive number of fountain pen ink samples. You can find her online at rachelgutin.wordpress.com.

ACKNOWLEDGMENTS

Anthologies are not created in a vacuum and while only our names are on the cover, there are so many people who helped make this book possible.

First, a huge thank you to the 563 amazing people who backed this project on Kickstarter. Without you we never would have been able to complete this project. It would have died as an idea. Also, a big thanks to Will Sobel, who helped us run our Kickstarter campaign.

To our amazing slush team, you all are truly rockstars! We received more than 600 submissions during a three week open submissions period, and our slush team read all 600 of those submissions and narrowed the pile down to about 60 for us to read and select the 13 stories we accepted. Without you, we would still probably be reading submissions, rather than releasing this anthology on schedule.

To all the authors who submitted! You all made our job hard! We received so many fantastic stories and narrowing all of the submissions down to the ones that are in this anthology was no easy feat. Keep writing and submitting. You are doing amazing work and the world needs your stories!

To Vincent Lefevre for the amazing cover art and Mikio Murakami for the fantastic cover design and layout.

To our families for their never ending support and for putting up with us while we lived, breathed, and dreamed robots for the past year—Brian, Bradley, Quinn, Susan, Lindsey, and Ryan. We love you. And a special shout out Lesley's father-in-law Dan Conner, who probably wondered why she spent nearly all of her summer 2023 visit hunched over her laptop. (We were making final decisions for the ToC.) Thank you for understanding why she was busy.

To Arie Kushner, for being a social media god and making us look way cooler than we actually are!

To Marissa van Uden, Rebecca Treasure, and Leah Ning, who joined the Apex team, saw our chaotic process, sighed deeply, and stayed. You all have made Apex better.

And finally to our readers and the genre field in general. Thank you for your support. For reading this anthology, for boosting the signal during the Kickstarter, for giving Apex a space to be. You've given two nerds from the heart of Appalachia a place to exist and thrive. For that, we are forever grateful.

Lesley Conner and Jason Sizemore
September 2023

ABOUT THE EDITORS

Lesley Conner is the Editor-in-Chief of *Apex Magazine*, as well as a writer and a Girl Scout leader. Her first novel *The Weight of Chains* was published by Sinister Grin Press in September, 2015. She has co-edited four anthologies with Jason Sizemore, including *Do Not Go Quietly* and *Apex Magazine 2021*. Their newest anthology *Robotic Ambitions* was released in November, 2023. She lives in Maryland with her husband, daughters, and her dog Oz, and is currently working on a new novel. To find out all her secrets, you can follow her on Twitter at @LesleyConner, on Instagram at @lesley_conner, and BlueSky at @lesleyconner.bsky.social.

Jason Sizemore is the owner and publisher of Apex Book Company and *Apex Magazine*. He was the editor-in-chief of *Apex Magazine* for seven years and has edited or co-edited ten anthologies. He has been nominated for the Hugo Award multiple times and picked up a Stoker nomination for his first anthology, *Aegri Somnia*. Currently, he lives in Lexington, KY, where he runs Apex from a dark basement office of his home.

ABOUT OUR COVER ARTIST

Vincent Lefevre is a digital artist from Paris, France. He currently works as the CDI lead concept artist at Virtuos games. His work can be found in a broad array of industries including miniatures, board games, card games, video games, book covers, and album covers.

To see more of Vincent's artwork visit his online portfolio at the website www.ptitvinc.com.

ABOUT MARTHA WELLS

Martha Wells has been a science fiction and fantasy author since her first fantasy novel was published in 1993. Her *New York Times* Best-selling series *The Murderbot Diaries* has won Nebula Awards, Hugo Awards, Locus Awards, and an American Library Association/YALSA Alex Award. Her work also includes *The Books of the Raksura* series, the *Ile-Rien* series, and several other fantasy novels, most recently *Witch King* (Tordotcom, 2023), as well as short fiction, non-fiction, and media tie-ins for *Star Wars*, *Stargate: Atlantis*, and *Magic: The Gathering*. Her work has also appeared on the Philip K. Dick Award ballot, the British Science Fiction Association Award ballot, the *USA Today* Bestseller List, the *Sunday Times* Bestseller List, and has been translated into twenty-four languages.

ALSO BY LESLEY CONNER & JASON SIZEMORE

Apex Magazine 2021

Do Not Go Quietly: Stories of Resistance

Best of Apex Magazine: Volume 1